MW00985593

the KEEPER *of* FLAMES

JAYNE THORNE, CIA LIBRARIAN BOOK THREE

TWO TALES PRESS

NEW YORK TIMES BESTSELLING AUTHOR

JOSS WALKER

AND R.L. PEREZ

PRAISE FOR THE JAYNE THORNE, CIA LIBRARIAN SERIES

"Vivid world-building, a page-turning mystery and a smart, adventurous heroine in the process of discovering her own power and learning from her mistakes makes for another great addition to an outstanding urban fantasy series."

— **Jayne Castle,** *New York Times* **bestselling author of the Harmony series, on** *Master of Shadows*

∽

"Light-hearted books can get a bad rap, as though making readers smile is somehow a weakness on the author's part... Walker has a light touch with [her] prose, and the likable characters breeze through many of their interactions. Which isn't to say that Tomb of the Queen lacks gravitas. No, there's a good story here with real edge-of-the-seat moments... It's fun from start to finish, and I'm going to keep my eye out for more from this "new" author."

—**Charles de Lint,** *The Magazine of Mystery & Science Fiction* **on** *Tomb of the Queen*

～

"Writer Joss Walker brings the magic back! It will take a witch with heart, humor, and book smarts–plus some killer kick-boxing skills–to save the world, and Jayne Thorne is the witch we need now. Hold on tight, you urban fantasy fans, because once you open *Tomb of the Queen*, the action doesn't stop until the last thrilling page."

— **Laura Benedict, bestselling author of the** *Bliss House* **trilogy, on** *Tomb of the Queen*

～

"A librarian gets recruited by the CIA to help track down rare and magical books... Jayne Thorne has just discovered that magic is real, and the CIA needs her help. After a crash course in Magic 101 she's sent to Ireland to investigate a rare manuscript. The start of this series is everything I love about urban fantasy: a wise-cracking heroine who diffuses tense situations with a joke, plenty of adventure, and an interesting magical world that exists alongside our own. I can't wait for more adventures with Jayne!"

— **John McDougall, Murder by the Book, on** *Tomb of the Queen*

～

"Joss Walker's debut had me completely under her spell. Part cleverly plotted fantasy and part thriller, I was drawn in by her charming bookworm of a librarian with magical powers, dashing Irish rogue, and the complicated battle between 'good' and evil. Addictive and utterly delightful, this is a book to treasure."

— Paige Crutcher, author of *The Orphan Witch,* on *Tomb of the Queen*

～

"*Tomb of the Queen* is a relatable, fun romp of a thrill ride! The characters are lifelike and well fleshed out, and the magic is done in a unique way that I have never seen before. I loved this book, and I'm sure that I will read it over and over again!"
— **Julie L. Kramer,** *USA Today* **bestselling author of** *Of Curses and Scandals,* **on** *Tomb of the Queen*

～

"This book was just my cup of tea! Or perhaps, my slice of pie? 😊 Jayne Thorne, CIA Librarian is a relatable, lovable, and smart heroine dead set on vanquishing evil. A genius mythology twist, swoony budding romance, and gorgeous library imagery, paired with non-stop action, makes *Tomb of the Queen* a winner for fans of urban fantasy. Stop everything and read this book!"
— **Ashley McLeo, author of the bestselling** *Starseed Trilogy,* **on** *Tomb of the Queen*

ALSO BY JOSS WALKER

Jayne Thorne, CIA Librarian Series

Tomb of the Queen

Master of Shadows

The Keeper of Flames

The Prophecy of Wind

A Betrayal of Magic (short prequel)

The Eighth Road (short prequel)

Discovery of Magic (bundle)

The Guardians Mini-Series

Guardians of Silence

Guardians of Fury

Guardians of Power

Writing as J.T. Ellison

Standalone Suspense

It's One of Us

Her Dark Lies

Good Girls Lie

Tear Me Apart

Lie to Me

No One Knows

Also by R.L. Perez

Timecaster Chronicles

Twisted by Time

Devoured by Darkness

Bound by Blood

Nightcaster Chronicles

The Cursed Witch

The Fallen Demon

The Lost Phoenix

Bloodcaster Chronicles

The Demon's Kiss

The Angel's Vow

The Reaper's Call

Ivy & Bone series

Ivy & Bone

Thorn & Ash

Oak & Ember

The Keeper of Flames
© 2023 by J.T. Ellison
Digital ISBN: 978-1-948967-58-7
Trade ISBN: 978-1-948967-66-2

Cover design © The Killion Group, Inc.

For more, visit Two Tales Press.

PROLOGUE

LAYERS OF DARKNESS

Rome was made of layers, ancient to modern, all stacked upon one another, waiting patiently to be found by those with a mind to search. So many treasures were hidden in those golden chambers, buried under centuries of dirt and rubble. It took money, and fortitude, and a burning desire to discover the truth of the city, to make even the tiniest dent into the past.

The Basilica di San Clemente had a head start. The masterpiece was five minutes from the Colosseum, a beloved stop for tourists and antiquarians alike. The archeological dig burrowed into the earth and held regular tours to show fascinating layers of the city time forgot.

It was to this place, deep under the streets of Rome, that Ruth Thorne found herself drawn. Something there, though she didn't know what. A voice inside her pushed her to go, and so she went. She knew not what she was looking for, and it didn't matter—whatever the voice wanted, it would show her when she arrived.

She entered at the assigned time, hooked up with a tour

group, listening to the guide's excited patter with half an ear. Ruth followed in the tour's footsteps through the main basilica, down a narrow flight of stairs to the second basilica, the foundation for the newer building, then down farther still. Her feet on the stone made a whisper, and she bit back a laugh.

Of course, she was entering a tomb. It was cold. Dark. The tunnel was long, and smelled of dust and rock, minerals and mold, elemental, the very earth itself. The rock ceiling was low and sloped, cut into hand-carved archways above the chamber. A hole bored through the rock let in light from above. A pattern spilled out from the center; it looked like a five-petaled flower.

The voice reverberated through her, so loudly she jumped, expecting heads around her to turn, but no, it was inside her; only she could hear it. It was in her mind now, her conscience, her very being. They were one creature.

"This," it intoned.

She was standing in front of a stone edifice with what looked like carvings of winged Mercury on his rounds, but the guide said the word "Mithras" and Ruth felt a thrill go through her. Mithras. The hidden god. The leader of a religious movement that predated Christ himself. Some called it a cult. But what Ruth saw now—what she felt in her bones—was not a cult figure but the markings of a powerful magician. This was where he'd conducted his magic, and his followers sat on the channels of hard rock lining the chamber to gape in awe at his powers, ancient Adepts who wanted some of that dark power for themselves and worshipped the god who could bring them closer to his immaculate strength. A true Master. One of those rare creatures that the Kingdom sought.

The god himself was gone, disappeared into the aether where all things go when no one believes in them any longer, but the power he'd left behind... Oh, the power thrummed in her veins.

She shivered with happiness. The power emanating from the edifice made her entire body tingle.

"Take," the voice inside her demanded.

With a cold, delighted smile, she did.

CHAPTER

ONE

ALL HANDS ON DECK

Crystal City, Virginia

"We have a situation. We need you to come in."

Amanda Newport, director of the Torrent Control Organization, pressed the red End button on her encrypted phone and frowned at the now dark screen. She never liked being summoned to the boss's office, but especially not on a Sunday. She was in the middle of making pancakes, had just folded in the egg whites, which meant the batch would be ruined if she put the batter in the refrigerator. No help for it, though. She dumped the batter down the sink, put the blueberries and cashew milk back in the fridge—*at least I hadn't put the blueberries in yet; that would truly be a waste*—and headed to her bedroom to dress. Urgent it might be, but she wouldn't show up without at least putting her hair in a bun and pulling on some jeans.

Her apartment in Crystal City had several advantages—one being a spectacular view of the Washington Monument and the

5

various marble buildings that made up the DC landscape. It was also less than a fifteen-minute drive to Langley.

She was on campus twenty minutes after the call, striding past the Kryptos sculpture with barely a glance at its magnificence. Three of the codes had been cracked, but the fourth remained a mystery. She'd often wondered if its significance was related to her division, the TCO. There was magic in codes, too, after all. Sunlight caught the edge and flashed as she passed. If she'd stopped to watch, she might have noticed how the sun's reflection made the corner glow green for the barest of moments. But she was in a hurry, and Kryptos would have to wait for another day.

She presented herself to Joshua's admin, Gladys, a lovely but intimidating relic from the agency's golden age of the Cold War, and was waved through. Joshua was the CIA director's direct report and Amanda's immediate boss. She spied him standing behind his desk, back to the door. What she wasn't expecting was the director himself, long body hunched into one of the leather chairs. Joshua turned when she entered and waved Amanda to the sofa, taking the chair next to the director.

"Amanda," the director greeted her. "Thanks for coming in."

"Isaac," she replied, just as coolly. While Joshua had always been a steady presence in her career—he wasn't a presidential appointee but actual CIA staff—the directors changed almost as often as the country voted in new leadership. Isaac Fitzgerald was the latest in a string of directors, and she got the sense he considered her division a bunch of mumbo jumbo. Just to make him sweat, she flicked a Fire spell at the gas fireplace against the far wall, and flames rose, crackling merrily. She wasn't above showing off a little to get her point across. *Magic is real. Get used to it, buddy.*

Isaac stifled the comment she knew he wanted to make. "Sorry to drag you in on a Sunday, but there's a problem in

THE KEEPER OF FLAMES

Rome. It seems there was an explosion and building collapse at the Basilica di San Clemente."

Uh-oh. Jayne...I'm gonna kill you.

"A terror attack?" she asked, hoping against hope he said yes.

"Unknown," Joshua replied. "This just happened. We've sent a team. There are casualties. Witnesses reported seeing a blue light encompass the area before the explosion happened. Similar reports came in after the earthquake at Fontainebleau. We thought this might be your people."

With a sigh, Amanda nodded. "That is entirely possible. I do have a team in Rome as we speak. I will reach out immediately, and—"

The director sat forward in his crumpled-leather chair.

"Amanda, to be frank, it feels as if your...*division*...is slipping. The president has expressed his desire to see these international accidents stop. It's making his foreign policy difficult to manage. Not to mention the extreme outlay of money that it takes to clean up your messes. If you can't get control of your people—"

Her back straightened. "Sir. With all due respect. My people are the only reason the world hasn't collapsed into chaos. The attacks we've thwarted far outstrip the few that have occurred. We're lucky to have found a very powerful magician, who we are in the midst of training. She—"

The director scoffed. "Jayne Thorne? The twenty-three-year-old librarian? You can hardly be pinning your hopes to save the world on *her*. I've seen the video feeds. She takes nothing seriously, she shows a disturbing lack of respect for authority, she only partially follows orders. Now you have her completely untrained sister and an Irish national boyfriend on this team, not to mention a French national whose allegiance has been in question more than once? I'm not sure I am comfortable telling the president things are under control."

Amanda grasped her necklace, running her thumb along its ridges. Agitation burned in her chest, igniting a fire within her. *Careful...* She cleared her throat.

"I understand your concerns, sir. But this is an international problem, and we need an international team to combat it. Yes, the Thorne girls are young. But they are the most powerful magicians we've seen in years. They can do things in their sleep that officers twice their age and experience can only dream about. They are the key to our future, and to saving the people we are sworn to protect."

"*Your* people. The magical folk. *Adepts.*" The word sounded like a curse from his lips.

"Everyone, sir. We would never put magical *or* nonmagical people first. We believe in equality. The people we are fighting, though, do not. They are committed to ferreting out every last nonmagical being on this planet and eliminating them. We are at war, sir. War for not only our *way* of life but our very lives."

"And you're putting that responsibility on the back of a girl who's barely out of diapers."

Amanda could feel her magic rising in Jayne's defense and balled her fists so as not to unleash hell here in her boss's office. "Sir. You're being quite unfair to Officer Thorne. She's shown herself to be not only talented but courageous, selfless, and dedicated to our cause. She's growing more powerful by the day. She is the path forward."

"Not powerful enough to stop these attacks! And they must be stopped. These terrorists must be eliminated. We can't chance a world war. The midterms are coming up, we'll lose the House and the Senate, and in two years—"

"You'll lose your job. Meanwhile, we will still be battling the forces of evil to save as many people as we can. Forgive me for saying it, sir, but this is bigger than you. Or me. Or the CIA. The fate of the free world hangs in the balance. We need more funding, more autonomy, and me in the field instead of here, pushing papers."

Joshua raised a brow at this last. "You need to be in the field? It's become that bad?"

"Yes." She touched her necklace again; she couldn't help herself. "I have a lead on a magical power source that will tip the scales in our favor. But I have to be the one to track down the lead. With Sofia Thorne. And as many TCO officers as we can spare."

Joshua was up and pacing now. "With the violent attacks and natural disasters of late, the president wants to distance us from these magical threats as quickly as possible. He believes they are escalating due to our involvement."

"They aren't," Amanda argued. "If not for our involvement, these attacks would have been far worse and far more deadly. We're fighting three wars, gentlemen. Against the Kingdom and La Liberté and Goddess knows how many more splinter factions that are growing in their nests. Against a secret society of magicians who are seeking the power of the Torrent for themselves. And against a shadow world that we're only beginning to understand, where mythological creatures and the gods and goddesses of old reign supreme. The necromantic texts we seek are no longer the only path forward. We need them, yes. But there are even more challenges ahead."

"It still sounds as if things are getting worse, Amanda. Not better," the director said. The skepticism in his tone was impossible to miss.

She allowed herself a chilly nod. "It's always darkest before the dawn, sir. But trust me. If any of these factions succeed before we do, the world as we know it will end. Magicians will reign. Non-Adepts will serve, or die."

"I'd think you'd want that."

She narrowed her eyes, again tamping down the surge of power coursing through her. "Quite the contrary. The Torrent freed would cause the level of destruction we might see from a bilateral nuclear war. Mutually assured destruction. That is not in anyone's best interest. We want to control it, not unleash it."

Fitzgerald steepled his meaty fingers, and Joshua watched them both. This was more than a battle of wills. Amanda had to get the director on board. She needed the resources the CIA provided.

"What can I do to convince you, sir?" she asked, more softly now.

He glanced at the fireplace. She snapped her fingers, and it turned off.

"Parlor tricks," he muttered, standing. "You have our full support, Amanda. Money, officers, whatever you need."

"Thank you, sir."

"But."

Ah. There was always a *but*.

"You get that loose-cannon Thorne girl under control. Get in the field. Deal with Rome. Clean up your messes. Stop these fools from hurting anyone else. Or else I will."

A FEW MINUTES LATER, Amanda blew past a shocked Pierce into her office, calling him as she went. "Get in here."

Chipper as always, he scurried in behind her. "What's wrong? Why are you here today? It's your day off."

She whirled, holding her necklace. "Later. Where is Jayne Thorne right now?"

CHAPTER

TWO

A MASTER AND A FRENCHMAN WALK INTO A LIBRARY...

Rome, Italy

Nothing like falling flat on your face to ruin the peaceful ambience of a beautiful library.

But Jayne Thorne, CIA Librarian, was nothing if not resilient. If she got knocked down, then she'd get back up again, just like in the Chumbawamba song. Jayne hummed it to herself, using the beat to time her moves as she staggered to her feet, narrowly missing another spell in the face. She teetered, her back colliding with the steel railing that caught her just before she tumbled off the balcony and crashed into the innocent and studious civilians below. Jayne needed to get out of there, pronto—before any books were damaged!

Yet this opponent was different. Not like the usual clueless goons Jayne could fight off in her sleep. No, it seemed the Kingdom, the terrorist organization that had sent the thugs after her, had upped its game; this guy had a glowing lasso rope like

Wonder Woman herself. That same lasso had just snagged Jayne's foot, leading her to fall on her face. Unhelpfully, the goon in question guffawed at her wipeout, his voice loud and boisterous.

"Oh, *ma poupée*, did you smear your makeup?" jeered the Frenchman to her right, nimbly dodging spells Matrix-style by arching backward with flawless grace.

Her nose and jaw still throbbing from the clumsy impact, Jayne gritted her teeth from the gibe of her partner. "If anyone wears makeup, it's you, Captain Guy-Liner."

Tristan Lowell, her aggravating partner, shot her a bemused look, arching a single eyebrow, before facing his assailant once more.

Jayne rolled her eyes. It was a pitiful insult, to be sure. She'd have to work harder next time. Tristan didn't actually wear any makeup; she was merely drawing attention to his luscious black lashes that any girl would envy. Of course the fates would decide to bestow them on a douchebag like Tristan instead of someone more worthy.

"You still have the grimoire?" Tristan called over his shoulder as he edged closer to the staircase.

"What do you take me for?" Jayne cried, pulling an Attack spell and flinging it toward the Wonder Woman wannabe, but the man jerked out of the way just in time. "Of course I have it!"

"Then follow my lead!" Without waiting for her response, Tristan ducked down low as a shower of sparks burst just above his head, narrowly missing his scalp. He rolled and jumped to his feet before dashing down the stairs, his lithe figure quickly sprinting the length of the reading room before he disappeared from view.

"Follow your lead," Jayne grumbled, straightening her blouse and climbing to her feet. "Easy for you to say, when you move like a damn acrobat."

The lasso snaked toward her feet once more, but Jayne hopped out of reach, reaching for the Torrent to find something new, something different. She pictured an ice cube with the lasso trapped inside, and the Torrent presented her with the Freeze spell.

Perfect.

She grabbed it, the pale blue light shimmering in her hands before tossing it on the lasso, effectively freezing it in place. The Wonder Woman thug grunted, his beefy hands tugging fruitlessly at the rope to pull it free, but it was useless. A glistening blue glow encased the lasso and it was stiff as a board, no longer the flexible whip of death he'd been using. Slowly, the icy magic began to climb up his hand, spreading along his skin. The man's eyes widened in alarm as he struggled more intensely against the spell.

Jayne smiled and blew him a kiss before hurrying down the staircase after Tristan. The reading room was roughly the size of a large cathedral, with towering bookshelves neatly lining each wall. She said a silent prayer to any gods and goddesses watching that every single shelf would remain intact during this fight. Thankfully, the civilians in the reading room were none the wiser, though they did look up occasionally as Tristan or Jayne shouted. It seemed the Torrent's knack for masking spells did not extend to carefully barbed insults. Pity.

A burst of heat seared past Jayne's left ear, so she started bobbing and weaving, knowing her Wonder Woman assailant had decided to ditch the frozen rope and come after her. She rushed out of the reading room and clambered down another set of stairs, muttering a quick "Later, Giro!" to the statue of Cardinal Girolamo Casanate that stood sentinel in the next room.

She quickly caught up with Tristan, who hissed, "What took you so long?" before they bolted out the door.

The Biblioteca Casanatense was tucked away in a side street, concealed from view—the perfect hiding spot for a magical grimoire. Jayne dodged the bikeshares and Vespas parked on the narrow street, following Tristan up the road toward the Piazza di San Macuto. While it was advantageous for them to steal a grimoire from an inconspicuous location, it did make them easy targets. The streets were far too quiet.

Sure enough, the two goons burst out the door after them, and it took no time at all before more spells were launched in their direction.

"Down!" Jayne shouted, and she and Tristan dropped to the ground to avoid getting hit. When she heard the spells explode against the concrete in front of them, Jayne jumped up, arms raised, palms out as she conjured a massive Block spell. A transparent dome surrounded her and Tristan, and the incoming spells ricocheted, bouncing off the shield and flying in different directions. Jayne sliced her hands through the air, layering an Attack spell with a Cloaking spell as she launched an offensive attack. The Cloaking spells masked the spells from view, so the goons stared, wide-eyed and clueless, as the invisible Attack spells smacked them in the face.

"Taste of your own medicine, bastards," Jayne said, rubbing her nose in memory of her own face-plant.

She and Tristan bolted, taking advantage of their enemies' momentary lapse in concentration. They reached the Piazza and turned, winding down Via del Seminario, the crowd thickening as they drew closer to the Pantheon. After a few minutes of sprinting, they easily blended in with the horde of pedestrians swarming the streets of Rome, chattering away as if there weren't two magical baddies lurking nearby.

Jayne honestly couldn't believe tourists were still out and about after the explosion at the Basilica di San Clemente. Then again, it wasn't like they had any idea that magic was behind it; as far as they knew, it was just some freakish natural disaster. The blue light in the sky was so clearly magical, any Adept in the area would know immediately. Jayne was only slightly relieved that she was across town at the moment it happened. She'd been tempted to leave her post, but had resisted. Tristan wouldn't have played along, anyway.

Because everything about the basilica collapse felt like a Ruth Thorne/Kingdom attack. Distract the masses with some huge, violent act of terror so the minions could get to this library undetected. It was meant to distract Jayne and Tristan from their mission. She was sure of it.

And that she hadn't run off to help showed how much she had grown. She'd stayed focused on the grimoire they'd been sent to retrieve, like she was supposed to. *See, Amanda? I can listen to orders.*

A tourist in a gray baseball cap shot her a look as she darted past him. They were drawing the nonmagicals' attention.

"Okay, okay. When in Rome, do as the clueless nonmagic folk do," Jayne muttered, slowing her stride to catch her breath —and so she didn't stick out. She nudged Tristan's elbow to indicate he do the same.

"We need to reach the safe house," Tristan panted, his brows lowering.

"We need to blend in and play it cool," Jayne shot back. "If we run, we'll draw their attention. They don't care about casualties, and they'll shoot down anyone in their way."

"Exactly. Which means we should be putting distance between us and these innocent civilians."

Jayne gave him her most withering glare, refusing to back down. She put a hand on his shoulder, perhaps digging in her fingernails a bit too much as she swept a Cloaking spell over him. His clothes and skin glimmered like a sparkly vampire, and he blinked at her.

"Should help us stay invisible," Jayne said before mimicking the same spell over her own body.

"You call yourself a Master magician?" Tristan scoffed. "Cloaking spells don't make a person invisible. It only adds camouflage."

"While this is a lovely time to learn all the specifics about the inner workings of Cloaking spells, can we do a rain check?" This wasn't the first time Tristan had lectured her about her inexperience, and it certainly wouldn't be the last. Her patience was already wearing thin.

"You shouldn't wait until you're in the field to learn the inner working of spells," Tristan said, his tone laced with irritation.

Jayne ignored him, though she balled her hands into fists, if only to keep herself from punching him in the face. The air behind them crackled with energy, and warmth tickled Jayne's brow in the same spot her totem glowed when Medb, the dead Master magician, was speaking to her.

The Earth goddess. She was trying to warn her.

Jayne stopped in her tracks, going perfectly still, her eyes closing as she opened her senses and listened. The chatter of the surrounding crowd died away, and her consciousness plunged into the earth, searching, seeking out the energies the totem gave her.

Then she heard it. Someone was whispering an enchantment, and a familiar ashy smell tickled Jayne's nose.

"Shit," she muttered, her mind crashing back to the present where Tristan was waving a hand in front of her face. She smacked his hand away and said, "They're casting a Tracking spell. They'll find us in the crowd in minutes."

Tristan's brow furrowed. He searched his pockets before

withdrawing a spray canister. Without warning, he spritzed Jayne up and down her body before doing the same to himself. Gagging, Jayne coughed and wheezed, trying to get the nasty sharp cologne smell out of her mouth. "God, what *is* that, Axe?"

"The foulest body spray I could find," Tristan said, wrinkling his own nose. "But the most pungent of aromas will mask a Tracking spell."

Jayne scowled. "You can't be serious. That sounds more like an old wives' tale."

"I *am* serious. A Tracking spell is like putting a bloodhound on someone's trail. If you mask the scent of the target, they are harder to track." He glanced over her shoulder. "Come on. We should keep moving."

As much as Jayne didn't trust his judgment, she knew he was right. The longer they stood still, the more attention they would draw to themselves. Besides, those Kingdom thugs were getting closer.

"If you're wrong, you're buying dinner," Jayne said, resisting the urge to look over her shoulder. "And dessert. Which will be lots of pie."

Tristan shot her a lopsided grin. "Deal. But I'm not wrong."

Oh, the male ego, Jayne thought to herself. *Such a fragile, stubborn thing.*

The hairs on the back of Jayne's neck stood on end, and she suppressed a shiver. Without thinking, she muttered, "Take off your jacket."

Tristan raised an eyebrow. "Shouldn't you take me to dinner first? You know, since you'll be losing the bet?"

Jayne elbowed him in the ribs. "If your old wives' tale proves correct, then removing our scent and tossing it somewhere else will throw them off our trail, right?"

Pride glimmered in Tristan's eyes. "That's...very smart."

"Did you just compliment me? Good Lord, the sky must be falling."

Tristan chuckled. "I know. But don't get used to it. I'll be back to insulting you in no time."

Despite his promise, Jayne found herself laughing as she yanked off her scarf and cardigan, leaving her in just a tank top. Thankfully, the air was warm, so it didn't bother her; if anything, it helped her fit in with the gaggle of college girls alongside them.

"Where to?" she asked, holding up her bundle of Jayne-scented clothes.

Tristan eyed her up and down, whether in disapproval or satisfaction, she couldn't tell. Then he gestured to the gelateria around the corner. "Fancy some gelato?"

Jayne's mouth watered at the sight of the delicious cones the other tourists were enjoying, but she quashed down her desire for sweets and nodded. Without further ado, Tristan took her cardigan and scarf and casually dropped it on the bench outside the gelateria, alongside his jacket. He strode nonchalantly down the street, a hand in his pocket, his face the picture of innocence.

Jayne didn't realize she was staring at him until he raised his eyebrows at her. "What?" he asked.

She shook her head, part annoyed and part impressed. Not for the first time, she imagined him as a model for a French perfume commercial. Flawless. Smooth. Masculine. "I don't know how you do that."

"Do what, exactly?"

"The whole *confident Frenchman* thing."

"Well, I am a confident Frenchman."

"Yes, yes. Confident. Irritating. Condescending..."

"Come now, don't be mean."

"Pompous. Difficult. Conceited."

"Please stop." Despite his request, Tristan was laughing.

They approached the Pantheon, and Jayne's breath caught in her throat as she gazed up at the magnificent architecture. Even from behind, it was awe-inspiring: the ancient concrete that spoke of hundreds of years of history, the domed rotunda on top, the half-circle windows that reminded her of a dungeon...

Before her yearning could blossom into a full-blown obsession, Jayne shut it down, remembering from her research that there was a strict dress code for entering the Pantheon, and her tank top simply wouldn't cut it. Even if she had the time to go inside and drink everything in, she wouldn't be allowed.

"You finished drooling yet?" Tristan asked.

"You uncultured swine. How can you not drool over something as breathtaking as this?"

"Because I have some semblance of self-control and focus. We're on a mission, remember?"

"Right." She shot one last parting glance at the Pantheon. "Another time," she promised.

"Stop making romantic promises to a building."

"You can't tell me who to love. I'll proposition whomever—or whatever—I please, thank you very much."

Tristan opened his mouth to reply, his eyes glimmering with the promise of another insult, when he stopped, his gaze snagging on something over Jayne's shoulder. "They took the bait," he muttered.

Jayne followed his gaze and found the two Kingdom operatives lingering by the bench outside the gelateria. One of them lifted up Jayne's cardigan and spouted something in loud, rapid-fire Welsh.

"Time's up." Jayne grabbed Tristan's elbow, and they burst into motion, weaving between tourists and civilians until they reached the front of the Pantheon, heading toward the Piazza della Rotonda. They passed the Macuteo Obelisk and a vendor shouting something about purchasing tickets to the Pantheon. Jayne shot one last look behind them, ensuring the goons hadn't spotted them, before she followed Tristan down a side street, away from the crowd and out of sight.

CHAPTER

THREE

A DARK ALLY

London

Ruth Thorne rubbed her forehead for the fourteenth time that day, the spot marking her totem irritating her profusely. If her clueless daughter could handle the weight of a totem, surely she, the Head of the Kingdom, could manage it just fine.

But the dark and persistent voice rumbled inside her, clawing at her insides, struggling to get out. It had consumed her in Rome just before the explosion at the basilica, and it was trying its damnedest to take her once more.

Ruth gritted her teeth so hard her head began to throb. The raging fire inside her was incessant.

And she knew exactly why. Before she'd even begun seeking out the Master magicians and their totems, she had unleashed something from within the Torrent. A presence she could not—*would not*—name. This presence had been her ally. Her ace in the hole. Her secret confidant. A voice so vibrant she could do nothing but acquiesce to its every demand.

At first, she'd thought it was the Master of Shadows. But no, her daughter Jayne had quite thoroughly banished the Master, sending him back into his resting place.

This was something different. Something that had been lurking in Ruth's mind since she first discovered her powers.

When she'd struck a bargain with it, she hadn't thought very far ahead. All she knew then was she needed to locate the Master magicians and their totems before the TCO did. By any means necessary.

And for that, she needed to locate the remaining necromantic grimoires. They were the keys to locating the totems.

But now, her dark ally was calling in its debts. And Ruth had no choice but to pay them herself. She couldn't very well introduce this powerful presence to others within the Kingdom; they would want that power for themselves, and Ruth couldn't risk it. She had to be in control. She had to be the most powerful. The most feared.

A cold sweat broke out on her skin, making her feel clammy and feverish. Her mouth turned dry, and she swallowed down another bout of nausea. It felt like her body was literally at war with itself, trying to combat the foreign presence inside her.

Because there was no doubt about it. The *thing* she'd unleashed from the Torrent...was now living inside her.

Not even the peaceful ambience of her flat in London could soothe the beast writhing within. Ordinarily, this place was a haven, a sanctuary for her to escape to. Something separate from the world, from the Kingdom, from her enemies. Her eyes went over the expensive paintings she'd acquired over the years —some illegally, of course, but that was part of her trade as an art dealer. After all, the Kingdom's efforts had to be funded somehow, and she couldn't exactly acquire the funds by bussing tables or selling appliances door-to-door.

Ordinarily, the Monet, Van Gogh, and Renoir paintings on the living room wall provided her comfort, reminding her of her status in life. She was elegant and wealthy. Powerful. Feared. The Head of an organization whose power grew day by day.

But today, gazing at these paintings brought her no peace. Only a sense of foreboding.

Her cell phone rang, an obnoxious trilling that made her jump. Her skin crawled as if she expected the foreign presence inside her to leap out if startled. But of course, it remained inside her, hiding away, biding its time...

Ruth brought the phone to her ear and snapped, "What?" Her usual phone was silenced; this one was only to be used in emergencies.

"You asked for us to send word when we tracked down the Guardian," came Lars's gruff voice. "We found her."

Ruth's mind was abuzz. For the moment, the presence inside her was silenced as plans took root, spreading and growing with fervor. The opportunity she'd waited for was hers for the taking. At last.

A cruel smile crept across her face. "Where?"

CHAPTER
FOUR
A VERY MINOR GRIMOIRE

Rome

Tristan Lowell stood in the safe house, waiting for Jayne to open the sibylline texts they'd just acquired from the Biblioteca Casanatense. The infuriating woman was sitting there, eyes closed in concentration. She was taking far too long to just open the damn book. Tristan would have done it himself, confident in his magical prowess that he could fight off whatever dark influence might be contained within. But orders were orders. And Jayne was his superior. Much as he disliked the thought.

Ruger Stern, Jayne's mentor and superior, stood next to the sofa, his eyes on Jayne as he, too, waited—much more patiently than Tristan.

A full minute passed, and Tristan tried his very best not to snap at the powerful Master magician. Knowing how much she disliked him, it would probably only delay things further.

Besides, Jayne had no way of knowing just how desperate

he was to open the grimoire and see what was contained within. She didn't know what was at stake.

And he couldn't tell her.

He was already uneasy with the idea of working with a Master magician—the first one the world had seen in decades. Never mind the fact that Jayne had just discovered her powers mere months ago. The girl was a bomb set to go off at any moment. Without the years of training most Adepts underwent, there was no way she could handle such volatile power. It was bound to burn her up, along with anyone else standing too close to the flames.

She was a means to an end. No matter how charming or quirky or witty her comebacks were. Once Tristan got what he needed, he intended to leave her far, far behind to avoid whatever disaster was sure to find her.

So, Tristan stood on the opposite end of the living room of the safe house, arms crossed as he waited for her to assess what was inside the grimoire. Though his head was spinning with anticipation and anxiety, his body remained perfectly composed. Years of shielding his true intentions from his power-hungry mother had taught him well.

It wasn't until Tristan felt a powerful magical presence permeate the air that he realized what Jayne was doing. The Earth totem from Queen Medb gleamed brightly on her forehead, and her brows were knitted in concentration.

She was summoning her Earth magic instead of relying on the Torrent. How interesting.

Jayne straightened on the sofa, her eyes opening and fixing on the grimoire sitting on the coffee table in front of her. The book looked quite innocent. Almost insignificant. Its leather bindings were worn with age, the edges frayed and tattered. The pages contained within were stained and weathered. It looked like it might fall apart from a single touch.

"Brace yourselves," Jayne said, her gaze never straying from the grimoire. "Last time I opened a powerful grimoire, it tried to eat me."

Tristan's brow furrowed. He was unsure if she was being serious or not. He could never tell with this woman.

"I'm not sensing too much power from it," Tristan said. "We should be fine." The words were meant to be reassuring, but he couldn't help the disappointment lacing his tone. He could already tell there wasn't nearly enough power contained in this book, despite what he'd originally thought. Which meant this wasn't the grimoire he was looking for.

Even so, he had to be sure.

"Whenever you're ready, Jayne," Ruger said in a soft voice.

Jayne took a long, steadying breath and puffed out an exhale with a resolved nod. Then, the motion quick as if she feared the book would burn her, she flipped open the cover. Gold light shimmered from the pages, casting a warm glow on her skin. Her face was ethereal in the light, and as the Earth totem brightened on her forehead, she almost looked like a goddess herself. Despite his reservations about her, Tristan couldn't keep his breath from hitching.

Just as suddenly as it appeared, the gold light faded, leaving the air cold and dim in its wake.

Tristan blinked, and Jayne reared back with a bewildered "What the hell?"

He took a wary step closer. "What's on the pages?"

Jayne extended a hand and pressed it against the parchment. She closed her eyes, and magic hummed in the air. The marking on her forehead burned brighter.

"There is...magic in here," she said, her voice distant. "But not a lot. As you said." She frowned. "Damn it. Really?" She yanked her hand back, her eyes opening as she leaned forward to inspect the pages. "It's just an anthology of prophecies."

Tristan could hold back no longer. He strode forward, his heart leaping in his throat as his senses confirmed what she had said. *There's not very much magic here.* He took the seat opposite Jayne, leaning forward with his arms propped on his knees. Careful not to touch the pages directly, he inhaled, focusing on the particular scent of the magic.

"Are you...sniffing it?" Jayne asked.

Tristan ignored her.

"I mean, no judgment. I sniff books all the time. It's kind of a thing among the bookish community."

Again, he said nothing. Each individual strand of magic had a signature flavor. He took another breath, isolating each odor, each aura the magic had left behind.

At long last, he sat back in defeat. "It's a minor grimoire."

"A what?"

Tristan rubbed the bridge of his nose. He didn't have the patience for this. Not when his only lead had turned out to be a dead end. "A *minor* grimoire."

"Yes, I heard you," Jayne snapped. "What is that?"

"Most of the grimoires you've encountered have been major ones," Ruger provided. "A couple were necromantic, full of the powerful, dark magic that can raise the dead. But not all magic is that powerful. Some lesser magics can still bewitch a book and grant it magical properties."

Jayne's eyes lit up. "Fascinating." She gazed at the book, her fingers hovering over its pages. "It's a cute little baby grimoire."

Tristan scowled. "Which means it's not the necromantic grimoire we were searching for."

"Hey, the Kingdom was after this, too. So if we don't know what it is, neither do they. It's still a win in my book. No pun intended."

"Still, this doesn't warrant something as drastic as blowing up the basilica," Ruger said thoughtfully. "If they went to such great lengths to cause a disturbance, I would think they would've made certain this was the right grimoire first."

Tristan ran a shaky hand through his hair, rising from the sofa. He needed to escape before he bit this woman's head off.

All he could think of was his utter and complete failure. Years of searching, and he had failed *again*.

He would never find it. He was doomed to spend the rest of his life searching for what couldn't be found.

"Tristan?"

Tristan realized he'd been pacing and stopped abruptly, looking at Jayne's concerned blue eyes. He felt Ruger watching him as well.

"Setbacks happen." Jayne's voice was gentle. "We'll find the real one. It's not like we have a list of lost necromantic grimoires we can pick and choose from. We have to discover them, one by one, using rumor and innuendo and—"

Her patronizing tone only incensed him further. "I've been doing this for years, and you started what, two days ago? Spare me your lecture."

"Tristan," Ruger growled in warning.

Jayne's eyebrows shot up. She lifted her hands, palms out. "Ooooookay," she said, drawing out the word. "I get the feeling you need to blow off some steam. I'll leave you to...brood." She huffed in exasperation and stood, not bothering to glance at him once before she left the room.

Tristan buried his face in his hands. He regretted snapping at Jayne; she was kind and didn't deserve that. But he couldn't be around her right now.

He sensed movement and looked up. Ruger was approaching, his face unreadable.

"Amanda says you asked for this assignment," the burly man said.

"I did."

Ruger watched him, unblinking. "Why?"

"Rumor and innuendo, remember?" Tristan said automatically. When Ruger didn't rise to the bait, he continued. "I've heard there's a necromantic grimoire hidden in Rome just like you have. I thought this grimoire might be the key to stopping the Kingdom. If they're after it, too, it looks like I was right."

Ruger's dark eyes continued to scrutinize him, and Tristan resisted the urge to avert his gaze. After a long moment, Ruger only hummed thoughtfully before leaving the room.

Damn that man and his sixth sense. Ruger always had a way of reading people. He'd been the only one who could see through Tristan's facade—the very mask that fooled his own mother.

But Ruger had good reason to be suspicious. In all his years of working for the TCO, Tristan had never deviated from or questioned a direct order. It had been Tristan who'd proposed an alternative plan to head off the Kingdom. He told them he'd received intelligence from one of his people in the splinter group of former La Liberté members he was in charge of, that one of the powerful necromantic grimoires they were seeking had surfaced in Rome and they couldn't pass up the opportunity to investigate. Thankfully, Amanda had jumped on the idea, but Ruger must have known something was up, especially now that the grimoire turned out to be worthless.

He ran a frustrated hand through his hair. His real mission was too important and too delicate to risk sharing with anyone else in the TCO, especially when there was a supposed mole in their midst. If Ruger started sniffing around, he could expose Tristan's entire plan.

He'd hoped it wouldn't come to this. But this was taking too long.

Desperate times called for desperate measures. And he was out of options.

FIVE

AN OLD FRIEND

Patagonia

S ofia had the strangest sense of déjà vu as she knocked on the door of a teal-roofed house halfway down the narrow street in Ushuaia, Argentina. This wasn't the first time she'd gone to great lengths to track down the powerful Adept named Xiomara de la Vega. Not only was the air saturated with power and magic—it thrummed along Sofia's skin, reverberating down to her bones—but the streets here looked similar to those in Miami's Little Havana. The climate, however, was quite different. Sofia still couldn't get over the vast mountain backdrop or the kaleidoscope of various-colored houses in the area.

Not to mention the temperature. Good Lord, it was freezing. Even with her sweater and scarf to keep her warm, Sofia couldn't keep her teeth from chattering. The chilly wind did nothing to help the situation. Though her blonde hair was tied back into a bun, several strands had pulled free and were whipping about her face with all the energy of those inflatable balloon-man things usually found at car dealerships.

Generally, when Sofia thought of Argentina, she thought of warm climes. But this place was nicknamed "The End of the World" for a reason. It was one of the closest cities to Antarctica.

Of course Xiomara would be hiding out here. Because it would be too much to ask for her to hide herself away in a quaint, pleasant city like Bismarck, North Dakota.

"You scent anything off?" she asked Cillian, who stood next to her. Though he wasn't shivering as severely as she was, his body was still tensed, indicating his discomfort.

His blue eyes grew distant as he inhaled deeply. As a Rogue who could shift into wolf form, Cillian had an impressive sense of smell. After a moment, he frowned and shook his head. "It's strange. I smell...nothing. Normally I can get a whiff of *something*, whether it be food or dust or traces of magic. But this place has an eerie absence of scents."

Sofia nodded. "It's probably warded." Xiomara was smart. With as much magic as she possessed, she would have likely taken precautions. Sofia resisted the urge to wrap her arms around herself. She still wasn't accustomed to *so much* magic pulsing through her body. Every hair seemed to stand on end in response to the potent presence of all that otherworldly energy. In Little Havana, her powers had been buried so deeply she had barely noticed the change in the air. But here and now, it was as intense as someone screaming in her ear.

Sofia rapped on the orange door once again, her knuckles brushing against the peeling paint. She resisted the urge to glance over her shoulder at the TCO officers lying in wait in case things went awry. Amanda had thought it best not to draw too much attention to themselves in case the Kingdom or La Liberté were nearby. And since Sofia was the only member of their team who had actually met Xiomara before, everyone thought it was best if she approached Xiomara first so as not to spook her.

But from what Sofia remembered of the formidable woman, she was not easily spooked.

Cillian, of course, was backup. Because as a Rogue, he had bonded with Sofia's Master magician powers.

She suppressed a shudder at the thought. *He's your Rogue,* Amanda had said just before sending them into the field. But those words sounded foul to Sofia's ears. Less than a month ago, Cillian had been her sister's boyfriend, and they too had supposedly bonded as Master and Rogue. Now, because of one crazy, inexplicable moment of converged magic, Sofia had not only stolen her sister's Rogue but she had managed to break them up as well.

Swallowing down her disgust and self-loathing, Sofia focused on the task at hand, staring at the door as if she could force it open by sheer willpower. She listened hard, but it was difficult to make out any sounds over the roaring wind in her ears. She wasn't sure if she was disappointed or relieved that no one seemed to be home...

Until the door swung open, and her heart lurched in her throat.

Her unease quickly melted into confusion as she found herself staring at a small child. The boy was probably no older than eight, and he stared up at Sofia with wide, dark eyes. Dirt smeared his cheeks, and his black hair was wild and unkempt around his face.

"¿Quién eres?" the boy asked, his voice faint but curious.

"Um," said Sofia, exchanging a bewildered glance with Cillian, who shrugged. "Is Xiomara here?"

"Juanito!" called a voice from within the house. *"¿Quién es?"*

"¡Estoy tratando de averiguarlo!" Juanito shouted back.

But Sofia had gone stiff at the sound of the second speaker. It had been so long, but she remembered the timbre of that deep, strong voice like it was yesterday.

"Xiomara?" Sofia called, squinting past the boy toward the darkened hallway behind him. "It's Sofia Thorne." She figured the best strategy was to be up-front and announce herself right away.

Silence met her words. Juanito muttered something else in Spanish before throwing his hands in the air and striding away from the door, leaving it wide open. Sofia rubbed her arms, wanting nothing more than to warm herself inside the house but feeling uncomfortable on the threshold since she hadn't been invited in yet.

Slow footsteps drew nearer. Then, at the end of the hallway, a familiar white-haired figure emerged. She leaned on a cane, but aside from that, she looked exactly the same as Sofia remembered. Same dark, fearsome eyes. Same wrinkles and hair. Same impatient scowl.

"You shouldn't be here, girl," Xiomara said when she reached the doorway. Her eyes flicked briefly to Cillian before she focused on Sofia.

Sofia bristled at the word *girl*. She might have been young and naive when they'd last seen each other, but that was almost a decade ago. So much had changed since then.

A low growl rumbled from Cillian's throat, and his lips curled back as he bared his teeth. His cold blue eyes flashed, his furious gaze pinned on Xiomara.

Sofia decided to cut right to the chase before Cillian shifted and pounced on the woman. "How long have you known my father was alive?"

Xiomara eyed her shrewdly. To her credit, she didn't flinch or gasp at Sofia's direct question. The older woman arched a single eyebrow before jerking her head toward the hallway. "Come in."

This is going well so far, Sofia thought, stepping inside. Cillian followed her and shut the door. Warmth immediately enveloped her from the wind's absence, and she sighed with relief.

"¿Así que es una amiga?" Juanito's small voice echoed from one of the bedrooms.

"Cállate," Xiomara snapped, hobbling down the small hallway with Sofia trailing behind her. *"Hazte escaso."*

A quick scuffling sound, and then...silence.

"Where did he go?" Sofia asked uncertainly, glancing around like she expected the boy to pop out. But it was as if he had vanished completely.

"Don't mind Juanito," Xiomara said, leading Sofia and Cillian to a small sitting room with worn couches and a coffee table missing a leg. "He's an orphan I've taken in. He knows when to make himself scarce. As you can imagine, the work I do involves a lot of secrecy."

"Which is why I'm surprised you have a small child running about."

"Would you prefer I leave him on the streets?" Xiomara barked.

"Of course not."

Xiomara's scowl deepened as she gestured to the couches. Slowly, Sofia sank down on one, and a plume of dust rose from the cushion. With a groan, Xiomara sat opposite her, the movement looking like it pained her deeply.

"I would offer tea," Xiomara said, "but my hands aren't as nimble as they once were."

"Don't worry about it," Sofia said at once. "We won't be long."

"Did Ruth send you?"

Sofia's blood ran cold at the thought of her power-hungry mother. "No," she said sharply. "The last time I saw Ruth, she tried to kill me."

Xiomara nodded as if this didn't surprise her.

Sofia leaned forward, meeting Xiomara's gaze. "How long have you known about my father?"

Xiomara sighed, propping her arm on her cane. "A year. Ever since I found out, I've been trying to locate him."

"Seems to me you did."

Xiomara's eyes narrowed. "You aren't working alone, are you?" Her gaze cut to Cillian in accusation.

"No."

Xiomara swore under her breath. "You brought them here, didn't you?"

"You can trust them," Cillian said defensively.

"Don't tell me who I can trust. I've been betrayed by too many to believe it."

"Just tell me where my dad is and we'll be on our way," Sofia said quickly. "We'll leave you in peace."

Xiomara shook her head, her expression souring. "It's far too late for that, girl."

"Why?"

"The Guardians are under attack from all sides. If Henry Thorne hasn't been targeted yet, he will be soon. I found him, so it's only a matter of time before they do."

"Who is *they*?" Sofia demanded.

"It's a long story."

Sofia sighed, growing impatient. "I didn't come all this way for riddles and vague replies. Did you find Henry or not?"

"I did find him," Xiomara said. "But during our travels, we were separated. I don't know what became of him. Our mutual friend was captured, and I had to flee before I was taken, too."

"What mutual friend?" asked Cillian, frowning.

"Another Guardian. He's probably dead by now. And he's probably told them your father is alive."

Sofia felt the blood drain from her face. "Who is *them*?" she asked again.

"Years ago, one of our own turned on us, rebelling against the Guardians and their calling. He's amassed a following and is trying to end us and our mission."

Sofia remembered what Amanda had said about the Guardians—that they had a sacred mission to protect the natural pockets of energy within the Torrent. Around the world, there were eight of them—eight magical hot spots that needed to be guarded lest they become unstable and threaten civilian lives.

"We already lost the pocket in Miami," Xiomara went on, her tone morose. "It was overrun by the Kingdom years ago. And before that, Mumbai. We are losing more and more ground every day."

Sofia went still. *The Kingdom.* She remembered seeing Aaró, a powerful member of the Kingdom, when she'd been in Little Havana. Aaró was dead now, but it seemed his presence in Miami had done its damage.

"So, what are you doing here? In Argentina?" Sofia asked.

"Guarding Henry's pocket." Xiomara said it like it was the most obvious thing in the world.

A sharp prickle of surprise swept through Sofia's body. The hairs on her arms stood on end. "Are you...are you saying my father is a Guardian?"

"Was," Xiomara corrected. "He gave up his mission when he went in hiding." She waved a hand, dismissing this earth-shattering news. "Another long story."

"So, why aren't you trying to get him back?" Sofia found her voice rising. "Why aren't you helping him? He's in hiding for a reason... My psychotic mother and several other terrorists are after him!"

"I have a sacred duty to uphold. Now that Guardians are being targeted and pockets are being seized, it is imperative that we protect our own. We cannot risk more pockets falling into the wrong hands." She glared at Sofia. "Which is why you shouldn't be here. I can smell the power on you. You'll attract them like flies to honey."

"I am not leaving until I have some clue where he is," Sofia said, determination flooding her.

"Well, I don't trust you, your boyfriend, or your team hiding out there." Xiomara waved a wrinkled hand toward the front door. "My kind are at war. I'm not telling you anything until I know for certain you can be trusted."

"I'm not her boyfriend," Cillian said. "I'm her Rogue. And how can we prove it to you?" He sounded far more patient than Sofia felt. Perhaps it was best if he did the talking.

Xiomara's gaze remained pinned on Sofia, who glowered in response. This woman knew where her father was. Sofia didn't care if she had to wait all night; she was determined to get answers.

"Let my magic commune with yours," Xiomara said. Her voice was so soft that Sofia wasn't certain she'd heard her right.

"I'm sorry?" Sofia asked.

"There is Guardian blood running through your veins. I felt it in you years ago. Why do you think you and your sister are so powerful? If my magic makes contact with yours, I'll be able to sense if you're being truthful."

Sofia's impatience fled her in an instant, leaving behind a cold dread. She still didn't fully trust her own magic. Now she had another kind of magic running through her veins? She didn't like the sound of that at all.

Cillian seemed to sense Sofia's hesitation, because he spoke for her. "What would she have to do?"

Xiomara offered a withered hand, palm up, toward Sofia. "All you have to do is take my hand. Our magic will do the rest."

Sofia shifted uncomfortably on the sofa. It seemed too easy. And putting her trust in this strange magic—in Xiomara's magic—didn't sit well with her.

"I'll be here," Cillian reassured her. "And the team is close by. It'll be all right, Sofia."

This reminder sent a tendril of warmth through Sofia's chest, despite how much she resisted it. She shouldn't be comforted by Cillian's presence; he was still pining for Jayne. He didn't belong to Sofia at all.

He's your partner, said a small voice in her head. *Not your lover. This is a professional relationship between two colleagues.*

Even so, a bond between Master and Rogue felt...intimate. It felt like a violation of the Girl Code for Sofia to bind herself to Jayne's ex.

Squaring her shoulders, Sofia lifted her chin and met Xiomara's gaze. "Fine. I'll do it." Before she could change her mind, she leaned forward and clasped the old woman's hand.

At first, nothing happened, and Sofia felt like a complete idiot, sitting there holding this woman's hand. Then, a flash of gold light burned in her gaze, momentarily blinding her. She gasped as the light intensified as if the sun itself was blasting its way through the tiny house. Sofia was weightless, floating in the burning glow, soaring among the smooth flow of magic.

Then, she touched the Torrent. She didn't know how else to describe it. There was the gleaming river of stars, sparkling and shimmering. She extended a hand, dipping her fingers into the river, only to find it wasn't liquid at all but thousands of tiny particles. Almost like a river of sand or glitter.

The Torrent hummed from her touch like a cat purring in

contentment. And something inside Sofia sighed as peace and tranquility took over.

I'm home, her magic seemed to say. *Home at last.*

Her body jerked forward, and the magic, the stars, the gold light all vanished. She slammed back to reality with such force that her breaths came in sharp pants. Sweat beaded along her forehead and down the back of her neck. The room suddenly seemed so dim and dank compared to the glorious light she had just beheld.

"Ah." Xiomara sat back against the sofa cushions, her eyes closing and her face smoothing into a look of serenity and ease. "I have not communed with such pure, untainted power in decades. Your tether to the Torrent is strong, Sofia Thorne."

It was the first time Xiomara had used her real name. Sofia swallowed hard, feeling as if she should be uneasy or alarmed or confused. But her emotions matched the look on Xiomara's face.

Joy. Peace. Understanding. Contentment.

I'm home.

"I can tell you're being truthful," Xiomara went on, sitting up straighter. Her eyes opened, her dark pupils slightly dilated. "I will answer your questions. But only you two." She gestured to Cillian and Sofia. "No others."

Sofia should have been relieved, but she was still processing the mind-boggling journey to the Torrent she'd just experienced. "What...what's happening to me?" she whispered.

Xiomara's lips twitched with the ghost of a smile. "You've just unlocked your Guardian magic."

CHAPTER
SIX
THE MAGIC OF A TIME CATCH

Cillian didn't know what to make of this ancient woman before him. He could smell the magic on her—now that they had passed through whatever wards surrounded her home, the scent was as pungent as his smelly gym socks after a workout, though far less unpleasant.

And when Sofia had clasped Xiomara's hand... Well, he wasn't sure what Sofia had experienced, but Cillian could've sworn he'd seen the Torrent itself beckoning him forward.

It had been alarming, to say the least. He wasn't sure if he liked it. But his Rogue magic certainly had.

Oddly, it felt like a betrayal. Not just to himself, but to Jayne. Her magic had its own unique signature, and this...was so different. He was accustomed to the rosy tang of her energy, and to be so wrapped up in this foreign new magic felt like he was wearing someone else's skin.

His chest tightened with the strange sensation of his body detaching itself from his mind, as if he were no longer in control of how he felt and what his magic did. He felt like he was seconds away from his insides bursting free and flying all over the place.

His fingers curled into fists on his lap as he forced himself to focus on what the old woman was saying. This was important. This was why they were here.

Not for the first time, Cillian wished Jayne were with him. She would think of something clever or funny to say to defuse the tension.

"Henry was hiding in Time Catches," Xiomara was saying. "His magic is untraceable that way, but he has...aged. Significantly."

Sofia tensed beside Cillian. "Aged how? Is he like eighty years old now?" Her tone betrayed her fear. Cillian couldn't imagine the idea of being reunited with a long-lost father only to find he was at death's door.

"Not exactly," said Xiomara. "Spending that much time in a Time Catch can alter your mind. He is not who he used to be."

"What was he doing there?" Cillian asked. "In the Time Catches?"

"I don't know," Xiomara admitted. "But whatever project he was working on, he became obsessed with it. So much so that he abandoned his Guardianship. I always thought he'd return, but no. He did not."

"Doesn't entirely seem like a bad thing to me," Sofia said. "You just said the Guardians were at war. Maybe he wanted to get away from all that."

Xiomara shook her head. "You don't understand. But you will. A Guardian's sacred calling is protecting the Torrent. It calls to our blood." She leveled a gaze at Sofia. "It calls to *your* blood, too."

Sofia went perfectly still, but Cillian could sense unease rippling off her in waves.

"Where would he have gone?" Sofia asked. "When you were separated, where do you think he might have headed?"

Xiomara frowned. "All the Time Catches I knew about were

41

either collapsed or already discovered by our enemies. If he has another hideout, then I'm not aware of it."

Cillian swore under his breath. Blessed saints, what was this woman good for if she couldn't give them helpful information?

"But," Xiomara went on, "Valeri Rudik knows."

"Who?" Sofia asked.

"The Guardian who was traveling with us. He and Henry made plans to work together on Henry's secret project. I heard them muttering in coded phrases all throughout our journey."

"Your journey where?" Sofia asked.

"When I lost the pocket in Miami, I came here. Convenient, for when Henry left, I took over his guardianship."

"These coded phrases...they didn't let you in on it?" Cillian crossed his arms, finding this hard to believe.

"They said it was too dangerous." Xiomara shrugged one shoulder. "I'm old. I cannot blame them for keeping vital information from me. If I was younger and more capable, perhaps they would have asked for my help and included me on their mission. But I can understand why they did not. And the less I know, the safer I'll be."

"This Valeri Rudik," Sofia said slowly. "Where is he?"

"La Liberté." Xiomara's voice was stony. "He was captured."

Shit. Cillian and Sofia exchanged a dark look. The last they'd seen of the French terror organization, there had been a falling-out between Gina Labelle, its head, and her son, Tristan, who secretly worked with the TCO. The organization had been quiet ever since, which was no surprise; half its forces betrayed Gina to work with the CIA.

"He has likely endured all manner of torture," Xiomara continued in a grim tone. "I have no doubt that whatever Henry was working on, La Liberté now knows of it."

"Great. Just perfect." Sofia rubbed her temples and groaned.

"Our enemies know more about my father than I do, and our allies know absolutely nothing."

"Maybe Tristan knows," Cillian said hopefully.

Sofia dropped her hands and looked at him, her eyes turning thoughtful. "Maybe he does. I can ask Jayne to talk to him."

A ripple of awareness swept over Cillian at the mention of Jayne, but he quashed it down. She wasn't his girlfriend anymore.

Still, if he could just *see* her... An aching desperation filled his chest, and it wouldn't leave no matter how he attempted to redirect his thoughts.

"Thank you for the information," Sofia said quietly, and Cillian forced himself to focus on the conversation. "I'm sorry for everything you've been through." She hesitated before continuing, "My boss will want to speak with you. If that's all right."

Xiomara stiffened, her eyes narrowing. "I do not—"

"Her husband was a Guardian," Sofia said in a rush. "We're on the same side, Xiomara. We want to protect the Torrent, too."

Xiomara's expression remained hard as she stared down Sofia. To her credit, Sofia didn't back down, either; her chin lifted in defiance, and Cillian couldn't help but be impressed. Old as this woman was, she was still formidable, her dark eyes shrewd and calculating. And yet, Sofia refused to cringe away from her intimidating scrutiny.

These Thorne women are dangerous as well, Cillian thought with no small amount of respect.

At long last, Xiomara nodded stiffly. "Very well. I will speak with her."

Relief bloomed in Cillian's chest, and he relaxed against the sofa.

"I'll reach out to Jayne and see if she can get information out of Tristan," Sofia said, pulling out her cell phone.

Xiomara extended a hand to stop her. "Have a care. The more people we involve in this, the faster this wildfire will spread. War is on our doorstep. We can't avoid it much longer."

Sofia's eyes turned steely. "War is already here, Xiomara. And it's time we made our move."

CHAPTER
SEVEN
PICK A SIDE ALREADY

Amanda Newport clutched at the necklace around her throat, the habit unconscious and yet so very fitting given whose company she was in. She sat directly across from Xiomara de la Vega, the legendary Guardian and fearsome Adept, at the small breakfast nook in the CIA safe house. It was modest, since anything ostentatious would stand out in the insular city, but based on what Sofia and Cillian had reported, it was much more spacious than Xiomara's tiny home. Two steaming cups of untouched maté sat on the table in front of them as the silence stretched on.

Amanda had only read about Xiomara in reports back when her husband, Karam, had served as a Guardian. Karam himself hadn't known the woman, but Amanda had heard of her exploits. She once singlehandedly stopped the Kingdom from accessing the pocket in Miami. In the end, it hadn't mattered. A few years later, the Kingdom had taken the territory anyway.

How times were changing... Once, the TCO and their allies outnumbered the terrorists. Now, the enemy was swarming them on all sides, cutting them off from supplies and assistance.

This truly was a war. And Amanda and her team were deep in the trenches.

"We need you on our side," Amanda said, cutting to the chase. She sensed Xiomara, like her, didn't want to beat around the bush.

"I am only on the side of the Torrent," Xiomara said coldly.

"Perfect. So are we."

"You misunderstand me. I am only devoted to my assignment. My Guardian blood. As such, I am only on the side of the Guardians. That's all it ever will be."

"Bullshit," Amanda said.

Xiomara blinked, momentarily stunned.

"My husband was a Guardian," Amanda went on. "He and I were on the same side. Yes, we had different assignments, but we were united against the forces intent on destroying us. You want to know why you're at war? It's because of this stuck-up belief that you must isolate yourselves from the other Adepts in the world. And I tell you, it's utter bullshit."

Xiomara's cheeks reddened, her eyes darkening with fury. "Don't you dare patronize me. You know nothing about our calling or our magic."

"What part of *I was married to a Guardian* did you not understand?" Amanda said coldly. "My husband sacrificed himself for your calling. I was there."

A chilled silence filled the small space between them. A tendril of satisfaction worked through Amanda's chest at the look of shock and regret that flashed across Xiomara's face, but it was fleeting compared to the onslaught of terrible memories associated with that day.

"So don't *you* patronize *me*," Amanda went on, smoothing the wrinkles in her skirt. "The time for coddling is over. Sacrifices must be made, Xiomara. You can either work with us and accept the benefits and intel we have to offer. Or you can sit here by yourself and watch as you and your fellow Guardians are picked off one by one."

Xiomara's lips grew thin as she glared at Amanda. But she said nothing.

"In the end, do you think the Torrent will care about your exclusive Guardians-only club if our enemies win?" Amanda's voice was soft. "I think you understand it's more important to preserve the Torrent, even if it means revealing yourselves and your secrets."

Xiomara's nostrils flared as she pointedly looked away from Amanda. But Amanda didn't care. She wasn't going to walk on eggshells around this woman. Time was running out. They needed allies now, and if Xiomara was going to throw her out for being direct, then good riddance.

Finally, Xiomara sighed, the sound heavy and exhausted. "I can only speak for myself," she said. "But I will work with you. And I know of a few others who might be willing as well. But this will be an uphill battle, Ms. Newport. Convincing other Guardians to join you will not be easy."

"I know. I assure you, our team is—"

"Not your team," Xiomara interrupted sharply. "I work only with you and Sofia. I don't trust anyone else. Do I make myself clear?"

Amanda's mouth clamped shut. Ordinarily, she would have argued, would have sworn on her life that her entire team could be trusted.

But that wasn't true. Not anymore. They had a mole in the TCO, someone who had helped smuggle a dangerous grimoire from a secure location. Until she knew the traitor's identity, nothing was safe. Given how secretive the Guardians were, Amanda couldn't blame Xiomara for insisting on this caveat.

"Fine," Amanda said. "But where Sofia goes, Cillian goes. The Rogue is bonded to her."

47

Xiomara's eyebrows lifted at that. "Ah, yes. The tension was unmistakable."

Amanda had to refrain from rolling her eyes. Yes, the tension. She didn't even want to delve into the nasty mess that was Cillian and Jayne's breakup or the uneasy bond with Sofia due to their own stubborn reluctance. Goddess, sometimes it was a nightmare working with young adults. They were not far enough removed from the wildly emotional teenagers they were so recently.

"First, I'll need information about the other Guardians you're in communication with and how I can reach them," Amanda said, pulling out a pad of paper and a pen. She wished Pierce, her assistant, were here to take notes for her. But, per Xiomara's request, their collaboration had to remain classified at the highest level.

It was a small price to pay. As Xiomara began speaking, a buzz of energy prickled through Amanda. They had allies. They actually stood a chance. Perhaps the tides were turning.

CHAPTER
EIGHT
A REJECTION

Rome

J ayne inspected the sibylline texts more thoroughly, just to ensure she hadn't missed anything, before calling Amanda on a secure line to report. After Cloaking their conversation from anyone who might be listening in, Jayne filled in Amanda on the results of their mission. Sadly, the grimoire was, as it turned out, a minor one and held nothing significant other than vague prophecies. It was not, in fact, the droids they were looking for.

"That's truly unfortunate," Amanda said in a clipped tone. "What of the Kingdom?"

"In the wind," Jayne said. "I sent a Tracking spell after them, but their trail vanished. Ruger thinks they might have portaled somewhere."

"It's just as well. We received intelligence that Gina Labelle is searching for a necromantic grimoire in Rome. Since you and

Lowell are already there, I need you to track her down and head her off before she finds it."

"Wait, what? You told me I could search for my dad after this. I need to find him, Amanda. Have you found out anything in Patagonia?"

"Nothing particularly helpful. It turns out Xiomara doesn't know where he is. But the Guardians are powerful, and we need to ally with them if we want to protect the Torrent. I fear a storm is brewing, Jayne, and it's imperative that we prepare ourselves."

Jayne's head was reeling as she stared at the phone on the desk. "Amanda, I need to find my father. We agreed: one more assignment and then that would be the priority."

Amanda sighed on the other end. "Yes. I know."

Something about her tone made Jayne hesitate. She had never heard her boss sound so...dejected.

"It is important," Amanda said slowly as if considering each word carefully, "that you follow my instructions to the letter, Jayne. Now more than ever."

"I always follow your instructions."

A loud and very un-Amanda-ish snort sounded from the other end.

"Okay, most of the time," Jayne amended.

"I'm serious," Amanda said. "The director has expressed doubt that the TCO is making any headway in this war. We need to devote all our time and resources to stopping these terrorist attacks and putting an end to this once and for all."

"What does he think we've been doing this whole time?" Jayne asked with an incredulous laugh.

"Look at it from a non-Adept standpoint, Jayne. From our side, we've stopped massive catastrophes from happening, but the only tangible results we can show for it are the side effects and retaliation of our enemies—which are also catastrophic."

Jayne thought of the tidal wave in Rosses Point and the earthquake that leveled the city of Fontainebleau. So many innocents dead. Yes, to an outsider, these events did look pretty bad...

"We need to start showing more productive results," Amanda went on. "Immediately."

Alarm bells rang in Jayne's mind at the urgency in her voice. "Amanda, are you suggesting the CIA might shut down the TCO?"

Amanda sighed. "The director has suggested it might be beneficial for the Agency to distance itself from magic."

Jayne's heart turned to stone in her chest, sinking rapidly down to her stomach with all the weight of her horror. "*What?* But the TCO—"

"I know," Amanda said. "Now, more than ever, the Torrent needs to be protected. I made the seriousness of our situation clear, and I do believe Joshua is on my side on this. I've bought us some time...for now. But the final decision rests with the director, and he wants more proof that our time, effort, and resources are not being wasted."

"What can I do?"

"You can follow orders."

"Come on, Amanda. When have I ever done that?"

"I suppose never." The hint of a smile laced Amanda's words. "But you're a smart woman, Jayne. I figured if you knew what was at stake, you would make a solid and reasonable decision."

Jayne stifled a groan. "Damn it, Amanda, why'd you have to get all sensible and logical on me?" She shook her head, gritting her teeth against the desperate desire to find her father.

But Henry Thorne had survived this long on his own. Surely, he could survive a bit longer. At least long enough for Jayne to complete this mission and help keep the TCO alive.

She rubbed the space between her eyebrows, feeling a headache coming on. "All right. What do we know about this grimoire?"

"I've sent all the intel to Ruger. He'll brief you on the assignment. Can you put him on so I can speak with him?"

"Yeah, sure." Jayne paused. "Amanda?"

"Yes?"

"I know this is the right thing to do, but after this..." Jayne bit her lip, hesitating. "If the CIA continues to stand in the way of me finding my father, I'm walking."

Silence. Then Amanda said softly, "I understand. And I don't blame you, Jayne. I'll do everything in my power to ensure we get your father back."

"Thank you." Jayne's throat throbbed, tears stinging her eyes as she left the room to seek out Ruger.

JAYNE SAT in the living room, rereading *Eragon* and sipping a steaming cup of chamomile tea to soothe her nerves. But neither the delightful story nor the tea could quench her anxiety as she waited for Amanda and Ruger's lengthy conversation to end. For a while, she took pride in her impressive restraint, resisting the urge to eavesdrop. But then, twenty minutes later, she thought, *To hell with restraint,* and pressed her ear to the door—only to curse when she realized the whole room was Cloaked.

Figures.

Her cell phone chimed, and she whipped it out, thinking it might be a message from her other TCO buddies, like Seo-joon or Tamara, perhaps with some news about this rift with the CIA.

But it was from Sofia.

Jayne's heart twisted at the sight of her sister's name. God, she missed her so much. Every piece of her yearned to go to Patagonia despite what Amanda had ordered, just to be with Sofia again.

And yet, Sofia would have wanted Jayne to find their father. They had both agreed to do whatever it took to get him back.

Jayne frowned as she stared at the message, rereading it several times to ensure she understood.

Valeri Rudik. Ask Tristan.

Was this a code of some sort? Who was Valeri? And why would Tristan know about them?

She couldn't exactly ask Sofia for clarification. It was dangerous enough to send those four words. And if Sofia couldn't call to tell her this, it probably meant she wasn't supposed to share the information at all.

Jayne tapped her phone against her palm as she considered her options. Her pacing became more agitated by the minute. Amanda had promised to do everything in her power to help find Henry Thorne. Jayne had agreed to do one more mission before focusing on finding her father.

But still, it wouldn't hurt to do a bit of digging on her own, right? After all, if Jayne found out any helpful information about Henry Thorne's whereabouts, it could speed things along.

Once again, she stared hard at Sofia's message. *Ask Tristan.*

The man in question had been surprisingly quiet since they discovered the sibylline texts weren't part of a necromantic grimoire. Jayne just assumed he was sulking over their quasi-failed mission. The last thing she wanted to do was poke the bear.

But Sofia's message was clear, and Jayne had to follow this trail. She had to find out what Tristan knew.

She sent back a thumbs-up emoji, and the text vanished. Sofia had deleted it.

Damn. This *was* important.

She casually made her way to the kitchen, hoping to find him fixing his lunch.

No such luck.

Jayne made herself a BLT—well, it was really a PLT, as the bacon was replaced by salty, delicious prosciutto—arguing that she couldn't very well interrogate Tristan on an empty stomach. In truth, she was just stalling. After devouring the sandwich and a slice of pie, Jayne forced herself down the hallway to his closed door. With a deep breath, she knocked softly.

After a moment, Tristan asked, "Yes?"

"It's me." She paused. "Jayne. Your partner." *Good God, Jayne, just stop.* She cleared her throat. "Can I come in?"

Tristan said nothing, and Jayne shifted her weight from one foot to the other. Was he just going to ignore her? Was he *that* pissed?

At long last, the door cracked open, and Tristan's disheveled head came into view. His normally flawless hair was wild and untamed as if he'd just woken up. Very un-Tristan.

Jayne frowned, trying to catch a glimpse of the room behind him, but his broad frame took up all the space.

"What?" Tristan asked, a bit breathless.

Jayne arched an eyebrow. "What, you got a girl in there?"

Tristan rolled his eyes. "Did you just come here to pick a fight? Because I'm not in the mood."

How broody. Jayne straightened, summoning a fresh dose of resolve. "I need to ask you some questions."

Tristan's eyebrows lifted. "About?"

Really? He was going to make her just stand in the hallway? Well, fine. "About Valeri Rudik."

Confusion clouded his gaze, followed quickly by alarm, then suspicion. "How do you know that name?" he asked slowly.

Jayne forced her most pleasant smile. "Let me in and I'll tell you."

Tristan's lips thinned, but he stood back and let her into his room.

Jayne wasn't sure what she expected—perhaps a scientist's lab with broken glass vials as a product of an experiment gone wrong. Or maybe a man in a gorilla suit that Tristan had just finished wrestling into submission.

What she *hadn't* expected was to find dozens of books sprawled along his bedspread, along with several notebooks filled with his neat and crisp handwriting. Most of his notes were in French, but Jayne made out words like "grimoire" and "location unknown."

Jayne shot an accusing look at Tristan. "What the hell is all this?"

"It's a messy bedroom. Most men are slobs, Jayne. Surely, you know this."

"You're researching grimoires. Why?"

"I assumed we'd continue our search, since it seems we hit another dead end."

"Actually, we're getting another assignment. Amanda just told me. Ruger will be briefing us on it soon."

Tristan raised his eyebrows, but he didn't seem surprised. "Really?"

Jayne narrowed her eyes, suspicious of his far-too-nonchalant reaction.

Tristan crossed his arms. "What about Valeri Rudik?"

He wasn't getting off that easy, but Jayne would allow the brief diversion. "I think he knows where my father is."

Tristan's face went slack with surprise. "Why do you think that?"

"I have my sources. But he was captured by La Liberté, yes?"

"Yes," Tristan hedged.

"Did you interrogate him? Did you find out anything that could lead to my father's whereabouts?"

Tristan stared at Jayne, his expression unreadable. For a long moment, he said nothing, but she could see the gears in his mind turning as he considered her words. *What is that clever French brain thinking right now?* she wondered.

Finally, he said, "I can't help you."

Jayne leveled a hard look at him. "I find that hard to believe. You were Gina's second-in-command. Her most trusted soldier. I highly doubt you weren't privy to whatever information was gathered from the interrogation of prisoners."

Tristan leaned against the wall, again looking like a French model posing for a magazine. He flashed the cocky grin she hated so much. "I didn't say I didn't know anything. I just said I can't help you."

Jayne balled her hands into fists, struggling to keep her anger in check. "Are you that heartless? This is my father we're talking about. Besides, I thought your allegiance was to the TCO now, not La Liberté. But perhaps you feel your loyalties are divided? Are you feeling regrets about leaving?"

That wiped the smile right off his face. He straightened, his expression hardening. "You don't know anything about me or my loyalties."

"Then prove it. Tell me what you know."

"I don't owe you *anything*. Our superiors know where my allegiance lies, and that's all that matters."

Jayne huffed a dry laugh. "Wow. You really are a bastard, aren't you? I'm on your side, Tristan. I'm your partner. And this is really important to me."

"Does it have anything to do with this mission or this assignment?"

Jayne scowled. "No."

"So, it's personal?"

"Yes."

That cocky grin was back. "Ah, I see. And...what personal

THE KEEPER OF FLAMES

things have *you* helped me with lately? Have you taken a vested interest in my goals and desires?"

A sour taste filled Jayne's mouth. Damn it, he was right. She was only here because she needed something from him. How could she expect him to care when she didn't reciprocate? She hadn't given two flying craps about him until now, and he knew it.

"We aren't friends, Jayne," Tristan went on, his expression morphing into a sneer. "Our relationship is strictly professional. So, let's not cross that line. Otherwise, you might not like what you find."

Jayne's suspicions returned, and she glared at him. "Are you threatening me?" And also, what was he hiding? What didn't he want her to find?

Tristan only shrugged, his mouth spreading into a satisfied smile. A look of triumph.

He believed he'd bested her.

Asshole.

Jayne's anger flared back to life, roaring in her chest. This arrogant man was keeping her from her father. On purpose. She would *never* do the same if the roles were reversed.

"You don't want me as your enemy, Tristan." Her voice was low and quiet. "There's a difference between two partners working together amicably and two rivals forced to work with someone they hate."

Tristan snorted. "It's always been the latter, Jayne. We were rivals from the beginning, and your opinion of me has never changed."

"As you said, I might not know anything about you, Tristan Lowell. But I damn well guarantee *you* don't know anything about *me*."

"Fine. Then we understand one another." He crossed his

arms and raised a brow. She wanted to punch that look right off his face.

"Yeah, I guess we do." Jayne turned to leave, then paused. "Your fly is open, by the way."

The satisfaction of seeing his panicked expression as he glanced down to his crotch was fleeting compared to the aching disappointment festering in her chest as she left the room.

CHAPTER
NINE

YOUR MISSION, SHOULD YOU CHOOSE TO
ACCEPT...

R uger Stern took a few moments to go over the files Amanda had just sent to him in an encrypted email. He rubbed his jaw, the hairs of his goatee tickling his hand. He needed a shave. They had been holed up in this safe house for days, expecting to be able to return to the States after the grimoire was acquired.

But they hadn't found the right one.

And, it seemed, the Kingdom was no longer the only player on the board.

He needed an extra minute to process everything Amanda had told him. With the possibility of a mole within the TCO, Ruger's mind was running haywire, the pieces not quite adding up.

Perhaps the magical duel between the TCO and the Kingdom had lured Gina Labelle from her hiding spot. But it seemed too convenient to Ruger that this intelligence should reach them at the precise moment when they had hit a dead end.

He'd mentioned as much to Amanda, and she'd agreed. But they wouldn't learn any new information by sitting by and doing nothing. She advised they follow this trail, but with caution. Eyes wide open for any clues they might have missed. In the meantime, Amanda planned to investigate the intel they'd received to try to weed out its source; perhaps that would give them more information.

Aside from the stolen Book of Shadows, the TCO traitor had been strangely quiet as of late. Ruger had no doubt the spy was lying low after such a big heist. Still, it made it hard to track down leads. It could be *anyone*.

Ruger didn't like the idea of suspecting one of his own. It put a foul taste in his mouth. But he'd learned the hard way that people weren't always who you thought they were.

After a panini and an espresso—the cup tiny in his mighty hands—he tracked down Jayne and Tristan to debrief them. They were on opposite ends of the safe house, oddly enough doing the exact same thing—reading. Jayne was curled up on the armchair of the sitting room, and Tristan was at the desk in his bedroom. Ruger gathered them both into the living room, where they sat as far apart as possible on the long sofa.

Tension rippled in the air between them. Ruger suppressed a sigh at the animosity emanating off the two officers. Hopefully, they could get past this latest argument and focus on the mission. Tristan and Jayne were capable Adepts, but they often rubbed each other the wrong way.

"I know Amanda already told you there was intelligence that Gina Labelle was in Rome, searching for a necromantic grimoire," he said. "It's been confirmed."

Jayne shot a wary look toward Tristan, who'd bolted upright in his seat.

"It seems she caught wind of the grimoire we're searching for here and is sending her own team after it. With this many opponents at play, we'll need to alter our strategy."

"How is Gina able to pursue this?" Jayne asked. "I thought

over half her forces were depleted, thanks to this guy." She waved an idle hand toward Tristan without even glancing his way. He responded with a dry smirk.

"My guess is, she's desperate," Ruger said. "The grimoires we seek hold a lot of power, and if she's able to harness that power, she won't *need* stronger forces."

"This doesn't change anything," Tristan said, spreading his hands. "We still have no idea where the grimoire is. We have no leads."

"We do now." Ruger handed each of them a stack of papers. "Our network of spies was able to bug a conversation between Gina and one of her lieutenants. It appears she's come across this particular grimoire before. This will help us narrow down our search."

"Unless Gina happened to leave a diary lying around of all her evil-overlord exploits over the years, I don't see how that will help," Jayne said, her nose buried in the pages.

"Actually," Tristan said, dragging out the word. "We have a logbook of all the magical artifacts La Liberté has encountered over the years."

Ruger nodded, not at all surprised by this. Tristan was a careful record keeper, which he had proven after staging a coup against his mother. "Tristan, we'll need you to cross-reference all the data we have on local grimoires with the logbook from La Liberté."

"And what about me?" Jayne lifted her head, her eyes glinting with the eagerness of a challenge.

Ruger hated to disappoint her, but there was truly only one option, at least until they had narrowed down their target. "Training."

Jayne's face fell. "I'm not sure how I'll be able to contain my enthusiasm," she dead-panned.

"It's not an insult," Ruger said. "You have the strongest

connection to grimoires. We need to utilize that. And our discussion earlier about minor and major grimoires made me realize how little you actually know about them."

Jayne's jaw went tight, and Tristan shot her a smug grin. Ruger rolled his eyes. God, these two were like children.

"My hope is that if I can train you to identify the signatures of various forms of grimoires, you will be able to track them down more easily," Ruger said.

Jayne crossed one leg over the other and nodded, her expression relaxing. "I get it. Makes perfect sense. I can be your grimoire bloodhound."

Ruger offered a half-smile. "For tonight, I want you both to patrol the area. Sniff out any unfamiliar magic in the air. See what you can dig up. If La Liberté is here, I want to know how many there are and where they are positioned. Do *not* cause a scene. And do not attract attention. You are to observe and report only. Understood?"

Jayne and Tristan both muttered their agreement.

"Any questions?" Ruger steepled his fingers together.

"I have one," Jayne said, lifting a hand. "If La Liberté and the Kingdom are searching for the same thing, what are the chances this conflict could escalate? *We* might be unwilling to cause mass destruction, but these are terror organizations we're talking about; they have no qualms about collateral damage. What precautions can we take to ensure they don't destroy the rest of Rome and all the people living here?"

Ruger nodded, acknowledging her point. "We're portaling in a surveillance team as well as backup for you two. They know how to be discreet and remain unseen. We're hoping that they can help manage damage control and keep a handle on things during the mission."

"With this one, it might be impossible." Tristan jerked his thumb toward Jayne, who glared at him.

"What's that supposed to mean?" she asked.

He only offered a shrug. "You're messy."

Jayne scoffed, opening her mouth to retort, but Ruger interjected.

"I think we have enough on our plates to worry about," he said, crossing his arms. "I want you two patrolling the area within the hour. We'll rendezvous back here for a late dinner and research." He paused. "And try to keep things civil. We're on the same side here."

Jayne and Tristan both nodded stiffly before rising from the sofa and striding in opposite directions. Ruger sighed, feeling like a long-suffering parent trying to separate two feuding siblings. He rubbed a hand down his face, wondering if he'd made the right decision pairing these two together. Their magic complemented each other perfectly; in battle, they were an unstoppable duo.

If only they didn't want to constantly tear out each other's throats.

CHAPTER

TEN

ON OFFENSE

Patagonia

T o Amanda's intense frustration, Xiomara refused to relocate to the TCO safe house. Not only was her house warded with powerful spells, but the old woman didn't trust the TCO farther than she could throw them. She flat out refused to leave her home, and Amanda was reluctant to leave Xiomara's side, given how much power she possessed and how much of a target that made her.

So they struck a deal. They'd work within the confines of Xiomara's home, and she reluctantly agreed to allow in a few additional members of Amanda's team.

It was rather crowded—between Xiomara, Juanito, Amanda, Cillian, Sofia, and Seo-joon, plus Pierce, Amanda's assistant, who had portaled in to help with the mission. Sofia had to admit it was a little unnerving seeing the eager assistant scribbling away constantly.

For one thing, Sofia didn't appreciate having an audience to

64

her training, even someone as enthusiastic as Pierce. These Master abilities were still so new and foreign to her, and seeing Juanito's dark little eyes peering curiously around the corner while she was trying to cast a spell was quite off-putting.

For another thing, Sofia was secretly hoping her training would be put on hold until this whole Guardian situation was sorted out. She would never admit it to anyone, but she was afraid to train with Cillian as her Rogue. He had always been *Jayne's* Rogue, and Sofia detested the idea that she had stolen her sister's boyfriend, even if she knew it was more complicated than that.

"Our enemies are multiplying," Amanda had told her tersely when Sofia objected to training. "We need as many trained and able-bodied Adepts on our side as possible to fight the battle to come."

Sofia wondered if the battle she referenced was against La Liberté, the Kingdom, or both. God, they had a lot of enemies...

Amanda had stressed to them the importance of providing tangible results in their efforts—working twice as hard to prevent disasters from occurring while also apprehending the criminals so the CIA could question them. This meant round-the-clock surveillance and a much more rigorous training schedule. Amanda was adamant that nothing fall through the cracks. Sofia could tell the woman was paranoid that another Fontainebleau disaster might happen right under their noses.

Sofia knew what Jayne's reaction would be: *Hell yes.* Jayne wanted a fight. She always saw a challenge as a puzzle to solve. She never balked at hard work. In many ways, Cillian was the same. He was a fighter, too.

But Sofia wasn't, not in the same way. Yes, she'd taken kick-boxing lessons for years—but as a defensive measure, not to play offense. She had always played it safe, avoiding risks, keeping her head down. But this was the first time the thought of hiding didn't feel right. Her gut twisted at the idea of putting her head in the sand while innocent Adepts—and non-Adepts—suffered. She couldn't just stand by and do nothing. Perhaps her time with Amanda and the TCO had shown what good she could do.

Or perhaps Jayne's reckless "save the world and all the books in it" mantra was rubbing off on her.

"Again," Seo-joon said, his eyes alight with excitement. He had taken on the role of unofficial mentor to Sofia. While she knew it was mostly because the TCO had been unable to assign her one on such short notice, she was still grateful it was someone she was already comfortable with. It made things so much easier.

The furniture had been pushed up against the wall, eliciting much grumbling from Xiomara. Cillian stood opposite Sofia in the living room, dressed in a T-shirt and gym shorts and looking ready for a boxing match. Sofia was in yoga pants and a tank top, her hair tied into a messy fishtail braid. They had already paused for a quick bite to eat—chorizo served on a marraqueta roll and topped with chimichurri. It had been divine, but now the food inside her churned uncontrollably. She was so not ready for this.

But she forced a determined expression and rolled her shoulders back. She had to try. Focusing on the immense power she had felt when fighting Ruth in the catacombs of Paris, Sofia shut her eyes and pictured the Torrent. The river of stars appeared immediately, drawing her in. She reached for it, envisioning Cillian as a wolf.

Something tangible yanked from the center of her chest, and Sofia stumbled forward, eyes wide as energy rippled around her. The air smelled of pine and strawberries, and the scent triggered a memory within Sofia: a bond snapping into place. Power flowing between them. Cillian's thoughts shared with hers, his magic a part of her body like an extra limb.

Sofia sucked in a breath, and the river of stars vanished. She whirled to find Cillian in wolf form beside her, serene and huge in all his white-furred glory.

"Oh my God," Sofia blurted, clapping a hand over her mouth. Had it been like this with Cillian and Jayne?

As a wolf, he was enormous, his head almost to Sofia's shoulder. She'd certainly seen him in his wolf form before, but she'd forgotten how impressive he was. Back then, he had been Jayne's Rogue. Looking at him through new eyes, Sofia couldn't help but feel intimidated.

Seo-joon let out a whoop, fist-pumping in the air. "Damn, Sofia! You've got some power in you, that's for sure."

Sofia only offered a weak smile. Seo-joon had meant it as a compliment, but all Sofia could think of was her mother and what that immense power had done to her. Was Sofia on that same path now?

"Let's try something other than a wolf," Seo-joon suggested. "That was what he had trouble with when training with Jayne."

Sofia flinched, and from the corner of her eye, she sensed Cillian stiffen. The wounds were still too raw for him, and Sofia didn't want to force him to relive those memories.

Seo-joon noticed, though, and immediately backpedaled. "I mean…it would be cool, right? To do the whole griffin thing again?" He made claws with his hands and cawed like an eagle.

A bewildered laugh bubbled up Sofia's throat before she could stop it. She covered her mouth again. Thank God for Seo-joon's good-natured humor and his uncanny ability to defuse the tension in the room.

"Can we try something simpler?" came Cillian's voice.

Sofia jerked, not expecting to hear this giant wolf speaking to her in Cillian's normal human voice.

"What did he say?" Seo-joon asked.

"You can't hear him?" Sofia gestured between Seo-joon and the wolf. When training with Jayne, there had been one instance when Sofia had heard him communicate, his voice as clear as if Cillian-the-man stood right next to her. Based on Jayne's reaction, this wasn't common.

When Seo-joon shook his head, Sofia translated Cillian's request. To her surprise, Seo-joon laughed. "Sure, buddy," he said. "Sofia, why don't you pick an animal?"

"Just...pick a random animal? That's it?" Sofia frowned, wracking her brain. What animal would be easy to shift into? To her, it seemed like shifting into *anything* besides a human sounded difficult and painful. "Um, okay. How about a cat?"

She looked at Cillian with raised eyebrows, hoping this was acceptable to him. But instead of sharing a glance with a wolf, she found herself looking at a gray cat with a striped tail.

"A cat?" he asked. "Really?"

"Hey. I like cats." Sofia's tone was defensive. "Besides, I figured it would be a nice break from something as massive as a wolf." She glanced over the cat's shining fur that looked so sleek it was almost silver.

"Who's a pretty kitty?" Seo-joon crooned, but Cillian-the-cat recoiled from him.

"Back off, or I'll claw your face off." Cillian fixed his eyes on Sofia, and she marveled that they were gray speckled with green. If he were a real cat and not a Rogue, she would be tempted to take him home with her. "Please get me out of this body."

"Fine. An owl." Sofia pointed to him, and this time she saw it: a burst of white light shimmered over the cat's body like sparkles, and in a flash, Cillian had transformed into a tawny brown owl. He ruffled his feathers and hooted, almost in indignation.

Sofia found herself laughing again. This was kind of fun. She pointed again and said, "A squirrel."

Another flash, and the small rodent appeared, reminding Sofia of her backyard in Nashville.

"Rabbit." Cillian turned into a fluffy white hare. "Raccoon." He shifted again. "Cockroach."

Nothing happened.

Sofia frowned, and then came Cillian's irritated voice.

"I flat out refuse to shift into a cockroach. No chance in hell."

Seo-joon was laughing now, too.

"Fascinating," murmured a voice from the doorway.

All three of them—including Cillian the raccoon—whirled to face Xiomara, who stood leaning against the doorframe, her gaze speculative.

"I know, right?" Seo-joon said with a grin. "I've never seen such instant and powerful magic."

"I mean that he has a choice in the matter." Xiomara hobbled forward, her gaze pinned on Cillian. "I have seen many Rogues in my day. None of them could shift as effortlessly as you, and none could resist the call of their Master, even if they wanted to."

Sofia suppressed a shudder at the grimness in Xiomara's words. She didn't want to dwell on what awful things Rogues might have been subjected to just because they were bonded to a corrupt Master.

"Some say this is why Master magicians died off," Xiomara went on, sinking into a chair by the door with a soft groan. "Because of their misuse of power."

"So, what's your theory about why they came back, then?" Sofia asked.

"Magic needs them." The answer seemed so simple.

"And what of the risk of misusing the power again?" Sofia feared the answer, but she had to ask. *Will I end up like Ruth?*

Xiomara's dark eyes shifted to Sofia, and she felt a whisper of power rush down her spine from the intensity of the old woman's stare. "It seems the Torrent decided the risk was worth it."

"Can I please not be a raccoon anymore?" Cillian asked as he nibbled at his paws.

"Right. Sorry." Sofia turned to look at him, envisioning his normal, human self. In a flash, he was standing upright, wearing the same T-shirt and shorts as before. His face took on a greenish hue, and he teetered.

"Hold on there." Without thinking, Sofia lunged, catching him before he could fall. He was bulky and heavier than she anticipated, but she hadn't spent hours training at the dojo for nothing. He smelled like sweat and musk and sage, a faint whiff lingering from his Rogue magic.

"I'm...all right," Cillian panted, closing his eyes briefly. "Just a lot of shifting in one go. My body's not used to it."

"You both did a lot today," Seo-joon said. "I'm impressed. But we don't want to push it too far. Go rest up, and we'll carry on tomorrow."

Cillian's eyes opened and fixed on Sofia. Her cheeks heated as she realized how close they stood. Damn it, what the hell was she thinking? After ensuring he was steady on his feet, she withdrew a step. Then another. And one more for good measure. At last, she could breathe again without filling her nose with his scent. It was too distracting. And she couldn't afford to forget what had happened between him and Jayne.

Not that Sofia was interested. Not in the slightest. But she didn't want Cillian to get the wrong idea. What would he think of her if he imagined she wanted something more than friend-ship? She had to ensure their boundaries were clear.

"You look a bit flushed, girl," Xiomara commented lightly from her chair.

Sofia fixed a scowl on her, hating the mirth shining in the old woman's eyes. Yes, Xiomara knew exactly what was going through Sofia's head.

"Just overexertion," Sofia forced herself to say. "Like Cillian. I—I need some fresh air." She nodded at Seo-joon. "Thanks for the training session. You're a great teacher."

Seo-joon beamed with pride as she strode to the door, not glancing back before she stepped outside.

ELEVEN

THE BROTHERS GRIMOIRE

Rome

Jayne had managed to remain quite civil toward Tristan when they were first assigned to work together. But after his brutal denial of her plea for help and his general attitude about her carelessness and lack of magical know-how, she was done trying to be friendly to him.

He wanted to be an asshole? Fine. She wasn't going to sit back and play nice anymore, either.

It did make for an uncomfortable few hours of patrolling, though. Jayne refused to break the silence, focusing instead on the amber-tinted streets of Rome, bathed in the warm glow of the setting sun. It wasn't hard to get lost in the breathtaking architecture, the trinkets and souvenirs on display, the smell of garlic and marinara as they passed by a piazza stuffed with charming restaurants...

"I can still scent those henchmen from the Kingdom," Tristan murmured, breaking Jayne's starstruck reverie.

She glanced in his direction. "Do you, now?"

She felt his eyes on her. "Do you not?"

That sounded like a challenge. Jayne took a deep breath, both to steel herself and to see what she could smell in the air. The strongest scents were the foods nearby that made Jayne's mouth water. But she pushed it aside and inhaled more fully, trying to sift through the overload of sensations surrounding her.

"Focus on your magic," Tristan advised. "Whatever powers you sense in the air will have a similar signature to your own. It will help you track it. Like calls to like."

"I don't need a lecture," Jayne snapped.

Tristan raised his palms. "Not trying to lecture. Just trying to help."

Jayne sighed. She was being a bit unreasonable. The wound of his denial to help her find her father still stung, and she hadn't moved past it yet. But Tristan wasn't her friend, and he didn't owe her anything. It was unrealistic of her to expect him to jump at an opportunity to help her.

He was like that annoying colleague you were forced to work with. Surely, Jayne could handle another Pete Mitchell, that snobby curator from the Harry Elkins Widener Memorial Library at Harvard University, who claimed only "lesser scholars" attended Vanderbilt and that their library was "mediocre" compared to the *real* Ivy Leagues.

Yet Jayne still managed to charm the socks off Pete Mitchell. She could be pleasant around Tristan Lowell, too. No problem.

"You're right," Jayne said, swallowing down her bitter feelings. "I'm sorry. I shouldn't have snapped at you. Can you describe to me what it smells like?"

"It's different for every Adept. We all have our unique scent and signature, and it conjures different feelings and emotions."

Jayne thought of her own magic and how it smelled like

roses and woodsmoke. She frowned, wondering if she could use that... Closing her eyes, she sniffed the air once more, channeling the powers stirring in her chest. Warmth radiated inside her, spreading through her whole body, from the top of her head to the tips of her fingers and toes.

The smell of her magic filled her nose—roses, woodsmoke, and something else—vanilla and soap. It was vaguely familiar.

Tristan cleared his throat, and Jayne's eyes flew open. She didn't realize she'd turned her head toward him or drawn closer, following the scent of his magic.

"Oh," she breathed, stepping back. "Sorry."

Right. That was *Tristan's* magic she had sensed. She'd forgotten what it smelled like. She turned away from him and tried again, sifting through the fragrances of her magic and his, trying to detect something new. Something unique.

Energy swirled inside her, and her forehead prickled with awareness. She knew her totem was glowing from her efforts, and that soon it would attract attention. Sure enough, she felt Tristan reposition himself, no doubt to block her from the view of passersby.

But after a moment, she sensed it. A faint whiff drifting along the wind. Jayne sniffed three times before she could fully identify it. Old lemons and rubbing alcohol. It smelled almost exactly like the cleaning solution she kept in the kitchen, plus the barest hint of dying flowers. Something like rotten tulips, or...

Her eyes snapped open once more, and she sucked in a sharp breath. Rotting violets. That was the smell of her mother's magic.

Did that mean Ruth was here, or just that her henchmen carried her scent with them? Tingles erupted along her arms, and she suppressed a shiver, all warmth fleeing from her instantly.

"What is it?" Tristan asked.

Jayne didn't want to admit her fear of Ruth, but if anyone would understand what it was like to have a psychotic mother, it was him. "It smells like Ruth Thorne. Just barely."

Tristan scented the air once more. Jayne couldn't help but be reminded of Cillian and his keen sense of smell. His uncanny senses would be able to tell her immediately if it was really Ruth. Her stomach ached with an unexpected pang. She missed Cillian. Not romantically. Physically, maybe a little; the bedroom had never been their problem. No, she missed having his companionship. His friendship. He was a good guy, and she felt a little homesick without him.

After a moment, Tristan stretched his arms, wiggling his fingers slightly. Under his breath, he murmured, *"Suscito."*

Frowning, Jayne stared at him. That wasn't French. It didn't even sound Italian. "Is that Latin?"

Tristan didn't answer. His eyes closed, and tiny white sparks danced from his fingers. The magic was so faint that Jayne had to squint to see it clearly; hopefully, none of the bystanders would notice it. It blended in so well with the shimmering gold light of the setting sun.

Power jolted through Jayne like static electricity. She sucked in a sharp breath, her spine going stiff. Tristan's magic washed over her like an ice-cold tidal wave, the shock tangible and unexpected. But with it came a flood of new sensations. Hot, prickly warmth that made the air feel stifling; a cool breeze that carried floral smells and ancient words whispered in Jayne's ear; more white lights that floated from the ground and hovered in front of her like tiny sprites.

"What is this?" Jayne murmured, reaching forward to touch the sparks, just to see if they were, indeed, sprites. But Tristan stilled her hand, somehow sensing her movement without opening his eyes.

"I'm awakening the magic around us," he said quietly. "Just wait a moment. Don't be alarmed, but don't disturb the forces in the air."

"Yes, Master Jedi."

Jayne stared, awestruck, as the white lights multiplied and danced around them both, swirling like winged fairies in a fairy circle. She thought of the will-o'-the-wisps and wondered if they had found a way to follow her from Dublin. Or perhaps they were *everywhere,* and Tristan's specific spell made them visible to her. Her chest swelled with delight and amazement and pure, glorious *wonder.*

Never a dull moment in the life of an Adept, she thought with a small smile. She would never tire of this. No matter the danger or the terrors of her job, she would never regret discovering magic existed.

Tristan suddenly dropped his arms, and the white lights vanished, leaving the street darker than it had been before. The sun was lower now, the buildings shrouded in shadow, and her body felt colder from the lack of power in the air.

"It isn't Ruth," Tristan said, reminding Jayne why he had cast the spell in the first place. He started forward again as if nothing unusual had happened.

She tugged at his elbow to stop him. "Wait. What *was* that? What did you just do?"

"I cast an Awaken spell."

Jayne shook her head. "I've studied that spell before. That was not an Awaken spell."

"It's a modified version." He seemed cagey and wouldn't meet her eyes.

She pulled more forcefully on his arm. "Tristan."

He sighed and met her gaze. "I often experiment with new spells. That was one of my own making. Ages ago, Adepts used to use Latin and other languages to summon certain spells.

We've since done away with that practice, but I've noticed it does help to enhance my magic."

Enhance was an understatement. Jayne had never seen anything so captivating in all her life. She remembered Hector, her stand-in mentor when Ruger was captured, mentioning how Adepts didn't use fancy languages anymore because it got too complicated and hard to remember.

"Can you teach me?" she asked eagerly.

Tristan shot her a wary look. "I thought you were a Master magician and didn't need training." His voice was deadpan and dripping with sarcasm.

Jayne glared. "I never said that."

"No, but you certainly scoffed at the idea of learning from me."

She bit her lip. Well, that much was true. "I shouldn't have. Ruger's right; more training couldn't hurt. Please? I'd like to learn." She shot him her most award-winning smile.

Tristan held her gaze, his expression unyielding, for a long moment. After a while, he exhaled. "All right. I'll teach you what I know."

Jayne clapped her hands together, eager to expand her magical knowledge. "Thank you! Oh, this will be fun."

"Yes, because we've proven to get along *so* well together in the past."

Jayne shoved his arm. "It'll be great. You'll see. I'm always in a better mood when there's research involved. Just saying."

Tristan grumbled something noncommittal, but the corners of his lips twitched, which Jayne took as a victory. Her mood significantly lighter, she followed him down the street as they continued with their patrol.

JAYNE KNEW the instant she stepped into the safe house that something was wrong. Beside her, Tristan stopped, no doubt sensing it as well. The air quivered with a foreign energy, tickling her skin and bringing her senses to high alert. On reflex, she threw a quick Shield spell over herself and Tristan.

"Good thinking," Tristan muttered, his eyes darkening as he scanned the surroundings. The foyer was dark, and the living room looked empty. But looks could be deceiving.

"I'm sorry—did you just compliment me?" Jayne accused.

"There's a strange magical presence lurking in our safe house, and *that's* what you're focusing on?"

"Honestly, it's the more shocking of the two."

They crept forward slowly, each step silent and careful. Jayne thought of Ruger—was he here? Was he in danger? She knew he could take care of himself, but if she could feel the power of a foreign magic lingering in the air, that didn't exactly seem promising.

A distant thrumming filled the air, making Jayne's eardrums throb. The farther into the house she went, the more intense the vibrations became, until it felt as if her very bones were rattling from the impact. She followed the energy, clenching her fingers into fists and raising her arms slightly, prepared to knock down whatever came at her.

Her gaze landed on the coffee table in front of the sofa, and her entire body froze.

Two grimoires rested on the surface, each one trembling and emitting a faint green glow.

Jayne dropped her arms in surprise, then glanced around again. What were these books doing here? And where was Ruger?

As if on cue, the big man himself strode into the living room as casually as if he was planning on ordering pizza and watching a movie. His expression was relaxed, and he was the picture of ease as he sank onto the sofa, draping one arm over the back and glancing up at Jayne and Tristan as if just noticing they were there.

"I made dinner." He waved a hand toward the dining area. Only then did Jayne see the steaming bowl of pasta on the table, alongside a pot of Alfredo sauce. She'd been so distracted by the grimoires that she hadn't even noticed.

"Anything out of the ordinary?" Ruger asked.

Jayne sputtered a sound that was a half scoff, half laugh. "Um, you mean besides the two *glowing grimoires* in front of me? No, everything is perfectly normal right now."

Ruger only smirked, and Jayne had the sneaking suspicion he was toying with her. "I meant on the streets."

"We caught a whiff of the Kingdom," Tristan supplied. "Someone close to Ruth. But we confirmed it's not her. She's not in the city—at least, not anymore."

Ruger nodded once.

Jayne threw her hands up. "Is anyone going to explain these grimoires? Because if not, I'm opening those bad boys up and seeing what's inside."

Ruger ignored her and turned to Tristan. "Help yourself to some dinner first. Then I need you to start cross-referencing data from La Liberté. We need that information as fast as possible."

"Right away." Tristan made his way to the dining room table and spooned heaps of pasta and sauce on a plate before he disappeared down the hallway.

Jayne huffed in exasperation. Was everyone else insane? Did she suddenly develop this sixth sense where she could see grimoires but other people couldn't? She rubbed her temples, wondering if this was an ocular migraine gone horribly, horribly wrong.

"Aren't you hungry?" Ruger asked.

"Ruger," Jayne said weakly, mumbling incoherently as she gestured from the grimoires to him and back again.

"Have a seat, Jayne. Eat. Then train."

She shoveled in the pasta, savoring the cheesy sauce, then wiped the bowl with a warm piece of focaccia.

"Okay."

"You could compliment the chef."

"I could," she said, tone dangerous, and Ruger laughed. "It's a long way from the burnt eggs in Dublin, all right? Now, if you've stashed a raspberry pie in *la cucina*, then I'm all yours."

"Fair enough." Ruger patted the cushion next to him. "This is part of your training. You'll be more focused if you're not hungry. And I need you focused."

Training. Jayne stared at him, then looked at the grimoires again. *Oh, right.* Major and minor grimoires. She relaxed, not realizing how stiff her limbs had been until now. With a heavy sigh, she collapsed onto the sofa next to Ruger.

"You could've mentioned that up front," she grumbled.

"Where's the fun in that?"

Jayne arched an eyebrow at Ruger, whose eyes glinted. She almost chewed him out for it, but how could she blame him? She gave him a heart attack every other day with her antics.

"Point to you, Ruge," she relented. "So, what do I need to do?"

"Describe the grimoires to me. Use your magical senses. Tell me what you can feel from them."

Jayne took a deep breath to steel herself. She remembered what Tristan had said about magic having a similar signature to her own powers. Her eyes closed as she inhaled, sifting through the ordinary human smells—the lingering scent of warm cheese from a grilled sandwich, a faint whiff of soap from the dishwasher, a faint aroma from the mint tea she'd made earlier... As she focused inward, trusting her magical senses, she felt her forehead prickling with awareness as her totem flared to life. Energy churned in her chest, swelling and rising, and she sucked in a gasp from the intensity of it.

"Easy," Ruger coaxed. "You don't need that much of your magic for this."

Jayne nodded, reeling in her magic. The powers inside her seemed eager to burst forward like a gushing river, but she pictured turning the handle of a faucet and slowing the flow to a small trickle. The magic quieted, the waters within her going still. Energy leaked forward with less intensity, a tendril of power stretching forward to inspect the grimoires.

When her magic made contact, she jumped from the jolt of electricity that coursed through her. A flood of images appeared in her mind, too fast for her to process. She made out an ancient building, a crowd of scholars poring over tomes, a sobbing woman, and a raging fire. She flinched away from the images, withdrawing her magic as she shifted to inspect the second grimoire. This one had a gentler aura to it, its power feeble in comparison. No images came to mind, but this book had a similar signature to the first: the same citrusy scent mingled with ink and parchment. Warmth traveled up and down Jayne's arms as she mentally inspected the surface, wondering what was contained within.

Her eyes opened, and she didn't realize she was breathing deeply until she wiped sweat from her brow, suddenly exhausted.

Ruger arched an eyebrow. "Well?"

Jayne took a moment to catch her breath. She eyed the two grimoires, suddenly seeing them more clearly. They looked nearly identical, with chocolate-brown leather coverings. But now that her magic was more acquainted with theirs, she could see the stark differences between them.

She gestured to the first one with the vivid images. Now

that she was focusing on it, this one glowed more brightly than the other. "That's the major grimoire."

"What makes you say that?"

"Its magic responded more powerfully to mine. It has a stronger glow. More forceful energy."

"And what about the second one?"

"It's...similar. I want to say they were from the same time period? Or authored by the same Adept?"

Ruger nodded. "Yes, they are born of the same magic. I was wondering if you would notice that."

A swell of pride bubbled up inside her chest. *Nailed it.* She pointed to the one on the right. "That one is definitely a minor grimoire. It felt a lot like the Sibylline texts. Quieter. More unassuming. Less obtrusive." She cocked her head at that sneaky second grimoire. "It makes me wonder what it's hiding. That first grimoire was shoving its power on me even though I didn't want it. But this one? It feels like it's hiding secrets. Secrets I want to uncover."

Ruger smiled. "Very good. I was going to save this for our next lesson, but you're right on the money there. Just because something is a minor grimoire does not mean it is any less powerful or dangerous. In some cases, Adepts have been known to cloak a grimoire to make it appear minor when the magic it contains is quite deadly. It lures people in under the guise of something small and harmless."

Jayne pointed her finger at the minor grimoire. "You know, I've met kickboxers like you. Some of the best fighters I've met are petite women who really pack a punch. Cunning and crafty, they are." When Ruger raised his eyebrows at her, Jayne went on, "We were taught early in our training to use perceptions to our advantage. I might not be small, but I'm still a woman, and that alone would make male opponents underestimate me."

To her surprise, Ruger gave her an impressed look. "That could work in a magical battle as well."

"Maybe. But by now, our enemies know I'm a Master magician. I feel like the cat's out of the bag."

"There will always be new enemies. New threats."

"That's comforting."

Ruger sat forward, bracing his arms on his knees. "This is excellent progress, though. You are learning to trust your magical instincts instead of your human ones. I could feel a different sort of energy emanating from you. Still your normal magical aura, but with more complex layers. With the amount of power you possess, it's good to let your magic stretch out once in a while. Like exercising a muscle."

Jayne nodded. "I've heard that metaphor before."

"Well, it's a good one. You're an athlete; treat this like you would a training regimen."

Jayne's head bobbed up and down again. "How long can we keep these?" She gestured to the grimoires.

"Only a day or two. I promised Katie I'd get them back to the TCO library as soon as possible."

Jayne smiled fondly at the memory of the quirky librarian. The woman was a kindred spirit. "Great. I'd like to practice on these a bit more. And I don't mind returning them myself when the time comes. I'd love to catch up with Katie."

"Just don't open that one." Ruger pointed to the major grimoire. "Really nasty stuff in there."

"Color me intrigued."

"Jayne," Ruger said, his voice taking on a lethal edge.

"Kidding! I promise I won't open Pandora's box."

"Good. I'm going to check in with Tristan and then turn in for the night. I'll see you in the morning."

Jayne bid him good night, her gaze still pinned on the major grimoire. After a moment, she stood and got herself another plate of noodles, then pulled out a frozen cherry pie that some kind soul from the TCOs safe house prep team had stashed for her, and cut out a slice. As she ate, she kept watching the two grimoires, expecting them to start trembling or emitting that strange humming sound again.

But they were eerily quiet. Almost *too* quiet.

She thought she'd understood the dangers of these books, especially since she'd encountered two necromantic grimoires. But this, like most magic, had so much more contained beneath the surface.

How many secrets could one book hold? And how long before Jayne unearthed something she wasn't strong enough to fight?

CHAPTER

TWELVE

TACKY TOURISTS

"Most of the grimoires La Liberté has encountered are within this five-mile radius." Tristan laid out a map flat on the dining room table and pointed to several areas marked in red.

Jayne, still munching on her bowl of cereal, frowned and leaned forward. "Those are all near the Pantheon. Looks like we were on the right track."

"My thinking exactly."

Ruger sat back in his chair and crossed his arms. "I've been mulling this over. I think the safest option is for you two to go undercover. With the Kingdom still at large and now La Liberté getting involved, a good cover will help you stay invisible."

Jayne was already rubbing her hands together, eager for the assignment. "Goody! Which library will we infiltrate this time?"

Ruger shook his head. "There are too many libraries to search, and inserting yourself as an employee for one might not guarantee we find the book. No, I think you and Tristan should go undercover as a couple. Tourists."

Jayne frowned at the word *couple*. "You mean like a brother and sister, or..."

"Your covers." Ruger handed them each a packet full of briefing papers, which included driver's licenses, passports, and American money. And, disturbingly, each held a simple gold band, and Jayne's also had a large but tasteful solitaire diamond. Wedding rings.

Jayne put hers to the side with distaste, pulled out the briefing document, and wrinkled her nose. "Jenny and Thomas Lowe? We're a married couple?" She scowled at Tristan and found his shoulders shaking with amusement.

"On your honeymoon in Rome. Yes. You can use the Disguise spell we worked on in your training," Ruger went on, ignoring Jayne's reaction. "And Tristan, your packet contains a spell to improve your American accent. We can still hear the French undertones; don't want to give you away."

It was Tristan's turn to look annoyed.

"It's true," Jayne said, happy as always to needle him. "You exude *French* from your very soul."

"I take that as the highest compliment," he said haughtily, looking down his nose at her. "The French always have been a superior culture."

"Bosh. America—"

"Focus, please," Ruger snapped. "We pulled in a favor and booked you at the Hassler, which is at the top of the Spanish Steps. The owner is an Adept. It's full of tourists at this time of year. You'll blend right in."

Jayne gaped at him. "We're sharing a hotel room? Now hang on, Ruger..."

Ruger leveled a stare at her. "I'm assuming you two can be professionals about this. This is a cover only. It will help keep you alive, undetected by our enemies for as long as possible. Right now, with so much attention on this grimoire, we need to fly under the radar. I'll be discreetly checking in with you frequently, but if I go with you, I'm afraid I'll draw too much attention."

Jayne's eyes roved over his bulky form, and she had to agree. Besides, so many of their enemies already knew Ruger's face and build. Whereas Jayne and Tristan could almost blend in with the college-aged tourists.

"How long?" Tristan asked, clearly unperturbed by the assignment.

"The suite is booked for two weeks, and if we're still searching, we'll move you to a different hotel. Assuming your cover isn't blown by then, of course."

"I wouldn't hold your breath," Tristan muttered.

Jayne shot him a glare, remembering how he'd referred to her as *messy*. "Hey, I happen to rock at undercover assignments. I lasted several weeks in Dublin."

Tristan gave her a look of mock pride and mimed enthusiastic applause.

"Jayne," Ruger said, redirecting her attention. "You still have that burner phone I gave you, right?"

Jayne pulled it from her pocket and wiggled in the air. "Yessiree."

"Good. Keep it on you at all times. I'll be using that to check in. If you don't return my call within two hours, I'll come find you." He gestured to the map on the table. "Start with these locations. If I receive any further intelligence, I'll send it your way."

Tristan nodded and rolled up the map. "I'll get a bag packed."

He left the room while Jayne stared vacantly at her empty bowl.

"I know this is hard for you, working with him," Ruger said in a low voice.

"I can be civil," she insisted. "He's an ally now."

"But it can't be easy to remember what he did."

Jayne resisted the urge to flinch. Tristan had taken part in abducting and torturing Ruger *and* Cillian. It was hard to see past his role as her enemy.

She knew it had all been a ruse. A ploy to keep his mother from getting suspicious while he fed information to the TCO.

But the torture? That had been all too real for two people she cared about deeply. And she couldn't just let that go.

"He can help you with your magic," Ruger went on. "He's been training since birth. I thought you two might be able to help each other, between your connection to grimoires and his Adept know-how."

Jayne sighed, remembering Tristan's agreement to teach her ancient spells. Ruger had a point, and she couldn't deny she *was* curious.

Besides, the sooner they found this grimoire and finished the mission, the sooner she could locate her father. With or without Tristan's help.

Jayne and Tristan took an Uber to the hotel Ruger had booked for them. It felt strange to Jayne, not having access to a private flat like she had in Paris and Dublin. But that would be too conspicuous—a beacon for La Liberté and the Kingdom to follow. Posing as tourists, not natives, they needed to have a hotel. In the car, she put on the rings, trying like hell not to look at them.

The car ride was too short. When the driver pulled up to the Hassler after only a few minutes in Roman traffic, Jayne blanched. It was time to pretend.

"We should have walked," she said to cover her discomfiture.

"With all the bags? Calling an Uber helps with our cover. It's a very American thing to do."

Jayne arched an eyebrow. "You're an American now? Perish the thought."

Tristan had donned his ring and seemed cool as a cucumber. Damn him.

The grand building had tourists and civilians bustling about, making their way to the famous Spanish Steps. An elegant stone archway framed the entrance, flanked by two pillars and rows of neatly trimmed shrubs.

Jayne's jaw dropped at the sight of it. "Holy Hera."

"It looks like we're posing as *rich* tourists," Tristan said with a chuckle.

"You can say that again." She gazed out the window again. God, this place was enormous. It looked like the Roman emperor himself lived here. "As long as there's free breakfast, I'm in."

They slid out of the car and grabbed their bags. After thanking the Uber driver, they started for the entrance. Just before entering the lobby, Jayne grabbed Tristan's arm and pulled him off to the side, pretending to admire the shrubbery.

"Wait," she said. "We should Cloak ourselves."

Tristan frowned. "Cloak? Why? I don't sense any magical threats nearby. Besides, Ruger only mentioned a Disguise spell."

"Trust me." Jayne reached for the Torrent and found the standard Cloaking spell. She caught hold of it and imagined a domino mask, the kind for a masquerade ball. A shimmering triangular mask appeared—the Disguise spell—and Jayne layered it on top of the Cloaking spell before releasing the Torrent.

Tristan was livid. "You can't just access the Torrent in broad daylight like that."

He drew closer to her—too close—and she tensed, eyes wide with alarm.

"The cover, remember?" he whispered. Then, in a loud and surprisingly convincing American accent, he said, "Come here, love, you've got something on your forehead."

My God, how did he still manage to sound like a sexy model even with an American accent? Curse this man and his undeniable charm. Scowling, Jayne allowed him to rub the pad of his thumb along her forehead, resisting the urge to shudder under his soft touch. But she knew what he was doing; he was masking the totem that was no doubt glowing for all the world to see.

Right. Maybe Jayne should've done this in private first. But unless they wanted to risk alarming the Uber driver, this was the only time for them to do it. They didn't want someone identifying them from the lobby.

"If you're quite finished," she said tersely before pressing her palm against his chest. She called on the two spells she'd conjured and funneled them into Tristan.

Tristan jerked, his arms going rigid. Faint white lights shimmered along his face before vanishing, leaving him looking pale and horrified. "What—what did you do?"

"Cloaking spell layered with a Disguise spell," Jayne said, trying not to sound smug. "You're welcome." She pressed her palm to her own chest and felt energy trickle down the back of her neck as if someone were running a wet comb through her hair. This time, she did shudder. The hairs on her arms stood up in response to the magic rippling over her.

"Jayne," Tristan said, a bit breathless. "You really shouldn't spontaneously layer spells together like that."

"Why not? I do it all the time."

Tristan shook his head. "It's dangerous. I know you are

90

more powerful than I am, but that doesn't mean you shouldn't exercise caution."

"I had a need, and the Torrent filled it. What's the problem?"

Tristan growled something unintelligible before glancing over his shoulder at the nearby tourists shooting them curious looks. "We'll discuss this later. Come on."

He took her hand, and Jayne resisted the urge to snatch it away, knowing they had a cover to maintain. As they entered the lobby, she had to crane her neck to take in the floor-to-ceiling travertine marble walls. A red carpet lined the floor, and cream leather chairs and sofas created conversational groupings. Elegant. Old school. Maybe this wouldn't be so bad after all.

Tristan approached the front desk and spoke in broken Italian, fumbling with an Italian phrase dictionary. "Uh, ciao, um, la camera..." before the woman said kindly, "I speak English, sir."

"Oh, wonderful," Tristan said in his American accent, sighing with relief. "My wife and I are checking in. It should be under the name Lowe."

"Like Rob Lowe," Jayne added helpfully.

The woman's gaze flicked to Jayne, her eyebrows puckering slightly. Jayne only grinned. If there was any moment for her to act quirky and chipper, it was here and now while she posed as an obnoxious American tourist.

"*Allora,*" she said, typing, "you are honeymooners?"

Jayne glanced at Tristan, swallowing nervously, but he had already taken on the role. He flashed his ring, then a wide smile. "Oh, yes. Hard to believe the deed has been done after all this time together, right, sweetie?" He pulled Jayne to his side in a one-armed hug, and she beamed at the woman while stepping hard on his instep. He gasped, covered it with a nuzzle to her neck. "My beautiful bride," he murmured, and Jayne's stomach nearly upended its contents on the lovely marble desk.

The woman—her name tag said Rosa—smiled indulgently. "*Sí*, Signore é Signora Lowe, I see your reservation. You are all checked in." She slid a folder to Tristan. "There is all the information for your stay as well as your room keys."

"Thank you so much." He spilled out the papers. "Look, dear, free breakfast is included!" Tristan's eyes glinted as he looked at Jayne, who couldn't help but laugh at his enthusiasm.

"I do love waffles," she supplied.

Tristan, ever the gentleman, hefted Jayne's suitcase and they took the elevator to the third floor. She ignored his ridiculous repetitions of their married name—"Signore and Signora Lowe; Signore and Signora Lowe"—until she couldn't stand it anymore.

"Oh, do shut up, Signore Lowe."

"*Mi amor,*" he responded with a wicked grin, holding a hand to his heart.

"Jackass," she replied.

After unlocking the door to their room, Jayne strode inside and gasped. The living room was elegant, understated but opulent, with cream carpets and a luxuriously plush sofa that she wanted to stretch out on immediately. The balcony had a view of the Spanish Steps that was awe-inspiring. The bedroom was just as luxe, with a four-poster king bed that clearly could sleep them both comfortably.

Jayne felt like she was staying in a castle. This place was simply too much.

"So...we'll be here for two weeks?" she asked weakly.

"That's what Ruger said."

Jayne raised an eyebrow at him. "You seem suspiciously okay with all this."

Tristan scoffed and gestured to the room. "It's not exactly a dumpster, Jayne."

"I mean this assignment. Aren't you upset about being stuck with me for so long?"

He sighed and waved an idle hand, and her eyes couldn't help but go to his ring. It looked very natural upon his elegant hand. "It's the mission, Jayne. I'm used to doing assignments I don't particularly like."

"Oh yeah, like capturing and torturing your colleagues?" The words were out before Jayne could stop them.

Tristan's shoulders tensed. His back was to Jayne, his head angled slightly, and she could tell from the curve of his jaw that he was gritting his teeth.

"Is that your problem with me? That I played my role too well?" The bitterness in his tone made her mouth taste like ash.

"Sorry, I didn't mean that," Jayne said quickly. "I'm tired and flustered. Just ignore me, please."

She turned away from him and began unpacking her belongings. The bathroom was gorgeous, the floor and walls clad in green marble that looked like a physical representation of the Torrent on Earth, accompanied by a massive bathtub and two sinks. Jayne always appreciated a bathroom large enough to fit two people side by side without knocking elbows.

"About your spells," Tristan said from the bedroom.

Jayne rolled her eyes, smelling a lecture coming.

"You really should practice in a safe environment before you layer spells like that."

"Hmm," Jayne said noncommittally, taking her time arranging her toiletries on the sink.

"Some spells are incompatible, and you won't realize this until you've already combined them. The results would be catastrophic."

Realizing Tristan wouldn't stop until she acknowledged him, Jayne said in a clipped tone, "Okay. Got it. Thanks."

A pause. "I'm just trying to help."

Remembering what Ruger said, Jayne sighed. "Yes, I know. But sometimes you act like I haven't already gotten all the basic training."

"But you haven't. That's the problem."

Frowning at the edge to his voice, Jayne emerged from the bathroom and crossed her arms. Tristan's jaw was set, his eyes flaring with emotion. Perhaps he was still upset about her earlier comment.

"Out with it, Tristan," she said. "What's this really about?"

"Fine. Most Adepts get years of training before they take assignments like this."

Jayne nodded. "You're right. But the situation was dicey, and the TCO needed me in the field sooner. Besides, I'm not like most Adepts."

"No, you're not." The words were laced with accusation.

"What's that supposed to mean?"

"We haven't seen a Master magician in decades, Jayne. You're the first one. Everyone else might be wowed by your prowess and abilities, but I'm not. If anything, your excess of power only concerns me. It's like handing a loaded gun to a toddler."

Jayne's head reared back. "A *toddler*? Are you serious?"

"Oh, I'm sorry," Tristan sneered. "You discovered your powers a few months ago, yes? I meant an infant."

Jayne dropped her arms, her body quivering with rage. "So that's why you hate me? Because I'm powerful? God, talk about toddlers! You're pissed because I have the shinier toy and you can't take it for yourself!"

"I don't hate you, and it's not just about your power. It's how you wield it carelessly, like you're invincible! You're clueless, arrogant, and powerful, which is a dangerous combination. If you don't take precautions, you're going to kill someone. Or yourself."

Jayne couldn't believe what she was hearing. *Clueless? Arrogant?* What an ass! She didn't ask for this power. And here he was, blaming her as if she'd swiped it from right under his nose or something. He didn't know her or what she'd been through. He was an ignorant douchebag, and Jayne had had enough. She strode past Tristan and pulled out her laptop and ear buds from her duffel bag.

"If you'll excuse me, *Signore Lowe,*" she said coldly. "I have some Roman libraries to research." She stuck in her earbuds and drowned out any protests by blaring her epic Hans Zimmer movie soundtrack playlist. Turning away from Tristan, she sat in the chair in the corner and got to work.

The sooner they found this grimoire and parted ways, the better.

THIRTEEN

MENDING FENCES

A few hours later, after much research and a quick break to grab a cornetto and espresso from a nearby bakery called Grano, Jayne was feeling much better. She'd spent the better part of the afternoon making copious notes about the libraries on the map as well as the grimoires from the files Ruger had given her, and the epic movie soundtrack blaring in her ears made her feel like she was doing something adventurous and daring instead of just researching. Then again, to Jayne, researching *was* adventurous. It was like diving into a good book; you could go on an adventure without ever leaving your seat. Oh, the wonders and secrets available at her fingertips, only a quick database search away...

Tristan had kept to his corner of the room, also working on his computer, though Jayne didn't spare him a single glance. Looking his way would have only resurrected her anger, and she didn't need that kind of hostility right now. They were partners, after all. They were fighting for the same side. She had to remember that. His personality might grate on hers, but he was still an ally.

Jayne took her time at Grano, needing a few minutes of solitude to clear her head. She may have read a chapter or two of Anne McCaffrey's *Dragonflight* as well—simply because enjoying pastries in a small café in Rome demanded diving into a good book, if only for a few minutes.

When Jayne returned, she handed Tristan an espresso and a *panna cotta* topped with strawberries she'd bought for him from Grano. A peace offering. There might not be pie as readily available as she would've liked, but *panna cotta* was a close second.

He glanced up at her with raised eyebrows before accepting them. After taking off the lid and sniffing the contents of the cup, he asked lightly, "Did you spit in it?"

"Of course not. I just poured in some cyanide."

Half his mouth quirked in a smile. "Thank you."

Jayne only nodded before settling into her seat by her computer. Now that the air was clear—well, not so much clear as slightly less murky—she sifted through her notes. "I've made a schedule of the libraries we can tackle first, as well as a list of some of the more noteworthy manuscripts we can ask for. We'll need a proper cover in order to get in and view the archives."

Tristan took a bite of his *panna cotta* and groaned with satisfaction. "That is good."

"The plan, or the dessert?"

"Both."

Jayne snorted. Well, at least he was enjoying the peace offering. She stood and handed him her list. "The schedule is arranged by location. The first ones are closest to where we are."

Tristan frowned, eyebrows raised as if impressed. "Wow. How...organized."

"Thank you."

"That wasn't necessarily a compliment."

"Of course it isn't, coming from you, but I'm choosing to accept it as such."

Tristan chuckled as he looked over the list, his expression sobering.

"You know," Jayne said slowly, "since you were with La Liberté for so long, isn't it possible *you* came across the grimoire we're looking for?"

Tristan stilled. After a moment, he said carefully, "It is possible."

"So, do any of these libraries look familiar?" Jayne asked, trying to adopt an air of mild curiosity.

Tristan shook his head. "No. But grimoires get moved around all the time."

Jayne eyed him, her suspicions rising. Tristan was still perusing the schedule she'd made, but his eyes weren't moving. It almost seemed as if he was avoiding her gaze.

She would bet good money that he *had* seen this particular grimoire before.

So why was he hiding that from her?

Silence fell between them, and Jayne didn't want to push, not when they had just formed an unsteady truce. She checked her watch and grimaced. "Most libraries here will be closing soon. But how about we scope out the ones closest to us, make some more detailed plans, and then come back here for dinner? I would kill for a plate of *cacio e pepe.*"

Something softened in Tristan's gaze, his expression turning unreadable. He often wore a mask that was hard for her to decipher. She couldn't tell if it was because he was always hiding something or because he was so used to wearing it as a double agent. Deceiving his own mother on a regular basis couldn't have been easy.

The reminder of what he'd endured cooled some of Jayne's frustration toward him. Tristan had been through a lot. For years, he had actively worked against those closest to him. No wonder he had such a rough exterior.

"Sounds like a plan," he said at last, setting aside her schedule to rise from his chair. He stretched, and Jayne, already scrutinizing him, noticed the peek of his muscles under the unbuttoned collar of his shirt. He was lean—certainly not as beefy as Cillian—but still fit in a way she couldn't help but admire.

Jayne snapped her gaze away, chiding herself for such silly thoughts. The last thing she needed to be doing was admiring Tristan's physique.

Besides, these kinds of thoughts only reminded her of the pain she'd put Cillian through. She tried not to dwell on it, but how could she not? She'd broken his heart. Anytime she remembered that moment in the Luxembourg Gardens when she'd ended things, she wondered if it would have been better if they'd never gotten together at all.

But no. They'd wanted each other. To put off that yearning and longing would have caused them both pain and would have been an even bigger distraction. She just didn't feel love for him in the way she knew she wanted to feel love. Cillian was a great guy. He was a powerful Rogue, and sexy as hell to boot. There was just something missing between them, and she'd been brave enough to admit that before things got too intense.

He'd find someone. So would she. The discovery of their individual magics would tie them together forever, and they'd find a way to be friends eventually.

Even so. How was this better? Cillian was hurting, and because she did love him as a friend, Jayne was hurting for him. Now, Sofia was caught in the middle of an incredibly awkward situation. It was just a mess. A mess of Jayne's own creation. She needed to guard her heart, gird her loins, and stow her hormones. Magical romances were for the birds.

"Jayne?"

Tristan had donned his coat and was looking at her expectantly. His brow was furrowed, his eyes contemplative. They didn't know each other well yet, but Jayne was certain he was thinking, *Where were you just now?*

"Right." Jayne snatched her scarf and tied back her hair before following Tristan out the door.

They only had time to check out two libraries before Jayne's stomach started grumbling for something more substantial than just sweets. They'd inspected the Library of the Chamber of Deputies and the Biblioteca di Archeologia e Storia dell'Arte, both nearly identical buildings. The former contained a sleek and modern series of rooms on the inside, but she felt nothing magical. The latter, Tristan dismissed immediately, and Jayne couldn't blame him; it just wasn't large enough to hold a major grimoire. A minor, perhaps, but that wasn't what they were looking for. Jayne knew from experience that a magical text like the ones she'd encountered was most likely locked away in a vault of some kind for security purposes, and this smaller library didn't seem like it had even that.

Jayne and Tristan outlined a thorough plan of attack for getting into the Library of the Chamber of Deputies again the following morning to search deeper in the stacks. To her surprise, as far as their cover went, they were of the same mind; Jayne would pose as a curator from Vanderbilt, and Tristan would be her backup, loitering as an ordinary civilian and lending his magic as needed.

It was the spells that they disagreed on. Jayne thought a simple Tracking spell would be enough; she'd used it plenty of times without issue. But Tristan argued that since she hadn't seen the grimoire before, the spell would be faulty.

"It's worth a try, right?" Jayne said as they strode down the street back to their hotel. "I mean, even if it leads us to the wrong grimoire, it's better than nothing."

"I disagree," said Tristan.

"Shocker."

"Not only will it alert any other Adepts to our presence," he went on censoriously, "but our efforts would be better put to use in gaining access to their vaults. You'll be able to sense any grimoires immediately without having to use any magic."

"Gaining access to a library vault is harder than you might think," Jayne said, her inner librarian roaring at the idea of an average Joe just waltzing in and asking to touch all kinds of valuable and ancient texts.

"What if we compromise?" Tristan asked, stopping to face her fully.

Jayne crossed her arms. "I'm listening."

"You convince them to take you as far as you can get, and I'll send my magic after you to Track the grimoire."

Jayne frowned. "But you just said—"

"If you cast the magic yourself, with your power, it will be a beacon alerting others to your presence. But sending a severed strand of magic, detached from the caster, will help mask the unique magical signature. It will come from me, but I'll be inconspicuous. You, however, will be trying to get into the library's vaults, which is very conspicuous."

Jayne's frown deepened at what he wasn't saying: *Also, I'm much more skilled at casting spells than you are.* She really wanted to argue that her magic was more powerful than his, but this would be beating a very dead horse.

Mend fences, Jayne, she told herself. *Give him a chance.*

"Fine," she said. "We'll try it. But if it doesn't work, we're doing it my way for the next one. Deal?"

Tristan flashed a grin. "Deal."

THEY DINED at an exquisite restaurant on the sixth floor of the hotel called Imàgo. Jayne started off with a dirty martini and then enjoyed a ridiculously tasty gnocchi with beef ragu. Tristan was more adventurous, ordering the raw rossini, followed by the rabbit raviolo and the wild boar. They each devoured a chocolate soufflé for dessert and finished a bottle of Louis Roederer Rosé sent over by the owner to celebrate their honeymoon. It was ridiculously good.

She'd always said it was impossible to argue with a delicious meal in front of you, and this proved correct, even with someone as snobby as Tristan. They talked of mundane things, not just to maintain their cover but to give themselves a break from the mental strain of their research and planning. Tristan had been to Rome before, but it had been over a decade, and he missed it terribly. Italy, it turned out, was one of his favorite places in the world, aside from France, of course.

After a meal like that, Jayne couldn't blame him. Her taste buds were singing.

It wasn't until they returned to the hotel room and changed into pajamas that Jayne finally faced the predicament before them: Two strangers. One bed.

If she were reading a romance novel, it would be easy; the couple would be forced to sleep side by side in a strained night of sexual tension and restrained passion, only to discover near the end of the book that they both yearned for more.

But Tristan was already prepared. He grabbed a spare blanket from the closet and headed for the sofa in the living room. He offered her a quick smile before bidding her good night.

She'd sat on that sofa. A glorious piece to look at, but cozy it was not. It might as well have been full of nails. It was fine to watch a movie, but to sleep all night?

She waited. Heard him tossing, turning, punching pillows.

Part of her thought he deserved to wake up with a crick in his neck. She finally got out of bed and followed his trail, almost laughing when she saw the ridiculous position he'd been forced to contort himself into as he struggled to contain all six feet five of his limbs and muscles in the makeshift bed.

"For the love of God," Jayne snapped. "Don't be an idiot. Just get in the bed."

Tristan, who had been wriggling around on the sofa in hilarious fashion, froze and looked up at her, his dark hair disheveled. "But..."

"We're partners, Tristan. We aren't from a different species. I can sleep side by side with anyone on my team without a problem." Although, to be frank, the idea of sharing a bed with him made her bristle. But she would never tell him that.

He seemed to sense the lie and arched an eyebrow at her.

"It's a king-size bed," she went on. "I don't move much when I sleep. But if you kick, I swear to God I'll kick you back."

Tristan chuckled and finally rose from the sofa. "If you say so. But at the first sign of discomfort, I'll sleep on the sofa. Or even the floor. I've endured worse."

"And how would it look if someone from housekeeping came in and found evidence of you sleeping somewhere else? Trouble in paradise on our honeymoon might cause gossip. We need to lay low and stay in our cover."

Tristan frowned. It was clear he hadn't considered this.

Jayne huffed a sigh and snatched up two long, plush pillows before cramming them directly in the middle of the bed as a sort of cushioned barrier. "There. Your side. My side." She pointed, then looked at him expectantly.

Tristan's mouth quirked. "I usually sleep on the right side."

Jayne shot him her fiercest glare.

He raised his palms. "Kidding." He eased into the left side, and Jayne was pleased to see he still had plenty of room despite the Great Wall of Pillows next to him. She climbed onto the opposite side, sighing with contentment at the softness of the comforter and the fluffy pillows.

"Good night, Jayne," Tristan said. She could barely see him over the massive pillow fort that separated them.

Sexual tension my ass, Jayne thought, smug that she had easily evaded a romance trope all on her own. "Good night."

FOURTEEN

CHANGE OF PLANS

Patagonia

Lars followed the narrow road to the house described by his contact. His source was rock-solid, so he had no doubt that Sofia Thorne was staying here.

Lars understood immediately what had drawn the oldest Thorne girl here; the air was simmering with power. It made his skin prickle. What he wouldn't do to have a taste. But no. He had a mission. He could not deviate.

Not for the first time, he wished he had a comfortable life like the Head of the Kingdom where he could lounge around and give orders to others.

Maybe someday.

He found the house easily. Humble, but warm, the lights inside glowing with familial warmth. He took a step toward the door and something tangible slammed into him, sending him stumbling backward.

Wards. Damn. Of course the Guardian in residence would have taken precautions.

Muttering curses under his breath, Lars reached into his pocket and withdrew a lighter. When he flicked it, energy bubbled from within. The air shifted and twisted around him, becoming thin and suffocating him. But he could see tendrils of green magic seeping from the house and floating into the lighter.

The tool was developed by the Kingdom's top technicians. Although their mantra was to reset the world back to archaic times, as long as their enemies had technology, they needed a means to keep up. And this little invention was one of the finest Lars had ever seen.

When the wards were successfully penetrated, Lars pocketed the lighter and drew closer. Already, he could make out loud voices from within.

"I *am* trying! This doesn't come as easily for me as it does for Jayne." A woman's voice. Sofia Thorne, most likely. Lars's ears perked up at the mention of her sister. Jayne Thorne had vanished after her altercation with the Kingdom in Rome. He was here to find out where she'd run off to. Sofia was making it easy.

Thank you, sister.

"Stop comparing yourself to Jayne," said a male voice. "You are your own unique person."

"I'm sorry. It's just—I miss her, that's all. It's hard not to think about her."

Lars frowned. If Sofia missed her sister, did that mean they weren't together? If so, then where was Jayne?

"We have our best team assisting her in Rome," said a cool female voice. Authoritative. Strong. Why was Amanda Newport here? "You have nothing to worry about. Jayne can take care of herself."

Lars typed quickly into his phone, eager to report all this information back to the Head. Jayne Thorne *was* still in Rome. Fascinating indeed...

"I know that," Sofia said. "I'm just eager for her to be done with the mission so we can track down my dad. Ever since we found out he's alive, I just... It's been driving me crazy, not knowing where he is."

Lars straightened. The Thorne girls knew about Henry Thorne? He made another note on his phone and waited, eager for more.

"Maybe if we talked to Xiomara about it again," Sofia said slowly.

"She doesn't know anything else," said Amanda. "She's given us all the information she has. We need to accept that and table this for later."

Sofia paused. "Maybe Jayne will find something."

Amanda seemed to sense something different about Sofia's tone. "What do you mean?" Her voice was laced with suspicion.

"I asked her to look into it," Sofia said quickly. "That's all."

Lars's head buzzed from this revelation. This changed everything. Ignoring the exasperated response from Amanda, he feverishly typed, *Jayne has a lead on H.T.*

After a moment, footsteps faded as one of the women stepped out of the room, but Lars remained frozen in place, mulling over this information.

Sofia wasn't searching for Henry. *Jayne* was. Lars wasn't sure why Sofia remained here, but the Head had made it that clear that locating Henry Thorne was the Kingdom's top priority. Her urgency on the matter led Lars to believe Henry had vital information; possibly something life-changing that could finally bring the Kingdom into full power.

And Jayne was still in Rome. The Kingdom still had operatives stationed there. It would be easy to track her down, now that they knew she had never left the city.

He stepped away from the house and farther down the road before casting a Cloaking spell and dialing the Head's number.

"What?" Her voice was strained. Every time Lars spoke with her recently, she sounded ill.

"You didn't get my text? I found Sofia. But she isn't looking for our target. Jayne is." He shared what he'd heard.

The Head was silent for a long moment. Lars could hear the gleeful smile in her voice as she said, "Excellent. Send Hans after Sofia. I'll handle Jayne."

CHAPTER
FIFTEEN
PARTNERS AND CONFESSIONS

"Again," said Seo-joon. The patience in his voice only exacerbated Sofia's nerves.

For the fifth time that day, Sofia reached for the Torrent and found the Block spell. She drew it closer, cupping it in the palm of her hand. When the river of stars vanished, the magic lingered on her palm. But as soon as she stretched out her hand, the spell vanished.

"Damn it!" She curled her hands into fists. It had been like this all morning. She could get Cillian to shift effortlessly, but wielding magic on her own was still difficult. "I fought off Ruth Thorne! I'm a Master magician! Why is this so impossible for me?" She wiped the sweat from her forehead. "It's so much easier for me to fight with my body instead of my magic. Can't I just kick you?"

Seo-joon snorted. "Well, as *fun* as that sounds..." He crossed his arms and scrutinized Sofia, his mouth twisting in thought.

"What?" she demanded.

"I think you're doubting yourself."

Sofia sighed and rubbed her temples. "Well, that's certainly true. But it's not like a switch I can flip, ordering myself to be more confident."

"Maybe you can channel that same feeling you had when you were fighting Ruth. Focus on that power."

"Every time I do, Cillian ends up shifting." The last time Sofia had focused on the euphoria she felt after bonding with him, a howl from the next room told her she'd accidentally called him to shift. She still felt guilty for interrupting his nap. It couldn't have been pleasant for him to wake up and suddenly realize he was a wolf.

"Don't focus on Cillian," Seo-joon said. "Focus on *you*. How *you* felt wielding that power. Not how Cillian's Rogue magic felt. Can you separate the two?"

Sofia frowned, gnawing on her lower lip. Could she? The events of that night were so muddled, it was hard to isolate one feeling from everything she'd gone through. When she thought of her own magic, it had been inexplicably entwined with Cillian's. But perhaps that was the problem. Was she relying too much on him?

Maybe it was better he wasn't in the room. Sofia was conflicted enough about coming between Cillian and Jayne; she didn't need that kind of distraction.

God, she missed Jayne. She knew her sister's mission was important, as was Sofia's; tracking down the Guardians and training alongside them would provide much-needed advancement for the TCO. And Jayne was trying to prevent two powerful terrorist organizations from getting their hands on a deadly grimoire.

Even so, the time apart from her sister was wearing on Sofia's already thin patience.

"Okay." She took a cleansing breath and closed her eyes. "Let's try again."

"Whenever you're ready," Seo-joon said.

Instead of reaching for the Torrent, Sofia took a moment to remember that day. Jayne had gotten swept aside by the Master of Shadows as if she'd been nothing more than a rag doll. And something had *clicked* between Sofia and Cillian.

She shut down that line of thinking, and the sensations it caused. No, something had snapped within Sofia. A well of power she had only just begun to uncover. Her protectiveness of Jayne had kindled a fire within her, bringing to life a formidable force. Something unstoppable.

In a flash, the green river of stars appeared in Sofia's mind. Before she had the chance to doubt herself again, she found the Block spell and grabbed it, then flung it straight at Seo-joon.

He was so startled that the spell hit him squarely in the chest before he could react, knocking him to the ground.

The Torrent vanished, and Sofia yelped, rushing to Seo-joon's side to help him to his feet. He rubbed his chest and groaned, but his eyes were alight with pride. "Damn, girl. You did good." He raised his hand for a high five, and Sofia obliged him.

"That was impressive."

Sofia turned to find Cillian watching from the doorway, eyebrows lifted. His expression was part satisfied, part awestruck.

Sofia rubbed the back of her neck, unsure how she felt about him watching her train. How long had he been standing there? "Um, thanks."

"I'm starved," Seo-joon announced. "Anyone else want some empanadas?"

"Yes, please." Sofia's stomach rumbled in response.

And just like that, she was alone in the room with Cillian. Well, crap. Sofia took a step back, putting a safe distance between them.

Cillian's brow furrowed. "Why do you do that?"

"Do what?"

"Back away from me like I'm about to hit you."

Sofia flinched. "It's not that. It's just—" God, how could she explain it? She felt like a fool. "I don't want you to think I'm trying anything with you. Romantically. And I'm worried all I do is remind you of Jayne." The words came out in a rush. As soon as they were out, she clamped her mouth shut, wishing she could take it all back.

A war of emotions surged behind his eyes, but Sofia couldn't read them all. She thought she sensed hurt, anger, and guilt, but she couldn't be sure.

"What happened between Jayne and me isn't your fault," Cillian said, his voice soft.

Sofia gave a dry laugh. "Yes, it is."

"No, it's not. I loved her. She didn't love me. That's why it ended."

She didn't know that. "I—oh."

"I heard what Seo-joon was saying about separating yourself from my Rogue magic," Cillian said. "What do you think he meant by that?"

Grateful for the subject change, Sofia shrugged. "Just that it's easy for me to envision my magic tethered to yours. I have to learn to isolate my powers so they can function on their own."

"No, I understand that. But what does he mean by *Rogue magic*?"

"The magic that allows you to shift." Sofia didn't understand what he was getting at.

Cillian only looked more confused as he sank onto the sofa. He ran a hand through his golden hair and sighed. "Do you think...it could be more than that?"

Sofia sat down next to him. "I'm not sure what you're saying."

"In Paris, Gina Labelle said something to me about

exploring my Rogue magic. She implied there was more to it than just shifting. She offered to help me with it."

Sofia's insides turned cold at the reminder of when Cillian had been imprisoned and tortured. God, the pain he must have endured... She resisted the urge to take his hand, worried he might misinterpret the gesture. "She was manipulating you. She wanted you to trust her."

"But that's the thing. It doesn't feel like a lie. Sometimes, I can sense the presence inside me, even when you aren't calling me to shift. The TCO makes it seem like Rogues only exist to serve their Masters, but I don't think that's true. I mean, look at Gina. She's bloody powerful, and she's not bonded."

"That we know. She's still quite the enigma." She chewed on her thumbnail. "I don't think all Rogues are the same. We know there's some Adept blood in that family. Tristan is an Adept, after all."

"If all Rogues aren't the same, then how does anyone know that my magic isn't something...more?"

Sofia remained silent as she considered his words. She knew firsthand how it felt to have something strong and powerful writhing inside you. She knew how terrifying it was to know nothing about it, to fear that it might be dangerous to those she loved. Shutting out her insecure thoughts, Sofia pressed her hand to Cillian's, trusting he would understand it for the gesture that it was.

"We don't know," Sofia said gently. "But I promise you, Cillian, I will work with you to figure out the answers you need. Okay?"

He met her eyes. His gaze was filled with a helplessness that made Sofia just want to wrap him in a bear hug, but she quashed the urge. As their eyes locked, Cillian's expression softened in relief and gratitude. He visibly relaxed, letting go of the tension that weighed him down.

"Thank you, Sofia." He squeezed her hand. "For what it's worth, I don't blame you at all. And I don't think of Jayne when I look at you. I just think...of Sofia."

Sofia's face heated at his words, and she dropped her gaze, suddenly embarrassed. Even so, she appreciated him saying this. It loosened the growing ache in her chest that she'd clung to ever since bonding with Cillian.

It's not your fault. Cillian and Jayne had both told her as much, but somehow, it hadn't sunk in until right now.

Sofia wasn't sure how long they sat there, hand in hand, but for the first time, she was comforted being there with him. They were a team. Partners. They would fight this battle and face these uncertainties. Together.

CHAPTER
SIXTEEN
THE LIBRARY, AT LAST

Rome

J ayne was swept up in a sea of lightning, her arms flailing, her body weightless as the storm carried her. She screamed, but the explosion of thunder swallowed up her cries.

Orange streaks lit up the sky, burning and scorching. As they drew closer, Jayne realized it wasn't amber lightning—it was *fire*. The flames lashed at her, melting her flesh and boiling her blood. A torrent of agony consumed her, and she screamed again.

Another voice joined hers. A woman. The sound of her terrified shouts startled Jayne into silence. Still floating in the wind, still overcome by the flames, she listened for another cry.

"Aidez-moi!" the woman wailed. *Help me.*

Jayne's body trembled with fear and awareness. Whoever this woman was, she was caught in the firestorm, too. Jayne tried to shout, to assure the woman she was coming, that she would save her—

Jayne jerked awake, her body coated in a cold sweat. Her heart pounded so loudly the rhythm seemed to reverberate into her bones. For the briefest moment, her pulse was so frantic she couldn't breathe. She wiped sweat from her brow, finally drawing breath, huffing in relief as she tried to get her bearings. The blackout curtains were drawn, blocking out the window, so she had no idea what time it was. On the other side of her pillow barrier, Tristan snored softly.

Right, she thought as her brain slowly caught up. *I'm in Rome with Tristan.*

God, that dream had been so real. So vivid. If Jayne didn't believe in magic, she would've chalked it up to too much sugar.

But she *did* know about magic. And this felt powerful. Different. Certainly not an ordinary dream. More like...a vision.

Her forehead prickled, and she rubbed at it by instinct before realizing it was likely her totem. Jumping out of bed, Jayne lunged for the bathroom and slipped inside. She didn't even have to turn on the light to see the golden glow of Medb's Earth totem gleaming on her forehead.

Her heart thundering anew, Jayne brushed her fingers over it, wondering what Medb was trying to tell her with this dream.

"Are you there?" she whispered, feeling like an idiot.

And, of course, Medb didn't answer.

Jayne briefly thought of waking Tristan. But he would probably lecture her about some magic she was supposed to know about but didn't.

No, she needed Ruger.

She withdrew her burner phone, shut the bathroom door, and dialed the number she had memorized. Ruger picked up after only two rings.

"Third-level code word?" He didn't even sound tired. Did he *ever* sleep?

Jayne didn't miss a beat. "Anaconda. Which was a terrible movie, by the way."

Ruger sighed, but Jayne wasn't finished with him yet.

"What's *your* code word, Mr. Stern?"

Ruger paused for only a moment before grumbling, "I'm too sexy."

Jayne snickered at her own invented code word. But Ruger had insisted he recite one, too, in case someone was impersonating him. And Jayne had jumped at the opportunity to come up with the most embarrassing phrases, claiming it would be safer if one of them avoided the TCO's boring and nonsensical codes. Especially since there was a suspected mole within the organization.

"What's up, Jayne?" Ruger asked.

Jayne quickly filled him in on her wacky dream and the glowing totem. He was silent for several moments as he mulled this over.

"I'm portaling you to the TCO Library," he finally decided.

Jayne lit up. "Really? Oh, yay! What a treat!"

"This isn't a reward, Jayne. I think Katie might be able to help you find a book or two that might help shed some light on your situation. You need the Italian translation spell anyway—we didn't think you would be in-country so long or I'd have routed you through the library before you portaled in. And you can return those grimoires we were practicing on."

Jayne nodded, remembering the insta-language spell when she'd basically absorbed a French dictionary in a minute before her Paris assignment. "Okay. When?"

"You and Tristan take the morning to get situated. Have breakfast. Do some touristy things in case anyone is watching. Then, before lunch, I want you to discreetly come to the safe house. I'll portal you from there."

"Ten-four, Boss Man." She was about to hang up when Ruger stopped her.

"And Jayne?"

"You did the right thing, calling me."

Jayne smiled. "I know." Even so, it was still nice to hear.

AFTER ENJOYING a basket of cornettos for breakfast—a pastry that was much sweeter than the croissants of Paris, but Jayne loved it just the same—and a couple of Americanos, Tristan and Jayne toured the Pantheon, which seemed like the obvious thing to do. Besides, she was eager for the excuse to view the interior of such a magnificent building.

Oh, the joys of working undercover. Getting paid to tour Rome? Not so bad.

She suppressed a swoon as they followed the line of people through the entrance. The domed ceiling towered high above them, and elegantly sculpted pillars framed the massive room. Pews lined the floors, all facing an impressive display of statues and intricately carved iron candlesticks.

Tristan had to nag Jayne often to quicken her pace, otherwise they wouldn't be finished before lunchtime. But how could she rush an experience like this? She wanted to stop and drink it all in, to savor this... God, all the history contained in each room was enough to make her want to weep with joy.

After gazing at the Cappella dell'Annunciazione for the fifth time, Jayne finally relented, feeling like the parent of a wayward child who was anxious to leave. Tristan touched her shoulder as he led her back outside, and she resisted the urge to shrug away from him.

Undercover, remember? She relaxed against him as if it were the most natural thing in the world.

"We'll be in Rome for a while, dear," Tristan said in his outrageous American accent. "There will be plenty of time."

Jayne shot him her most sickly sweet smile. "Any time spent with you is a vacation, my darling shepherd's pie."

Tristan's mouth twitched, but he kept his gaze fixed forward as they left the Pantheon.

They stopped in the piazza to admire the obelisk, dawdling as tourists are wont to do. After ensuring they weren't being followed, they ducked down a narrow side street, swiftly following the previously mapped-out course toward the safe house. They approached the back door, and Jayne knocked gently. After a few moments, the door swung open and Ruger gestured them inside.

"I feel like a real spy now," Jayne said with a grin. "All cloak-and-dagger and everything."

"I'm so glad the possibility of enemies following us is amusing for you," Tristan said.

Ruger shut the door and bolted it. "The portal is in the kitchen for you, Jayne."

"Perfect." She rubbed her hands together. "I can sneak a slice of pie before I go." She moved toward the kitchen, then faltered when she realized Tristan wasn't following. "Aren't you coming?"

Tristan crossed his arms and shot her his most infuriating smirk. "I'm already fluent in Italian."

Jayne rolled her eyes. "Of course you are."

"Tristan will stay here with me, and we'll go over the plan you two came up with," Ruger explained.

Jayne shrugged. Truth be told, if they were pretending to be annoying American tourists, she didn't see why she needed the Translation spell. But she wasn't about to pass up the opportunity to visit the glorious TCO Library, so she made no objections.

Ruger gestured to the coffee table where the two grimoires sat, untouched, as if they had been waiting for her this whole time. Jayne hesitantly approached, wondering if the major grimoire would try anything on her if she touched it.

"It's perfectly safe," Ruger said, reading her mind. "I've spelled them, and their magic is dormant right now."

"Aw, sleepy little grimoires," Jayne cooed as she scooped them into her arms. They were warm against her skin and emitted a faint humming sound, but it was subtle compared to the onslaught of magic she'd felt earlier. This almost reminded her of holding a purring kitten in her arms. She resisted the urge to press her cheek against the leather cover.

"Should we leave you alone for a moment?" Tristan joked.

"Books hold an allure and charm that you men will never be able to compete with," Jayne said as she made her way to the kitchen. *"Ciao!"*

True to her word, she snagged the remaining slice of cherry pie before glancing around in search of the glowing gold portal. It took her a moment to find it, but eventually her eyes landed on a mysterious shimmering light gleaming from underneath the pantry door.

"Sneaky Ruger," Jayne said with a chuckle. She gathered the grimoires against her chest once more and swung open the pantry door. A wall of rippling liquid gold stood in front of her, and without preamble, she stepped through. Magic roiled over her, as shocking as a wave of ice-cold water. With a gasp, she shook her head, almost expecting gold droplets to fall from her hair.

Slightly disoriented, Jayne glanced around and found herself in the hallway just outside the TCO Library. She grinned. She would never cease to be amazed by the concept of portals. One second, she was in Rome; the next, she was in the CIA headquarters in Langley.

"Jayne!" called a familiar voice.

Jayne's smile broadened as she recognized the blonde woman racing toward her from the other end of the hallway. Still juggling the grimoires, she leaned into Sofia in an awkward embrace. Her sister's familiar raspberry scent mingled with something new that awakened the magical senses inside her.

Jayne leaned away and scrutinized her. "What is that?"

"What's what?"

"That... *sense* about you? Have you done something different with your magic?"

Sofia's smile faded, and her face paled slightly. "Oh yeah. That. I, uh, kind of awakened my Guardian magic."

Jayne nearly dropped the books in her arms. "*What?* Since when do you have Guardian magic?"

Sofia laughed nervously. "We have a lot to catch up on. Come on, I'll get the door for you."

"Hang on. What are you even doing here?"

"Ruger called to tell Amanda you'd be here. They both thought we could use the sister bonding time." Sofia's smile was soft.

"Bless them!" Jayne made a mental note to give Ruger a great big bear hug when she returned.

Sofia pressed her palm against the biometric fingerprint reader on the wall. It glowed green, and she swung open the library door, then frowned. "Uh, not to alarm you, Jayne, but this kind of looks like a dump."

Jayne laughed. "Give it a second. Trust me."

Sofia shot her a doubtful look but stepped forward to allow Jayne to enter. The door closed behind them, and as they moved further inside, Sofia's look of confusion only intensified.

Jayne couldn't blame her. When she'd first set foot in this library, it had appeared just the same: dusty shelves, a disorganized array of books stacked haphazardly upon one another, and an armchair shoved into the corner. Overall, the place looked cramped and was pretty much exactly what Jayne's nightmares looked like. It almost gave her hives just looking at it, even though she knew it was an illusion.

The air began to shimmer, and Sofia gasped. With each step, the library expanded, stretching deeper and wider like an opening file cabinet drawer. The shelves elongated, the books righting themselves into an organized array of tomes. Sofia's arms stretched out as if she might fall over from shock, and Jayne laughed again.

When the transformation was complete, the sisters stood in a two-story hallway with magnificent shelves from floor to ceiling. Just ahead of them was a reception desk where a familiar older woman in a gaudy Christmas sweater sat poring over books.

"Katie!" Jayne shouted eagerly, drawing forward to greet the woman.

To her surprise, Katie jumped, then shuffled books around as if she'd been caught reading the raciest of romances. "Oh! You startled me there, dear." She slid her glasses on and squinted, then broke into a smile. "Jayne, darling. So nice to see you again!"

Jayne didn't miss the way Katie's hand shifted over her stack of books to block the spines from view. What on earth was this woman reading? "Katie, this is my sister, Sofia. Sofia, meet Katie Bell."

"How do you do?" Sofia stuck out her hand, and Jayne marveled that Sofia was so blind as not to see the woman's obvious Harry Potter–related name.

Katie smiled warmly and shook Sofia's hand, giving Jayne the perfect opportunity to glance over the books she was trying to hide.

"What the what?" Jayne asked as she read the titles aloud.

"H.G. Wells' *The Time Machine,* Einstein's *Theory of Relativity, The Magic of Wormholes, An Adept's Guide to Quantum Physics,* and *The Grandfather Paradox*? Wow, Katie, are you brushing up on your Doctor Who research?"

Sofia tilted her head to read the spines as well. "H.G. Wells? I hated that book."

"Yeah, for a book about time travel, it wasn't all that exciting," Jayne agreed.

Katie sighed in good-natured exasperation, her cheeks turning pink. "Just...branching out on my reading repertoire. Come, come, let me help you find the books you need."

Jayne shot another curious glance at the stack of books, wondering what Katie was hiding. But the older woman bustled forward, and Jayne hurried to keep up with her brisk pace.

"What are we looking for this time?" Katie asked, turning to face them with an eager grin Jayne could not help but reciprocate.

Without the cover of the reception desk, Jayne now got a full view of the glory of the woman's holiday sweater. It was cherry red with a gleaming green Christmas tree in the center. Actual bells dangled from the tree's edges, and they jingled slightly with her movements.

Jayne bit back a laugh, admiring the librarian's undeniably festive nature. "I came to return these to you, and to see what you have on magical visions and dreams. And I'll need access to your Italian dictionary, if you can manage it." She extended her arms and offered the grimoires to Katie.

The woman shook her head vehemently. "Oh no, I wouldn't dare touch those unless they called to me. You can return them yourself down there." She gestured to the second row of shelves, barely visible on the other side of the entrance. "As for your other request, let me see what I can find! I'll have a few books ready for you after you send those back." She fixed a bright smile on Sofia. "And you, dear?"

"What do you have on Master magicians and their training? And maybe...Guardian magic?" Sofia asked.

"Let's see what the library will show us, shall we?" Katie tucked Sofia's arm in hers and led her away through the stacks.

CHAPTER

SEVENTEEN

I DARE YOU

Though Jayne yearned to hear the specifics of what her sister was hoping to research—was she having issues tapping into her newly discovered abilities?—she hurried down the second aisle of bookshelves to return the grimoires to their rightful place. Her thoughts turned to Katie's words: *I wouldn't dare touch those unless they called to me.*

She loved how the woman spoke of books as if they were sentient things with their own thoughts and minds. But now that Jayne knew a bit more about grimoires, the thought was less intriguing and more...terrifying. Sure, it was fun to sit at home and think to oneself, *this book sure has a mind of its own!* But to witness it firsthand and see the dangers a single book could hold was quite alarming. In a sense, Jayne almost felt let down. She had always held a reverent respect for all books, and this felt like a betrayal of sorts. How could her precious books turn on her like this?

Not all grimoires are bad, Jayne, she chided herself. But she was reminded of the horrifying incident in Paris when the Book of Shadows tried to devour her. Whatever entity lived inside had certainly wished to do her harm. And, if it weren't for Medb's strength, it would have succeeded.

Suppressing a shudder, Jayne hurried down the aisle, anxious to get these grimoires and her negative thoughts as far away from herself as possible. She was just wondering where exactly to place them when the air began to hum and the books quivered in her grasp. With a sharp intake of breath, she loosened her grip on them, and they darted out of her arms, floating toward the shelves until they slid neatly in place in a gap that seemed to be waiting for them.

Jayne grinned. Of course the TCO Library had self-shelving books. Was there no end to the magical wonders of this place? She kept her gaze fixed on that spot on the shelves, waiting for the two grimoires to act up or show some sign of distress. But they remained silent and still, obviously content with their new home.

"So long, boys." Jayne waved before turning back down the aisle in search of Sofia.

The other women were not where she'd left them. After a few minutes of perusing the stacks, admiring the way they grew and morphed as she walked past, Jayne finally found the two in the cozy sitting area hidden behind a large bookshelf. Sofia was already helping herself to a blueberry scone and a steaming cup of tea, her expression so relaxed that Jayne had to stop and smile for a moment, relishing the delight on her sister's face. It wasn't often that Sofia looked so at ease, especially when it came to things of a magical nature.

But right here and now, Sofia looked at home. And it made Jayne's heart swell.

Katie brightened at Jayne's approach and gestured to the coffee table, where a stack of thick tomes rested. "Here are some books for you to start with. When you finish, let me know, and

I'll find some more for you! Oh, and that Italian dictionary is at the top of the pile when you're ready for it."

Jayne gawked at the massive pile. How had the woman retrieved so many books so quickly? She glanced at Sofia, who was getting situated in front of a table with her own monster mountain of books.

Damn, that librarian was quick. Jayne could learn a thing or two from Katie Bell.

"You two have fun," Katie said, waving over her shoulder as she vanished around the corner.

Sofia chuckled to herself as she took a long sip from her cup. Jayne fixed herself a mint tea and set up a research station next to her sister. When she pulled the books closer, she noticed the Italian dictionary hummed with power. Tendrils of energy crept toward her as if beckoning her to open the book, but they were much less abrasive than from the major grimoire she had assessed earlier. Frowning, Jayne inspected the ancient book and its worn leather cover.

"Minor grimoire," she guessed.

"What?" Sofia asked.

Jayne smiled and shook her head. "Nothing."

"God, I bet you could live here, couldn't you?" Sofia asked with a smile as she gazed around at the cozy seating area.

"It's basically a library straight from my diary." Jayne peered at Sofia's collection. "Magic trouble?"

Sofia shifted in her seat, avoiding Jayne's gaze. "More like confidence issues. I just don't *feel* like a Master, you know?"

Jayne nodded. Her Master magic was different from Sofia's mainly because of the Earth totem, but she could absolutely understand feeling overwhelmed by your own powers.

"What about you?" Sofia asked. "Visions and dreams?"

"Yeah. I had this crazy-ass dream before I got here. It felt like something more, though, and I thought I should look into it." She raised her eyebrows at her sister. "So...your Guardian magic?"

"Right. It's a long story..."

Sofia dove into the lengthy tale about tracking down Xiomara and finding out their father was actually a Guardian. In return, Jayne filled in Sofia about her mission and Tristan's blatant refusal to help.

"Jackass," Sofia muttered, but Jayne shook her head.

"It was a big ask from someone who's been pretty rude to him, so I can't say I blame him. We've never gotten along, and it's not like we're friends. He didn't owe me anything."

"Still. If he'd asked you for help, you would have given it."

Jayne shrugged. She wanted to say, *the hell I would,* but truth be told, if she knew Tristan was in trouble or he was searching for a long-lost family member, she would not hesitate to jump to his aid.

Sofia's eyes turned warm, and she placed a hand on Jayne's arm. "I missed you."

Emotion swelled in Jayne's throat, and she squeezed Sofia's hand. "Me too! I'm so glad we get to hang out today, even if it is to research. If I can help in any way, let me know."

"Oh, trust me, I will undoubtedly utilize your expert research skills before the day is over."

THE RESEARCH DIDN'T PROVE as useful as Jayne had hoped, but she couldn't be upset about it; she got to spend the afternoon with her sister, which was a treat in itself. Most of the texts about visions and dreams referenced famous Seers in the history of Adepts, and Jayne was fairly certain that didn't apply to her. There was one mention of the usage of powerful visions to communicate with dead Master magicians—and Jayne, of course, immediately thought of Medb—but her firestorm dream hadn't featured the Celtic goddess at all.

Even so, Jayne felt certain Medb had something to do with it. She vowed to reach out to the goddess and demand answers from her.

Sofia's research yielded few results as well. Even with Jayne's assistance, all they could find about Master magician training was archaic and horrifying, usually having to do with animal sacrifices or blood rituals (which, as it turned out, were now banned). In addition, all the Master magicians noted in historical texts knew of their great powers from birth and began rigorous training programs early on.

"I honestly think it might be a mental block," Jayne said after a few hours of studying and several cups of tea. "You spent so many years fearing your magic, and it was suppressed for so long, that of course you're not going to bounce back immediately. There's no magic formula for that."

Sofia sighed and rubbed between her eyebrows. "You're right. I guess I was just hoping to find some magical method to help speed things along."

"Are you working with Cillian on it?"

Sofia straightened, her eyes widening in alarm. "Cillian? No, why?"

Jayne laughed. "Relax, Sofia. You two are partners. Maybe he can help with this. He used to be great at it when we trained."

Sofia relaxed slightly, but her expression still held that deer-in-the-headlights panic. "I actually think he's part of the problem. I'm relying too much on his Rogue abilities to fuel my own."

Jayne frowned. She'd never had that issue. Then again, she'd discovered her Master abilities *before* bonding with Cillian. For Sofia, the two came hand-in-hand. "Well, he may be your Rogue, but he's still your partner. Talk to him about this. See what he thinks. He knows firsthand what your magic feels like."

Sofia rubbed the back of her neck and said nothing.

Jayne put a hand on her shoulder. "Listen, it's fine. You don't have to act so skittish around him—or me. We're not walking on eggshells here, Sofia. Cillian and I are over, and it sucks, but it is what it is. I don't blame you, and neither does he. Let's just move on and get past this like adults, okay?"

Sofia exhaled and nodded. "You're right. I know you're right. It's just..."

"Another kind of mental block?" Jayne offered a wry smile. She could understand that, too. Anytime Sofia flirted with a guy, Jayne would automatically classify him as off-limits and she would keep her distance. She couldn't imagine what Sofia was feeling, having to rearrange her perception of Cillian without crossing any lines. Training together as Rogue and Master was a personal, intimate thing. It had made it so easy for Jayne when she and Cillian were together, but what if they weren't?

Jayne squeezed Sofia's shoulder. "Do what you have to do, okay? And trust me when I say that communication is key. If you're uncomfortable, explain to him why. He'll understand. You don't want anything getting in the way of the bond you two share."

Sofia's gaze turned distant. "I know." She shook her head, then gestured to the last remaining book on the table. "Are you going to open that? I've been dying to see how this works."

"Subtle subject change there," Jayne complimented, but she shifted in her seat to hoist the massive Italian dictionary onto her lap. It pulsed in her fingertips as if it had its own heartbeat. The energies inside drummed against her pulse, making her blood sing with awareness. But the magic emanating from the book was a gentle coaxing, a soothing companion to her own. Nothing obtrusive like from the major grimoires she'd encountered.

Jayne hadn't practiced much with minor grimoires, but already she was amazed at the differences she could discern between them and the majors.

She flipped open the cover, and a burst of white light filled her vision. She gasped as words and phrases filled her mind. A calm Italian voice whispered over her, brushing against her awareness.

Just as suddenly, the light vanished, and the grimoire went still in her grasp. Jayne panted as if she'd just run a mile, her heart racing and sweat forming on her brow.

"Wow," she muttered. "That was an experience."

Sofia's brows knitted together. "Jayne?"

Jayne blinked and looked at her. "What? Do I have something on my face?"

Sofia snorted, then covered her mouth. "Good God. That's incredible."

"What?" Jayne spread her palms, then faltered as she remembered what had happened when she'd become fluent in French. She hesitated, considering her words carefully. In her mind, she conjured the words *what's going on?* But as she spoke, concentrating fully on the words, they came out in flawless Italian: *"Cosa sta succedendo?"*

Sofia's mouth widened in an amazed smile, and she laughed again. "Jayne, that's amazing! I kind of want to do one, too..."

Jayne's mind spun with Italian gloriousness, and she clapped her hands together eagerly. *"Che bello!"*

They played with their newfound linguistic prowess for a few minutes, but a gentle nudge from the Torrent reminded Jayne that her portal was going to close if she didn't get it in gear. She hated leaving Sofia, but she had to get back to Rome, to Tristan. She felt a little thrill at the thought of him, then tamped it down with a stern mental stomp.

Partner. Annoying. Arrogant.

Handsome. Funny. Smells good.

No! No. Insufferable French prig with an attitude.

Tall. So tall.

Called me a toddler!

Furious at him again, she gave her mind a thorough shake and prepared to portal back. With a last wave at Sofia and Katie, she stepped through the glowing door into her suite at the Hassler.

Tristan was asleep. She stood in the doorway to the bedroom for a moment, watching him. How he managed to look thoroughly dangerous and heartbreakingly innocent at the same time was lost on her.

"Um, creepy as hell, stalker," he said in that outrageous American accent. She spit out a laugh.

"Sorry. Just ascertaining if you were still alive."

"Very much, *merci.*" He yawned and rolled toward her. "Did you find what you needed?"

"Adesso sono abbastanza fluente, grazie."

"Brava," he said admiringly. "You sound like a proper Roman now. Why don't you use that charming accent to tell me a bedtime story?" He wiggled an eyebrow, and she rolled her eyes.

"In your dreams, Frenchie. Go to sleep," she replied.

CHAPTER

EIGHTEEN

BIBLIOTECA ANGELICA

J ayne was protecting a veil, a shimmering moving pool of aether that rippled in front of her. She didn't know anything else except that she was duty-bound to protect this veil...or die trying. Alongside her, three faceless Guardians joined her in this sacred task. The space behind them was a yawning void of black matter, threatening to swallow them. But their magic kept them grounded. Focused.

Until...she tumbled into nothingness. The free fall of her body sliding forward, the terrifying sensation of being sucked into the churning, gaping river before her was enough to wrench a scream from her throat. It felt like falling through milky swirling clouds and fog, but thicker. Denser. Enough to slow her down, to surround her with a sludge that obscured her vision.

She could sense the other souls in the viscous aether with her. Faceless bodies bumped into her. Hands grasped her limbs and hair. Moans and wails echoed in her mind like the cries of the dead. She was drowning, being pulled under by their despair and agony. She screamed and screamed, jerking uncontrollably, trying to wriggle free from the grip of the souls and the tangy fluid surrounding her. At long last, she felt her limbs moving more freely. With a gasp, she climbed out of the pool, her body dripping with a strange, sticky substance like she had dived into a tub of melted frosting.

Choking on the thick liquid still in her mouth and nose, Jayne reached forward and found a pair of feet in front of her. Slowly, she gazed upward and found her father, Henry Thorne, standing above her. His kind eyes were fixed on her, but sorrow tinged his expression.

"You're almost there," he murmured.

With a gasp, Jayne awoke, her heart drumming and her body quaking with chills like she had a fever. Her limbs shook as she slid out of bed, rubbing her arms to ground herself in the present.

Just another crazy dream, she told herself.

And yet...something told her this wasn't ordinary. Just like her dream of the firestorm.

After glancing over her shoulder to ensure Tristan still slept, Jayne crept into the bathroom and shut the door. Sure enough, in the reflection of the mirror, her totem glowed like a night light in the darkness.

"Medb," Jayne murmured, still breathless from the horrifying dream. "Are you there? What the hell was that vision about?"

Silence.

Gritting her teeth, Jayne dived down deep within her reserve of magic, summoning Medb's powerful Earth energy. Her totem glowed brighter, and Jayne said firmly, "Queen Medb. What was that vision?"

More silence. Jayne was ready to fling something against a wall, when a somber voice echoed in her mind, *A Time Catch.*

Jayne stilled, her chest tightening. "What Time Catch?"

Henry Thorne is dabbling in dangerous magicks, my child. Have a care. This vision is the most dangerous passage through a Time Catch imaginable. If he isn't careful, he will drag you down as well.

Horror prickled along Jayne's spine as she vividly recalled the sheer panic of falling into the aether. This place...was *real?*

"How do I stop it?" Jayne asked urgently. "How do I save my dad?"

Medb said nothing, and Jayne slammed her hands on the counter.

"Tell me!" she cried.

A knock sounded at the door. "Jayne?" came Tristan's tired voice. "Are you all right?"

Jayne swore under her breath and smoothed her sticky hair away from her face. "I'm fine. Just give me a moment."

They had a big day ahead of them. After her return from the TCO Library yesterday, Jayne, Tristan, and Ruger had made a solid game plan for infiltrating the first library on their list. She couldn't afford to mess this up.

She took her time washing her face and taking deep breaths. She even did a few calming yoga stretches to scrub the nightmare from her mind.

But no matter what she did, surrounded by the green marble so reminiscent of the Torrent itself, the vision of her father and that void of souls was still burned into her mind.

~

"REMEMBER THE PLAN," Jayne whispered to Tristan as they approached the magnificent Biblioteca Angelica, its massive towers stretching toward the sky. The sheer grandness of it reminded Jayne of the libraries she'd visited in Paris. "Let me take the lead on this."

Tristan's jaw was clenched. It was obvious he didn't like deferring to Jayne when he believed himself to be the Most

Talented and All-Knowing Adept in the Universe. But he offered a stiff nod, and she knew that was the best she would get out of him.

Jayne felt certain everything would go smoothly, but she could tell he did not share her optimism. She tried not to take that personally. After all, he'd called her messy and reckless. It was clear he thought she would screw things up on their mission with her impulsive spell-casting. She lifted her chin, determined to show him just how mature and careful she could be.

Even if the screams from her nightmare still echoed in her mind.

Jayne adjusted her glasses—fake, now, after the magical LASIK spell Amanda had subjected her to. They felt comfortable on her face; a reminder of simpler times when she worked at Vanderbilt and had nothing to worry about in her life except ocular migraines and difficult manuscripts. After ensuring her Disguise spell was still in place, she strode into the library with an air of confidence. She didn't look over her shoulder to see that Tristan was playing his part; she had to be fully immersed in her own mission for this to work. She had to trust he was smart enough to follow the plan.

The smell of ancient texts and vellum filled Jayne's nose the instant she set foot in the library, and she found herself smiling as if coming home from a long day. The familiar scent of books was like a comforting embrace, and the quiet stillness of libraries soothed her soul. The outside world seemed chaotic, constantly in motion. But here? The world seemed to stop, just for her.

The woman behind the front desk looked up with a friendly smile, already easing Jayne's nerves. Jayne grinned in response and asked hesitantly, "Do you speak English?" She knew Italian now, of course, but she was playing the part of the American librarian who only spoke English.

"Yes," the woman said with a thick accent. "How can I help you?"

"I'm the curator for the Vanderbilt Library in Nashville, and I'd love to take a look at the Codex Angelicus. We are thinking of acquiring similar manuscripts, and this would really help us with our research."

The woman grimaced, just as Jayne expected. "Unfortunately, without a formal request, I cannot—"

"I understand," Jayne said quickly. "I'm only in Rome for a day, and I'm in a bit of a time crunch." She offered a nervous laugh that wasn't entirely forced. "If you could help me out, I'd really appreciate it. I can provide you with references if you need them."

The woman hesitated, her expression conflicted.

Time to sweeten the deal, Jayne thought. She sent the briefest sliver of awareness to the Torrent, seeking the spell she'd found the day before: the Siren spell. Or, at least, that was what Jayne called it. It almost resembled rippling waves in an ocean, and the effect was similar to that of a siren, but much less deadly. Jayne cupped it in her hands and unleashed it in front of her. Faint green wisps of magic floated toward the woman, but Jayne knew she had to speak first in order for it to work.

"I hate to put you in a difficult spot," Jayne said softly, afraid she'd frighten off the magic. It seemed so frail and delicate, capable of being carried away on the wind. "I know you have protocols for this sort of thing."

Lime-green energy swirled in the woman's eyes, and she suddenly straightened, looking at Jayne as if just seeing her. A fog clouded over her gaze, and she smiled faintly.

A wriggle of guilt worked through Jayne's gut for manipulating her, but she had to remind herself she wasn't hurting anyone. This woman would forget the encounter entirely.

"Of course," the woman said in an airy tone. "Follow me, please." She rose from her desk and strode away, the green wisps trailing after her obediently.

Jayne hastened to follow, catching sight of Tristan casually gazing at the paintings hanging on the wall. He met her gaze and nodded. She felt a whisper of his power fill the air, the presence thick and heady as it followed her. It smelled foreign and familiar all at once; Jayne had used the Tracking spell before, but this time it had Tristan's unique signature entwined with it. Mint, and something earthy, mixed with vanilla and soap.

It wasn't entirely unpleasant.

Jayne had suggested just using the standard Tracking spell to find the grimoire, but Tristan had said this was too risky; some grimoires reacted to the presence of unfamiliar magic, and they didn't want to risk setting off dark magic and endangering innocent civilians. Or, of course, the precious books contained within the library.

She followed the librarian through a narrow hall adorned with paintings taller than Jayne herself. Tiny filing cabinets lined the walls, and already the smell of old texts filled her nose. It smelled like home.

The hallway opened up to a massive room with floor-to-ceiling bookshelves. The domed ceiling was adorned with elaborate sculptures and beautiful blue embellishments that made Jayne crane her neck just to see it better. Three levels of shelves wrapped around the walls, curving perfectly around the windows as if the building and bookshelves had been destined to be together, like soul mates from across time.

Easy, Jayne, she chided herself, trying to ignore the pricking of tears behind her eyes. *Get it together. This isn't a romance novel.*

But in a sense, it felt more awe-inspiring than any romance novel she'd ever read.

The librarian led her through the reading room and into an adjacent room with a stanchion placed at the doorway to keep random patrons from straying inside. The woman easily unclipped the velvet rope and stood by to let Jayne through, the misty fog still clouding her gaze.

"Thank you," Jayne said quietly. "I'd appreciate a moment of privacy as well."

"Of course," the woman said again. She reattached the rope to the stanchion and retreated obediently back to her post.

Jayne watched her leave and heaved a sigh. Behind her, Tristan's magic swelled, using her presence as a deflector to any powerful grimoire magic lurking nearby. According to Tristan, any magic tethered to an actual warm body was less alarming to a grimoire than a disembodied spell. Grimoires had failsafes to protect them from unwelcome magic, but if a person was close by, it had no way of differentiating the magic from the body. So, in theory, his ghostly energies shouldn't cause any problems.

Jayne inhaled deeply, sensing the warmth from her totem prickling along her forehead as her magic surged to life. She stretched her awareness, spreading it all around the room, sniffing out any other presences. She felt her magic sweeping over every text like invisible fingertips brushing past them. In Paris, she hadn't been able to do this, though she wasn't sure what had changed. She'd definitely gotten a firmer grip on her magic and spells; but she hadn't fully bonded to Medb's totem then.

Sending a quick prayer of gratitude to the Earth Goddess, Jayne continued her search with soft and gentle strokes of her magical awareness. She whispered to herself, eyes closed, as she used her powers to see each manuscript. She didn't need to read anything to know if it was a grimoire or not. The quivering energy emanating from a magical text would be distinguishable right away.

It's not here, whispered a voice.

A shiver ran down Jayne's spine from the voice in her head. Was that Medb? Or Jayne's own magic?

Jayne. We should leave.

Jayne's eyes flew open. It was *Tristan.*

What the freaking hell?

She whirled around, her body rigid at the thought of finding him standing right behind her, though she had no idea why that would set her on edge. It wasn't like she was stark naked or anything.

But he wasn't there. Instead, she saw threads of white light shimmering in the air.

Ah. Tristan's magic. It was talking to her. Of course.

"Um, hello, Magic of Tristan," Jayne said uncertainly. "Nice to meet you."

You can't sense any power here, right?

Now that Jayne could focus better on it, the voice in her head sounded exactly like Tristan. Stiff. No-nonsense. Infuriatingly smug. She paused to evaluate her magical senses. As she closed her eyes, her perception immediately shifted; the transition from human awareness to magical awareness was becoming easier every time.

The air was still and empty. Void of any kind of power, whether major or minor.

Jayne sighed. "Right. A dead end."

Let's get out of here before someone finds you in a restricted area.

"All right, Filch," Jayne grumbled, striding for the doorway. Just as she stepped over the stanchion, a hulking figure appeared in front of her. She froze, straightening in alarm. An uneasy laugh bubbled to her lips before she could stop it.

Then she realized she knew this fellow. He was the Wonder Woman wannabe, the same thug who had chased her out of the Biblioteca Casanatense.

"Oh, hell," Jayne muttered.

The meathead grinned at her, his teeth yellow and positively horrifying.

Jayne raised her eyebrows. "What, no clever quip? You're just gonna stand there, leering at me? I must admit, I'm a bit disappointed."

The man's smile faded slightly, and Jayne took advantage of his hesitation. She launched an Attack spell straight into his chest. He leaned backward, barely even jostled, but it was all the delay she needed. Jayne lunged, legs swinging as her foot connected with his jaw in a roundhouse kick. He fell to the ground, and she took off, sprinting through the reading room and toward the foyer.

Warmth tickled the back of her neck, and she instinctively dropped to the floor just as a spell whizzed past her head, singeing the top of her hair.

"Not my hair, you asshole," Jayne growled, climbing to her feet. She waved a hand in the air to cloak herself, but the library patrons were deeply absorbed in their work, not even glancing her way.

The Torrent is keeping them in the dark, Jayne thought. She'd always wondered what it meant that every magical fight was obscured from innocent eyes, but some ingrained part of her knew the Torrent was protecting itself, like a survival instinct.

As if the Torrent was sentient. A creature of its own.

Yes, murmured Medb in her head.

Of course the Earth Goddess would choose *now* to chat with Jayne.

Kinda busy, Medb, Jayne thought. Not only did she not want to dwell on the creepiness factor of knowing the Torrent was alive, she didn't have time to catch up with Medb right now. Not with the Kingdom thug lumbering toward her with murder in his eyes.

"Bring it," Jayne said, beckoning with her hand for him to come closer—the universal gesture that badasses used in action movies all the time. She'd always wanted to try it.

"Jayne!" cried a voice. She didn't need to look up to know it was Tristan coming to her aid.

But she didn't need his help. This pain-in-the-ass thug was hers.

Jayne reached for the Torrent and envisioned a Blood Choke, one of her favorite kickboxing moves that compressed the opponent's carotid arteries. A crimson ribbon of power soared toward her, and she layered it with an Attack spell, then sent it spiraling toward the beefy man. He unleashed his whip, using it to sever right through the magic.

Jayne's eyebrows lifted. Handy. What she would give for a magically infused weapon that could cut through magic itself... Cataloging that thought away for future fights, Jayne repeated the same strike, but sent the Attack spell and the Blood Choke spell in two different directions.

The thug used his whip to slice through the Attack spell, but the Blood Choke still soared forward before claiming him. He made a nasty gurgling noise, his body going stiff from the blow. He struck out with his whip again, taking out the spell before it could render him unconscious.

Before he could attack again, Jayne reached for the Torrent and found a spell that resembled a hand mirror. She grabbed it and layered it with another Attack spell, then flung it toward the man.

Green light spun and twisted toward the thug, who raised his whip...and faltered. His eyes clouded with confusion, and Jayne grinned. The Reflector spell. It was quite literally a mirror, reflecting the attacker's own image so all he saw was himself and his own magic.

The spell hit the man in the face, sending him flying. Jayne wove a net with her magic to catch him before he crashed into the precious bookshelves, then tied strands of power around his mouth and wrists like rope. For good measure, she threw a Cloaking spell over him to make certain no one came across him while he was tied up.

With a satisfied smile, she turned and found Tristan right behind her, eyes blazing. *"Qu'est-ce que l'enfer?"* he shouted, raising his arms.

Jayne didn't need her inner French translator to understand his meaning. His entire posture said, *What the hell?*

"You can lecture me later. Let's get out of here before he follows us." She grabbed Tristan's arm and all but hauled him toward the front doors.

CHAPTER
NINETEEN
AMBUSH

Patagonia

S ofia wasn't sure if clearing the air with Cillian had freed her magic somehow, or if her chat with Jayne had given her the confidence she needed. But somehow, miraculously, her magic now flowed freely. No restraints. No hesitation. Training with Seo-joon was a breeze, and Sofia had never felt so light, so unburdened. It wasn't just power; the enormity of her magic had always felt like a heavy weight to her, something to fear and tiptoe around. But this felt like she was floating, like there was nothing inside her but air. It was deliciously liberating. Not only did she feel more capable, but she felt assured she wouldn't hurt anyone because that sickening dread wasn't perched on her shoulder, warning her she was a danger to herself or someone she loved.

A week after they arrived at Xiomara's house, Sofia had just successfully knocked Seo-joon off his feet for the third time when something unfamiliar rippled in the air. She halted, the hairs on her arms standing on end, responding to some other presence lurking nearby. "What is that?" she whispered.

Shuffled footsteps thundered down the hall, and Xiomara appeared. "The wards have been penetrated," she rasped. "Someone's here."

Sofia exchanged an alarmed look with Seo-joon, who sprang into action. He reached for a spell and released it into the air, but nothing happened. His face drained of color. "The wards are there," he said slowly, "but they aren't yours, Xiomara. They belong to someone else, and they're blocking my magic."

Xiomara gritted her teeth. "That explains why I didn't sense the intrusion. My wards are designed to block Adept magic. They don't know about Sofia's new abilities. Let's keep it that way."

Seo-joon nodded and caught Sofia's arm as she hurried down the hall. "Don't use your Guardian magic," he whispered. "They don't know about you yet."

Eyes wild, she nodded in agreement. Cillian emerged from one of the bedrooms, his grim expression indicating he knew something was happening. She grabbed his hand and led him farther down the hall, intending to sneak out the back. Amanda had warned them to be prepared, and this was their escape plan. Unfortunately, their escape plan had also included Guardian magic, but that wasn't a possibility.

Whoever was after them had been well-prepared, and the thought frightened Sofia.

Ruth, she thought. *It has to be her.*

"Amanda!" Sofia shouted.

"I know!" came Amanda's voice from the kitchen.

"Where's Pierce?"

"I sent him back to the safe house."

Thank God. The last thing Sofia wanted was to endanger any more people in this fight. She found Amanda waving her hands toward the kitchen window, no doubt trying to ward it from trespassers.

"It's too late for that," Sofia argued. "We need to get out *now*."

"We can't lose Xiomara," Amanda said, her eyes full of fury.

"She can handle herself." Sofia took Amanda's hand, and, thankfully, the woman didn't argue further.

The three of them had just reached the back door when it flew open, revealing a tall, thin woman. Sofia's chest spasmed, her first thought of her mother and how unprepared she was to face her again...

But it wasn't Ruth. In fact, Sofia had never seen this woman before. She was cadaverous and bony, her brown hair tied into a tight bun. She smiled, the gesture cold and cruel as she drew closer.

Sofia staggered backward, but Cillian strode forward, clearly not intimidated. "Hello there," he said just before lunging for the woman.

Gold light flashed, slamming into Cillian's chest and sending him crashing into Sofia. Together, they fell, sprawled in a heap on the floor.

"Shit. Get back," Amanda hissed, her voice full of dread.

Sofia knew it was serious when Amanda swore. She extracted her limbs from Cillian and climbed to her feet, raising her fists. She might be without her basic Adept magic, but she could still kick ass.

More gold light gleamed, and Amanda raised her fist, identical gold sparks flashing from her fingertips.

Sofia froze, momentarily caught off guard. What the hell was this magic? She had never seen it before, except...

Except when Xiomara awakened her Guardian magic. Her blood ran cold at the thought.

Was Amanda...using *Guardian* magic?

Shaking her head, Sofia shoved the thought away, knowing now wasn't the time. Instead, she searched within herself for that glowing power, her direct link to the Torrent. If Amanda could wield it, so could Sofia. Her brow furrowed, and sweat trickled down her back as she pulled from this foreign source. She still wasn't accustomed to it, but she knew she could do it. She *knew*.

Power roared in her blood, making her bones quiver, and Sofia unleashed the magic, sending it directly into the skinny woman's chest. Amanda joined in, weaving gold threads together in a complicated maneuver that made Sofia stare in awe. The threads twined around the woman's neck and arms, effectively tying her up.

"Come on," Amanda urged, and the three of them hurried forward.

"You two are making me seem incompetent," Cillian grumbled as they flew out the back door.

"What *was* that?" Sofia demanded. They emerged in a narrow alley and rounded a corner, shimmying between buildings to get back to the main road.

"Guardian magic," Amanda said. "That woman was a Guardian."

That hadn't been Sofia's question, but it certainly explained a lot. The wards against Adept magic rendered it useless. Guardian magic was unaffected. Relief filled her as she thought of Xiomara, who wouldn't be completely defenseless.

Sofia stopped in her tracks. "Seo-joon!"

"He's tasked with defending Xiomara," Amanda said, her fingernails digging into Sofia's arm to keep her moving. "He'll be fine. He's trained for this."

"But he can't use his magic! He's not a Guardian, he—"

"He is a trained officer," Amanda said tightly. "He can take care of himself."

She sounded more like she was trying to convince herself than Sofia.

Just before they reached the road, several figures emerged, blocking their path. Sofia shrieked, and Cillian sprang into action. He swung his fist, then ducked to avoid another blow. Jets of gold light filled the air, but Cillian was light on his feet, quicker than Sofia would've thought. He landed a blow to one man's shoulder and another's jaw before a spell took him down. Amanda was already drawing gold magic into her hands, and Sofia followed suit.

"Enough!" roared a voice.

Sofia stilled, dread filling her chest as she found a muscular white-blond man holding Juanito by the scruff of his neck. Juanito thrashed and shouted in Spanish, but the man didn't relent. His cold gray eyes were fixed on Sofia. "Make a move, and he dies." His voice was slightly accented, but she couldn't place it. Scandinavian maybe?

Who the hell *was* this guy?

"Release the child," Amanda barked, still keeping a spell suspended between her fingers, ready to launch it. "Your quarrel isn't with the locals."

Amanda seemed to know this man somehow. Sofia resisted the urge to shoot a questioning look her way, trying to sift through her confusion and formulate a plan.

"Hans!" bellowed a voice. From around the corner came Xiomara, walking lithely without her cane, her voice as strong as a twenty-year-old's. "Terrorizing innocent children? Don't be ridiculous. You're better than this." The older woman sported a bloody lip, but her eyes were dark with fury and power. Behind her was Seo-joon, his hair tousled and one eye already bruising. But they were otherwise unharmed. Thank God.

Relief swelled in Sofia's chest, but it was short-lived as the man—Hans—tightened his grip on Juanito.

"You're outnumbered," Xiomara said. "We've already taken down your accomplice. She won't be spelling anyone for quite a while. Come now, Hans, be reasonable. I'm willing to talk. That's why you're here, right? To talk?"

Hans sneered. "Don't be so naive, Xiomara."

"Say your piece," Xiomara said. "I will listen. Just let the boy go."

"The only way I'm letting him go is if you give yourself up!" Hans spat, his face contorting with rage. His fair features twisted into something hideous, like from Sofia's nightmares. He reminded her of the dark fae from the fantasy books she and Jayne loved.

"Hans." Xiomara's voice was calmer now. "We were once allies. We have the same blood flowing through our veins. Let us discuss this like civilized people. Like the friends we've always been."

"Friends," he spat, gesturing to Sofia and Amanda. "You made your choice, Xiomara. You are a traitor for putting mere Adepts before your Guardian brethren." Hans's gaze darkened, and his hands moved ominously.

"No!" Sofia shrieked.

At the same time, Cillian pounced. Sofia's gold light enveloped him, and he shifted into a panther, slashing at Hans with vicious, three-inch claws. Xiomara's magic wrapped around Juanito, tugging him out of the way just as Cillian made contact. His claws raked down Hans's face, and the man screamed. Cillian pinned him to the ground, tearing at the man until a burst of gold light slammed the panther backward.

Sofia hurried forward, prepared to destroy this man herself, but in another explosion of gold light, Hans vanished. Chest heaving, she whirled around, expecting to find Hans lurking in the alley behind her. But he was gone.

"Who the ruddy hell was that?" Cillian demanded, suddenly back in human form and just as winded as Sofia.

"His name is Hans Kaufmann," Xiomara said solemnly, clutching a trembling Juanito to her chest. "He was once a Guardian. Like me and Henry." Her eyes shifted to Amanda. "And like you."

Amanda's lips thinned. "I am not a Guardian."

Xiomara's eyes flashed. "Your magic says otherwise." Her gaze fell accusingly to the necklace dangling from Amanda's throat.

"How?" Seo-joon asked. "How are you using Guardian magic?"

Amanda clutched her necklace. "Before my husband died, he gifted this to me. It holds a kernel of his powers. I didn't think it worked anymore. It's been so long, but all this Guardian magic—and with my Adept magic blocked—it must have awakened those powers somehow."

Xiomara's lips thinned as she stared hard at Amanda. Sofia couldn't tell if the older woman doubted the story, or if she simply disapproved. After a long moment, Xiomara nodded stiffly. "Come inside. I'll reinforce the wards. We have much to discuss."

"But what if he comes back?" Seo-joon asked.

"I have no doubt he will. But I have a duty, and I can't abandon it. I wouldn't last very long as a Guardian if I fled from every attack." She glanced at Cillian, then Sofia, then Amanda. "Besides, I think we had that well in hand. And claw."

"I'm not going anywhere until you send him somewhere safe," Sofia said, pointing a shaking finger at Juanito. "He's in too much danger being here."

"He has nowhere else to go," Xiomara snapped. "There is no one to take care of him."

"That can't happen again!" Sofia gestured wildly to where Hans had disappeared. Juanito's stricken and terrified face burned into her brain, making her eyes sting with tears. All she could think of was Jayne as a toddler, submitting to the whims of their psychopath mother as she tried to drain the life out of her daughter.

Xiomara stared hard at Sofia, her eyes searching. At long last, she deflated and nodded. "I know another Adept who can take him in. I'll make contact and ensure he's cared for."

Sofia exhaled, her chest still constricted with terror and grief. She couldn't tear her gaze from Juanito, whose dark eyes were full of tears. Swallowing the lump in her throat, Sofia approached the boy slowly, offering her arms to him. "It's all right."

To her surprise, he broke free of Xiomara's grasp and ran into Sofia's arms. She hugged him fiercely, surprised by his affection. She hadn't thought he'd warmed up to her, always hiding during their training and only peering out of his bedroom occasionally.

The boy looked up at her and touched her cheek, muttering a single word in English: "Safe."

Sofia's eyes welled. The boy's meaning was clear. He felt safe with them. Safe with *her*.

But this wasn't true. No matter how powerful Sofia was, she couldn't stop every threat. She couldn't keep everyone safe. Not herself. Not this boy. Not even Jayne.

Something cracked in Sofia's chest, and she clutched the boy tighter as if she could blot out her fears in this single embrace. But her terrors continued running circles in her mind, telling her the worst was yet to come.

CHAPTER
TWENTY
THE ANTI-GUARDIANS

With one hand pressed to the bleeding cuts on his face, Hans Kaufmann stumbled into the house they were renting, seething with rage.

Three Guardians? Lars hadn't bothered mentioning it, the bastard.

Hans thought he knew all the Guardians, but it seemed there were some who had not yet been called. Or perhaps they were defectors, like him? Interesting... Perhaps he could recruit them to his cause. The young blonde woman in particular seemed unsteady with her magic, as if she had just come into her powers.

He could use her. That much power flowing from her could greatly help his cause.

When Hans entered the house, several figures hurried forward to tend to his wounds. "Enough!" he roared, sending them staggering backward with his fury. His steely eyes found Katherine, his comrade who had accompanied him to Xiomara's house. A bloody wound spread from her eyebrow to her temple, and she was panting as if she'd only just escaped from the house. She flinched under his gaze. She knew she had failed him. Even if she had avoided capture and interrogation, she had still been bested.

And she knew she needed to be punished for it.

"What happened?" he demanded, glancing among his seven followers.

"Our magic seems to have been confused by the wards," Katherine ventured. "We only sensed the Adept, not the Guardians. And the Rogue was a surprise, too. The blonde is unfamiliar, but we know the redhead. Amanda Newport. Her husband was Karam Newport."

Hans ran a hand along his face. "Ah, Karam. I remember him." Karam had been one of the first Guardians Hans had betrayed. He had seen that man's death as a true victory in his vendetta against the Guardians. "That doesn't explain her Guardian blood, though. If there were Guardians in her bloodline, I would've known about it. Karam would have, too."

"She wears a Guardian token," said a short and stocky man standing in the back. "I could sense its power."

Hans frowned. Only those with Guardian blood could wear a Guardian token. But if Amanda was a Guardian, why hadn't her powers manifested earlier? Why *now*?

"I don't care, Alexei. This changes nothing," Hans said stiffly. "We still must acquire Xiomara's access point. Our plan cannot continue without it." His jaw set, and zealous determination flooded his veins, empowering him. Nothing would stop the plan.

The Guardians would be brought down. Their selfish, misguided cause of trying to protect the pockets into the Torrent would fail.

And they would suffer for what they had taken from him. Hans had lost *everything* because of his devotion to this foolish calling.

"If we must end her life, we will," Hans said, his voice deadly soft.

"But to kill another Guardian—" Katherine started.

"I know," Hans snapped. "But the transition takes time. If we kill Xiomara and seize her territory before another Guardian is called, then we will have control. The new Guardian will be powerless against us." He inhaled deeply, sending his magical awareness outward. "I can feel the pocket's energy in the air. It knows we are here. Even if we can't kill Xiomara, it's ours for the taking. She is protecting it, yes, but she is not the Guardian bonded to it."

"Henry Thorne," Alexei said with disgust.

Hans nodded. "Yes. And with him missing, the energy here is volatile. Unstable. It wouldn't take much to set it off." A slow smile spread across his face. "Let's see how our new Guardian friends react when their precious Torrent revolts against them."

His subordinates nodded, looking eager. But when his gaze landed on Katherine, her face paled.

"Come." He jerked his head, and she followed him into the back room, where a metal chair rested on a blood-soaked floor. Obediently, she sat, her entire body trembling in anticipation of her punishment.

As her screams filled Hans's ears, all he felt was pure, raw power. An unstoppable force swelling through him, taking no prisoners and devouring everything in its path.

TWENTY-ONE
THE WHOLE UGLY TRUTH

Rome

"Do you realize what you've done?" Tristan bellowed once they were in the privacy of their hotel room. The door slammed shut behind him as he whirled to face Jayne.

"I took care of that asshole," Jayne countered. "You're welcome. If I'd let him follow us, we would have had to find a new hideout. I like it here. The food's good. I don't want to move again."

"This is about more than just a hideout." Tristan scrubbed a hand down his face, his eyes full of frustration. "When you layer spells like that, it essentially sends a beacon through the Torrent, alerting our enemies of a strong magical presence in the area."

Alarm twisted in Jayne's gut. "What? No way. I've done this plenty of times."

"Yes, you have. And how long has it taken for an enemy to track you down?"

Her mouth clamped shut. Was he right? Was she being careless? Or was Tristan just being his usual overprotective self? She tried again.

"Regardless, I couldn't have him following us. Besides, the Kingdom already knows we're here in Rome. That ship has sailed. They just don't know where *exactly* we are."

"No thanks to you. We can hardly work undercover with you setting off beacons like this. It won't be just the Kingdom coming after us," Tristan said darkly. He shook his head. "Jayne, the point is, if you layer spells without caution, without precision and practice, it flags down anyone watching the Torrent. And I mean *anyone.*"

She suppressed a shiver at the intensity of his words, her mind turning to the powerful presence inside the Book of Shadows that had tried to devour her. She still had no idea what that entity was, but she really didn't want to think of it spying on her while she was searching for grimoires.

"Look, I'm sorry," Jayne said, spreading her palms. "I didn't know. But you've already agreed to train me, and I'm willing to learn from you. If you can manage to teach without patronizing me, of course." She offered a sickly sweet smile.

Tristan rolled his eyes. "I don't know how to act around you. I didn't realize I was being patronizing."

Jayne only arched a single eyebrow.

Tristan smirked. "Fair enough. I'll try to...be more understanding and less..."

"Insufferable? Arrogant? Self-righteous?"

Tristan laughed. "I get it. I'll work on it, okay?"

Jayne crossed her arms. "I think we need to change tactics, especially with the Kingdom now hot on our trail." She paused, choosing her next words carefully. "You need to tell me everything you know about this grimoire."

Tristan frowned. "What do you mean? All the information we have is from the files—"

"Not the files. You've seen this grimoire before. Please don't lie to me. I can tell you're hiding something."

Tristan's mouth clamped shut, his jaw working as he stared at her. His hardened expression revealed nothing.

"If you want to succeed with the mission, you need to be open with me," Jayne urged him. "Tell me what you know. Please. I'm sure it will help us."

Tristan ran a hand through his hair and strode toward the window, his back rigid and his arms stiff. "I can't share that with you."

Jayne threw her hands in the air. "Why not? Because of some misguided loyalty toward La Liberté? Pick a damn side, Tristan!"

"It's not that," he said, suddenly sounding exhausted. "It's... personal. I've never shared it with anyone before."

She stilled, her mind whirring from this information. Personal? What dark secrets could Tristan possibly be hiding in relation to this grimoire?

He turned to her, and she tried to arrange her face into her fiercest, most determined expression. She would *not* budge on this.

But seeing the haunted and devastated look in his eyes, her resolve faltered. What demons was he carrying? This was the first time Jayne had gotten a look at the true darkness lurking inside him. It was a heavy burden, and it shone plainly right now. His usual mask was gone.

This was not the arrogant, confident Tristan she knew. This was someone tortured and hurting.

"Tristan," she said gently, stretching out a hand toward him. "Let me help you."

He moved so swiftly she jumped backward.

"I have a sister—Vivienne—" His voice cracked, and he swallowed hard. "She's a Rogue. Like our mother. But...she also possesses strong Adept magic. I've seen you with your Rogue; you understand how that bond works."

Jayne resisted the urge to correct him. Cillian wasn't her Rogue. Not anymore. Besides, her head was still reeling from the knowledge that Tristan had a *sister*.

"*Maman* wanted to utilize that bond herself," Tristan went on, shoving his hands in his pockets as he ambled around the room. To an innocent bystander, the movement seemed casual and lithe, almost like a swagger. Jayne understood he needed to be in motion right now. "She believed she was a strong enough Adept and that her connection to the Torrent would allow her to bond with Vivienne."

Needles of dread pricked at Jayne's skin. She had a sinking feeling she knew where this story was going...

"They tried," Tristan said. "They didn't have enough power between them. That should have been proof enough that the bond couldn't be forged, but *Maman* was insistent. She sought out a powerful grimoire to use to fuel the spell. Vivienne, so eager to please our mother, went along with it. I vehemently opposed the idea—enough that my mother had her men restrain me to keep me from interfering." His jaw was rigid, his eyes flashing with anger and guilt. "They opened the grimoire and attempted to force the bond, and..." He trailed off, eyes shining with grief.

Jayne held her breath, her heart hammering in anticipation. *God, please don't say it. Please don't.*

"The grimoire sucked her in."

Jayne shut her eyes, swearing inwardly.

"It threatened to take the rest of us, too. I was too far away to do anything but scream my sister's name. *Maman* bound the book, sealing it shut before it devoured us all."

Jayne opened her eyes at the tart bitterness in his tone. "You think she shouldn't have?"

"I would have jumped in after Vivienne," Tristan said, his voice hard. "She should have left it open a little longer before giving up on her daughter."

Jayne didn't argue. How could she? If it had been Sofia, she would have felt the exact same way, the rest of the world be damned.

In that moment, she realized how similar she and Tristan were. Both had psychotic mothers intent on ruling the world and sisters they would sacrifice anything to protect. Something in her heart softened toward him as she saw echoes of herself. If Sofia had been trapped inside a grimoire, Jayne would have done anything—*anything*—to get her back.

She thought of Tristan's disappointment when they'd discovered the sibylline texts. It hadn't been just a morose reaction to failing a mission; he'd realized they hadn't found the grimoire that held his sister captive. That was why he'd shut himself in his room for so long afterward.

"How long ago was this?" Jayne asked, her voice almost a whisper.

"Five years ago. Vivienne was only seventeen."

A lump formed in Jayne's throat at the thought of someone so young losing their life and freedom to a power-hungry grimoire.

"And why is the grimoire missing? If your mother had it—"

"The Torrent took it. When *Maman* sealed the grimoire, the Torrent opened and swallowed it whole. We've not seen a hint of it since. Or of Vivienne."

"That... I'm sorry, Tristan."

"My mother insisted she would help me find Vivienne," Tristan continued, looking so much older in this moment, his face tight with agony. "But it became one task after another.

'Find this weapon for me, and then we'll search for Vivienne. Interrogate this prisoner first, Tristan. Track down our missing comrades.'" He shook his head, and a muscle worked in his jaw. "It took me two years to stop believing her lies. By then, I realized she had no intention of finding Vivienne. To her, Vivienne was dead and she got what she deserved. According to my mother, if Vivienne wasn't strong enough to resist the pull of the grimoire, then she didn't deserve to live." He spat the last words, his face twisting in disgust.

Jayne winced. God, that was harsh. Gina Labelle was a piece of work—cut from the same cloth as Ruth Thorne.

"That was the moment I decided to leave," Tristan said, finally meeting Jayne's gaze. "From that point, I made my plans and amassed my followers, biding my time for the right moment to stage a coup. Before I could, Amanda Newport found me. I didn't need much convincing to join her cause and betray my mother. After all, she betrayed Vivienne first."

Jayne pressed a hand to her chest, her heart aching for the suffering he and Vivienne had endured. What was it like, to be trapped inside a grimoire? She thought of that powerful magical presence lurking within the Book of Shadows that had beckoned her closer. With a shudder of dread, she knew she didn't want to imagine what horrors Vivienne was facing. Was that same entity with her now? Was she even alive?

She dropped her hand and forced a calming breath. Tristan was hurting enough; she needed to be the levelheaded one. "I— Tristan, there are no words. I'm so sorry for what you and your sister have been through. Thank you for sharing this with me." She reached out to touch his arm, but then thought better of it. "What do you remember about this grimoire? If you were there, can you remember its signature? You can use that in a Tracking spell."

Tristan shook his head. "My mother put a dampener on me. I didn't have access to my magic at the time."

"Dampener?"

"The same weapon we used on Ruger to stifle his magic. She didn't want a conflict. She didn't want me to interfere."

Icy coldness seeped into Jayne's chest at the reminder that her friend and mentor had been imprisoned by Tristan's people.

No, she reminded herself. Tristan worked for the TCO at the time. She had no doubt he was trying to help Ruger but couldn't afford to blow his cover.

"Right." Jayne cleared her throat. "Okay. So, what *do* you remember? What did it look like?"

Tristan gave a dry laugh. "How did you function without your magic in France? It's like removing one of your five senses. Everything else seemed dimmer. I couldn't even focus on my sense of smell or sight."

"Yeah, I remember how much that sucked." Jayne couldn't keep the bite from her voice. After all, Tristan was the one who had poisoned her magic.

He offered a sideways grin. "Sorry about that."

"You don't sound very sorry."

He sighed. "No cover. The pages were worn and yellowed with age. It was old. And thick; thicker than the sibylline texts we found. Honestly, that should've been my first clue that we hadn't found the right grimoire. But I was so hopeful..." He trailed off and ran a hand through his hair again.

That was why he'd been so eager for the assignment in Rome. He'd hoped the grimoire they were looking for was the same one that had trapped his sister. It all made sense now.

"The whole point of this mission is to get this grimoire before anyone else," Jayne said slowly. "The Kingdom *and* La Liberté are after it. Do you think that has anything to do with your sister?"

Tristan shook his head. "The whole reason *Maman* wanted to use this grimoire was its power. It was so powerful it overwhelmed her own abilities. But she's stronger now; I have no doubt she thinks she's capable enough to siphon its energies and use it for herself."

Jayne sucked in a breath. "What would that do to Vivienne?"

Tristan shuddered. "I don't want to think about it. We just have to get to it first."

"Who else knows about this grimoire?" Jayne asked, determined to find something, *anything*, they could use to aid their search. "It's obvious the Kingdom doesn't know much, since they're scrambling just like we are."

"The men working with my mother were killed a few years later. The only ones still alive who saw the full power of the grimoire are my mother and Vivienne."

Damn. Well, that certainly made things difficult. No wonder Tristan hadn't made any headway in five years. Jayne started pacing the small room, chewing on her lip as she thought through their options. They had already searched three of the seven libraries from the files Ruger had given her. Even if they searched all seven, that was no guarantee they would find it. What if the manuscript had been moved? What if it wasn't even in Rome anymore?

No, they needed to resort to more drastic measures. And after everything Jayne had just learned about Gina Labelle, she felt no remorse in suggesting this.

With a bright expression, Jayne turned to Tristan. "Sounds like our best option is to question the only available witness to the incident." She cocked her head at him. "We need to interrogate your *Maman*, Tristan."

TWENTY-TWO

"Absolutely not," Tristan snapped. The girl was out of her mind.

Jayne spread her hands as if this was the most obvious solution in the world. "There's no other way."

"I will *not* interrogate my mother!" Rage boiled within him. It had been years since he'd reopened the wounds of losing Vivienne. He felt unstable and on edge. Seeing his mother was the last thing he needed. And he was not about to risk Jayne Thorne's pretty little neck by getting the two face to face again.

Jayne crossed her arms, her expression stern. "You need to make a choice. What lengths are you willing to go to in order to find Vivienne?"

Tristan said nothing, but the answer was clear to him. *Anything. I will do anything.*

Jayne seemed to read this in his face. "Then you need to get over it and help me."

Tristan shot her a dark look. "It's so much more complicated than you think, Jayne."

"No, it's not. Your mother is the key to finding this grimoire.

163

Simple as that. Do you still want to rescue your sister? With the Kingdom on our tail, time is running out. Make a choice."

Tristan ran a hand through his hair, but Jayne had a point. If it would locate his sister faster, he had to do it. *Even if it means sacrificing Jayne?* his mind unhelpfully provided. *Because you know what your mother will do to her. Or at least, try,* he amended, looking at Jayne's smooth forehead. The glimmer of the Earth rune showed a ghostly white. She was angry with him. Well, he was angry, too.

"Fine."

"Excellent! Good boy. Now. I need your help finding her. Do you know where she might be?"

"The Domdaniel," Tristan said at once. "It's...our home."

Jayne shot him a bewildered look. "You live in a cavernous hell filled with mythical creatures? In France?"

He rolled his eyes. "No, it's what we call our hideout. In the Time Catch. You've been there before. And if you call me a good boy ever again, I will drop you off the balcony. You may be powerful, but I don't think you can fly. Are we clear?"

Jayne nodded, but her expression darkened, and Tristan knew she was recalling the day she'd rescued Ruger—and lost Cillian to La Liberté. As much as it pained him to see the fury written on her face, it served as a reminder of who they were to each other. Tristan was her enemy. No matter that he had been secretly working for the TCO for years; he had played a crucial role in the suffering of the people she loved.

Neither of them could forget that.

"But how?" Jayne asked finally. "How can you *live* inside a Time Catch? My friend once got stuck in one, and it wasn't pretty." Emotion flashed in her eyes again, and Tristan found himself wondering what friend she was referring to.

"It all depends on how you construct it. Some are more

dangerous and volatile because they aren't constructed properly. But we built ours to reflect the real world as much as possible. There are still some side effects, but living safely was worth the price for us."

"Okay, so this...Domdaniel," Jayne said. "Where can I find it?"

"It constantly moves. For our protection."

Jayne sighed. "Of course it does. Can you be a little more specific, please?"

"We always settle near water to help our magic recharge. Rivers, oceans, lakes. Generally, in Western Europe, as that's where most of us are from."

"Ah. The Water God, right?"

Tristan nodded stiffly. La Liberté were devout worshippers of the Water God, also known as the Master of Shadows. Tristan had never been particularly enthusiastic about the religion, but he still felt rattled about the incident in the catacombs when he'd seen the true brutal nature of the Master of Shadows. It had been nothing like the benevolent god he'd been raised to believe in.

And now Ruth Thorne held the god's totem. All of it was a betrayal like no other. His heart ached for his comrades who were grieving that loss. He knew all too well how it felt to place all of your faith in one entity only to be callously cast aside in favor of another.

"And you all live together?" Jayne asked uncertainly.

"Yes. We crafted a complex of buildings within the Time Catch. Those are our homes."

Something softened in Jayne's eyes, and he wondered what it must have been like for her, growing up with Ruth Thorne. Not pleasant, that was for sure. "That's—I mean, you guys must really be a family, then. If you all live together."

Tristan arched an eyebrow. "What did you think, that we lived in a deep, dark cave somewhere, sharpening our claws?"

Jayne scoffed. "Of course not. But the Kingdom's Time Catch is..." She faltered, at a loss for words.

"Different?"

She snorted. "To say the least. It's...cold. Unfeeling. Mostly used for training and interrogations. Nothing like the homey atmosphere you're describing."

Tristan shifted his weight, suddenly uncomfortable. "Well, erm, we use ours for training and interrogations, too."

"Right, right. But still. It's different." Something clouded her expression again, and Tristan wondered what this other Time Catch had been like to affect her so. She clearly had negative memories about it—negative enough to overshadow the trauma she'd endured at La Liberté's hands.

"We are not like the Kingdom," Tristan said sharply. "We value Rogues, while the Kingdom enslaves them. We have always sought to empower magic users, yes, but we do not approve of the Kingdom's methods."

"You leveled the entire city of Fontainebleau," Jayne accused. "You *poisoned my magic.*"

"Fontainebleau was a tragic accident. Even my mother agrees that shouldn't have happened. As for the poison, you may recall I helped you overcome it."

Jayne spit out a laugh. "Oh, okay. I suppose I should thank you for almost killing me just because you gave me some cryptic clue about how to save my own damn skin."

"I was working *undercover!*" Tristan felt his fury bubbling over once more. He couldn't control it. "What would you have me do? Blow my cover? For *you?*" He laughed, but it was more like a sneer. "I had people depending on me. Their lives were on the line. Forgive me for not dropping everything just to help the first pretty face I saw."

"God, you're so insufferable." Jayne rubbed her temples and shut her eyes.

Tristan turned away from her, hoping that by averting his gaze, his emotions would settle. He needed a clear head for this. And her perpetual attitude was distracting. "The Domdaniel will be fairly close to France. After what happened in the catacombs, they won't have enough power to move the Time Catch very far."

"But La Liberté is chasing after this grimoire, too," Jayne pointed out. "They can't be too far away."

Tristan nodded distantly. He took a deep, steadying breath. "I can help you find it. I still have access to the magic woven within it."

"You do?"

"Of course. It was my home for nearly three decades." Tristan shot her a grim look. "That kind of familiarity is hard to lose, no matter where my loyalties lie. Assuming they haven't entirely cut me off, that is."

"Okay." Jayne crossed her arms. "So, what's our plan?"

"I need a map. A real map, not digital. And, for the love of God, please be silent. The last thing I need is for your incessant chattering to get in the way of my spell."

To his surprise, Jayne grinned. "You're saying I'm a distraction? A pretty distraction? I'm so flattered."

"Don't put words in my mouth."

"Oh, no, Captain, my captain. Never."

Insufferable. The girl was utterly insufferable.

Jayne started digging through her duffel bag. After a few minutes, she shouted, "Eureka!" and withdrew a folded map. Tristan took it and smoothed it out on top of the small bedside table. It was worn and wrinkled, but it displayed all of Europe. It would do just fine.

He glanced at Jayne, who mimed zipping her lips and

throwing away the key. In spite of himself, his mouth twitched. He grabbed a safety pin from the table and used the point to draw a bead of blood from his thumb. Rubbing his fingers against the blood, he closed his eyes and murmured, "Dom-daniel, *je t'invoque*."

He heard Jayne's quiet intake of breath as energy swirled in the room, the air thick with magic. Energy prickled along Tristan's skin, and the smell of seawater and mist and *home* filled his nose. A mixture of nostalgia and regret seeped into him. All at once, he felt a yearning for the life he had known before he got mixed up with the TCO, for the place where he'd grown up with Vivienne, for his comfortable life before the loss and betrayal. But at the same time, he couldn't think of his home without remembering the trauma, the manipulations of his mother, the lies and deceit... It left a sour taste in his mouth, tainting those pleasant memories and twisting them into something dark and treacherous.

Gina Labelle had done this to him. She had taken away his home, shattering his peaceful illusion of home and family. She had taken everything from him.

He gritted his teeth, feeling no guilt as he tugged on the shining white threads of power from the Torrent. When the familiar pattern came into view, he snatched it and brought it forward. His eyes flew open, only to find Jayne staring at him in wonder. The glow of the spell still in his palm reflected off her face, illuminating the glowing totem on her forehead.

Fascinating. His magic had called to hers. No time to examine that now, he couldn't lose the spell.

With slow, careful movements, Tristan lay the spell flat on the map, pressing the magic into the paper until it sank through as if absorbed by a sponge. He and Jayne hovered over the map, staring as the white lines spread along the map like veins, finally settling on...

A mixture of surprise and dread filled Tristan's chest.

Much closer than I thought...

"They're in Italy."

TWENTY-THREE

IF YOU WANT SOMETHING DONE RIGHT...

London

R uth Thorne's hands shook as she stepped over the maimed and twisted bodies of the henchmen she had just executed. Ordinarily, she would let one of her subordinates handle the task of debriefing her people after a failed mission, but the dark magic festering inside her was begging to be unleashed. If she didn't appease it, it would take over her mind again. She couldn't risk it.

The debrief had turned into an interrogation, and just as quickly, as she realized they'd let Jayne slip through their fingers yet again, an intense fury burned through her body. The interrogation became an execution.

Their fear of her overreaction pulled at her, and she felt a moment of remorse for losing her temper in such a dramatic way. Only a moment; the force inside her had roared with satisfaction when she'd killed them.

Her legs felt heavy with each step as she made her way to

the kitchen sink to wipe the blood from her hands. It took several minutes of scrubbing, but the tedious monotony soothed her mind and helped ground her in place. She was here, in the Kingdom's Time Catch, safe from her enemies. No one could touch her here.

I can, hissed a voice in her head.

Ruth shut her eyes, blocking out the presence threatening to emerge again. No. Not now. She wouldn't allow it.

By the time her hands were finally clean, her head was throbbing. Fools. She was surrounded by utter fools. How hard could it be to find a twenty-three-year-old librarian who had only recently come into her powers? She didn't even have her pet Rogue with her. Why were her people so incompetent?

Perhaps you must locate her yourself, whispered the voice inside her. *You share blood, after all. A Tracking spell would be all too easy.*

Ruth went still, the towel suspended in the air as she considered this. As much as she didn't trust the voice inside her, it made an excellent point. She hadn't performed blood magic in a long time, but the potential was still there. Using her own blood would not only provide Jayne's location, it would empower Ruth and hopefully allow her to shut out this demon's presence completely.

Resolve pulsed through her as she emerged from the kitchen to find Lars waiting expectantly in the sitting room. He looked over her shoulder at the carnage, and to his credit, merely raised an eyebrow. Ruth was relieved to find she was no longer trembling.

"Assemble our strongest team," she ordered. "We're going back to Rome."

CHAPTER
TWENTY-FOUR
HOWDY, PARTNER

Rome

"It's perfect," Jayne said, tracing the white lines of Tristan's magic on the map with two fingers. The spell felt like Tristan, warm and capable, and the room was scented with vanilla and something smoky, like incense. The lines converged over Bari, which was right next to the Adriatic Sea. It made sense; after the fight in the catacombs, only a strong and powerful body of water could help replenish La Liberté's magic.

"At least we're close," Tristan muttered. His voice was quiet and strange, and Jayne felt a spike of sorrow for what he'd been through. She touched his hand, and he withdrew it as if the touch burned. She frowned but let it go.

"You know, if Gina is truly after this grimoire too—if not for Vivienne, then for the power contained inside it—she's going to try her damnedest to get to it first, even if the Domdaniel is still weak."

"That seems likely," Jayne replied.

"At least we're close," Tristan muttered. His voice was quiet and strange, and Jayne felt a spike of sorrow for what he'd been through. She touched his hand, and he withdrew it as if the touch burned. She frowned but let it go.

Perhaps this was a sign indeed that they were on the right path. His mother and former home were only a train ride away.

Or maybe...

Jayne looked up at Tristan, only partly seeing him in her concentration. He'd shaved off his goatee sometime recently; the skin around his mouth was a tiniest bit paler than the rest of his face. *Stop looking at his mouth, you dweeb.* She looked into his eyes instead (mistake, there was something indefinable in them), then away again quickly when they narrowed. He was no doubt suspicious of her Thinking Face.

"What is it?" he asked.

"Well...why don't I just create a portal and grab her right now?"

Tristan looked alarmed, his face turning a shade paler. "Jayne, no—"

"It's Medb's power." Jayne tapped the totem on her forehead. "I won't be alerting anyone within the Torrent."

Tristan scrubbed a hand down his face. "God, Jayne, have you learned nothing?"

"Yes, I have." Despite his frustrated tone, Jayne was determined to keep her cool. "Which is why I'm telling you instead of diving in head-first."

Tristan opened his mouth, then shut it, his caramel eyes calculating as he scrutinized her.

"I'd like your input," Jayne said. "As my partner."

Something unreadable flashed in his eyes, and his expression softened. "You've...done this before?"

"Yes. But only once. So, I can understand if you have doubts

173

about it. But I assume there are wards in place that will alert those in the Domdaniel as soon as we arrive."

"You assume correctly. I was hoping I could distract them by showing up first under the guise of reconciling, but they would still detect the powerful magic within you." He rubbed his jaw, his gaze turning distant. Jayne could tell the appeal of simply creating a portal and snatching Mommy Dearest was tempting him.

Tristan dropped his hand with a sigh. "We'll do a test run first. If the test proves successful, then we'll move forward with your plan."

Jayne could hardly contain her glee. She beamed at him and punched the air with her fist.

Tristan rolled his eyes, but his mouth curled in a reluctant smile.

"I'll win you over," Jayne said, leaning closer to show him the breadth of her grin. "I'll wear you down one day at a time, Tristan Lowell. Just you watch."

His gaze locked onto hers, pinning her in place. She didn't realize how closely she stood, both of them still hovering over the map on the table. She'd just touched his magic; the smoky vanilla scent of it twined around her, and she could still feel the remnants of the spell lingering on her fingers. They were near enough to share breath. This shared space wasn't a line they'd ever crossed before; at least, not like this.

Jayne felt her smile slowly fade as something genuine and sincere took its place. As she stared at him, this enemy-turned-ally-turned-friend, she realized something was shifting between them. She took a breath and said, "I don't hate you, you know."

His lips quirked. "Excellent news. I don't hate you, either."

Jayne laughed. "I find that hard to believe."

Conflict twisted his features, making him look haunted and

devastated. Just like he had when he'd told the story of Vivienne. "I...worry about you."

Stunned, Jayne couldn't reply. She hadn't expected that.

He surged forward, speaking quickly now. "Your power is unprecedented, and..."

"Dangerous. I know. You've told me."

"It's not just dangerous. It's...magical and beautiful and awe-inspiring."

Her chest tightened at his words. Was he complimenting her? She might just drop dead from shock.

"You have a good heart, Jayne," he went on. "You're one of the fiercest fighters I know. If you were an ordinary Adept, I'd have no doubt you would change the world with your willpower and determination. But with this much magic inside you, I worry about what it might do to you. I worry how it might...change you."

An unexpected pain sliced through Jayne's chest. He sounded like Sofia, who was always afraid that powerful magic would turn them into replicas of Ruth Thorne. While her fear was built on irrational thoughts, it was still valid. Ruth hadn't always been evil. At least, that's what Jayne had been told. But somewhere along the road, her growth and power had twisted her into someone different. Someone bloodthirsty and ruthless and brutal.

"I'm afraid of that, too," Jayne admitted in a soft voice. "I guess it's a good thing I have you to keep me on the right track." She offered another smile, but this one felt less humorous and more...earnest. It held a new kind of depth, of understanding and trust, that she'd never felt with Tristan before.

He must have sensed it, too. Clearing his throat, he withdrew, putting a more respectable distance between them. "Right." He smoothed his hands on his pants, and Jayne wondered if his palms were sweaty, just like hers. Avoiding her gaze, he said, "I think we should start with an object first. But it has to contain magic. Otherwise, it can't come through the portal on its own."

"What about the sibylline texts?"

Tristan arched an eyebrow. "You want to steal the minor grimoire?"

Jayne shrugged one shoulder. "It's small magic, so it's less likely to explode and kill someone, right? Besides, the TCO just lock grimoires away in the vault once they were properly shelved. It wasn't the grimoire we were looking for anyway."

Tristan offered a pained grimace but said nothing.

"Unless you know of some other small, magical item we can snatch." Jayne held out her hands in an open invitation. "By all means."

Tristan exhaled, then waved a hand. "Fine. But we're running this plan by Ruger first. If and *only if* he approves of it, then I'm on board."

"Deal."

TWENTY-FIVE

THE RECRUITER

Houston, Texas

Hans Kaufmann pressed a hand to his chest as he pursued that gleaming gold thread linking him to his Guardian magic. He followed it like a trail leading him to greatness; to glory and power.

Those fools who blindly protected the Torrent knew nothing. If Hans wasn't meant to rebel, then why did he still possess this power? This much magic was granted to him for a reason, and if he was making the wrong choice, it would have withdrawn. Just like the pockets had.

But no, this was fate. Hans was only following the path put before him.

Darkness clouded his form, but the gold light still shone brightly, lighting the way like a beacon.

Desperate times called for desperate measures. Katherine wouldn't like it, but Alexei had been saying for years they needed to recruit fresh Guardians. The knowledge that Amanda

Newport possessed Guardian magic, and now this new blonde Guardian was on their radar, meant that Hans had to resort to more-drastic methods of acquiring power.

Hans followed his magic until it led him to a tidy two-story home. The streets were lit by a single, faded lamp, and the neighborhood was so quiet that his own breathing blared in his ears.

This was it. No turning back now.

Hans sent his gold power into the air. It ignited like fireworks, but he wasn't worried; he already knew this particular spell was only visible to those with Guardian magic. And, assuming his energy had correctly found his target, she would see it. She would come looking.

He only had to wait a few minutes before the back door opened and a girl about ten years old emerged, dressed in a pink nightgown and rubbing sleepily at her eyes. She stared, wide-eyed, at the gold light bursting in the sky, her face full of awe.

Hans straightened with pride. Of course, she should be awestruck by this power; who wouldn't be?

"You like it?" he asked.

The girl froze, her eyes finally snapping to him as if just realizing he was there.

Hans lifted his hands in a gesture of peace. "I mean you no harm. I have magic just like you. If you like, I can show you how to use it."

The girl eyed him warily. "Who are you?"

"I'm called a Guardian. Do you know what that is?"

Slowly, the girl shook her head, and Hans silently cursed the fools who had raised her in ignorance. How could they not tell her what she was? What immense power she possessed?

"Come with me, and I can train you," Hans said, inching

closer to her. To his relief, she didn't back away from him. "I can show you what you are capable of."

The girl's brows knitted together. She cast a glance over her shoulder to the back door, which stood open. "But...my family."

"They don't know you," Hans said. "Not the real you. You hide it from them, don't you?"

The girl pressed her lips together but didn't deny it.

"They would fear you," Hans went on. "They would turn on you. Do you really think you're safe here with them?"

"Of course," the girl said quickly, but her voice trembled.

"What's your name?" Hans asked, trying to calm her. "My name is Hans."

"I shouldn't tell you my name."

Technically, he already knew her name; it was Rebecca. But he didn't want to frighten her further by stating this.

"Come with me." Hans stretched out his hand to her. "Let me show you the potential of your powers. And if you don't like it, I'll bring you straight home. No questions asked."

The girl's eyes roved over his face. "How did you get those scars?" She sounded afraid, and Hans cursed that damned Rogue for permanently marring his features.

"It was an accident," he said quickly, trying to brush it off. "Please. You must come with me."

Uncertainty flickered in the girl's gaze, and she took a step backward, shaking her head. "N-no. I can't. You're a stranger. I don't even know you."

"You do, though." Hans gestured to the lights still shining in the darkened sky. "I'm just like you. Your magic can sense that. You have to trust that instinct."

Rebecca continued to shake her head. His patience was wearing thin. If she wouldn't come with him willingly, then he would take her by force if he had to. The cause was too great.

"Alexei," he said quietly.

Rebecca looked at him in bewilderment. "What?"

But Hans wasn't talking to her. A dark shape moved behind the girl. She whirled, a scream building in her throat. But before she could cry out, Alexei's gold magic swept over her, lulling her into a deep sleep. Alexei caught her before she fell to the ground, her limp body draped over his arms.

"Why didn't you just do that to begin with?" he demanded.

"I don't like the idea of kidnapping children," Hans said. "I wanted to give her a chance." He didn't bother pointing out that it had been for nothing; they were still kidnapping her.

But it was for her own good. Someday, Rebecca would see that. She would be grateful for what Hans had done for her.

He left the back door open. Let the girl's parents believe she ran away. It would be easier that way. Hans waved his hands in the air and summoned a shimmering gold portal before he, Alexei, and the girl were swallowed up by it.

CHAPTER

TWENTY-SIX

MORE THAN MEETS THE EYE

Rome

Shockingly, Ruger had agreed to their plan. The sibylline texts hadn't fully been processed yet, so they were prime for the taking. Jayne had asked him to supervise their snatch-and-grab portal, but he insisted it was more important for him to be at TCO headquarters to ensure everything went smoothly on their end. Jayne couldn't blame him; if the TCO analysts were hard at work testing and evaluating grimoires when, out of nowhere, the sibylline texts vanished without explanation, that would probably be chaos.

Jayne perched on the sofa in the suite's living room, taking deep breaths as she channeled her energy to Medb's totem, allowing her usual Torrent magic to lie dormant for the time being. Tristan had already cast Cloaking spells and warded the hotel room thoroughly. He stood by the chaise, his back stiff and his eyes alert, prepared for anything that might go wrong.

It was better they had someone there to run interference. Just in case.

That now familiar icy presence gripped Jayne's heart, and she almost couldn't breathe. She stifled the panic that had been her automatic response for so long. Medb's presence was powerful, but it wasn't something to be feared.

Hello, darkness, my old friend, Jayne thought as Medb's power arose inside her.

Images flashed in her mind. Roots spreading through the earth, vines stretching, flowers blooming... Earth magic swept over her, and the smell of damp soil and spring blossoms filled her nose.

Tristan inhaled sharply, and Jayne knew he sensed it, too. She was also well aware of the totem burning against her forehead, but she focused solely on the powers inside her.

Hello, Master, came Medb's deep voice.

Hey there, Medb, Jayne thought back. *Can you help me make a portal?*

She wasn't sure if she expected Medb to respond to her or not, but white light shimmered in her palms as if waiting for Jayne to command it.

Excellent.

Jayne took another deep breath, steadying her nerves. She could do this. She thought of the sibylline texts they'd stolen and remembered every facet, every detail about it. The leather cover, the smell of worn and ancient parchment, the traces of magic lingering. She envisioned the elegant script on the pages and could almost feel the vellum along her fingers.

She swept a hand through the air, and a glowing portal appeared. The scent of woodsmoke and roses permeated the air. Tristan straightened, his mouth falling open. Jayne's gaze remained pinned on the portal, never losing focus. Without hesitation, she stretched out her arm, and her hand slid through the portal. The grimoire fell into her palm, and she closed her hand around it before pulling it straight through. Immediately after, the portal closed, and Jayne exhaled, her shoulders slumping. She hadn't realized how tense she'd been until she relaxed. Sweat pooled down her brow and neck, and her spine felt stiff.

"Piece of cake," she said, though her quick breaths said otherwise.

Tristan continued to gape at her, his gaze falling on the grimoire in her hands. "Remarkable," he whispered, taking a knee to inspect the sibylline texts more fully. "I can't believe it."

"So little faith in me? I'm offended."

"It has nothing to do with you. It's magic in general. It takes a monumental amount of effort to craft a functioning portal, but to pull something *through* like that is...unheard of. I've never seen it done before."

"Oh. Really?" She hadn't exactly meant to invent some new magical concept. She was certain Adepts had done this before.

"Really." Tristan met her gaze, his eyes wide with wonder and awe. Instead of the chastisement she expected to see, she found nothing but amazement and almost reverence in his gaze.

For some reason, this made her uncomfortable. She was so accustomed to his ire, already prepared with a quip of her own if he chided her for using magic recklessly. But she didn't expect *this* from him.

"So, what do you think?" Jayne asked, keeping her eyes cast on the floor. "Can we use a portal to kidnap your mother?"

"It will take a lot more power than what you just did," Tristan said. "The grimoire didn't have the means to fight back —she will. And we can't do it here; we'll have to find a more secure and ambiguous location in case she's tracked."

"Right." Something faint tickled Jayne's ears, and she frowned. "Do you hear that?"

Tristan stared at her for a moment. "No." His voice was slow and uncertain.

Jayne strained her ears to listen. After a moment, she realized it was the sound of someone singing. The longer Tristan stared at her, the more she understood it was something only she could hear. She glanced around, searching for the source. But the hotel room was as ordinary as ever. Her gaze fell on the sibylline texts on her lap, and she froze.

The pages were glowing.

"Um." Jayne touched the grimoire gingerly, expecting to be burned. But they felt the same as they had a moment ago. Ordinary, if a bit fragile.

"What is it?" Tristan asked, his voice edged with concern.

"I hear singing. And the grimoire is glowing."

"Nothing is happening for me." Power filled the air, and Tristan's hands glowed green. His eyes closed as he weaved a spell in the air, an intricate swirl of threads and knots. When he opened his eyes, he stared hard at the grimoire. "I can sense... another presence here."

"Medb," Jayne said at once.

"Her power allows you to see what I cannot, Jayne."

"But I used her power to open the grimoire the first time."

"Not like this. I didn't feel nearly as much power the first time. It *smells* like earth magic in here. Grimoires are tricky things. Fickle, even. If this grimoire didn't want to be read, it would have withheld its magic from you. But now..." Tristan shrugged. "Perhaps your portal passed the test. Perhaps this time it can sense the full extent of your earth magic. Maybe it was impressed enough to open up to you."

"You speak of grimoires as if they are sentient."

"Aren't they?"

Jayne couldn't argue with this. Her hands shook as she brushed her fingers against the leather bindings. "Is it safe to open it?"

"My magic is ready. Go ahead."

Jayne flipped open the cover, expecting a dark voice to invade her thoughts like it had when she'd opened the Book of Shadows. Instead, the singing dissolved into incoherent whispers, the sound tickling her ears and making her shiver. She focused on the glowing pages, trying to find what the grimoire wanted her to see.

Follow, one voice hissed.

Look and see, said another.

"I don't understand," Jayne muttered aloud. "What do you want me to see?"

See beyond the ink. Beyond the pages.

Treasures to behold. Secrets to find. Truths to uncover.

"It's riddles," Jayne said. "All riddles." Medb's cold power swelled in her chest, and she clung to it, knowing it might be her only link to this strange and unpredictable grimoire. By instinct, she laid her palm flat on the page, reminded of that fateful moment in the Vandy vault when she'd accessed magic for the first time.

Seek the Keeper of Flames, the voices urged. *Seek the Goddess.*

The hairs on her arms stood on end, and goose bumps erupted along her skin. The Keeper of Flames. Who was it? Another Master magician? The last one Jayne had encountered hadn't been friendly at all.

She closed her eyes and focused on the feel of her fingers on the page. The Torrent's glowing green river of stars flowed in her mind, but it mingled with Medb's icy powers, swirling and twisting into a kaleidoscope of snow and flurries—as if the Torrent itself was now frozen solid, a winding ribbon of hardened ice. As Jayne reached for it, the surface cracked and splintered like shards of glass. Gold light filtered through the cracks, enveloping her in warmth and a surge of power she'd never felt before. She drew in a sharp gasp, and a warm hand pressed against hers, grounding her.

Tristan. She squeezed his fingers, clinging to him like an anchor. *Keep me here,* she silently begged even as she felt her body floating, being swept away by this strange gold power. *Don't let me go.*

Never, came his reassuring voice.

Only then did Jayne realize they were communicating telepathically again. But she didn't care. His voice in her ear sent a bolt of clarity through the haze of the gold light and broken river. Had something happened to the Torrent? Or was this grimoire doing something to her?

Jayne returned to the present with a jolt, her face dripping with cold sweat. Breathless, she found Tristan crouched in front of her, one hand clasped in hers and the other pressed to her cheek. Her heart was hammering so painfully her bones seemed to echo with each pulse. God, she couldn't breathe. Couldn't get enough air. She was going to pass out, she just knew it.

Tristan placed his other palm on her cheek, framing her face with both hands. Jayne shivered, suddenly unbearably cold. She couldn't stop trembling.

"Stay with me," he murmured, his deep voice soothing. "You are here. You are safe."

Jayne's teeth chattered, but she tried to focus on his words. She was here with Tristan. She searched within herself and found a faint echo of the cold power from Medb. The magic was still there, but it was dwarfed by this foreign gold energy still flowing from the grimoire.

"What's...happening?" Jayne said between shivers.

"The grimoire unlocked something within you," Tristan

said, his voice still soft. "Don't let it take you, Jayne. You're more powerful than this."

She nodded, closing her eyes. *Medb, help me,* she pleaded. The cold power flared in response, but the energies of the grimoire engulfed it, quashing any assistance it could offer.

Don't fight, Jayne told herself. *Find out what this power wants.*

She exhaled deeply, releasing the tension in her body. She focused on Tristan's skin against hers and the warmth he provided, reminding herself she wasn't alone.

Show me, she told the grimoire. *Show me what you want me to see.*

She knew this was what it had been waiting for. The gold light twisted and coiled, spiraling in her mind before it began to fade. In its place was an elegant, sloping script penned not in ink, but in pure light itself.

"Pen and paper," she said to Tristan.

He jumped up and snatched a notepad and pencil from the table before thrusting it into her hands. Jayne's fingers flew as she transcribed the script imprinted on her mind, desperate to jot it all down before it vanished. The words flowed from her like she was a conduit for this strange power. Her body still quivered, but now it was from urgency. After she'd filled six pages with the words gleaming in her mind, the gold magic disappeared. A sudden darkness filled the room, and Jayne's mind and chest were empty and silent. All that remained was her labored breathing, now sounding far too loud.

She and Tristan were silent for a solid minute as they both processed what had happened. At long last, Tristan whispered, "What was that?"

"I don't know. But it seems there's more to this minor grimoire than meets the eye."

CHAPTER

TWENTY-SEVEN

TELL ME YOUR SECRETS

The words Jayne had transcribed were in a wholly different language. At first glance, it looked almost Greek, but something told her this was older.

"What do you think—"

"It's Etruscan," Tristan said in awe, running his fingers along the scribblings she'd made. "Well, Jayne, you certainly know how to surprise me."

"How do you know that?"

"Ancient languages are one of my many talents," he said. At her raised brow, he continued, less mocking. "I was fascinated by the Egyptians when I was a boy. There was an exhibit in the Louvre that I went to on a school trip. One thing led to another."

"As they seem to do with you." At his amused expression, Jayne smiled. "I'm starving. Can we eat something before you interpret this?"

"Yes. Of course. It's been quite some time since I studied the Etruscans. It will take me a bit to translate. Pizza? You admired the spot down the street when we passed yesterday."

"Yes, please."

SHE HAD to admit that the sausage-and-mushroom pizza certainly did take her mind off all things magical. When they returned, Tristan got to work while Jayne briefed Ruger on the development. Ruger unsurprisingly cautioned her against doing anything with the newfound power, and she readily agreed. The grimoire's secrets felt like an invasion to her. She wasn't excited to do it again.

After a few hours of research and translation, they were able to interpret the words.

"It's a poem," Tristan said.

Jayne frowned as she inspected the pages he'd translated. "It doesn't look like any poem I've ever read."

"Well, not everything is 'roses are red, violets are blue,' Jayne."

"Lowell, I will not hesitate to throw you through a portal into a hellacious inferno..."

He grinned. "Temper, temper. It's a linguistic puzzle. One that was not meant to be interpreted easily." He ran a hand over his face, his expression perplexed. "Whoever designed this wanted to keep it hidden from as many people as possible."

"But what does this mean?" Jayne looked up at him. "Do you think the grimoire we're looking for is actually right here? Disguised somehow?"

Tristan shook his head. "It's not the same one. I can tell. No amount of magic could disguise it so thoroughly. But..." He glanced over the pages, his eyes flitting back and forth as he skimmed. "I do believe they are connected."

"But how?" She read the words aloud. "*The river flows beneath the dark skies. A magnificent meadow to behold. Beware the lies of the Whispering Tree.* I mean, what the hell does all this mean?"

"I don't know." Tristan sat back in his chair and pinched the bridge of his nose. "Instead of giving us answers, it just brings up more questions."

Jayne was silent for a moment as she considered this new puzzle they'd uncovered. With a sigh, she said, "This changes nothing. We still need to find your mother. Maybe she can make sense of this."

To her surprise, Tristan nodded. "I agree."

"I think I might die of shock."

Amusement danced in his eyes, but his expression remained serious. "We should hold on to the grimoire. Just in case."

"Yes. Definitely." The last thing she wanted to do was give this thing back. It was clear the grimoire trusted Jayne enough to impart this riddle to her, and she needed to find out why.

BEFORE CONJURING the portal to the Domdaniel so they could interrogate Gina, Tristan and Jayne sought out a suitable location for them to do their dirty work. It didn't take long; after winding down alleys until the buildings became more run-down and less polished, they encountered an abandoned pizza parlor. A metal grate enclosed the entrance, and judging by the graffiti surrounding the place, it hadn't been maintained in months.

Jayne cast an Unlock spell to allow her and Tristan to step inside, then reversed it to lock it behind them. Just to be safe.

The darkened shop smelled faintly of butter and moldy bread along with some damp, rotten smell Jayne didn't want to identify.

"Lovely," Tristan remarked, hands shoved in his pockets as if visiting a disgusting, abandoned shop was the most normal thing in the world.

"Points for intimidation," Jayne muttered. "Hopefully, it'll help loosen your mother's tongue."

"Not likely. She's endured worse."

"I figured."

Together, she and Tristan cast Cloaking and Protection spells to ward the place against intruders and innocent bystanders. Tristan muttered an ancient spell in Latin that made Jayne's skin thrum.

"What is that?" she asked.

Tristan waved his hands through the air, and sparks shimmered from his fingertips. "A spell to seal this spot away from prying eyes." When Jayne continued to watch him expectantly, he said, "It's a Latin spell I often use. Very effective for warding places."

"Can you teach it to me?"

Tristan sighed. "Is now really the time?"

"Yes! You promised you would teach me. And maybe if I cast the spell, too, it'll be even stronger."

Tristan nodded, relenting. "All right. The words are *Signa spatium*."

"*Signa spatium*," Jayne repeated.

"Now, open your magical senses."

"It's hard to do that with this musty smell clogging my nose."

Tristan chuckled. "It's not just your sense of smell. You've heard of the phrase *open your third eye*? Well, that references all five of the senses, not just sight. So, these human perceptions you have of your surroundings have kind of an internal switch you can turn on to tap into your magical side. Sight, smell, taste, hearing, touch…but with your magical awareness."

Jayne's chest swelled from the solid *rightness* of his words. When she'd sensed Ruth Thorne's magic on the streets of Rome, she'd been able to identify the smells associated with it. But she had only just scratched the surface. There were other perceptions she could utilize; she just had to figure out how to do so.

Like Ruger said, it was like a muscle she needed to stretch in order to use it better.

"Open that third eye," Tristan said softly.

Jayne nodded and closed her eyes, allowing her mind to move into a state of magical awareness. The air shifted almost imperceptibly; the smells and sounds vanished, but something else took their place. A distant thrumming. A pulse in the air. A quiver of icy coldness that indicated Medb's totem was active.

"*Signa spatium,*" Jayne whispered, sweeping her hands through the air just as Tristan had. She *felt* the shimmering power before she saw it. Her eyes flickered open, and the air sparked with electricity. White lights danced in front of her, reminding her of the fairy circle Tristan had conjured before. A solid barrier formed around her and Tristan, like a clear, viscous film encasing them both. Jayne had the thought that if she were to reach out and touch it, it would feel like Vaseline.

"Incredible," she breathed as the lights faded from view. When she looked at Tristan, his eyes were glowing with pride.

"First try," he said. "I'm impressed."

"I've always been an overachiever." Jayne grinned in return, still awestruck by the power of the spell.

Tristan faced her, eyebrows raised. "Ready?" His dark eyes betrayed his unease, but his expression remained otherwise composed.

Jayne nodded "Ready."

She closed her eyes and summoned Medb's power, focusing on the earthy feel of the Goddess's power, just like when the sibylline texts had opened up to her. Tristan had been right; she hadn't fully tapped into that side of her magic the first time. She had only scratched the surface.

In order for this to work, she needed to immerse herself completely.

She momentarily transported herself to the Luxembourg Gardens in Paris, where she had first connected with the Earth totem. She focused on the blooming trees and blossoms, the smell of rich earth and soil and flowers. Grass and birds and insects. Pollen tickled her nose so fiercely she almost sneezed.

Medb stirred within her, and Jayne smiled.

Jayne thought of the location of the Domdaniel: Bari. She conjured images she'd studied online of the small city, the coastline, the Adriatic Sea, everything she could think of. With the wave of her hand, a portal appeared.

The air went still. Tristan drew in a breath as something powerful filled the room, clouding Jayne's senses.

"Your turn," she murmured to Tristan, keeping her eyes closed so she wouldn't lose focus. Her hand remained poised midair to hold open the portal.

Tristan didn't hesitate. A shuffling movement, then a loud *thump,* followed by a female yelp. A feline scent met Jayne's nose, and she knew Gina was here in the flesh. Another wave of her hand, and the portal vanished.

Only then did Jayne open her eyes and face her old foe once more.

Gina looked thinner than normal, which was an impressive feat, given she had already been stick-thin to begin with. Her sharp cheekbones stood out on her face, and her cold, gray eyes flicked from Jayne to Tristan and back again.

"Que se passe-t-il?" Gina demanded, practically spitting the words.

"Hello," Jayne said, smiling sweetly. "Long time no see. How are things? Your minions are well, I presume?"

"Jayne," Tristan warned, his eyes never leaving Gina. His jaw was clenched, his whole frame tense.

"Fine, we'll skip the pleasantries." Jayne sidled closer to Gina, who took a step back. "Tell me about the grimoire that trapped Vivienne."

Gina gave her son a venomous gaze. "You filthy traitor. You shared our secrets with *her*?" She pointed an accusing finger at Jayne as if she were the most hideous slug she'd ever seen.

"I'm asking the questions," Jayne said, her tone sharpening. "And if you don't answer, I will be forced to use other methods."

Gina laughed without humor. "You think you can frighten me, girl? You are nothing. A mere wisp of power compared to what I am."

Jayne cocked her head, assessing Gina like a predator would. Here, she saw a formidable warrior, a woman who had strength and power, who had endured all manner of misfortunes in her quest for control.

No, this woman would not talk easily. And time was of the essence. The longer Gina remained here, the sooner her people would track her down.

"Tristan, hold her," Jayne said.

Tristan grabbed his mother's arms and pinned them behind her. Gina thrashed against his grip, her eyes darkening, the skin around her face twisting and warping...

Damn. She was shifting.

Jayne pressed her fingers to Gina's forehead and sent a tendril of Medb's power into her temples. The air quivered, and Gina's head went slack, lolling forward with unconsciousness.

"What...what did you do to her?" Tristan asked breathlessly. Jayne couldn't tell if he was horrified or impressed.

"Just silenced her with some earth magic. She's likely wandering the grounds of the Luxembourg Gardens right now." Jayne dropped her hands, then looked at Tristan. "You have the spell ready?"

"It's powerful," Tristan warned. "It will alert the Kingdom and La Liberté to our presence."

"It won't take long."

He nodded and twirled one hand in the air, summoning a glistening green orb with twisting strands like DNA gleaming from within. Jayne caught the spell in her hands as Tristan returned his arm to prop up his mother's limp figure.

Jayne accessed Medb's magic again and withdrew the Tracking spell, layering it on top of Tristan's Memory spell. Layering spells still ran the risk of tipping off their enemies, but with two different magical signatures, plus the usage of Medb's power instead of the Torrent, it wasn't as hazardous.

The weight of the two spells dragged Jayne's hands downward like a heavy dumbbell. She sagged and groaned as Medb's icy power ran through her veins, making her shiver. Using the Earth totem to fuel her spells wasn't as comfortable as the Torrent; it was like a tight, cold fist wrapped around her heart, making it hard to breathe. She felt like she was trudging through a snowstorm.

Beads of sweat rolled down her forehead. Grunting with effort, Jayne raised the spell to Gina's forehead and unleashed it.

Gina's body twitched, jerking violently as if she were a zombie coming to life. Jayne flinched, backing away, and Tristan tightened his hold on Gina's arms, locking her in place.

Gina's head snapped up, her eyes open and a milky white as she stared vacantly at Jayne. Jayne suppressed a shudder at the sight; it really did seem like the woman was a zombie. Super creepy.

"Tell me about the grimoire and Vivienne," Jayne commanded. "What is the grimoire we seek?"

"The Codex Vaticanus. The Latin Bible." Gina's voice sounded sleepy and robotic, like a GPS device. Or a drunken Siri.

Jayne's chest twisted. *Good God. The Latin Bible? Isn't that in one of the Vatican Museums?* Her heart rate accelerated, and she struggled to breathe right. *Come on, Jayne! Tame your inner librarian and focus on the interrogation.*

"Show me," she ordered. She raised a finger to Gina's temple and pushed another tendril of Medb's magic into the woman's mind.

A rush of images overwhelmed Jayne's thoughts. She inhaled deeply, relaxing until the images slowed. She remembered drowning in memories when she'd tried finding the Master of Shadows, but that was before she'd fully bonded with Medb's magic. Now, she knew what to expect.

A collection of ancient, weathered pages drew Jayne's attention, and she mentally reached out to grasp it. Just as Tristan had described it, the withered pages yellowed with age. Her mouth grew dry at the sight of it. The Codex Vaticanus. A fourth-century manuscript of the Greek Bible. God, if her Vanderbilt or Trinity colleagues could see her now, they would faint with envy.

Swallowing the urge to peruse every page and document as much as she could, Jayne instead focused on the magic emanating from the grimoire. Through Gina's memories, she unearthed the familiar scent of ink and parchment, plus charcoal and woodsmoke, and a faint feline smell that reminded Jayne of Gina.

Vivienne. It had to be her. Jayne memorized the unique scent, sifting further until she could identify smaller details. Sage. Embers. Rain clouds just before a heavy storm.

A flash of flames seared through her vision, startling her. In an instant, she was transported to that mystical firestorm from her dream. The woman screaming for help in French...

Oh my God, Jayne thought, horrified. *That was Vivienne!*

Something jerked Jayne from the memories, and she stumbled, literally falling over from the intensity of removing her consciousness from the spell too quickly. She lost her grip on Gina and collapsed to the floor, her head spinning. With great effort, she climbed to her feet, only to find Gina, very much awake and holding Tristan by the throat. Her stormy eyes raged with fury, and her body twisted like a funhouse mirror.

"Gina, stop!" Jayne shouted, raising her palms. "He's your son. Don't hurt him."

"He is nothing to me," Gina spat. "He is my enemy now. As are you, Jayne Thorne. You will pay for invading my thoughts like that." A white glow burned from her eyes.

Before Gina could shift, Jayne launched an Attack spell at her. Gina raised her arms to deflect it, but her body was still mid-shift, and it disoriented her. She flew backward and collided with the dusty shelves against the wall.

Jayne hurried to Tristan's side. He massaged his throat but otherwise looked fine. "We need to send her back," he said hoarsely. "Before they come after us."

Jayne nodded and conjured Medb's power, prepared to summon the portal to the Domdaniel again.

A heavy crash echoed, followed by a loud shriek. Gina emerged from the piles of boxes, flying with inhuman speed until she tackled Tristan to the ground, pinning him with the force of her fury.

"You betrayed me!" she screamed. "You betrayed us all!" She waved one hand in the air and conjured a glowing green spear.

Jayne lunged, but she was too late. Gina shoved the spear into Tristan's chest.

"No!" Jayne roared. A gust of wind swelled in the shop, sweeping Gina away from Tristan.

But the damage was done. A choked, gurgling sound bubbled from Tristan's throat. Blood dripped from his lips.

Heal, heal, Jayne thought frantically. *I can heal him. I just need to...*

The ground shook, and a roar burst from the other side of the room.

Jayne's blood ran cold. Oh, shit.

Gina had shifted.

Without thinking, Jayne reached for the Torrent and layered a Shield spell, a Block spell, and her Healing spell. When she gathered all three spells in her hands, some small voice in her mind whispered, *Wait.*

I can't wait! Jayne wanted to scream. *Tristan is dying!*

The weapon, Medb's voice instructed.

Jayne's raging thoughts stilled as she zeroed in on the spear still lodged in Tristan's chest. It was glowing.

An *enchanted* weapon.

All Jayne had to do was alter the enchantment. It seemed so simple...

She weaved the spells together, threading them like a tapestry. Her magic crackled, splitting the air like lightning, dancing along her fingers. Electricity buzzed in her veins, intense and powerful. It was unlike any other magic she'd felt before. Her skin hummed from the force of it. Jayne couldn't help but stare at the electricity flowing from her fingertips before she draped the spell over the spear. The weapon shimmered and changed color—instead of green, it now glowed gold. Tristan inhaled a rattling breath, his body jerking from the magic embedded in him.

Heal, Jayne urged the magic. Rippling waves of light flowed up and down the spear. Tristan's whole body burned with the heat of Jayne's magic.

A low growl made Jayne whirl, arms raising just as Gina—in panther form—pounced for her. Jayne swept the animal away with her magic, but it rebounded immediately, undeterred.

Claws slashed, teeth flashed... Gina was relentless. She would tear Jayne apart.

Block after Block deflected Gina's strikes, but Jayne couldn't keep this up forever. She kicked at the panther, then slammed an Attack spell into her. Gina tumbled, buying Jayne a few seconds. She reached for Medb's power, summoned the portal to the Domdaniel, and threw it straight at Gina's snarling face.

A shimmering green sphere collided with the panther, then splintered and fractured into a kaleidoscope of light and magic. A feral whine filled the air, and the panther vanished from view, sucked into the spinning portal. With a *crack*, the light vanished, collapsing in on itself and leaving the abandoned shop in utter silence.

Out of breath, Jayne staggered to her feet, only then realizing she had several deep gashes running down her arm. Damn. Pushing aside the burning pain, she ran to Tristan. The spear had vanished, but his chest was still glowing. Jayne briefly wondered if the weapon was somehow linked to Gina and it had been pulled through the portal along with her.

"Tristan. *Tristan!* Can you hear me?" Jayne swiped the dark, sweaty locks out of his face. His eyes were wide, his face pale, but his breaths no longer sounded strained or choked. Slowly, his gaze fixed on her.

Jayne placed a tentative hand on his chest, feeling for a wound. He felt warm—warmer than usual—but there was no injury. His clothes were still soaked in blood, but after pressing against his abdomen and pectorals, she gathered he *had*, in fact, been healed.

Thank God.

Sagging, Jayne let her head droop, resting her forehead on his chest. She was suddenly exhausted, every inch of her aching and throbbing from the whole ordeal. She'd used so much magic... It would take several days to recover from this.

"Did...it work?" Tristan asked weakly. The glow had faded from his body, and some color had returned to his cheeks.

"Yes," Jayne whispered. "I know where we can find the grimoire."

"Good. Good." Tristan lay his head back with a groan.

Jayne's head whipped back. "Hey. *Hey.* That doesn't mean you can just go die now, all right?"

"I'm not," Tristan argued, his voice gaining strength. "I'm just so tired. Can't I rest? I was just impaled by my mother."

Jayne faltered. "Oh. Right. Um. I think so? It's not like you're at risk for a concussion or anything. I've never healed with a layered spell before."

"A layered..." Tristan blanched. "Jayne, what the hell did you do?"

"I layered the spells and then...sent them *into* the spear." It sounded so dumb when she put it into words, but it had made perfect sense at the time.

Tristan's mouth fell open as he glanced down at his chest where the spear had been moments before. "You imbued an object with the layered spells." His dark eyes turned fierce and calculating.

There was the Tristan she knew.

"Of course!" He sat up, then let out a low hiss in pain.

"Easy." Jayne caught his shoulders and eased him up against the wall, scooting so she sat beside him. "Don't push yourself."

"The layered spells serve as a beacon when they don't have a proper conduit to channel themselves into. It's like a defense mechanism; the magic is alerting others to the dangers of not having a proper conductor for that much power."

"You mean like electricity? Something to allow the flow and current?" Jayne remembered the way her magic had crackled just like lightning. So surreal.

"Yes, exactly. Normal spells don't usually require something to anchor them, but the complex spells you've been experimenting with require something more, something to ground them."

"Like...a magic spear." Jayne's thoughts turned to that thug from the Kingdom who wielded a whip like Wonder Woman. Was that why he used the weapon—to channel more complicated spells?

Jayne's head was spinning. As monumental as this revelation was, she was too weak to process it properly. She staggered to her feet, then extended a hand to Tristan. It took much more effort to get him to his feet. He pressed a hand to his chest, his face contorting in agony before he stood next to her, leaning heavily on her for support.

"Let's get you out of here," she muttered, draping one of his arms around her shoulder.

"Jayne."

She paused. "What?"

"You saved my life."

"I know." She smiled. "I was there."

Tristan hesitated. "Thank you. I owe you."

Jayne only nodded, ignoring the way her chest tightened. He had almost died. And she had been frantic to try to save him.

She didn't allow herself to dwell on it. Not now. They both needed to rest and heal. And report to Ruger what they'd found.

Shoving aside her pesky thoughts, Jayne hauled Tristan toward the door.

CHAPTER

TWENTY-EIGHT

AN UNEXPECTED DEVELOPMENT

Patagonia

"We need a plan," Amanda said firmly as the team sat together in Xiomara's living room, sharing *milanesa con papas fritas* for lunch. "Sofia, you and Cillian have trained enough. It's clear your powers as Master and Rogue are thriving."

"I'm not ready," Sofia said quickly, her head reeling. "My own powers..."

"We can't wait any longer." Amanda's voice was brisk. "Hans has made his move. It's only a matter of time before he strikes again. Your magic could use some work, yes, but for now, you are a powerful force on your own. I have no doubt you could hold your own in battle if needed."

Battle. The word made Sofia sick to her stomach. God, she was so not ready for this.

"We need more information first," Cillian said with a concerned look toward Sofia. No doubt he could tell she was on the brink of a panic attack. "How does Hans have Guardians working for him? What happened to their pockets?"

"When a Guardian turns away from their duty, from the calling thrumming in their blood, their connection to the access points withers away," Xiomara said. "Our magic is a living entity, and it senses our loyalty. If one of us were to turn against our responsibility, we would be cut off from the power of the pockets around the world."

"Wait, what?" Sofia asked, raising a hand to stop her. "So you're saying if you were to start having rebellious thoughts, like *This mission sucks,* or *I don't believe in the Guardian cause anymore,* you would no longer have a connection to your pocket?"

"It's not exactly like that," Xiomara said. "I can *say* those things, but if I don't mean them, my magic wouldn't change. Like all magic, our Guardian magic is tethered to our blood, to our very souls. It can sense our intentions and aspirations. Hans's descent into rebellion was slow and gradual. It did not happen all at once. Several small choices turned into one big act of betrayal. Once he made the decision to defect, to turn on his allies, to turn against the magic of his ancestors, it was a slippery slope from there. The true nail in the coffin was when he spilled innocent Guardian blood. After that, his connection was officially severed."

A solemn silence filled the room. Sofia's gut twisted at the thought of everything the Guardians had suffered because of Hans's actions.

"But Hans still wields his Guardian magic," Seo-joon said after swallowing a bite of his sandwich. "Flawlessly, I might add. It didn't seem like that connection was gone."

"It has no effect on the magic already in his blood," Xiomara clarified. "But the Torrent itself would refuse to cooperate with a corrupt Guardian. That is, after all, why we do this: to protect the Torrent."

"The Torrent...is alive?" Sofia asked uncertainly.

"Of course it is." Xiomara's tone was incredulous. "How could it not be?"

Sofia frowned at this and then sat backward, her gaze distant as she thought of everything she knew of the Torrent. Yes, it certainly did seem alive. The thought frightened her more than she cared to admit. She took a bite of her food but didn't taste anything as she mulled this over.

"If he can't use the Torrent, that means his Adept magic isn't working, right?" Seo-joon asked.

"Yes," Xiomara said. "That would explain why they tampered with the wards to block out Adept magic. It wouldn't apply to them. They can still use their basic Guardian magic. But they are not connected to the access points, and the magic of the Torrent is inaccessible to them."

"It seems like it should be a handicap," Sofia muttered, rubbing her temples. "But it's not. They're still extremely powerful."

"There's only so much the Torrent can take away from a Guardian," Xiomara said. "As I said, it's part of our blood and our souls. The only way to truly sever a Guardian from all of his powers is to kill him."

"Now there's a thought," Cillian grumbled.

"Everyone who follows Hans has turned away from their duty," Xiomara went on. "As soon as they made that decision, as soon as they actively plotted against that sacred mission, a new Guardian was called to take their place. But Hans is smart. He knows these new Guardians are inexperienced. As soon as they appeared at their new post, he was ready for them and intercepted them."

Cillian frowned. "Intercepted them? Or killed them?"

"He knew if he killed them, someone else would just take their place. No, he imprisons them. Locks them away. As long as they are alive and still pledge themselves to the Torrent, another Guardian will not be called. Hans seeks to take over each pocket, one by one."

"But *why*?" Sofia asked. "Why this vendetta against the Guardians?"

Xiomara hesitated for a moment. "Hans suffered a great loss because of his mission as a Guardian. He blames us for that. He believes our abilities are better served for another purpose. He wants to tap into the power of the pockets and utilize them for his own gain—alongside the Kingdom."

"The Kingdom? Since when?" Amanda asked, incredulous.

Xiomara's gaze was filled with grief. "I believe that Hans has been working with them from the very beginning."

Amanda pressed a hand to her forehead, her face suddenly bone-white.

Dread coiled in Sofia's chest. What was going through Amanda's head? What had she figured out?

"Hans was stationed in Switzerland, wasn't he?" Amanda asked, her voice nearly a whisper.

Xiomara frowned. "Yes. Why?"

"Karam's only contact was a Guardian in Switzerland." Amanda's fingers curled into fists. "Hans must have betrayed him, too. He's the reason my husband was killed."

When he spilled innocent Guardian blood... Xiomara's words echoed in Sofia's mind. *Karam's blood.* Her chest tightened with grief and sympathy for Amanda. She placed a hand on the woman's arm, hoping to comfort her, but Amanda drew away, taking a shaky breath.

"This—this doesn't change anything," Amanda said. "It was a long time ago, and we need to focus on our plan *now*. We need a preemptive strike. With our Guardian powers, we can track their magic. Seek out Hans before he finds us again."

"And do what?" Xiomara demanded. "Kill him? You cannot kill one of my own."

"He's trying to kill *you*," Sofia argued.

"I don't care. My magic is only meant to protect. Not kill. To preserve life, not end it. If we kill him, it makes us just like him. We'd be turning against everything we stand for."

A hushed silence filled the room. Sofia's heart raged within her, warring between Amanda's insistence to end the threat and Xiomara's pledge to protect all life—even someone as despicable as Hans Kaufmann.

At long last, Sofia murmured, "You're right. Xiomara's right. If we truly are called by the Torrent to protect these pockets, then we have to use this power for good, not evil. Otherwise, we are doing just as Hans did—we are twisting something great and honorable, and it will only make things worse."

"So, what do you propose?" Amanda's lips were thin, her eyes dark and full of rage. Sofia couldn't blame her; Hans was responsible for her husband's death, and she clearly wanted revenge. Even after all those years, those wounds were still fresh.

"We have to find a way to strip them of their power," Sofia said at once, though it sounded ridiculous when she uttered it. "Is this possible? Does the TCO have some kind of elixir or spell or device..."

"Quimby would know," Amanda said.

Seo-joon shook his head. "But...she's mortal. Nonmagical."

"A non-Adept?" Xiomara shook her head. "No. This is not her fight. We can't ask her to risk her life for this."

"Isn't that her decision?" Amanda challenged.

Sofia raised a hand. "Who is Quimby?"

"Our tech expert within the TCO," Amanda said.

"Is there a way to make contact with her?" Cillian asked.

"Yes," Amanda said at once. "She left me with a pager and a number."

"A pager? How archaic." Cillian laughed.

"The older the tech, the harder it is to track. We're trying to keep off the radar, remember? Though our enemies clearly know I'm in the field now."

Cillian sobered. "Oh. Right. Makes sense."

"If you drag her into this and she gets caught in the cross-fire...," Xiomara said angrily.

"She's a grown woman," Amanda said. "She can make her own decisions. If she decides not to be a part of it, she can ignore my message. But the time for walking on eggshells is over. This is war, and we will be slaughtered if we don't do something. Quimby is a part of our team. She understands the risks involved with these missions."

Sofia straightened. "I'm with Amanda. We can't afford not to try. It's worth a shot."

Xiomara's lips thinned, her fierce dark eyes shifting from Sofia to Amanda. After a moment, the older woman nodded slightly.

Amanda rose to her feet, disappearing down the hallway, no doubt to unearth this pager.

"In the meantime," Cillian said, "what's our contingency plan?"

Before anyone could respond, a distant *boom* split the air, and the ground shuddered in response. Cillian was on his feet in an instant. Xiomara's face paled, her eyes growing distant.

"Guardian magic," she said softly. "But...it's like nothing I've ever sensed before. Stronger than my own powers."

Sofia's blood ran cold. Xiomara was fierce and powerful; even Hans's powers hadn't matched hers. She shifted on the couch, parting the curtain to peer outside. A tiny mushroom cloud a few miles away drifted in the sky. "Oh my God..."

"It's go time," Seo-joon said, jumping to his feet. Without another word, he flew out the door.

Sofia's limbs went tense as she realized they were under attack. Seo-joon was in battle mode. The first wave of soldiers.

God, they were so outnumbered.

"Cillian." Sofia turned to him, trying to quell the fear rising in her chest. "Wolf."

Immediately, he shifted to his huge, white wolf form, padding forward with a growl rising in his throat. She steeled herself before reaching for the Torrent, clearing her head and focusing on her powers. Her strength.

I am not weak.

A soothing emptiness filled her mind as the flowing river of stars came into view. Sofia sifted through the magic floating around her until she found an Attack spell. She weaved it through her fingers, threading it around her wrist like a bracelet. She piled dozens of offensive spells on top of one another, envisioning all forms of attack she could think of: shrapnel, bullets, heavy ammunition, plus her favorite combat moves in a kickboxing match—Stranglehold, Groin Strike, Temple Strike. She recalled Seo-joon teaching her about Incendiary spells, so she pulled a Fire spell for good measure, layering the deadly combination together in a heavy sphere of death and destruction. It weighed in her grip, threatening to drag her down. From within the sphere, the magic crackled like lightning. A bomb, just waiting to go off...

Sweat collected on her forehead as she pressed the sphere together before wrapping it around her fingertips. An ashy residue formed on her palms, spreading along her hands and sparking with energy. Warmth tickled her hands, a product of the lethal power she weaved.

Fully armed, hands heavy with the intensity of her spells, Sofia faced Cillian. "I'm ready."

He inclined his huge, canine head to her.

"We'll be right behind you," Xiomara said, rising to her feet and leaning heavily on her cane.

Sofia nodded, her stomach twisting with uncertainty. Xiomara was powerful, yes, but she was also an old woman.

Amanda will protect her, Sofia thought. *Cillian and I are the second wave of soldiers. This is our job.*

With resolve burning in her blood, Sofia stormed out the door with Cillian on her heels.

Screams echoed in the street. Plumes of smoke filled the air, muddying the sky. Wind whipped at Sofia's face and hair, bringing the smell of burning and destruction in its wake. She clenched her fingers into fists, trying to isolate her thoughts, to separate herself from the chaos around her. She inhaled deeply and focused on that gold thread of power. Her Guardian magic.

It tugged her forward. To the west.

"Come on," she urged Cillian, and they broke into a run, weaving through frantic civilians and crumbling buildings. A fierce determination burned in Sofia's gut, piercing through her fear and bringing a rising fury inside her.

Attacking a city. Endangering innocent lives. This had gone too far.

Hans would pay for this.

It didn't take them long to find the source of the attacks. Even without the mushroom cloud to follow, Sofia could see the air shimmering with tiny gold threads of power.

What the hell had he done?

When Sofia and Cillian reached the main square, they stopped short. The area was clear of civilians, but a small crowd was gathered in the center. Hans stood there, arms outstretched and gold light flowing between his fingers. Surrounding him were more than a dozen children. It was hard to tell ages, but none seemed older than twelve.

And each child glowed with the same gold light as Hans. Their eyes were closed, their arms outstretched. Ropes of golden magic twined between them, linking them all together. Stationed around the children were several of Hans's followers, positioned strategically to keep anyone from interfering with the flow of magic.

Horror and anger churned in Sofia's chest. She wasn't sure if she was going to scream or vomit.

Hans was using *children*. To fuel his magic.

He truly was a monster.

As if sensing her arrival, Hans's eyes opened, and he smiled. "Welcome. Have you come to join our cause? We could truly use someone with your unique gifts." His hungry gaze shifted to Cillian, who uttered a low growl.

"Release them," Sofia snarled, the rage in her voice surprising herself.

"I'm afraid I can't do that. You see, they are bound to my life force now. If I disconnect them, all of us here will die."

Sofia shook her head slowly. He was lying. He had to be. She couldn't imagine anything more barbaric. Her eyes flitted over the square, searching for Seo-joon. Had he been captured?

No, Hans would've flaunted it if they had. Seo-joon must be lurking in the shadows, waiting to strike. Sofia would have to distract Hans.

"Why?" she demanded. "Are you really so low as to use innocent kids for power? It's pathetic, Hans."

The smugness in his eyes faltered for only a moment before his smirk returned. "They are part of my flock now. They are Guardians, just like me. Just like you." His steely gaze burned into her.

A lump formed in her throat. Guardian children? How?

"Each and every one of them was squandering their powers," Hans went on, gesturing to the children around him. "They were living in an environment that smothered their true potential. Some of them didn't even know who they were, or what they were capable of! Can you imagine?"

"Yes," Sofia said at once. "My sister had the same upbringing. I raised her in ignorance, but I regret nothing. It kept us alive. It kept us safe."

Hans's expression darkened. "Then you are just as bad as them."

"Maybe. But you have no idea what lengths someone will go to in order to protect those they love. How dare you? How dare you intrude on these innocent families and take what doesn't belong to you? How dare you presume to know better than their parents do?" Sofia took a step forward, and she felt Cillian do the same. "This power does not belong to you, Hans. Release it. *Now.*"

Hans bared his teeth at her. "Never."

Sofia's fists began to tremble. "Then you leave me no choice." She spread her arms and unleashed the full force of her fury. Power flowed through every inch of her, making her skin hum and her blood sing. The last time she had felt this much unrestrained magic flowing through her had been in the catacombs of Paris after Jayne had been struck by the Master of Shadows.

Hans had triggered something within her, some fiercely protective instinct. Talking of Jayne must have brought that out of her.

He had no right to question how Sofia had raised Jayne or what she did to protect her sister. He was just as bad as Ruth: grooming magicians for his own uses and power. For his own scheming, like they were just tools to be wielded instead of living, human souls.

He had to be stopped.

Sofia's magic struck out, pulling her with it. For the first time since Paris, she relinquished full control to her powers. She sensed Cillian shifting beside her, and she didn't need to look to know he took his griffin form.

Hans's eyes flickered with uncertainty.

Sofia gathered a Binding spell, spinning it through her fingers before flinging it toward Hans. He recovered just in time, his gold magic shooting forward to intercept the spell before it could contain him. Gold sparks showered in the air above them. Sofia moved with flawless grace, her body twisting and contorting, her muscles straining, but the pull of it all felt freeing—like her muscles had been sore and tight before and she was finally stretching them out.

The magic flowed freely from her. Green light exploded from her fingertips, coiling around Hans like gleaming cords. He writhed against the restraints, but Sofia's magic was stronger. She flexed her fingers, tightening her hold on him. Next to her, Cillian was roaring, pouncing from Guardian to Guardian, taking them out one by one. Sofia noticed he targeted the Guardians stationed near the children so as to free them.

Good boy, Sofia thought with a smirk, thinking of Jayne's pet nicknames for him.

"Stop!" roared a voice.

Sofia froze, not from the sound of the voice but from the crackling, deathly energy circulating in the air. She'd only felt this once before—when Jayne had killed Alarik at Medb's tomb.

Slowly, Sofia turned to find the same thin woman who had helped attack Xiomara's home. She clutched a trembling red-haired girl in one hand, and a shimmering spell in the other. The Spell to Kill.

CHAPTER
TWENTY-NINE
CAUGHT OFF GUARD

Amanda had just finished sending the coded message to Quimby Cain's pager when all hell broke loose.

But she didn't panic. Her team had prepared for this. Seojoon went first to assess the situation and make an attack plan. Sofia and Cillian followed after. Amanda gestured to Xiomara and they trailed after them, keeping to the older woman's pace.

Just like Amanda knew she would, Sofia tapped into her power, fueled by rage and determination. Even Amanda was caught off guard by the presence of children—*children*—in the square. She never expected Hans to cross that line.

And then, her eyes fell on a child with dark eyes, which flitted about in pure terror. Her lean, wiry frame trembled, and her light brown skin was covered in sweat.

Hans's colleague had the child in her clutches.

Amanda couldn't think. She couldn't breathe. A scream tore from her throat before she realized what was happening. She took a staggering step forward, arms outstretched as if she could snatch the child out of harm's way.

Everything crumbled from there. Sofia's face, white as paper, slackened in shock. Cillian faltered, his form quivering as he shifted back to human form, his eyes wild with part rage, part confusion.

In a flash, Seo-joon was there, emerging from his hiding spot, rushing forward to intervene before the child was killed.

"Grab her!" shrieked the woman holding the girl.

Amanda turned to Sofia. But it wasn't Sofia they were after.

A scuffling sound behind her made Amanda whirl in time to see three Guardians surround Xiomara. Gold spells flashed from the older woman's hands, but the Guardians were quick and brutal. In seconds, they had her arms pinned behind her back and kicked her legs out from under her. Xiomara cried out, and without ceremony, the Guardians tied her wrists together and hoisted her up, ushering her away from the scene.

The team snapped into action. Amanda, torn between the child and Xiomara, finally made a decision and leapt forward, weaving an Attack spell between her fingers. While the Guardians' attention was fixed on Xiomara, Amanda struck. Her spell hit the woman in the forehead, sending her sprawling backward.

Sofia and Cillian lunged for Xiomara, but Amanda only had eyes for the child. No longer supported by the weight of the Guardian, she slumped over. Amanda caught her just in time. The girl's head lolled, her eyes rolling backward as she fainted, no doubt from fear or shock. Sympathy and regret tightened Amanda's chest as she clutched the girl to her chest.

"Seo-joon!" Amanda cried out in a shaky voice.

He was already there, gathering the other children to him and incapacitating any lingering Guardians. But they'd gotten what they came for: Xiomara.

A few minutes later, Sofia and Cillian returned. Empty-handed. Sofia shook her head grimly, and Amanda knew the Guardians had portaled away with Xiomara.

Because of her.

Amanda shut her eyes against the grief and pain, the anguish of knowing the failed mission was her fault. How had she lost her head like that?

It was Hans. He'd abducted Guardian *children*. The idea rattled Amanda more than she liked to admit.

This was the perfect distraction. He'd known exactly what he was doing. He'd seen how Sofia had reacted with Juanito. What better way to immobilize them than to threaten *dozens* of children?

It was their weakness. And now, Amanda realized it wasn't just Sofia who was affected by it. She was, too.

"Amanda," Sofia was saying. Only then did Amanda realize someone was speaking to her. "What happened?"

Amanda blinked, still dazed as she met Sofia's panicked expression. The woman had a right to question what was going on; Amanda had completely lost her head. She still couldn't breathe. She only nodded numbly, her mind feeling so far away. She wasn't even sure if she still remained upright. In that moment, the trauma of memories she had buried so deeply now came flooding back in a rush of emotion. The emotions were so thick, so overwhelming, that Amanda didn't even know where she was anymore.

The raw, untethered pain threatened to consume her if she didn't stifle it. Now. With a deep breath and a shake of her head, Amanda said, "Later. I'll tell you later. But for now, we still have work to do."

"We've secured the children," Seo-joon said. "They're safe."

"But Xiomara...," Sofia protested.

"She's strong," Amanda said. "She'll be all right. They can't kill her, or another Guardian will be called in her place. We have time to get her back." She fixed her gaze on Sofia. "The pocket. Where is it?" Xiomara had never shared that information with them, claiming it wasn't safe. But now, more than ever, they needed to protect that access point to the Torrent. Before Hans's followers took over.

Sofia only shook her head. "I—I don't know."

"Your magic can tell you," Seo-joon said. "Both of yours. You can find it together."

Amanda nodded again, preparing to move, to set off with a purpose. But she couldn't. The girl still lay in her arms, her face an echo of the fear and horrors she'd already endured.

"I'll take her." Seo-joon seemed to read the uncertainty in her gaze. Gingerly, he swept the little girl into his arms.

Amanda forced her gaze away from the child who had unsettled her so much. She had a job to do. A problem to fix. She had to make this right. She *had* to.

"Sofia, with me." Amanda's tone was stronger now as she strode forward. Sofia met her halfway, her face still pale. Behind her trailed Cillian, but Amanda didn't object. Some backup wasn't a bad idea.

"Let's find the pocket before Hans does," Amanda said.

Sofia nodded, and the three of them hurried down the street to clean up the mess. Before it was too late.

CHAPTER
THIRTY
THE ACCESS POINT

Gold threads of magic led the way, and Sofia followed them down the narrow streets of the small village without hesitating. She didn't have time to doubt or question it; she had to trust this instinct within her.

And right now, her Guardian magic was the only thing left. Xiomara was taken. Hans would seize the Torrent access point next.

This way, the light seemed to say, beckoning Sofia forward. Every now and then, she exchanged a glance with Amanda, knowing the same power flowed through her veins.

Amanda's face was still ghostly pale.

"Want to talk about what happened back there?" Sofia asked quietly.

Amanda cut a glance to her. "I said later."

"If I know what triggered your panic, it could help. Clearly, you're rattled."

Amanda gritted her teeth. "Can we focus on this right now?"

Sofia shrugged, but she wasn't going to let this go. Amanda

was always calm and collected. She *never* lost her cool. Not like that.

But if she needed time before she talked about it, then Sofia could respect that.

Warmth tingled in Sofia's fingertips, and she knew they were getting closer. Behind her, in wolf form, Cillian kept their pace, his paws padding against the concrete.

It wasn't long before the air started to feel different. An intense citrus scent tickled Sofia's nose, and she slowed to a walk. Beside her, Amanda did the same. The air was warmer, and the brisk wind was nonexistent, as if the Argentina weather itself couldn't compete with the power lurking nearby.

"Be careful," Amanda murmured. "The strongest of Adepts have been burned alive by this magic."

Sofia nodded, swallowing her unease. She could do this. It was in her blood, after all.

Never mind the fact that most Guardians went through decades of training before facing their assigned pocket.

Sofia felt it before she saw it. A scorching presence, burning with the intensity of a thousand suns. Her skin felt too warm and tight on her body as she inched closer.

There, embedded into the wall of the house next to them, was a giant, glowing sphere of gold. It gleamed with such force that Sofia had to shield her eyes against it. Behind her, Cillian let out a shrill whine.

"Cillian, stop!" she said at once. "You can't go farther without it hurting you. Guard my back."

To her surprise, he did as she said. Perhaps he understood the gravity of the situation and knew he would die if he came any closer. Frankly, from the power burning against her flesh, Sofia was surprised she wasn't dead herself.

Magic whispered in the air, and Sofia whirled to find Amanda setting up wards around the pocket.

"What are you doing?" Sofia hissed. Some innate instinct told her that to cast a spell around this volatile source of power was the dumbest thing she could do.

"Xiomara's wards will have failed by now," Amanda said. "We have to do something."

"That's too dangerous. Amanda—"

"I'm using my Guardian magic. Besides, what choice do we have? Do we just leave it defenseless?"

Sofia had no argument for that. As she watched, sure enough, there were gold threads stringing across the alley, knotting together to form an intricate pattern. The swelling in her chest only grew at the sight, as if Amanda's magic was calling to her own.

It was beautiful. Mesmerizing. And utterly terrifying.

You know a Shield spell, Sofia told herself. *You can help.*

With a determined nod, she reached for the Torrent. The river of stars now glowed gold instead of green, as if Sofia had flicked a switch from Adept to Guardian. She summoned a Shield spell, and it looked different from the shape she was accustomed to. This one was three triangles layered over one another. The same symbol from Amanda's necklace.

The symbol of the Guardians.

"Protect this sacred area," Sofia murmured, weaving the spell along her fingers. "Guard this source of magic." She spread her arms, and the spell shimmered, twisting from wall to wall like a spiderweb. "Seal this from prying eyes. From those who would do it harm." A fierce wind tousled her hair, but she knew it wasn't natural; this came directly from her spell. She closed her eyes, breathing in the magic, her body absorbing it like a sponge.

"By the Goddess," Amanda whispered in a shocked tone.

Sofia's eyes flew open, her strength faltering. "What is it? What have I done wrong?"

"Your...eyes. They're glowing."

Sofia self-consciously raised a hand to her eyes as if to cover them. The gold glow surrounding her faded.

"Don't stop," Amanda said urgently. "You're almost finished. I...I can feel it, too."

Unease gripped her, but Sofia forced herself to continue. She pictured the golden river of stars again, and the spell returned. "Bind the magic contained within," Sofia murmured. "Let no others pass. I seal this with my vow." Energy burned into her, and she gasped, her blood boiling and her bones quivering. Magic exploded from her, stretching down the alley with long fingers, coating the area in a golden hue.

When the spell was finished, a burst of gold light crackled in the air, momentarily blinding her. The ground trembled, and the force of the magic made Sofia's very bones quiver. Her heart drummed an erratic beat inside her, and she waited for the powerful magic of the Torrent to devour her.

But it didn't. The gold light settled, then faded. Sofia deflated, her body sagging as she gasped for breath. In an instant, Amanda was there, her hands on her shoulders and her eyes wide with fear and awe.

"Where did you learn the words for that spell?" Amanda asked.

Sofia was about to shake her head, to say she didn't know, but that was a lie. In her mind's eye, she saw the pages of a journal. Henry Thorne's journal. She knew now those words had been coded somewhere on the pages.

The spell of a Guardian.

"My father's journal," Sofia whispered. "I don't know how, but it's like...they were embedded in my mind. I couldn't unlock them until now."

"Remarkable." Amanda's gaze swept over the alley, scrutinizing the spell with approval. "It's more powerful than any wards I've ever seen."

Sofia scoffed, knowing this couldn't be true, but Amanda looked at her in earnest. "Your magic is strong, Sofia. There have been thousands of Guardians over the years...but never a Master."

Sofia's stomach knotted at the thought. She was partly amazed, partly scared out of her mind. This power, this intense magic was overwhelming and frightening. But it was also beautiful.

She could do so much good with this.

Slowly, Sofia nodded, and Amanda smiled. Together, they rounded the corner and found Cillian pacing the street in human form, his brow furrowed and his hair mussed as if he'd run his hands through it several times.

"Thank God." To Sofia's surprise, he rushed to her and took her in his arms, embracing her tightly. She was too startled to protest, and she couldn't deny that his strength enveloping her felt like a balm to her injuries and fears. In his arms, she felt safe. She didn't feel alone.

He withdrew and touched her cheek. "Are you all right? I felt that spell go off, and I thought..." He shook his head, his eyes filling with sorrow.

Oh, God. Did he think the magic had killed her? Sofia squeezed her shoulders. "I'm all right. Really. I'm sorry to worry you, Cillian."

He blinked as if just registering that she truly was alive and well. An uncertain chuckle burst from his lips, and he took a step back. Sofia was suddenly aware of how close they'd been just now. It was silly, really. He only worried about her because they were partners. That was all. She would be distraught if anyone from their team was hurt—Amanda, Ruger, Seo-joon...

And yet, something different twisted in her gut at the

thought of Cillian hurt or dying. She couldn't process it. Couldn't see past her grief and rage at the idea of losing him.

"We still have work to do," Amanda called from the other side of the street. "Let's go see to those children." Her voice caught at the last word, and Sofia sobered instantly.

Yes. They had to see what damage Hans had inflicted on those innocent kids.

Avoiding Cillian's gaze, Sofia strode forward, following Amanda back to Xiomara's house.

CHAPTER

THIRTY-ONE

A LITTLE BIT OF ROGUE MAGIC

Cillian had never imagined Sofia Thorne as a warrior. He'd seen her fight, yes, and while that was impressive, it certainly wasn't anything like this.

The gold glow surrounding her was ethereal, giving her an almost angelic appearance. And to see Amanda exhibiting the same kind of power was startling. It made Cillian feel strangely inadequate. But not in a pitying sort of way. More in an awestruck way. As if he were in the presence of gods and goddesses.

Based on their previous conversation about where Guardian magic came from, perhaps he was.

As he followed the women back to Xiomara's house, he couldn't help but recall that feeling of utter terror and panic when he thought the magic had devoured Sofia. That something had happened to her...

He'd seen Sofia as Jayne's sister. Someone to care for, someone always there, but never his primary focus. A friend. An acquaintance. Nothing particularly special, but only because she was on the sidelines of Cillian's life.

The moment when he thought he'd lost her changed that. It changed everything.

He needed Sofia. He couldn't deny how much he needed her in his life. Not as a sidekick. Not as his girlfriend's sister. But as his partner. A solid fortress of strength he hadn't known until he thought he'd lost it.

Warmth tickled Cillian's throat, and his head was spinning. He forced himself to focus on the task at hand. Xiomara, the powerful Adept, the unstoppable force for good, had been abducted.

And those children—God, the notion that Hans Kaufmann had stolen them from their homes just to harness their magic... It was despicable. Cillian hadn't believed anyone in the world was as cruel as Ruth Thorne, but it seemed he was mistaken. Hans would give Ruth a run for her money.

When they reached the house, murmurs echoed from within, and Cillian could feel the energy rippling from inside. It seemed the children's magic was still on full blast. He suppressed a shudder. Would they be glowing, too? Somehow, it felt different than when Sofia, a skilled fighter, emitted that shimmering light. But to see it on children, who were innocent, who shouldn't be in battle at all? It made him feel ill.

Cillian steeled himself, his hand on the doorframe just before entering, his mind traveling back to a time when he was young and helpless, and his jackass father came home drunk *again*. The screams of his mother, the bruises, the raw feeling of helplessness...

You aren't helpless anymore, he reminded himself. It was the reason he started going to the dojo in the first place. He would never be a victim ever again.

But these children... They reminded him of himself so long ago.

If only I could give them some of my power, Cillian thought. *Just a bottle of it for them to use when they need it.* He thought of the insane technological advances from the TCO, the ingenious inventions of Quimby Cain that allowed them to develop magic into portable weapons.

Could Quimby do something like that for these kids?

Shaking the consuming thoughts from his head, Cillian entered the house, his eyes taking in everything all at once. A dozen or so children filled the small living room. Some were collapsed on the couch, dozing peacefully. Others were sitting in chairs, looking around with wide, terrified eyes. A few were chatting with Pierce, Amanda's assistant. He was waving his hands animatedly, and, judging by the kids' laughter, he was telling a funny story.

Someone had prepared several plates of empanadas, and Cillian grabbed one just for something to do with his hands. The steamed combination of meat and cheese melted on his tongue, soothing his nerves.

One girl in particular caught Cillian's eye. She stood in the corner, isolated from everyone else, an arm wrapped around herself as if hoping to appear as small as possible. Her hair was a fiery crimson and her skin was a light brown. She seemed older than most of the other kids, maybe ten or so.

Cillian felt the strangest urge to speak to her, to comfort her. Somewhere within the house, Sofia, Amanda, and Seo-joon were strategizing, and a small part of Cillian felt he should be there with them.

But the stronger part of him knew he belonged here, with these kids. They were scared and terrified and homesick. Lost and confused. A few kids were crying softly, leaning against each other for comfort. With Pierce's attention on the two kids next to him, Cillian couldn't comfort all of them.

Cillian knew in a heartbeat he would give all of his lifeblood to keep these children safe. He didn't know why or how this

JOSS WALKER

fierce sense of protectiveness overcame him so forcefully, but he felt it in his bones. He would be their protector.

He moved toward the red-haired girl, approaching slowly so as not to frighten her. He was a big guy, and a stranger; he wouldn't blame her for being terrified of him.

Sure enough, the girl tensed at his approach. Cillian stopped a few feet away, giving her plenty of space to withdraw if that was what she wanted. He raised his hands in a sign of peace.

"Just wanted to let you know, the empanadas are delicious." He handed her one. "You're probably hungry."

The girl gave him a wary look, but after a moment, she took the pastry and nibbled on it. Her eyes lit up and she took a few bigger bites, nearly scarfing down the entire thing in one go. A few other children, encouraged by her reaction, also grabbed some of the food.

"I'm Cillian," he said quietly. "What's your name?"

The girl's eyes scrunched together for a brief moment. "I— What is your accent?"

Cillian chuckled. Trust his endearing Irish charm to win her over. "Irish. I'm from Dublin, lass."

The girl's eyes brightened slightly. "I've always wanted to visit the castles in Ireland."

"Aye, they are definitely something to behold, that's for sure. Maybe you'll get to see them someday. I can tell you about some of my favorites."

A small smile flickered to life on her face. "My name is Rebecca. Rebecca Peters."

"A pleasure to meet you, Rebecca." Cillian stuck out his hand, and the girl shook it, her tiny fingers swallowed up in his calloused palm. "I know this must be scary for you, being here. You probably have a lot of questions."

Rebecca nodded vigorously. "Yes. Tons."

Cillian hesitated for only a moment. His instinct was to get permission from Amanda before answering questions. But these kids had already been shoved into this world. There was no going back. And he wouldn't leave them in the dark, not if explaining things might help them or keep them safer.

He crossed his arms. "What do you want to know?"

Rebecca blinked, startled, as if she hadn't expected such an open-ended offer. "That man. The one who... who..." She didn't seem capable of putting her thoughts into words, and Cillian couldn't blame her. What would she say: *The strange man who abducted me and stole my magic*? Did this girl even know magic existed before today?

"His name is Hans," Cillian said, starting with the easy part. "And he has a very special magic. Magic like yours."

Rebecca's eyes grew round as saucers. "Magic." She breathed the word in part awe, part fear.

"You've felt it before, yes?" Cillian asked, remembering the odd and horrifying sensation when he shifted forms for the first time. "Maybe not as powerful as in the square, but odd things here and there that made you wonder."

Rebecca nodded, her expression dazed. "Yes. I thought I was imagining things."

"Can you tell me about it? What was your magic like when it emerged?"

Her mouth clamped shut, her eyes turning wary.

Damn. He must have pushed too hard.

"Did you know I have magic, too?" Cillian asked, changing tactics. "Do you want to know what it's like?"

Curiosity sparked in her eyes, and she nodded again.

Cillian's gaze darted left and right before he leaned closer as if sharing a secret. To his delight, the girl leaned closer, too. "I can shift," he whispered, "into a *wolf*."

Rebecca uttered a soft gasp, her eyes sparking with delight and wonder. "Really?"

"Yep. And that's not the only thing I can shift into. I've been practicing."

"What else can you turn into? A cat? A lion? What about a unicorn?"

Cillian laughed. "I haven't tried a unicorn yet, but I don't think it would work." He frowned, thinking of the griffin. Well, why couldn't it work? Griffins weren't real, either. Perhaps nothing was off-limits. Could he shift into a dinosaur? A sphinx? A sprite?

He wasn't sure if he should laugh or retch at the thought.

"When I first discovered my magic, though, I was so scared," he continued.

"How did it feel?" Rebecca asked.

Cillian hesitated. How could he put this into words? The sick, feverish feeling, the sense of his skin growing too tight for his bones, the sweat, the blazing bright light... He didn't want to frighten her further, but he wanted to show her that even if magic was scary at first, it could be controlled and enjoyed.

I wish I could show her, he thought, his mind aching with the idea. Wouldn't it be so easy to just share those memories with her, so he wouldn't have to worry about phrasing it the right way?

The girl gasped again. "What...what was that?" Rebecca whispered.

Cillian froze, glancing around, expecting Hans to show up on their doorstep. But Rebecca was staring at Cillian in accusation. "What did you do to me?"

He raised his palms again. "Nothing. I swear."

"I just...saw you in my mind. You were standing in a parking lot, and you looked really sick."

Cillian's heart hammered madly in his chest. The description sounded like the first time he'd shifted, when he was with Jayne and Deirdre. Good God... Had he just shared a memory with this girl?

"I'm sorry," he said at once. "I didn't mean to."

"It's okay." Rebecca sounded uncertain. "Was that the first time you shifted?"

Smart girl. "Yes."

"Can... Can I see more?"

Cillian hesitated. "I don't know how this works. And I don't want to hurt you."

"I didn't feel anything. It was all in my head, and it didn't hurt." Rebecca looked positively eager now. "Please? It was like a movie!"

Now he felt uncomfortable. Did he have control over what this girl saw? What if she saw something inappropriate, like a romp in the sack with Jayne, or one of Cillian's fights over the years?

"Okay." He rolled his shoulders back. "Here's what we're going to do." He extended his hand, and she took it. "If you see something you don't like, you squeeze your fingernails into my hand really, really hard. Got it? Do your best to hurt me."

The girl cringed. "Why?"

"I'm very strong. I promise. You won't do any real damage, but the pain should jolt me out of whatever magic this is." *I hope,* he thought. "Got it?"

She nodded, that same spark of eagerness returning to her gaze.

"All right." *Bloody hell, am I really doing this?* He glanced around, but Pierce was still the only other adult in the room. He shot a curious glance toward Cillian but didn't intervene.

No one was here to stop him from testing out this strange new power.

So, he closed his eyes and focused on those same thoughts

he'd had earlier. *I wish I could show her the first time I shifted. I wish I could share how it felt. How terrified I was.*

A startled laugh bubbled up from her mouth, and Cillian's eyes flew open. Rebecca's eyes were closed, too, and a wide smile spread on her face. "I see you!" she said excitedly. "You're on a street with two other girls. You're talking. And... *Oh my God!*" She clapped a hand over her mouth and squealed loudly. "You're a wolf now! An actual wolf!" Her fingernails dug into Cillian's hand, but it was so faint it didn't jolt him from the warm power coursing through his body. He could tell it was just from her own excitement. Her cheeks were pink, her eyes crinkling with her smile. She looked positively overjoyed, and it made his heart lift.

"Cillian, you're beautiful!" she said, her voice full of awe. "Every time I think of wolves, I picture them as gray or black, but you're white as snow! So pretty... I just want to touch your fur!"

Cillian laughed again, his insides squirming. He clung to the energy flowing freely through him. Now that he was focusing on it, he could feel how different it was from when he connected to Sofia's power. Not the pine and strawberry scent he was accustomed to, but something else. Something uniquely...*his.*

Sage and moss and the hint of saltwater. Subtle but distinct. Instead of the sharp blast of power when he trained, this was a smooth current, flowing gently through his blood.

Rebecca giggled excitedly, and Cillian found himself laughing again, more out of amazement than anything else.

Apparently being a Rogue was more complex than merely shifting into other creatures. He had his own magic, too.

CHAPTER

THIRTY-TWO

FIND THAT GRIMOIRE!

Rome

Jayne was swept up in the firestorm again, but this time, she was grounded, merely watching as the lightning forked through the sky. In front of her stood a woman she had never seen before. She had shiny white hair that cascaded down her back in waves. Her back was turned to Jayne, but the sleeves of her crimson dress revealed a bronze skin tone that gleamed in the firelight.

"Hello?" Jayne asked, hoping the woman would turn so she could get a better look.

"I can sense him," the woman said, still facing away as if speaking to someone else. "Henry Thorne has emerged once again."

Alarm jolted through Jayne, and she took a step closer. "What do you know about my dad? Tell me, please!"

"He's meddling in dangerous forces," the woman went on,

ignoring Jayne's pleas. "He must be careful. Already, he attracts too much attention from powerful beings."

The woman lifted one graceful hand, her finger pointing to something in the distance. Squinting, Jayne followed her gesture, trying to see through the haze of fire and lightning.

Just beyond the storm, standing atop a cliff, was another figure. But Jayne didn't need to scrutinize to see who it was. She knew this woman's form too well.

Ruth Thorne.

Jayne awoke, her brain sluggish and muddled—worse than her first hangover. With a groan, she shifted, and pain ricocheted down her body. Her eyelids felt crusty as she forced them open to assess her surroundings.

She was back in the hotel room. Across from her, draped in the chair, was Tristan. He was fast asleep, his head against the wall as he snored softly. Shadows framed his eyes, and he still looked pale and weak. He'd changed out of his bloody clothes, though, and he looked vastly better than he had when Gina's spear had impaled him.

God. Gina!

In a flash, Jayne sprang out of bed, tripping over her duffel bag so loudly that Tristan jerked awake with a snort.

"Sorry. Sorry." She hissed as her head throbbed mercilessly. She extricated her legs from the bag's straps and stumbled over to Tristan. "Didn't mean to wake you."

He yawned and sat up. "No problem. How are you feeling?"

"I wasn't the one who got stabbed. Let me see the wound."

"There is no wound. I'm fine, thanks to you. Now, how are you, Jayne? Really?" Tristan's chocolate-brown eyes were filled with concern.

"I'm..." Jayne was about to brush off his question but thought better of it. "Woozy."

Tristan arched a single eyebrow.

"I'm not fully recovered," Jayne clarified. "But I'm fine. I'll survive. Does Ruger—"

"I've filled him in on everything. He's at TCO headquarters now, organizing a team to head off my mother and any possible retaliation. He told us to work on resting and restoring our strength."

Jayne nodded, relief filling her at the thought of Ruger being on top of things, as usual.

"I told him you'd check in with him shortly," Tristan went on, then hesitated. "Did you get what you needed from my mother? We didn't get to ask her about the sibylline texts." Guilt laced his voice, as if he felt responsible for this. Which was absurd. It wasn't his fault his mother was psychotic and powerful enough to overcome Medb's earth magic.

"Yes, I think so." Jayne crossed the room and unearthed the grimoire from her bag before placing it delicately on the table. "Gina showed me an image of the grimoire we're looking for."

"The Latin Bible," Tristan said. "I remember."

"It's in the Vatican Museum."

Tristan nodded, his gaze turning distant. "Yes, but we need to be certain. What if the one in the museum is a fake?"

Jayne thought of Deirdre, her friend and colleague within the TCO. Her job had been to create convincing forgeries of grimoires so no one would notice the originals were missing.

"I can do it," Jayne said. "I can use a Tracking spell to find it using the sibylline texts. We'll make sure it's there, and then we'll go and get it."

"Jayne—" Tristan rose to his feet.

"We have to do it this way, Tristan. We don't have time. Gina knows we're looking for it, and if she gets to it before us..."

Tristan's eyes darkened with rage.

"We don't have time to go hunting for it unless we are 100 percent certain it's there," Jayne said. "But if you have a better idea, I'm all ears." She looked at him expectantly. What if they burst into the Vatican Museum only to find the grimoire wasn't there? Their enemies could be several steps ahead of them...

The only alternative she could think of was sifting through the riddles from the sibylline texts, but that could take hours. Days, even.

Tristan sighed. "All right. But I'm Binding you to me first."

Jayne was vaguely familiar with a Binding spell. It had two purposes: to restrain an opponent or to link two Adepts together to harness their powers. "Are you strong enough for that?"

"My wound was physical. It didn't hurt my magic."

"Don't be an idiot, Tristan. You still need physical strength to cast spells."

"I'm fine," he bit out. "Will you just let me do this? You're as weak as I am."

Jayne waved her hand, too tired to argue. She straightened as he approached, his fingers already twisting a shape into the air. A complicated curlicue of white light formed between them. Tristan muttered something Jayne couldn't make out, but it sounded French. The light intensified, darting between them and crackling like...

Electricity.

Jayne's breath caught. Was it a coincidence that this was the second time the magic had seemed like lightning? She couldn't be sure...

Something warm latched onto her chest, jerking her forward. With a grunt, she held her ground as Tristan's magic locked onto her.

"Ready," he said in a tight voice, the warmth still pulsing between them.

Okay. I can do this. Jayne steeled herself with a deep breath before turning to the sibylline texts. Each movement gave her body a small tug as if she was tied to Tristan by a thick cord. She pictured the Latin Bible: the ancient, weathered pages, the elegant, curling script, the scent of magic contained within...

And the scent of Vivienne. Woodsmoke and charcoal and something unmistakably feline, similar to Gina's scent but less sharp. In her mind, Jayne heard Vivienne's frightened scream.

Jayne reached for the Torrent and easily found the Tracking spell. As she grasped it, she felt a weight tugging her from behind, as if she were dragging Tristan into the Torrent by force. Gritting her teeth, she grabbed the spell and cast it, keeping the mental image of the Latin Bible in her mind.

Show me, she commanded.

Her image of the grimoire twisted and quivered, shaping itself into something tangible. The manuscript flickered as if Jayne were watching a television with poor reception. But as she focused, drawing on more power, she found herself in a library vault.

Okay, now we're getting somewhere. Show me more.

She pictured herself zooming out like a player in a video game, and, miraculously, the spell obeyed. Jayne's consciousness floated backward until she made out a locked grate concealing the library archives. But this still didn't give her any clue where the book was being kept...

More, Jayne thought. *Back up, back up. We're going in reverse here.*

She felt herself flying backward, the motion unsettling because she knew she was still standing there, solid and whole, alongside Tristan.

When Jayne caught a glimpse of a clear blue sky, she thought, *Stop!* The spell obeyed, and she took in her surroundings, drinking in everything, memorizing every detail.

She didn't need to scrutinize for long. She recognized this magnificent building with its sweeping pillars and ornate sculptures and grand courtyard from her studies of Roman libraries.

The Vatican Museum.

Jayne released the spell and was thrown backward so violently that she collided into Tristan's hard chest. They both grunted, and his arms were around her, steadying her so she didn't fall. The Binding spell snapped, and Jayne's brain jolted as if it had been tethered to something heavy. She felt muddy and confused, her mind fogging.

"Well?" Tristan sounded just as strained as Jayne felt.

"It's there. The real grimoire is in the Vatican Museum." She shook her head, trying to orient herself. "This isn't going to be easy. They need an application in advance, so I need to—" She staggered on jelly legs until she reached her computer. Her vision still swam, and she shook her head again.

"Jayne."

She ignored him and pulled up a web browser. Thankfully, she had the page bookmarked. She pulled up the admissions page and started filling out an application when Tristan's hand came down on her fingers, freezing her in place. Slowly, she looked up to find his expression soft and open, revealing every emotion she'd been unable to read until now. Hope. Guilt. Relief. And something warm that made her stomach coil with uncertainty.

"What?" she asked, a little breathless.

"Valeri Rudik," Tristan said, his voice a low murmur, "said he was meeting Henry Thorne in Geneva."

Jayne's chest constricted, her sluggish brain struggling to keep up. "What—*what*?" She went from locating a powerful grimoire to submitting an application to go steal it, and out of nowhere, Tristan was talking about Valeri Rudik and her father. Her head throbbed from the whiplash of it all.

"There is a Time Catch that Thorne is hiding in there,"

Tristan went on, his eyes sharp with urgency. "All Rudik would tell us was that Thorne is obsessed with locating someone named Alexandra."

Jayne's mouth went dry as she recalled the woman from her dream who could sense Henry. "Who is Alexandra?" Could it be the same woman with the white hair?

"We don't know. Rudik's mind was scrambled by the time we extracted this information. He was muttering about things like the Whispering Tree and time travel. We couldn't get any more out of him."

Darkness clouded Jayne's thoughts, and she shook her hand free of Tristan's grasp. "Through torture, you mean," she snapped.

"My mother was in charge. There was little I could do for him."

"You said *we*. I didn't miss that. Tristan, you were a part of this, whether you like it or not."

Tristan flinched, regret in his expression.

Jayne couldn't hide from it anymore. Regardless of what Tristan had been through or where his loyalties lay, he still had worked for the enemy and did unspeakable things to maintain his cover.

Things like torturing a friend of Jayne's father.

He likely would've done the same to Henry, too, if La Liberté had caught him.

Jayne couldn't let go of that. She could never forget it. She and Tristan were too different. She had never hunted and tortured innocent Adepts, or decimated an entire city in a quest for power, or betrayed allies and comrades just to maintain a ruse that she was one of the good guys.

Did that truly make Tristan a good guy, if his actions painted him as one of the villains?

He seemed to sense Jayne's resolve, because he took a

healthy step away from her, his expression closing off into that unreadable mask once more. Something in her chest tightened at the sight, longing to see the real Tristan behind the facade, but she quashed that feeling down.

Being his partner had blinded her to his true self. She vowed to always remember the kind of man he truly was.

"Why are you telling me this?" Jayne's voice was hollow.

To her shock and unease, Tristan knelt before her so they were almost eye level. "Because I opened up to you about my sister. You didn't hesitate to help me find her. We're more than just colleagues now, Jayne. I trust you. And...I owe you this much at the very least. I shouldn't have kept this information from you. I realized that...I wouldn't want to be the one keeping you from your loved one. Because I would hate it if someone kept me from Vivienne intentionally." His eyes met hers. "If our roles were reversed, I would despise you for keeping that from me."

Jayne sniffed. "You're not far off."

Tristan's mouth curved into half a smile. "I figured as much. At any rate, you saved my life. What *Maman* did..." His eyes darkened, and something haunted took over his features.

Jayne's insides twisted. God, his own mother had tried to kill him. How horrific... And she'd almost succeeded.

Tristan shook his head as if to shake off the trauma of such an ordeal. "I think you've proven yourself a more loyal friend than I ever could be. I'm sorry I couldn't see that before." His voice turned soft. "You're a remarkable woman, Jayne."

Jayne tried to ignore the way her toes curled at the huskiness in his voice, the way his eyes burned into hers.

Evil, evil, evil, she reminded herself. *He's done evil things.*

This didn't quench the heat thrumming in her veins.

He's probably murdered puppies, Jayne! I bet he rips up ancient manuscripts in his free time and laughs as he burns the pages.

Still didn't help.

The heat became something tangible flowing between them, drawing them closer. Jayne leaned in, and so did Tristan.

A burst of magic swelled in the hotel room, sending a shower of water droplets flinging in all directions. A wave crashed into Jayne, and she flew backward, slamming against the wall, her head throbbing once more. She peeled her drenched hair out of her eyes, her heart drumming in her chest. On the floor next to her was Tristan, spitting out mouthfuls of water as he staggered to his feet.

Jayne raised her hands, summoning a Shield spell to protect herself and Tristan while they caught their breath from whatever had just attacked them.

But her resolve faltered when she saw who now stood in their hotel room, her chin lifted in defiance and her smile smug.

Ruth Thorne.

THIRTY-THREE
CHERNABOG

"At last," Ruth said with a sigh of relief and triumph. "Let's finish this, daughter. You've been a thorn in my side for too long."

"You mean, a *Thorne* in your side?" Jayne couldn't help but snort. "God, that's awful. What's next, you'll call me a *Jayne in the ass*?"

Ruth's eyes darkened, and only then did Jayne realize something was different about her. Her skin had an unhealthy green tint to it, and though the Water totem glowed freshly on her forehead, Ruth appeared rather sickly. Shadows lined her eyes, and she looked much thinner than when Jayne had last seen her.

Jayne cocked her head, swiping more wet hair out of her face. "Powerful magic doesn't seem to be treating you too well, Mommy."

With a shout of fury, Ruth sliced her hands through the air, but Jayne was ready for her. Before Ruth's spell hit her, Jayne blocked it, sending it ricocheting toward Ruth. A spray of water absorbed the spell, and more droplets splashed against Jayne.

Before Jayne could grab another spell, Tristan was there,

weaving his own spell. He muttered something in French just before a gleaming green orb sailed toward Ruth.

Perfect. Tristan could distract her. Jayne reached for the Torrent and searched for a spell to end Ruth's reign of terror, once and for all.

An almighty roar shook the walls and floor, making Jayne go perfectly still, the hairs on her arm standing on end. For the briefest of seconds, Ruth's eyes blackened, an inky darkness seeping from corner to corner until there were no whites left. Her skin turned the color of tough leather, and long fangs extended from her mouth.

But Jayne blinked, and Ruth was back to her usual uncheery self.

What. The. Actual. Hell.

Taking advantage of Jayne's stunned stupor, Ruth flung another spell her way, and Jayne was too slow. The magic collided with her, slamming her against the wall. Again. A painting hanging above her crashed over her head, making her vision go dark.

"Jayne!" Tristan shouted.

Jayne slumped over, feeling warm blood trickling down her forehead. *Get up!* she screamed at herself. *Ruth will kill you! Get the hell up!*

But she couldn't move. Her head lolled, and the darkness in her mind threatened to swallow her whole.

Really? This was how it would go for her? Death by painting... That was even more embarrassing than death by books.

Heal, said a voice, and clarity broke through Jayne's hazy thoughts.

Right. Yes. Jayne could heal herself. Bright lights burst in her vision, and for a moment Jayne thought it was from her injury.

But no. It was Ruth and Tristan sparring. And damn, but that Frenchman could hold his own against the psychopath.

Jayne raised a hand, which felt completely numb, to her temple and whispered, "Heal." Medb's power shot forward, rising obediently. The smell of earth and soil tickled Jayne's nose as her own magic warmed her body, spreading through her like a wildfire.

Gradually, the pain in her skull ebbed, and the fog in her head cleared. She pressed her hand to the carpeted floor. Medb's magic was still flowing through her, so she used it. Vines snaked along the carpet until they wrapped about Ruth's ankles and tugged.

With an unladylike shriek, Ruth fell, just as Tristan's glowing white ropes tied themselves around her, binding her arms and legs.

Jayne strode forward, meeting Tristan's gaze. Sweat gleamed on his forehead, but he looked unharmed. Relieved, actually.

"You all right?" he asked.

"Never better." Jayne crouched in front of her mother, who spat at her.

"You have no idea what you're dealing with," Ruth seethed, her voice deep and layered. It was not just Ruth speaking, and a chill went down Jayne's spine. This time, she wasn't imagining it. Ruth was changing before her. The tough, leathery skin. Inky black eyes. Fangs. Now, horns protruded from her temples, and great black wings extended from her shoulder blades.

Jayne staggered back with a cry of horror. "Holy shit!"

Tristan muttered a curse in French, his face white as bone. His hands fell on Jayne's shoulders as he tugged her backward, and she didn't object. The ropes binding Ruth's body snapped as the woman rose in height, now towering over Tristan and Jayne like they were nothing more than children. She was no longer Ruth Thorne but a monster. She now resembled a gargoyle, or Chernabog from the movie *Fantasia*.

The beast swiped its claws at them, and Tristan and Jayne barely ducked out of the way in time. Something shattered nearby—Jayne wasn't sure if it was a window or a lamp.

Tristan summoned another spell, something that looked like a cross between a pretzel and a crisscrossing pattern of threads. The spell sailed toward the creature, but it fizzled upon contact. As if...the monster was immune to magic.

Impossible.

Jayne's blood ran cold at the nightmare before them. If magic was no use against it, then what was?

To hell with this. Jayne lunged, aiming a roundhouse kick to the creature's face. She caught it by surprise, and it stumbled backward, crashing through the wall. Concrete and dry wood splintered and smashed, but Jayne wasn't finished. She aimed a punch, then ducked as the creature brought its meaty fist down.

The thing was huge—gargantuan, really—but Jayne was quicker. This was just like an opponent at the dojo. Except, you know, bigger, and more *demonic*. She could pretend this was just another meathead at the gym.

The beast lumbered to its feet and roared again before advancing toward Jayne, but she darted underneath its legs. Was it male? Would it react if she punched it in the balls? She gave the area a good *thwack* for good measure, but nothing happened.

Okay. That didn't work.

The monster whirled to face her just as Jayne struck it in the jaw, then elbowed it in the gut. The beast bellowed, its wings stretching wide. Long talons extended from the wings, sharp enough to pierce through flesh.

Uh-oh. There certainly wasn't room for that transformation.

"Tristan, look out!" Jayne shrieked as she dropped to the floor, making herself as small as possible.

The wings broke through another wall, the window shattering as they stretched wide. Jayne felt something tough and wrinkled brush against her shoulders. A talon grazed her back, cutting through the fabric of her shirt, bruising the skin, and Jayne bit back a cry of pain.

Tristan grunted in pain. Jayne peered from her fetal position, frantically looking for him. Had the hell-beast gotten him?

She was too distracted to see the claws coming toward her once more. A heavy force slammed into her, crunching through skin and bone. The monster's razor-sharp claws cut through her, deep and merciless, and she couldn't breathe. Blood bubbled up her throat, and she coughed and choked.

Can't. Breathe.

Distantly, she heard Tristan screaming her name. Her body was on fire, her insides scorching as the pain consumed her. She slumped over, her body hitting the floor hard. Agony quivered through her, making her tremble. She was dying, for real this time, she was sure of it.

Then Ruth stood before her, out of breath and covered in sweat but grinning in triumph. "As I said. You have no idea what you're dealing with." She raised a hand and pressed it to Jayne's forehead. Jayne screamed as Ruth's power cut into her, digging into her forehead.

Oh, God. She's trying to pull out the totem by force.

Pain blinded Jayne, white-hot and endless. Something tugged from within her chest, and Ruth flew backward. Only then did Jayne smell the soil and earth around her.

Medb had just thrown Ruth back. Good God.

Ruth clambered to her feet, rage burning in her gaze. From behind her, Jayne barely made out Tristan's inert form. Blood coated his forehead, trickling down to his chin. His eyes were closed, and he wasn't moving.

Tristan. Jayne tried to rasp out something, to reach for him, but she couldn't move. She couldn't do anything more than watch as Ruth conjured her own portal and leapt through it, taking Tristan with her.

THIRTY-FOUR

LET'S HAVE SOME FUN

London

The creature within Ruth Thorne roared its approval when she arrived at her flat, leaving Tristan Lowell draped over her couch like a limp wet blanket. He would wake shortly, but she wasn't worried.

God, the sheer power of it all... Ruth hadn't known anything like it.

Yes, said the voice inside her. *I told you, my child. I told you we were capable of so much greatness together.*

Ruth honestly didn't know why she'd fought it for so long. Seeing her daughter had brought out such uncontrollable rage, and in that moment, she had willingly relinquished control to the beast inside her.

And now Jayne was dying. Probably dead already. And Ruth had Gina Labelle's wretched son to use as leverage.

She would return to that hotel and claim the Earth totem for herself, once Jayne was well and truly dead.

Yes, everything was proceeding nicely. She would torture Tristan for information on Gina and La Liberté, then unleash the creature on them, eliminating them from existence. They would no longer be a pebble in her shoe, and without them and Jayne to defy her, she would be unstoppable.

She'd felt the power of Jayne's little spell just before she'd arrived. That girl had found another grimoire; she was certain of it.

And if she had, Ruth was steps away from acquiring another totem. Another presence to empower her. She was practically a goddess, possessing strength that made Adepts look like ants scurrying for cover.

Tristan groaned, turning over, and Ruth turned to face him, a smile already spreading across her lips. The beast inside rumbled, eager to be let loose again. And perhaps she would let it out to play. After all, the Lowell boy had been a nuisance for too long, flitting from La Liberté to the TCO, constantly thwarting her.

And if Jayne had found another grimoire—another Master to raise—then Tristan would know about it. The information was here, waiting for Ruth to extract it.

Yes, she thought as she freed the monster once more, its leathery wings crashing into the walls. *Let's have some fun.*

THIRTY-FIVE

BEHOLD, THE WATER TOTEM

Rome

Jayne felt the life seeping out of her, one drop of blood at a time. Each puncture, each tear in her flesh throbbed mercilessly. The wounds pulsed like a heartbeat of their own. All she knew was pain. She could do nothing but lie there and wait for death to take her.

Pathetic, she told herself. *You're better than this. Heal yourself!*

But she'd already tried. That creature, that beast, was from some other world; magic was struggling to work on the wounds. Wherever it came from, it was beyond magic.

My child, whispered a voice. *You are not alone.*

Oh, thanks, Medb, Jayne thought. *Nice to know I'll have someone to talk to in my last moments.*

Jayne could've sworn she heard the Earth goddess laugh. Well, that was a first.

Remember the gardens, Medb urged. *You have only used a fraction of my power. Unleash it all, Master. All of it, right here.*

248

Jayne tried to shake her head, but she still couldn't move, her body paralyzed. "I... c-c-can't," she managed, choking on more blood.

You can, Medb argued, her voice a low growl. *Do not give up. There are people out there who need you, just as I do.*

Jayne faltered at that. Sofia. Cillian. Tristan. Ruger. Amanda. They were counting on her.

And Medb... What would happen to her if Jayne died? Would Ruth come back to collect the totem? Or would Medb be destroyed as well?

I am stronger than this pain, Jayne told herself. *I am more powerful than these injuries. I am more than this.*

The smell of flowers and dew-moistened grass reached her nose, and she clung to it, immersing herself in the Luxembourg Gardens once more. Birds cawed, insects chirped, and the fresh spring air surrounded her, giving her strength. Jayne drew on it, pulling everything she could into her body.

More, Medb urged. *Take it all, my child.*

Jayne didn't hesitate. She drank it all in, absorbing the power fully, using it to fuel herself as she sat up. Instead of finding herself in the ruined hotel suite, she was sitting in an expanse of grass, surrounded by rows of blooming trees and neatly trimmed hedges. Her wounds were gone, but she knew it was just an illusion; she still had to heal herself. She pressed a hand to her chest and conjured the Heal spell. Her chest burned, her insides scorching, but she pushed onward, imagining her skin and bones knitting themselves back together, the wounds closing and sealing themselves. It was like mending the branches of a tree or repotting a plant to fresher soil. It was nothing more than feeding and healing the earth itself.

Jayne breathed in, and it felt like the breath of life. She was back, and she was whole. Her eyes opened once more, and she found herself surrounded by the rubble of the once ornate hotel room.

God, Ruth had really destroyed this place. Jayne's chest ached at the thought. It was a really nice hotel. She felt bad for the owners.

But as she lamented the destruction before her, Medb's earth magic inched forward, the dirt and broken concrete quivering as energy snaked through it. Shimmering white light glistened in the air, and before Jayne's eyes, the broken walls began mending themselves back together. Shards of glass rose up, fitting together perfectly to form the windows. The splintered remains of the furniture magically fit back into the proper placement, forming the elegant woodwork she had admired when they'd first arrived.

Jayne felt like she'd just waved a magic wand as the room healed itself one piece at a time. Her mouth fell open as she watched, awestruck by exactly how much power Medb's magic was capable of.

When it was all finished, Jayne found herself in an immaculate, spotless hotel suite, cleaner than she'd ever seen it. Had she hallucinated this whole thing? Perhaps she was still in the Luxembourg Gardens and she would wake up to find the place in ruins once more.

Never underestimate the power of Earth magic, came Medb's proud, rumbling voice. Though, to Jayne, it sounded a bit weaker than it had moments before, as if such effort had drained the great goddess.

But Jayne didn't have time to dwell on it. Ruth had Tristan. And Jayne had to get him back. Every ounce of her urged her forward.

"I have to find Tristan," Jayne whispered, rising to her feet. She brushed off dust and dirt from her clothes, but it did almost nothing—she was covered in blood, even if she'd been healed.

Medb's full powers still flowed through her, and Jayne used them to conjure her own portal. She focused on Ruth—on the rage twisting her expression, the dark beast lurking within, the power flowing through her—and dove head-first into the portal.

JAYNE WASN'T sure what she'd expected—maybe a villainous lair, a murky cave, or even the Time Catch from when she'd been chasing after Alarik when she was assigned to the Trinity library in Dublin. But it certainly wasn't this.

When the glow of the portal faded, Jayne found herself standing atop a bridge. On either side of her, dozens of civilians strolled past, chattering merrily as if there wasn't a care in the world.

Jayne's hands were in fists, her body poised for a fight. Why had the portal taken her here? Her eyes narrowed as she took in her surroundings. She recognized the huge statues framing the bridge, some of them almost gargoyle-like. And in the distance, she could make out the dome-shaped building of the Castel Sant'Angelo.

She was still in Rome. Standing on the Ponte Vittorio Emanuele. Beneath her was the Tiber. A sudden flashback of Paris filled her mind, reminding her of her battle with La Liberté on the Pont des Arts.

"I suppose I shouldn't be surprised."

Jayne whirled and found her mother standing on the opposite side of the bridge. A mark glowed green on her forehead, and her eyes emanated the same ethereal light.

The Water totem.

Jayne surged forward, ready to intercept Ruth before she took out the entire city. But Ruth was quicker. She raised her hands, and droplets of water ran down her arms. Underneath the bridge, the waters began to churn. Gasps and cries echoed around them as the alarmed civilians took notice of the water's movement.

"Stop!" Jayne cried, flinging her hands forward. She sent an Attack spell toward Ruth, who easily deflected it. But she didn't see the second spell Jayne had fired right after it, curling her fingers, using the Puppet spell she had learned earlier. Her magic followed the movement, coiling around the hair on Ruth's head before giving it a sharp tug.

Ruth screeched, her head jerking backward from Jayne's invisible hair-pulling. Sure, it was petty and reeked of middle school cat-fights, but Jayne didn't care. She used the opportunity to launch a spell mimicking the Throat strike she knew so well from her kickboxing training straight into her mother.

Ruth buckled from the force of the strike, jerking backward, choking on gasps. Jayne closed the distance between them, slamming the heel of her palm into Ruth's forehead, then ramming her elbow into her chest.

Ruth crumpled to the ground, but Jayne kept her fists raised, her chest heaving from her breaths as she waited for the woman to retaliate.

At first, nothing happened.

Then, the churning river gushed, the flow intensifying. The water swelled as it ascended, a huge tidal wave rising over the bridge.

"No!" Jayne screamed, stretching out her hands. She wasn't sure what she hoped to do, but she knew she had to stop the waters from flooding the city.

Medb's magic rose to her assistance. Lengthy branches extended from the trees lining the bridge, forming a tight web that trapped the water. The temporary dam wouldn't hold for long, though. Already, water was leaking through.

And Ruth was climbing to her feet, ready for more.

"Get out of here!" Jayne cried to the panicking civilians still on the bridge. "Now! Run!"

Several of them did just that, their screams echoing in the street. On either side of the bridge, cars stopped, their drivers pausing to gawk at the cyclone of water hovering at the edge of the bridge.

Jayne's arms shook from the effort of holding the water at bay. Medb's Earth magic kept funneling into the branches, thickening them, reinforcing the barrier. But the Water magic was stronger. After all, Ruth had the entire river at her disposal.

There wasn't enough Earth magic to combat it.

Ruth started laughing, as if she knew how useless Jayne's efforts were. The psychotic woman thrust the water forward until it lapped over the bridge.

A roar ripped at Jayne's throat as she summoned a Shield spell, slamming it into the overflowing river. It merely deflected the water, pushing it off to one side. But the river was too strong. Though Jayne layered Shield after Shield, trying to keep the waters at bay, they continued gushing around her, cascading down the streets of Rome until all manner of things —vehicles, garbage cans, and even people—started floating downstream. The cries around her intensified as several citizens were swept away by the tide, unable to fight the magnitude of power churning from within the river.

Tears streamed down Jayne's face as she flung another spell at Ruth, even knowing it was too late. The spell was easily deflected, and Ruth shot a triumphant smirk at her before conjuring a portal and vanishing.

Jayne couldn't control her sobs as she dug into her pockets, clumsily removing the burner phone. She dialed Ruger's number, not bothering with code words as she cried, "I need your help! *Now!*"

CHAPTER

THIRTY-SIX

BEAST MODE

R uger quickly assembled a clean-up crew and an extraction team to intervene. But the damage was done. Half of Rome was flooded. The catastrophe was all over the news, and no amount of damage control could erase what the nonmagical community had witnessed.

Jayne did what she could, cleaning up the streets with magical spells and wading through the water to help the struggling citizens. The people were too distressed and shellshocked to notice when they were suddenly dry and warm again.

But all the while, Jayne's limbs wouldn't stop trembling. All she could see was Ruth's twisted smile, the look of triumph on her face.

She had flooded the city for a reason—because she needed a distraction.

Jayne's mind immediately turned to Tristan. Ruth needed him for information. What if he'd told her where the Latin Bible was?

What if Ruth knew and was on her way now?

Or what if she was going to kill Tristan before Jayne could get to him?

"Can you hear me?"

Jayne blinked and found Ruger in front of her, his face haggard. His sleeves were rolled up as he, too, helped with the massive clean-up project.

"I said you need to go rest," Ruger said. "You don't look good."

"No. Tristan is still out there. I have to get him back."

"I've already sent a team. Let them do their job, Jayne."

"They can't track him like I can!" Jayne argued. "You know I'm the best person for this, Ruger. She'll *kill* him. I can get him back. I know I can."

Ruger rubbed his jaw and sighed. "You'll just go after him anyway, won't you?"

"Yes," Jayne said immediately. No point denying it.

"All right. But be careful."

Jayne nodded before hurrying down the street, finding an abandoned alley. After a quick glance around to ensure no one lurked nearby, she summoned a portal, focusing intently on Tristan. A shimmering gold sphere appeared, and without hesitation, she leaped through.

A glamorous flat opened up before her, decorated with the most stunning paintings Jayne had ever seen. Some hung from floor to ceiling and looked like they belonged in a museum. Others looked as if they had been painted by the gods themselves. Handsome throw rugs lined the floors, and the spotless furniture looked straight from the pages of *Architectural Digest*.

Jayne would have thought this was a staged apartment if not for the scent of blood and dark magic lingering in the air. She smelled the telltale sign of Ruth's magic—rotting violets and burning iron—but it mingled with something dark and sickly Jayne had never scented before.

It made her very bones quiver.

But energy thrummed in her veins, fresh from Medb herself. And Jayne was not afraid.

She inched forward, following that foul stench. She knew the blood in the air must belong to Tristan, but she shoved that knowledge into the recesses of her mind, refusing to dwell on it.

She was in beast mode right now, and she couldn't afford to be distracted. In her mind, she formed a plan of attack, knowing magic wouldn't work on whatever beast Ruth could change into.

How in the holy hell had Ruth managed to shift into that creature? Had it been a Rogue experimentation gone wrong?

Or was this exactly what the Kingdom was hoping to accomplish—tethering a creature to them permanently as a weapon they could wield?

Jayne suppressed a shudder, discarding those thoughts as well. She could ponder the vile inner workings of her mother after Tristan was safe.

Tristan. His name echoed in her thoughts with every foot-step, a rhythm to ground her, to remind her why she was here. The smell of him grew stronger, and Jayne didn't waste a thought marveling at how she could sense him so easily, but that soap-and-vanilla scent lingered in the air, tainted by blood and sweat and fear.

He was here. She was certain of it. It definitely wasn't the torture chamber she was expecting, but with Ruth, could she ever really be shocked? That woman was full of dark surprises. Like a murderous gift box that kept on giving.

Jayne crept through a living room, a small breakfast nook, then down a hallway and past several doors—a library, a small gym, a guest room. At the end of the hall, a light bled out from a closed door. Judging by the placement, this was probably the primary bedroom.

Ruth was keeping Tristan in her bedroom? Ick.

Okay, Jayne, she thought to herself, inhaling deeply. *Ruth may already know you're here, assuming she's warded the place. Remember the plan.* She waved a hand over her face, casting a quick Cloaking spell just for good measure.

And, because she knew it would be distracting, as Tristan always warned her, she layered a Block spell, an Attack spell, and a Blood Choke spell, just for funsies. Just to see what havoc she could wreak. Now that she was aware of it, a brief bolt of energy laced the air from the layering of spells. Faint, barely a tickle against her nostrils, but it was still there.

How fascinating. And she never knew.

As the magic wafted through the air, Jayne waited for one heartbeat. Then another. Once she was certain the smell of her magic had crept underneath the door, she kicked it down with a fierce thrust of her foot. The frame splintered, and the door crashed to the ground. Jayne leaped into action, wielding her layered spells together like a shield.

Her eyes swept over the room in one quick motion, noting everything—the furniture pushed against the walls, the lone chair in the middle, surrounded by a pool of blood, and the chained figure resting atop it. Tristan.

No time. Beast Mode, remember?

Jayne's gaze continued to rove around, searching for... There.

She ducked just as a heavy claw swiped for her. Ah, so Chernabog was back. At some point after flooding the city, Ruth had unleashed the demon again.

Oh, not today, beastie. You already got me once. It won't happen again. Jayne flung out her spell, spreading it through the air to create a thin transparent film. A barrier between her and the creature.

It might not work. But it was worth a shot. And if there was any piece of Ruth left inside this gargoyle thing, then hopefully, the potent magic in the air would distract her.

Sure enough, as the monster lumbered forward, it faltered when it reached Jayne's barrier.

She kicked forward, sliding her legs underneath it. It didn't do much—the creature was too big for Jayne's pathetic "sweep the leg" method to do any damage. But she easily ducked beneath the beast, then aimed a high kick squarely in its back. It buckled with a roar, and Jayne struck again—a kick to the back of its knee, then the lower back. She slammed the heel of her palm into the beast's spine and watched with satisfaction as it crumpled.

I need a weapon, Jayne thought. Immediately, the Torrent shimmered into view, revealing a display of the sharpest, most deadly weapons she'd ever seen. How in the hell? What, was the Torrent an arms dealer now?

Not something made of magic, she clarified. The list of items narrowed like a list of search results on the computer. Then Jayne saw it: a long, smooth, wooden bow staff. The wood was weathered and ancient, but strong. Rows of carvings lined the staff, reminding her of runes she'd studied during her training. Though the rod seemed thousands of years old, when Jayne gripped it in her hands, the wood was firm and unyielding.

Yes. Perfect. She swirled it in a circle, using the momentum until it connected with a loud crack against the Ruth-Demon's skull.

Part of her had worried it wouldn't work; it had come from the Torrent, after all. Shouldn't it be a magical item? But somehow, miraculously, the creature staggered backward, its eyelids fluttering.

It made Jayne wonder...

She layered another Block and Attack spell, plus a Sleeping

spell she'd only used once before. Because, why not? What was the creature going to do, kill her...again?

Jayne brought the spells forward, embedding them into her staff just like she had with Gina Labelle's spear. The staff trembled, and the air crackled with lightning again, zipping through Jayne's veins and warming her blood. God, the intensity of it... It made her teeth chatter as if she had, indeed, been electrocuted.

But it wasn't unpleasant. It made her whole body sing with awareness. With a *thwack*, she thrust the flat end of her staff directly into the creature's chest. A crack of thunder split the air, making the ground tremble. Jayne's arms shot out, expecting to topple from the mini-earthquake, but she remained upright. The beast fell to the floor with such force that the walls rattled, and several stunning paintings fell, their frames shattering on impact. Jayne hovered, her staff ready, waiting for the beast to rise.

It didn't. Its huge body still rose and fell with labored breaths, so it wasn't quite dead.

No time to waste. Still clutching the staff, she raced toward Tristan's limp and bloody form.

"Please don't be dead," she muttered in a rush. "Please don't be dead. Damn it, Tristan, I still have so much to yell at you for!" She dropped her staff, her hands shaking as the adrenaline wore off and she searched for the bindings around his hands.

Metal chains. Of course. Jayne conjured a quick Unlock spell and pressed it against the cuffs. With a loud clang, they split and fell to the ground, the chains clattering. Tristan groaned, his head turning. Blood covered half of his face, and crimson stains coated his sleeves. One arm was twisted at an odd angle, likely broken. A long gash ran from his eyebrow to his chin, and blood dribbled from his mouth.

If Ruth had extracted any of his teeth, Jayne would slit her throat.

Jayne tried to help Tristan to his feet, but he was too weak. She was hoping to save her strength until after they'd gotten out, but he needed to be healed. Now.

Jayne reached for Medb's power, but it flickered before vanishing completely.

Uh-oh.

"It's fine," Jayne whispered to herself. "I've healed without Medb before. I can do it again." She accessed the Torrent and found the Heal spell. Steeling herself, she grabbed it and pressed the warmth against Tristan's chest. His body jerked, and he inhaled a shuddering gasp as if he'd been brought back from the dead. Every muscle in Jayne's body throbbed, and she gritted her teeth against the heat burning against her flesh. Still, she pressed on, urging the magic forward, encouraging it to heal, to knit the flesh and bone back together again.

Something cracked, and Tristan cried out. That would be the bones resetting. The gash on his face vanished, and his eyes slowly blinked open.

"Jayne?" he groaned.

But the magic wasn't finished. With a bark of pain, Jayne hunched over, her insides on fire. The heat intensified, scorching her blood and melting her bones. She was an inferno. She was lava. It wouldn't stop, the flames licking against her, burning her to a crisp. Distantly, she heard Tristan's cry of alarm, just before darkness consumed her.

THIRTY-SEVEN

A MOMENT OF WEAKNESS

London

"J*ayne.*"

Jayne tried to shift, but she was immobilized. Her eyes opened, but all she could make out was amber dust surrounding her.

Oh God. She was back in the firestorm dream.

"*Agnes Jayne Thorne, pay attention. This is important.*"

Jayne tried to see through the fog, but it was impossible. Coughing, she asked, "Who are you?"

"*I am Vesta, the Fire Goddess. You must find me, Jayne. I know where your father is.*"

A jolt of awareness rippled over her, and she sat up straighter, desperate to find the voice speaking to her. "Where are you? How can I find him? Please, tell me where he is!"

"*I cannot. You are not the only one hearing my voice. It is too dangerous.*"

Jayne recalled the sight of her mother perched on the cliff in the firestorm. Was Ruth listening, too?

"How?" Jayne asked, her panic mounting.

"We are linking through divine magic. But you must find me, Jayne Throne. Find me before the others do."

Medb. The totems. The pieces slid together, and Jayne stifled a cry of shock. The Earth totem allowed her to communicate with other gods and goddesses.

But if that was the case...Ruth Thorne had the same power.

The air began to clear, and Jayne felt her consciousness shifting. "No! Wait, I need—"

Her body jerked, her eyes opening to find her face pressed against a soft cushion. She groggily shifted, and a sudden pain lanced through her. Hissing, she opened her eyes to find Tristan hovering over her. He'd changed into clean clothes, but his hair and face were still matted with blood.

"Where—where am I?" Jayne's tongue felt like sandpaper.

"A hotel in London."

Jayne sat bolt upright, ignoring the throbbing in her limbs. *"What?* How the hell did we wind up in London?"

Her eyes took in the double bed she rested on, along with the desk and chair, the plain blue curtains, and the mini fridge in the corner. A smaller and much less elegant room than their suite in Rome, that was for sure. But she couldn't complain— she and Tristan were alive, and the Ruth creature was...

"Ruth?" Jayne asked.

"Still at her flat, I presume," Tristan said. "You dealt her quite a blow. That was impressive."

Jayne scoffed. "How would you know? You were unconscious."

Darkness flitted over his gaze, and she regretted her comment immediately. No doubt it brought back painful memories of whatever torture he'd endured.

She needed to change the subject. "I saw Vesta, the Fire Goddess. The grimoire we're looking for will raise her. I'm sure of it."

Tristan frowned. "How do you know?"

Quickly, Jayne filled him in on her visions, Medb's voice, and now Vesta pleading for Jayne to come find her.

"In my first vision, I saw a firestorm and heard a woman calling for help in French," Jayne concluded. "It's Vivienne. It has to be."

Tristan rubbed his jaw as he paced back and forth on the carpeted floor. "It would make sense. Something as powerful as a Master magician could easily overpower my mother and sister —and pull Vivienne inside." He waved a finger at Jayne. "And if Vesta has another totem, it's no wonder *Maman* and Ruth are after it."

"I can portal us back." Jayne stood on wobbly legs, but Tristan grabbed her arm to stop her.

"No."

Jayne's eyes narrowed. "Excuse me? Didn't you hear what you just said? There's a *totem* connected to this grimoire. We can't allow someone to find it first!"

"You almost burned yourself up, Jayne. You need to rest and recover before you cast powerful magic like that again."

"I can—"

Tristan silenced her by raising her left arm. Jayne's words died on her tongue, her heart slamming painfully in her chest.

Along her wrist, like a huge scab, was a stretch of dark and leathery skin. The exact shade and texture as the skin of Ruth's gargoyle creature.

Her blood chilled, and she stared at Tristan in horror. "What is this?" Her voice was nothing more than a hushed whisper.

"Sit down, and I'll tell you."

Jayne was too numb to argue. Slowly, she sat back down on the edge of the bed, her whole body cold with the disturbing realization that part of her flesh looked just like that...that creature.

Was she—would she become that thing? Eventually?

"I wasn't certain before, but after being held in Ruth's flat and witnessing her transition, now I know for sure." Tristan turned the desk chair so it faced Jayne and sank onto it. "Centuries ago, there were stories of Master magicians who bonded themselves to other Adepts. Similar to Rogues and Masters, but the bond is more...forced. The Adept's powers are swallowed up in the Master's. They share a body, but only when the Master allows it.

"My mother kept texts detailing these accounts. We often read through them, searching for answers about Rogue magic. Only a few Masters performed this dark magic, and some who did were destroyed by it. They...they burned themselves alive from the force of such unnatural magic."

Burned themselves alive. Jayne stared at the dark stretch of skin along her arm, unable to tear her gaze away from it. "So you're saying Ruth did this to another Adept?"

"No. I'm saying Ruth *is* the Adept."

Jayne's eyes snapped to Tristan's. "What?"

"Ruth is no Master magician, Jayne. If this dark spell was performed, then she was the victim, not the perpetrator."

Jayne blinked at the concept of Ruth being a victim of anything.

"That creature we saw—that's what happens when a Master magician casts magic more powerful than they can wield. A normal Adept would just burn to a crisp, their body completely consumed. And for some Master magicians, they succumbed to the same fate. But a select few were...transformed. Their magic was strong enough to keep them alive, but the damage was done."

A hard lump formed in Jayne's throat, and she thought she might be sick. After swallowing twice, she finally found her voice. "Are you saying...that if I use too much power...I'll turn into *that*?" She gestured to the door, but Tristan understood her meaning.

"I don't know," he admitted. "But based on that, my guess is yes." He pointed to her injured arm, and she self-consciously covered the mark.

Jayne stood, her legs requiring movement. She paced the tiny hotel room as she sifted through her thoughts, muttering aloud to make sense of it all. "Ruth bonded herself to an ancient Master magician who used so much power they turned into a creature of darkness."

"They are called Wraiths," Tristan said.

"Wraiths. Of course." Jayne nodded like this was the most natural thing in the world, still talking to herself. "Half Ruth, half Wraith. So is the Master still alive, or is that just like a projection of its magic?"

"Everything I've studied tells stories of Masters binding themselves to Adepts while their bodies are still intact. I've never heard of a situation where a Wraith has been bound to an Adept."

"Well, what do you know of these Wraiths? When was the last time something like this happened?"

"Over a century ago. When our last Masters still walked among us. One scorched his entire body and shifted into this creature shortly before slaughtering an entire town. He had to be put down by the other Masters."

Jayne shuddered. Was that in her future? Would she become this unstoppable beast, too?

Sofia's fears had come to fruition. Jayne would become the

same creature that possessed Ruth. She was no better. She was dabbling in powerful, dark magicks that she had no business wielding.

"Jayne." Tristan's hands came down on her shoulders, halting her frantic pacing. "You're panicking."

"I'm not! I'm just…processing." But even Jayne could hear the wild edge to her voice.

"That will not happen to you." Each word was strong and forceful. Tristan's caramel-brown eyes held her own, pinning her in place. "I swear it."

"How do you know? You said it yourself, I'm reckless and destructive with my magic. It's only a matter of time, right?"

Tristan flinched, his eyes closing. "I shouldn't have said that."

"But you weren't wrong! I'm a loose cannon. A bomb about to go off. And then, I'll destroy a city, too, and—and—" She faltered, then glared at Tristan. "Why did you carry me out of Ruth's place? You should've just left me there. I'm doomed to become just like her."

"No, you're not." Tristan's voice was a growl, his eyes sharpening with anger. Good. She deserved his fury.

"I'm the reason you were abducted and tortured," Jayne said. "You should have left me. You could be on a plane to Rome right now, on your way to get your sister back."

"And if you had left me there, you could already be in Geneva, getting your father back," Tristan snapped, his gaze full of rage.

"Ruth is my fight," Jayne hissed. "Not yours."

"So, what do you care? You hate me anyway, right? We were just temporary partners, destined to part ways eventually. I was always just an irritant to you, so being rid of me should have been a welcome relief to you."

Jayne's head reared back. Where the hell was this coming from? "If you think that, then you don't know me at all! I would've gone back to rescue you even if you were my worst enemy." Well, that wasn't entirely true, but the statement sounded heroic.

"So I'm no better than your worst enemy?" Tristan chuckled wryly. "That's fitting, I suppose. I tortured your friends. Then, your mother tortures me. Karma, right?"

"Are you saying I *wanted* you to get caught? That I wished this on you? You're such an idiot!"

"So are you!"

"Well then, maybe we should—"

Tristan cut her off. He seized her, cupping her face in his hands and bringing her mouth to his. The kiss was brutal and bruising, hard and unyielding, but that kind of force was just what Jayne needed. Her insides melted from the motion, and she found herself clinging to his collar, her mouth roving over his.

Reality slammed into her, and she shoved him backward, wiping her mouth with the back of her hand. "What the hell was that? Why would you do that? You really *are* an idiot!"

She grabbed him, pulling him back to her, and they were kissing again. There was nothing soft about it. They clung to each other, mouths crushing and tongues colliding, their movements feral and desperate. Their chests pressed together, and Tristan's arms wound around her waist, their bodies molding so tightly it almost cracked Jayne's bones.

But she relished the feeling, the pain of it. Her lips were numb, and she wished she could put more force into it, more anguish... She guided him backward, their steps clumsy as they slammed against the wall. She pinned him there before kissing him again, and he groaned against her mouth, his hands exploring, teasing at the edge of her shirt as he hiked it up.

Flesh touched flesh, and the shock of his touch hit her skin like a lightning bolt.

No. No. This couldn't happen.

Jayne pulled herself away with a sharp gasp. Her body yearned to press against him once more, to finish what they started—and God, how she wanted to—but this absolutely *could not happen.*

"Damn it." She scrubbed her face with her hand, trying to ignore the tingling in her lips. They ached, and she couldn't tell if it was from longing or from the pain of such forceful kissing. She'd never made out like that before, not even with Cillian.

The thought of the Irish kickboxer sent a bolt of clarity through her hazy thoughts. She whirled away from Tristan, from those adorable, pink-smeared lips and the smoky dark eyes. Burying her face in her hands, she thought instead of Cillian and Sofia, Ruger and Amanda... They were all counting on her.

Tears stung her eyes. She was on a mission to rescue Tristan's sister and Jayne's father. Amanda and Ruger—all of them had risked their jobs and their lives to fight this battle, and Jayne was busy making out with Tristan. Part of her knew it was just her adrenaline and survival instincts pushing her, desperate for an outlet, but still... She was never like this. She was always level-headed. Always had a plan.

Jayne dropped her hands and huffed a deep breath before turning to face Tristan. He was smoothing back his hair and righting his wrinkled shirt, but she gazed at him with what she hoped was an apathetic expression.

"Fine, then," she said as if they were merely continuing their conversation. As if nothing had happened between them at all. "We won't portal. We'll book a flight back to Rome and finish this once and for all."

Tristan's expression smoothed, but not before a powerful

emotion glimmered in his gaze, igniting the heat that had consumed Jayne mere moments ago.

She shoved it down deep. There was no time for this. They were both truly being idiots, and that had to stop now.

She pointed toward the door. "Go take a cold shower. Then let's go find your sister."

CHAPTER

THIRTY-EIGHT

AMANDA'S TALE

Patagonia

B ack at Xiomara's house, Amanda kept her mind blank as she shut herself in a tiny bedroom with Sofia and Seo-joon, leaving Cillian and Pierce to watch over the Guardian children in the living room. Amanda tried not to focus on the traumatized children or Hans Kaufmann's attack or the inevitable looks of shock and betrayal she would find when her truth was finally exposed. No one, not even Ruger, knew what she'd been hiding all these years.

None of them would look at her the same.

But that was the burden she had to bear. It was what she'd agreed to when her husband passed away all those years ago. Her hand automatically went to her necklace, which felt warm against her fingers. It had heated from the use of her Guardian magic and still hadn't cooled off. No doubt the trinket she wore was old and worn from disuse. It would be dangerous for her to keep using magic so recklessly. She needed to practice, to hone these skills before using them more permanently. Goddess, what had the world come to? Amanda had fully planned on keeping these powers a secret until the day she died.

But war was on their doorstep. And how could she ask the Guardians to fight for her cause if she wasn't willing to do the same?

No, Amanda had hidden in the shadows for long enough. It was time to come forward.

When the place was cleaned up and the wards replaced and strengthened, there was nothing left for Amanda to do but tell the truth to her team.

Seo-joon and Sofia waited patiently, each of them watching her steadily as if they knew she was about to unearth some great secret. How could they not? They had seen her reaction in the courtyard.

You are strong. You are a warrior. Keep fighting.

That was what her husband had always said. And oh, how she needed his strength right now.

I'm sorry, Karam, she thought. *I hope I'm making the right choice.*

The necklace burned against her palm in response.

"I know you have lots of questions," Amanda began, clasping her hands in front of her. "And you deserve answers. Just understand that the secrets I've been keeping were not mine to share. I had others I was tasked with protecting. I also trust that you will convey this all to Cillian once we're finished. He deserves to know, too."

Sofia's brows knotted together, her eyes questioning.

"You all know my late husband was a Guardian," Amanda went on, trying to remain impassive as she told her story. But the grief welled up in her throat, threatening to suffocate her. All these years, and she still hadn't moved on from his death. Every day, the ache of his absence festered inside her. "What I said before was true—just before he died, he gave me this." She held up her necklace. "It's a Guardian token, and it holds a fraction of Guardian magic. But I didn't tell you everything. This trinket can only be worn by those who possess Guardian blood. It will burn someone without Guardian magic to ashes if they try to put it on."

"So...you..." Sofia's gaze clouded with confusion.

"Yes, I do have a small trace of Guardian blood," Amanda said. "Ordinarily, it wouldn't have been enough to allow me to channel the magic of this token, but...well, shortly after my husband was killed, I learned that I was pregnant with his child."

Sofia sucked in a sharp breath and exchanged a shocked glance with Seo-joon.

"The Kingdom was actively hunting down Guardians," Amanda said, now focusing on the faded curtains framing the window so she wouldn't have to meet anyone's gaze. She spoke the words as if rehearsing a speech, distancing herself from the story as much as possible. "I knew it wouldn't be safe to raise the child of a Guardian, especially with my active pursuit of the Kingdom. I...I sent the child away to live with a family I trusted. For her safety, the family moved often, and I insisted we sever all communication just in case I was compromised and the Kingdom forced the truth from me. The only time I met my daughter was when I first held her after giving birth. After that, she was mine no more. I had to do what was needed to protect her." She sniffed, her eyes welling. She blinked furiously, clearing her eyes before continuing.

Amanda finally looked at the stunned gazes of her colleagues. No, they were more than colleagues now. They were risking their lives to work with her. They were friends. Family. And she trusted them with her life.

"I am not technically a Guardian," Amanda said. "But I can

channel a portion of their powers thanks to the magic infused in my blood when I carried my child. After much research, I discovered that my daughter's DNA in vitro provided a bond between me and the token, allowing me to connect with the Guardian magic. And after I gave birth, that connection remained. I speculate that if I remove the necklace, the link will be broken. But I have never taken it off since Karam gave it to me."

"And your daughter?" Seo-joon asked softly.

"I've never spoken to her, and she doesn't know anything about me. It's far too dangerous for her to find out. Especially now. The war against Guardians is too fierce for me to risk it."

Silence followed her words. After a moment, Sofia sucked in a shaky breath. "Are you saying you just sat by all these years while someone you loved was handed off to a life with strangers?" She shook her head. "No way. I don't buy it."

Amanda's lips thinned. "I couldn't—"

"I heard what you said. And while it was a heartbreaking story and makes me want to wrap you in a hug, I'm still calling bullshit on you. There's no way you don't know exactly where your daughter is right now."

Amanda's eyes flickered closed for a moment. "I never said I didn't know where she was. I kept tabs on her, of course I did. I said I'd never spoken to her."

"That is...so sad," Sofia said. Amanda was grateful she didn't push more; the girl was too smart for her own good, and this was dangerous information.

"Why tell us this now?" Seo-joon asked, his face pale. "What does this have to do with that fight in the courtyard?"

"Because it's time we all chose a side. Just as I called for Xiomara to join the ranks, I felt I had to do the same. I couldn't live with myself if I stood by while you all fought this battle without me. And also..." She paused, glancing down at the symbol of the Guardians—three overlapping triangles—on her necklace. "Seeing those children reminded me of the anguish of giving up my own child. She would've had Guardian magic, too, because of my husband. What's to stop Hans from abducting her, too? It was...too close to those emotions I kept locked away."

"Hold on, hold on." Seo-joon raised his hand. "You're telling me that you have Guardian magic." He gestured to Amanda. "And so do you." He pointed to Sofia. "And Xiomara's a Guardian, too. This means we essentially have three Guardians on our side right now."

"Not necessarily," Amanda said. "Sofia and I are untrained. Acting on instinct. We would not be nearly as powerful as a fully trained Guardian like Hans. And remember, he has Guardians on his side as well. Not to mention Xiomara is being held captive."

"Right." Sofia shifted on her seat and glanced at Amanda. "But what about—"

"We have a bigger problem. The child—my daughter—" Amanda's head jerked toward the door, her eyes darkening with unease. "What is that?"

Sofia listened hard for some kind of disturbance, too, but she sensed nothing.

"I feel it, too," Seo-joon said.

Sofia stilled, searching inward for her magic, and then she felt the energy sweeping over her, familiar and warm, but also stronger than she was accustomed to. The smell of sage was so recognizable that she almost dismissed it as nothing at all. It was Cillian.

But she had never felt his magic swell like *this* before. And without her, too.

Without another word, Amanda burst out of the room. Sofia

hurried after her with Seo-joon close behind. They strode down the hallway until they reached the living room.

"What the hell is going on?" Amanda said loudly.

Sofia peered around Amanda and found Cillian standing with one of the Guardian children—the girl with red hair. They were clutching hands, and even before Cillian dropped her hand, Sofia could see the tendrils of gold magic winding between them. The warm magic in the air receded, leaving emptiness in its wake, and Sofia had to admit she yearned for it to return. She hadn't realized how comforting that presence had been until it vanished. It was like sitting in front of a cozy fire on a chilly day with a fabulous book.

Cillian stepped away from Rebecca, his eyes sliding to Amanda and Sofia, then darting to the children watching curiously from the sofa.

"I smelled magic," Amanda said accusingly. "Magic I've never encountered before."

Sofia needed to intervene before things got messy. It was clear Cillian was too flustered to defend himself. "I've sensed it before," she said breathlessly, drawing closer to him. "It was you, Cillian. Wasn't it? You tapped into your Rogue powers, didn't you?"

Amanda shook her head in surprise. "That can't be right. I've felt Cillian's powers before, too. It's nothing like this."

Sofia was grinning now, glancing from Amanda to Cillian. "That's because it's not his normal power. It's not connected with mine. It's his *own* magic. His Rogue magic."

"What did you do?" Seo-joon asked. His tone wasn't sharp like Amanda's; merely inquisitive.

"I—I—" Cillian gestured helplessly to the girl. "I was just trying to help her understand that not all magic is scary."

"He showed me his wolf!" the girl said eagerly, grinning broadly.

Sofia covered her mouth. Dear God, had he *shifted* in front of her?

"No, no!" Cillian said, reading the panic and alarm in the room. "I showed her *memories*. I don't know how. But I just felt this...desperation to show her something that might help, and before I knew it, she could sort of see into my mind, read the memories I was feeding her."

"It was amazing!" the girl gushed. "I've never seen anything like it!"

Sofia found herself smiling, too. Cillian could share memories? What did this mean? Could all Rogues do this? Could he expand the power and send other things telepathically as well?

She turned and met Amanda's stunned expression, followed by Seo-joon's overjoyed grin. As Amanda's shock faded, her shrewd eyes turned calculating.

"This changes everything," she murmured.

Sofia, unable to keep her gaze from straying back to Cillian, couldn't help but agree.

THIRTY-NINE

A NEW ALLY

Amanda had avoided the Guardian children for a good reason. Now, facing them once more, all the raw and festering emotions washed over her once more, weakening her. Dragging her downward.

Karam, I need you, she thought. *I can't do this alone.*

You are a warrior, Karam's voice seemed to say. *The strongest woman I know. You've faced worse battles head-on without fear. You can master this, too.*

His words sent rivers of warmth coursing through her as if he were indeed standing right next to her. She'd felt much closer to him upon the reawakening of her Guardian magic. It had remained dormant for so long. But now, it felt as if a kernel of Karam's presence swelled within her, twining with the gold threads of magic glowing in her blood.

"We need to get them out of here," Amanda said, finding her resolve at last. "We can't risk Hans finding them again, and they can't be a part of this fight."

"No," the red-haired girl said at once.

All the adults turned to face her.

"Listen—" Amanda began gently.

"No," the girl said again, her voice firm. "We aren't going anywhere. That man, that monster, took us from our homes. He can do it again. We want to help you stop him."

Amanda felt the blood drain from her face. "You don't know what you're saying."

The child's eyes locked on hers, and a tangible jolt raced through Amanda's veins. Judging by the way the girl's eyes widened slightly, she felt it, too.

Her resolve faltered. "I...I know you." She pointed an uncertain finger toward Amanda.

Amanda found herself shaking her head. "No, you don't. We've never met before."

Pink spread along the girl's cheeks as she said in a hushed voice, "I've dreamed about you. How is that possible?"

Amanda had no words. Her chest constricted more and more with each passing second, her breaths coming sharp and fast. An instinct told her to get out, to flee from this place and this confrontation.

I am not a coward, she thought, echoing Karam's words.

A hum burned within Amanda's chest, and when she lifted her hands, she realized why: she was glowing.

And so was the girl.

"Hot damn," Seo-joon muttered, rising to his feet, his face torn between shock and amazement.

"There are children present," Sofia snapped, but her eyes were on Amanda.

Amanda could do nothing but stare at her hands, her brain too muddled to make sense of any of this: her daughter, her unfamiliar magic, Xiomara's abduction, Hans's cruel plans... It was all too much.

"You're my...mother." The words were barely more than a breath.

Amanda stared at the girl, whose entire body was bathed in

an ethereal gold glow. She didn't have to ask how the girl knew. Her magic told her.

Their magic was connected. Because it came from the same source: Karam.

The idea sent so much warmth and love rising in Amanda's chest that it chased away her fear. Lifting her chin, she said in a calm voice, "I am. And I love you very much. I know this is confusing, and I will tell you everything I can. But by the Goddess, can I just hug you?"

Amanda stepped forward, but the girl stepped back, closer to Cillian. Amanda halted, yearning for the connection, understanding innately why it was not forthcoming.

Sofia gasped sharply, and Seo-joon swore again. Cillian ran a hand through his hair and took a step back, as if putting more distance between himself and the girl would incriminate him less.

From the moment Amanda had seen this girl, she'd known. Her name was Rebecca Peters, and until recently, she was living in the care of Amanda's close colleague who had retired right around the time of the girl's birth.

Yes. This was her daughter. And she couldn't hide from it any longer.

Amanda looked at Sofia's stunned expression. "I was about to tell you a moment ago that Rebecca is mine."

The gold glow around Rebecca faded and then vanished. To Amanda's surprise, her daughter's expression hardened, her eyes cold.

"That doesn't change a thing. I'm used to fending for myself," Rebecca said. "My parents—my *real* parents—never really understood what lives inside me. I don't care who you are. Nothing has changed. The only person who can protect me is myself." Her steely eyes turned to Cillian. "All of us here have magic. Magic you need. We want to stop that man before he hurts anyone else."

Around them, the other children were nodding, drawing closer to Rebecca in a sign of solidarity.

"Now, hold on a minute," Cillian began, but Sofia put a hand on his chest to silence him. He blinked, obviously startled by the gesture, and he wasn't the only one. Amanda arched an eyebrow, and Seo-joon covered his mouth to hide a smirk.

"They're right," Sofia said gently, withdrawing her hand. Was it Amanda's imagination, or were Sofia's cheeks turning red? "We need their magic. Hans vastly outnumbers us. And now he has Xiomara."

"We cannot use children like he did," Amanda said through gritted teeth. "That makes us just as vile as he is."

"We aren't using them if they're volunteering," Sofia argued.

"They are young and inexperienced!" Amanda went on, her blood heating. "They aren't trained soldiers, and some of them could die. Besides, you and I don't have much experience with Guardian magic, either. What if we accidentally leach it from them just like Hans did?"

Cillian's brow furrowed, his eyes turning distant. "Hang on. What if... What if we could ensure that wouldn't happen?"

Everyone turned to look at him.

"What do you mean?" Sofia asked.

"I mean, the magic I just used pushed a memory into Rebecca's mind," Cillian said, gesturing to the girl. "What if, instead of drawing power from them, we push our own energy into them, to protect them?"

A stunned silence followed his words. Several children looked around in obvious confusion, clearly not understanding what was being discussed.

"You mean like," Rebecca said slowly, "you will make me shift like you do?" A wide grin spread across her face. "Oh my

God, that would be amazing! Can you make *me* into a unicorn? Or what about—"

"I don't know if it works like that," Cillian said quickly, his ears turning red. "The only thing I sent to your mind were memories, right? But...what if I serve as a kind of conduit between one Guardian and the next, feeding magic into you? We've already seen that identical forms of magic can call to one another." He waved his hand between Amanda and Rebecca.

Amanda's thoughts were spinning. Cillian's idea was far-fetched and dangerous, but could he be right? Guardian magic was very unlike Adept magic; it was a living thing that grew between people, connecting them like the long-buried roots of a tree.

And if Cillian was correct, if he had indeed shared memories with Rebecca, then what else could he share with her? With all of them?

"He has Xiomara," Sofia reminded them. "He won't stop until he's seized control of the access point. He'll destroy the city if we don't stop him. We don't have time to get these kids away safely. And Rebecca is right—what if we fail? Hans will just kidnap them again."

"We won't fail," said a voice at the door.

Everyone turned to face the newcomer. Amanda lifted her hands, summoning a Block spell on instinct.

"Whoa, whoa!" The woman raised her arms to shield her face. "It's me, Quimby!"

Amanda relaxed, finally recognizing her colleague.

"I'm sorry," Quimby said quickly, adjusting the glasses on her nose. "I just, it always sounds so epic when people say that in superhero movies and stuff. I've always wanted to make a dramatic entrance." She broke off with a nervous chuckle.

"Quimby Cain in the flesh!" Seo-joon crowed, lunging forward to embrace the tall, slender woman. She giggled as

Seo-joon spun her in a circle. When they broke apart, Quimby glanced around, her face lighting up when she saw Pierce. "Oh, yay! Pierce is here, too!"

By then, the tension in the atmosphere had dissipated. Amanda drew closer to Quimby and took her hands—the only sign of physical affection she was comfortable with at the moment. "Quimby, how did you get here so fast? Did you portal?" Ordinarily, the TCO would contact her first about connecting a portal.

"I got your message." Quimby's brow furrowed. "It was on the emergency pager, so it sounded urgent. And with the TCO in a panic about this Rome incident, I—"

"What Rome incident?" Sofia demanded.

"Don't worry, Jayne is fine," Amanda reassured her. "There was a massive flood caused by the Kingdom. Ruger is managing the situation." She turned back to Quimby. "How did you get here?"

"Oh, that." Quimby laughed like Amanda had just told a hilarious joke. "I used my brother's private jet."

Several pairs of eyes blinked at her, uncomprehending.

"My brother?" Quimby said, her smile faltering. "Lionel?"

Sofia blanched. "Your brother is Lionel Cain? The tech mogul turned senator?"

Seo-joon laughed. "You guys didn't know that? Jeez, do you live under a rock?"

"I don't think it's called living under a rock," Quimby said, linking her arm with Sofia's. "She's got bigger fish to fry. Right?"

Sofia nodded. "You could say that."

Amanda wasn't thrilled at the idea of mingling mortal politics with Adept magic. Hopefully, Quimby hadn't told her brother the true nature of her work with the CIA.

She marveled at Quimby's eager expression, her obvious joy at being included in this mission despite the dangers and the impossible magic surrounding her. She was clearly not afraid. Amanda had said it before: Quimby was a grown woman who could make her own decisions—and if she decided to join them, Amanda would not stop her.

Her gaze shifted to Rebecca, and something clicked in her mind. These were children, yes. But they could still make their own decisions. They'd been dragged into this situation against their will. It was too late to undo that. They were in this fight now, just like Amanda and her team.

As much as she wanted to shelter them, to hide them from harm, to ensure she was the only one risking her life here...she couldn't make that choice for them.

Chatter had broken out among the crowd that filled the tiny house. Several children were muttering excitedly about the private jet Quimby had used. Rebecca was talking with Cillian about the different animals she would want to shift into.

Amanda steeled herself. When she cleared her throat, the room quieted. Goddess, she loved that power. She missed having the authority to silence an entire room. It was the little things, really.

"If any of you wish to stay and work with us," Amanda said, "I will allow it." Before cheers could break out, she quickly added, "But there are protocols that must be followed. I can't allow unaccompanied minors to roam wild without alerting their guardians. I won't be seen as an accessory to kidnapping." Her harsh tone left no room for negotiation. "I will be contacting all of your parents and ensuring they consent to you staying here. If they demand it, I *will* send you home in a heartbeat. Is that understood?"

Several faces fell, and Amanda had no doubt most of the parents of these children would insist they be sent home.

"Will you let us speak with them?" Rebecca asked. Several

other children nodded in agreement, and it was clear that Rebecca was becoming the ringleader of this group of kids.

"Yes," Amanda replied.

"Good. Because they will let us fight," Rebecca said at once. When Amanda didn't respond, she went on, "My parents might not understand the magic in me, but they understand its power. They've kept me safe, and sheltered, but now it's time for me to use this power to help you stop Hans."

Amanda couldn't help the pride that bubbled up. Her girl was brave. Strong. She thought of Peters, her colleague from years ago. He had given up everything. He and his wife had risked their own lives to keep Rebecca safe, to be parents in Amanda's stead. They took every precaution, and clearly, they'd done a stellar job raising her.

Amanda wasn't sure which she wanted more: for Peters to demand Rebecca's immediate return, or for him to give his blessing for Rebecca to fight alongside them.

"Your father—your birth father—would be proud of you," Amanda said, her voice almost a whisper. She wasn't sure what possessed her to say it, but the feeling of Karam's presence was so intense that it couldn't be ignored. *Oh, Karam. If you could see her now.*

Rebecca's eyes moistened, and she blinked fiercely, averting her gaze and rubbing her nose.

"Quimby," Seo-joon said loudly, obviously trying to defuse the tension, "tell us what toys you brought."

"Yes," Cillian said, jumping on the subject change. "Do you have any kind of magic dampener? Have you been able to develop anything from what La Liberté and the Kingdom used?"

Quimby's eyes lit up. "Of course! I brought a bunch of samples." She dug through her bag, and the clinking of glass indicated she had several jars stashed inside. "You know, since I wasn't sure what exactly you needed, I just brought a smorgasbord. With the emergency pager, I couldn't exactly be like, 'Hey, what kind of dangerous and possibly illegal weapons do you want me to bring?' because that's not exactly the kind of message we want people to intercept, right?"

Seo-joon snorted, and Amanda refrained from heaving a sigh, forgetting how chatty Quimby could be. But several of the children giggled, watching Quimby with starry eyes and bouncing on the balls of their feet.

Quimby beamed at their reaction, and Amanda knew they were in good hands.

"Seo-joon, I need you to collect names, addresses, and phone numbers," Amanda said, snapping back into battle mode. "Any information the children can provide. Make contact with their families as soon as you can. I'll need you to escort the children through a portal and ensure their safe departure. Only those whose parents demand them home, that is. Once they're safe, work with Quimby and ascertain what tech she's brought and how we can use it against Hans."

Amanda turned to Sofia, who straightened, her blue eyes fierce and glowing. She was every bit a lioness, as Amanda was. Karam would've liked her, too. "Sofia, Cillian, you'll be with me. We'll head off Hans. If it's a fight he wants, that's what he'll get."

FORTY
THE VATICAN MUSEUM

Rome

Jayne and Tristan spent the next few days canvassing the Vatican Museum, taking copious notes and making a solid plan to infiltrate and access the Latin Bible. Jayne had immediately put in a request to access the archives, and their TCO connections helped expedite the process, labeling their request as urgent and classified—a double whammy.

Ruger told them there were rumors of Kingdom operatives combing Rome for them, that Ruth Thorne was in hiding, but nothing materialized. It all felt...too easy.

While they waited, Jayne studiously avoided talking about The Incident between them, and Tristan followed her lead. They were cordial and stiff around one another. No longer friends. Not even enemies. Just very reluctant allies.

Jayne preferred being his enemy. She loved to hate Tristan. But that love-hate relationship was exactly what had led to their kiss.

Nope, Jayne thought. *Shut it down. Don't think about it. It didn't happen.*

When the museum sent its approval of Jayne's application, she and Tristan set their plan into motion.

This would work. It had to. Vivienne was waiting for them. And once they'd set her free from the grimoire in which she'd been imprisoned, Jayne would sever ties with Tristan. She had to locate her father. The mission had been put off for long enough. Henry Thorne was way more important than some fleeting notion of angsty make-out sessions with Tristan. The urgency of her nightmares was proof of that. Her father was in trouble, and he needed her. Sofia was counting on her, too. God, Jayne missed her. It had been too dangerous to make contact, between Gina's interrogation and Ruth's unexpected visit. And with Sofia, Jayne didn't trust herself to be careful enough not to give something away.

Besides, hearing her sister's voice would break her, especially after what she'd done. *Find Dad? Oh, right. Yeah, I've kind of been doing that. But really, I've just been flirting with Tristan. You know how it is.*

The guilt nearly consumed Jayne, and she strengthened her resolve. She would end her bargain with Tristan and find her father. This would be over soon.

"You have the spell ready?" Tristan asked as he donned his jacket. He wore fake glasses, just like Jayne. With his long hair slicked back, he looked like a very hot professor. Or maybe one of those delicious grad students that you secretly hoped would take charge of the lecture just so you could stare at him a bit longer.

Shaking her head to rid herself of those traitorous thoughts, Jayne nodded. "Of course." She grabbed her scarf, completing the studious curator look she was going for. After checking her hair to ensure her no-nonsense bun was in place, she turned and faced Tristan, only to find him staring, his eyes stirring with emotion.

Jayne kept her expression blank as she raised her eyebrows. "Shall we?"

Tristan cleared his throat and dropped his gaze. He pulled open the door and held it for her. Together, they left the hotel suite for possibly the last time.

Good riddance, Jayne thought bitterly, but she couldn't stop the ache of longing in her gut as she left the room.

When they exited the building, they both subtly gathered Cloaking spells around themselves, just to be safe. Kingdom operatives could still be lurking nearby, and Jayne shuddered to think of where Beast-Ruth was hiding right now. Would she find her way back to Rome? Or was she still stuck in London after the blow Jayne had dealt her?

They conjured a portal that took them to a narrow street, out of sight from witnesses, but close enough to the library for them to approach easily. When they reached the main street, Jayne's eyes were drawn to the area that Ruth had flooded mere days ago. The roads were still full of debris from the flood, but most of the public had returned in full force, clearly undeterred. It wasn't as crowded as a normal tourist day, but there were still enough people to make Jayne a bit nervous about their mission.

Before long, Jayne and Tristan stood in front of the towering fortress of the Vatican Museum. It was a bit...underwhelming, if Jayne was being honest. It looked more like a defense base in the middle of a medieval war than a series of impressive museums with the most glorious art known to man contained inside. The wall stretched on and on, and the buildings across the street were unassuming and plain. Trucks and vendor stands littered the small plaza as merchants advertised their wares. At the entrance, the words MVSEI VATICANI were etched above an archway, adorned with a sculpture of what looked like cherubs. The only indication of the magnificent art contained inside.

It almost seemed like a ruse; a guise to protect the treasures inside. Disguise the area with something ugly and unassuming to protect the true prize.

But Jayne was no fool.

She strode up to the entrance with Tristan and explained in flawless Italian that they had been invited to view the archives of the Vatican Museum. After showing their papers to the official, he waved them through.

They both remained silent as they entered, which seemed fitting. This was the climax of their mission. They both needed to focus. But when Tristan's hand brushed against hers as he handed her the ticket, a jolt of electricity buzzed underneath her skin.

Okay, maybe it wasn't just because she was trying to focus. Maybe she was just trying too hard not to think about how his hands would feel around her body or how warm his lips might feel against hers.

Now is not the time, Jayne, she chided herself. She looked away from Tristan and followed the crowd through the ornate archway and down the massive spiral staircase. Jayne rested her hand along the intricately crafted iron railing, her breath catching in her throat at the sheer grandeur of it all.

This would never get old. A dangerous and deadly grimoire was located in one of the most beautiful places in the world. The irony was not lost on her.

For a while, they trailed the crowd, glancing around the museum as if they were ordinary tourists. Jayne didn't have to pretend to admire the sculptures and artwork, craning her neck to drink it all in. The domed ceiling, the vast spaces painted from floor to ceiling with vibrant colors. Centuries of beauty preserved right here in this building. Her eyes followed the span of each painting, its canvas stretched along the wall as it told its own story. God, the sheer craft and detail put into it... She couldn't fathom it at all.

"I could come here again and again," Tristan murmured in her ear. "So magnificent."

Her blood heated as his breath tickled her ear. She cleared her throat and managed an idle "Is that so?"

Even though she didn't look at him, she could feel his smirk, as if he knew exactly how his proximity affected her.

When they entered a large room with pillars and barriers lining the edge of the walls to protect the art from grubby fingerprints, Jayne's eyes latched onto the hallways in front of her. Bingo.

"It's clobbering time," she muttered before striding forward.

Tristan caught her arm, forcing her to meet his gaze. "Be careful."

She nodded, ready to turn away. But if something happened to him, and she'd been this cold, distant bitch the whole time, she'd never forgive herself. Lowering her cold mask, she unleashed all the affection she'd been holding back these past two days. She took his hand and squeezed it. "You, too."

Surprise and admiration gleamed in his eyes, but Jayne didn't linger to revel in it. Before she did something she regretted, she turned from him and strode purposefully toward the narrow hallways. Tristan said something loudly in his ridiculous American accent, distracting the masses while Jayne made her escape. She fought back a smile. It had been fun to pretend to be obnoxious tourists with him.

But the time for pretending was over.

Jayne's steps were firm and purposeful, her head held high as she carried herself with the air of someone who belonged there.

It didn't take long for someone to stop her, though.

"Signorina, posso aiutarla?"

Jayne froze and turned to find a portly middle-aged man wearing a uniform, his thick bushy eyebrows lowered in suspicion.

She flashed a grin before withdrawing the papers she'd printed. She spoke in her perfect Italian, and the guard looked totally shocked. "Yes, my application was approved. I'm here to access the archives."

The man's frown deepened as he inspected her papers.

"I've been given explicit permission," Jayne went on brightly. "I'm the curator at Vanderbilt. Do you know where that is? It's in Nashville. Have you ever been there before? Lovely place. Highly recommend it."

"Signorina," the man said weakly, handing the papers back to her. His face was getting red.

"Do I need to call my superiors?" Jayne asked, plastering a look of innocence on her face. "I'm sure they could smooth things over. They don't speak Italian, unfortunately, so you'd have to do your best with American English. I could translate." She forced an airy laugh. With every passing minute, the poor Italian looked more and more uncomfortable.

Finally, he acquiesced. *"Aspettare qui, per favore."*

He shuffled off, and Jayne heaved a sigh. She didn't want to use magic on the poor man, but she would have if necessary. After he rounded the corner, Jayne hurried off in the opposite direction, following the map ingrained in her brain from her endless research of the place. The halls became narrower and winding, lined by shut doors with keypads on the handles. This area was definitely off-limits to the public, which meant Jayne was in the right place.

"Alrighty, time for the handy dandy Tracking spell," she whispered. With a deep breath, she reached for the Torrent and found the spell she and Tristan had crafted earlier that day. A Tracking spell layered with a Locator spell, plus a dash of the Memory spell they'd used on Gina Labelle for good measure. Jayne carefully gathered the spell into her hands and then summoned her trusty bow staff. It appeared in her hand, fitting perfectly against her palm. She ran her fingers along the smooth wood and already felt comforted by its presence, as if it had been crafted just for her.

"Hello there, friend," Jayne said quietly. In one hand, she held the staff. In the other, she held the spell. "Now, don't mess this up." She held her breath as she brought the two together.

A crackle of electricity split the air, and Jayne drew in a sharp breath as the bow staff hummed in her palm, quivering against her flesh. The staff absorbed the spell and began to glow green from the force of it. In an instant, the Torrent vanished, leaving Jayne panting in the narrow hallway with her staff.

Well done, said a voice.

Jayne jumped, even though she'd been expecting it. Behind her floated a tendril of Tristan's magic. Though Jayne knew she would be fine without it, he'd insisted, just in case things went poorly. And she couldn't deny that the presence of another Adept watching her back, even if it was just a ghost of his magic, was a comfort to her.

"Um, thanks, disembodied Tristan-fog," Jayne said, uncertain if he could hear her. A chuckle rumbled in her mind, and she gathered that yes, he could indeed hear her. A smile twitched along her mouth as she gripped her staff in both hands, following the reverberation of its magic leading her forward.

She paused often, waiting for the spell to guide her. It was so different from just conjuring the spell in midair and letting it float in front of her as she'd done at the Château de Chantilly. She couldn't believe how clueless she'd been back then. Yes, she'd known power before, but, as begrudging as she felt about it, Tristan had shown her some important nuances in the crafting of spells. And she felt she'd only scratched the surface. There was so much more to discover, and her skin tingled with the prospect of accessing more of her powers.

Jayne's staff pressed into the carpeted floor, the thump resonating down the hallway. The rhythm of her footsteps and the *thunk* of her staff made her blood sing with awareness. Magic flowed into her hand from the staff, and it was warm and unfamiliar all at once. Tendrils of energy prickled along her bones, steadying her nerves. She felt as one with the staff. As one with the spell. She no longer felt like the Master magician in charge of the magic; they were both in charge. Equal partners. Jayne followed the magic, and the magic followed her.

In this moment, she was Gandalf the Grey, wielding magic like a badass wizard with an ancient, powerful staff. The thought brought a smile to her face, and she spun the staff so quickly the breeze blew back the tendrils of hair that were escaping her bun.

After rounding another corner, Jayne felt it in her chest—a seizing tug, like the pull of a cord. She stopped short, facing a set of double doors with a keypad, just like all the others. Jayne summoned an Unlock spell and pressed it against the handle. Her eyes closed, and she felt the mechanisms inside click just before the door popped open.

"Thank you," Jayne whispered to the powers that be before she moved inside.

Careful, Tristan warned, his wispy magic trailing behind her.

"Stop nagging me," Jayne muttered as lights clicked on, no doubt motion-sensored. She heaved a deep breath, eyes roving over the shelves and locked safes. These were the archives she hadn't been able to see online. It wasn't like she could Google: *What does the inside of the deepest, darkest archives in the Vatican Museum look like?*

She would have to rely on her magic to guide her to the right place. Just like in Chantilly.

Jayne ran her hands along the bow stuff, trusting in the magic flowing through the smooth wood. *Show me,* she urged it.

Not a command. She wasn't in control of the magic. They were working together as equal forces.

The staff quivered in her grip, easing her forward like the tug of a leash from an eager puppy. Jayne followed the pull, edging around the vaults against the walls, her eyes scanning the archives for...something resonating with power. She searched within herself, waiting for the grimoire to call to her. She would know it when she saw it.

The staff halted halfway into the room, and Jayne turned and faced the biggest safe of them all, a towering gray fortress of steel. Yes, this was it. This was what housed the precious fourth-century Greek Bible.

Jayne summoned the Unlock spell again but faltered. The staff was trembling more intensely in her hands.

Something was wrong.

A crack of electricity split the air, and Jayne dropped to the ground by instinct as heat singed the top of her hair. Her bow staff buzzed with energy, and she twirled it in her hands before slamming it forward. But, unfortunately, it was imbued only with the Tracking spells. Not Attack spells.

Even so, a force of energy rippled in the air, ejecting from the staff and swirling toward the attacker, who blocked it effortlessly.

As she drew closer, Jayne's heart stuttered in fear.

"A pitiful attempt, I must admit," said Gina Labelle, her stormy eyes cold and full of fury. "To be honest, I expected more from you." She gestured to the safe in front of Jayne. "Now, be a good girl and unlock that door. There's a grimoire in there that belongs to me."

FORTY-ONE

FANCY SEEING YOU AGAIN, OLD FOE

Be cool, Jayne.

Tristan's words soothed Jayne's fear and allowed her to fix a dubious look on Gina Labelle. "What gave you the impression this is *your* grimoire? From what I've heard, you didn't get along with it that well before."

Gina remained unfazed, looking at Jayne with that air of superiority that infuriated her so. "Don't pretend you understand me or my past, girl. This is beyond—"

"Okay, I'm gonna stop you right there." Jayne lifted a hand, her rage boiling. "Quit calling me *girl*. We are both grown-ass women here."

Gina only scowled at her.

"Oh, and another thing," Jayne added with a smile. "Shut up."

Jayne dropped to the floor, covering her head with her arms. All she heard was Gina's startled yelp before Tristan's glowing magical orb assaulted her. Cautiously, Jayne peered up at the chaos from the safety of her arms. It was rather amusing, really. Gina was swatting at the misty fog that floated in front of her face like a swarm of bees.

Any minute now, she thought, feeling like an idiot crouching on the floor.

The fireworks entered. Light exploded in the air. Heat stung Jayne's arms.

And Tristan was there. Jayne wasn't sure how she knew, but her magic seemed to leap with excitement as he joined the fray. Gina grunted, then shrieked as Tristan attacked, shoving her backward.

When the exploding lights subsided, Jayne was on her feet, her mind racing as she scanned the safe that refused to unlock.

"Come on, I'm a Master magician and a librarian," she muttered to herself. "I should be able to get into this."

She reached for the Torrent and found the lingering remains of their layered Tracking spell. Focusing on Gina's memory of the grimoire, Jayne grabbed the spell and carefully pressed it against the safe's door. It didn't matter if casting a raw layer of spells would draw attention or not. The enemy was already here.

And if it managed to lure Ruth Thorne from her hiding spot, well, maybe she and Gina would just kill each other off. Problem solved.

The metal door hummed under Jayne's fingertips. She urged her magic forward, focusing on the thoughts and images that had swept over her from other grimoires.

I know you, she whispered in her mind. *I've seen your kind before. Open for me. Show me your truth.*

The lock clicked, and the humming died. Heart hammering, Jayne swung open the safe, her eyes fixed on the grimoire contained within.

She had but a moment to drink it all in—the collection of withered pages, stained with age, that familiar smell of vellum and ancient ink and parchment—before the grimoire moved. As if it had sprouted legs.

The book shifted forward, sliding out of the safe. Jayne yelped and staggered away from it as if it were a cockroach. Which was stupid, really. She was here for the very purpose of taking the grimoire. Why would she jerk away from it?

But it truly did seem to be alive. A strange orange glow emanated from its pages, and Jayne could've sworn she heard a voice echoing from within.

Shouts sounded behind her, and Jayne whirled to find half a dozen men and women flooding the archives, rallying to Gina's aid.

La Liberté. Not good. Tristan couldn't fight them all off on his own.

But what the hell was this grimoire even doing? Was this good or bad? Was it about to open for Jayne, or self-destruct and blow up the museum?

The voice from the grimoire magnified, and Jayne's bones rattled from the intensity of it. Her forehead warmed with Medb's awareness, and her blood seemed to thrum with anticipation.

Go ahead, psycho grimoire, she thought, assuming a fighting stance. *Do your worst.*

She was ready. And so was Medb.

But before the grimoire could try anything—and before Jayne registered how stupid it felt preparing to attack a *book*—La Liberté rushed Tristan, who was too busy battling Gina to notice.

Jayne swore and sprinted into the fray, deflecting a spell before it could hit Tristan's skull. Light flashed in the air as they exchanged blows. She alternated between Attack and Block spells and old-fashioned roundhouse kicks and punches. She loved the look of pure shock on their faces when she used a nonmagic move. Priceless.

Something heavy pounded on the locked door of the

archives. Jayne and her assailant froze, momentarily startled by this interruption. Only then did Jayne remember that she was in a secure vault, surrounded by baddies, in a museum.

Did she really think the officials on site wouldn't notice? Regardless of how cloaked the Adepts were, they couldn't stop people from coming in here.

A scream split the air, and Jayne's skin crawled, her eardrums throbbing. Her wide eyes fixed on the grimoire, which shuddered and shifted along the ground. Dear God, someone was screaming from *inside*.

"Vivienne!" Tristan shouted, dodging a blow from Gina and ducking past her to sprint toward the grimoire. But one of Gina's cronies intercepted him, swinging his fist so it slammed into his jaw.

Jayne reached for Tristan but before she could help, the screaming burned so loudly in her ears that Medb's Earth magic began to buzz and quiver.

Heal, Medb urged. *She is in pain. Heal her!*

Oh. *Oh.* Jayne finally put the pieces together. Perhaps Vivienne was trying to get out, but she couldn't because she was injured.

"Say no more," Jayne whispered, ramming her shoulder into the nearest goon and stomping on his instep for good measure. While he keeled over, howling in pain, Jayne lunged for the grimoire—just as Gina Labelle did the same. Jayne clutched one end of the binding while Gina tugged at the other. All of Jayne's librarian instincts screamed at her to protect the book, protect the pages... But she had to keep it out of Gina's hands. Even if it tore the vellum in half.

"Give it to me!" Gina roared, her face red and blotchy with manic fury.

"Do you even care that your daughter is trapped inside?" Jayne cried. "Let me help her! She could be dying!"

"She was already dead to me when she succumbed to its power," Gina snarled. "She got what she deserved for being so weak."

A fresh wave of anger rolled off Jayne, sending a spark of unexpected clarity in her mind. She released the grimoire.

Gina, caught off guard, stumbled backward from the force of her tugging. She crashed into the metal safe behind her with a sickening *thud*. The glowing book fell from her hands and dropped to the floor.

Jayne darted forward and pressed her hands to the book's surface. It was so hot it almost scalded her flesh, but she held fast and summoned the Heal spell. Darkness crept into the corners of her mind, threatening to take over. The magic from inside the grimoire was too powerful. It roiled off her like steam, scorching her skin and melting her bones. God, it was so damn hot! Jayne felt like she was burning from the inside out.

"Heal!" she commanded, drawing on the Torrent and Medb's power for an extra boost. Sweat pooled down her brow and neck, soaking her shirt. Heat seared against her skin, and she gritted her teeth. *Hold on,* she urged, pushing the magic forward. *Just a little longer.*

The scream faded before vanishing completely. The glow diminished until the grimoire was nothing more than an ancient text lying innocently on the floor.

Behind her, the brawl continued. Tristan grunted in pain, and Jayne feared he was seconds away from being beaten.

Or killed.

She couldn't let that happen.

Her bow staff was on the other side of Gina's unconscious form. She snatched it up, spinning it for momentum before slamming the flat end into the floor with a furious shout. The ground trembled, and magic speared forward. It was only the

Tracking spell, but it was powerful, and Gina's henchmen teetered on their feet, looking around in alarm.

Jayne called a Sleep spell and infused it into the staff, then shouted, "Tristan, jump!"

He didn't hesitate. Just before she slammed the staff into the floor again, Tristan leaped to his feet, nimbly grabbing hold of the shelves and perching atop them like a ninja. Blood trickled down his temple, and his shirt was torn and bleeding on his shoulder. But if he was agile enough to do *that*, then Jayne knew he was fine. He'd probably even brag about it later.

Unawares, the last remaining attackers were caught up in her Sleep spell as it shimmered in the air, rising from the floor until it seeped into the feet of the unsuspecting goons. She watched as it climbed from feet to legs and torso, their forms drooping one limb at a time until they fell over, snoring loudly.

Jayne laughed. "Never get tired of that. Pun intended."

"How is it you always have time for puns?" Tristan asked, hopping down from the shelves.

"It's never a good fight without puns."

His eyes were on the grimoire. "Did you…"

"I don't know." Jayne eyed it warily, waiting for it to start trembling and screaming again.

More fierce pounding on the door. Damn. They had to escape before the museum locked down.

"Can you get us out of here?" Tristan asked, glancing at the door.

"In a jiff." Jayne scooped the grimoire into her arms, marveling that it was now cool to the touch, and took Tristan's hand. Though his palms were slick with sweat, the warmth of his fingers twined in hers was a comfort. He was alive. He was okay.

Jayne thrust the grimoire into his free hand, then used her fingers to trace an oval in the air. She pictured the abandoned pizza shop where they'd interrogated Gina. Not the best location, but it would give them a bit of time and privacy.

A crash echoed from the door, and the frame bent from the force of it.

A golden white light burned against Jayne's eyes as the portal shimmered into view, revealing the familiar musty shop. Despite the grimy atmosphere, Jayne felt relieved to see it, as if it were home sweet home.

"Bombs away," Jayne said, and she and Tristan leaped into the portal just as the door to the archives burst open.

FORTY-TWO

Patagonia

S ofia strode alongside Amanda, Cillian leading the way in his wolf form as he sniffed out Hans. Though Sofia and Amanda could probably locate him with their Guardian magic, there was so much saturating the air, between the anti-Guardians and the children, that they were worried they'd get their signals crossed.

It had taken half an hour of careful and precise magic for Sofia and Amanda to craft the spell they would need to share magic with the kids, or Guardianitos, as Sofia had started to call them. The spell required even more complexity because it was something no one had done before—using a Rogue as a vessel for transferring power to other Adepts.

So much uncharted territory here. A mere month ago, Sofia hadn't even known Guardians existed. Now, that very same power thrummed in her veins, and she was willing to lay her life on the line for children she met only hours ago.

But she didn't regret any of it. Not a single thing.

As they rounded a corner, and Sofia's nerves jangled so intensely she couldn't breathe, she whispered, "Cillian?"

His voice was a low rumble in her mind. "Yes?"

"If this goes badly, I just want you to know, I've grown really fond of you. You're the best first partner I ever could've asked for."

Sofia felt Amanda's curious glance her way but kept her own gaze firmly fixed ahead, her cheeks burning with embarrassment. But she had to tell Cillian what he meant to her. She'd always regret it if she didn't.

"And I just want you to know," Cillian said softly, "that I don't regret what happened between Jayne and me. It only gave me more time to spend with you."

Now Sofia's face was on fire, and she was deeply grateful that Amanda couldn't hear Cillian's voice when he was in this form. Her heart thrummed painfully in her chest, no longer consumed by fear but something else. Something warmer that she hadn't dared to experience in ages.

Could she feel this way again? She had always been a shameless flirt, looking for the next tattooed hunk to wrap her arms around.

But she had never allowed herself a serious attachment. Mostly because of Jayne. But also because of her own fears. Living on the run didn't give a lot of time for relationships. And the secrets the Thorne women harbored could get an innocent man killed.

This is stupid, Sofia chided herself. She'd been watching too many romance movies, where in the heat of an action-packed moment, the hero seizes the heroine and kisses her passionately.

Yeah, that wouldn't really work with the wolf trotting in front of her.

Instead, Sofia forced away her nerves and said, "Thank you. That means a lot to me."

Again, she felt Amanda's eyes on her and dutifully ignored it. Amanda had never been one to pry; she always respected Sofia's privacy, for which Sofia was grateful.

"We're close," came Cillian's voice. His wolf head was bent low, nose to the ground as he sniffed out their foe. Sofia whispered his words to Amanda.

"Remember the plan," Amanda hissed, next to Sofia, who nodded.

Conjure the spell. Send it to Cillian. Stop Hans.

Ruger and Seo-joon would extract Xiomara as soon as possible. All but three of the Guardian children had been safely returned to their homes. Those who remained were with Quimby, their third line of defense. She'd prepared some rather wicked technology that Sofia found whimsical and over-the-top—perfect for the situation. It would be a distraction Hans would never forget.

"He's in that alley," Cillian said, his voice in her head barely above a whisper. They had turned on a narrow side street, and just ahead was an alley tucked between two buildings and shrouded in the darkening shadows.

Sofia frowned. "He's in that alley? No way can he fit all his goons in there."

"Trap," Amanda said simply. "But that's exactly why we're here. We're the bait."

Sofia swallowed hard and nodded. She'd known this, but it didn't stifle the panic rising in her chest. She and Amanda possessed Guardian magic, so they were the only things standing in Hans's way.

Amanda conjured a Cloaking spell and shrouded it over the three of them. The sensation of ice-cold fingers crept down Sofia's spine, and she shuddered. For good measure, she reached into the Torrent and found the spell Ruger and Amanda had crafted, waiting along the green river of stars. It was shaped like a sphere with a halo around it and a checkered pattern layered over it.

They called it the Projection spell. God, she hoped it worked.

"He knows we're here," Amanda murmured.

Sure enough, Sofia's gold magic ignited inside her, sensing the power of another Guardian nearby. Her chin lifted, and she confidently approached the alley, rallying her magic inside her.

At first, all she saw was darkness. As her eyes adjusted, she made out two figures: Hans and Xiomara. The former held the latter in a chokehold with a dagger pressed to her throat.

Sofia's heart seized, but she forced her expression to remain calm. Undeterred. "Still hiding behind others, I see," she said with a scoff.

Hans only smirked. "It's kept me alive, hasn't it?"

"For now. But soon, you'll run out of bodies to cower behind." She sensed Cillian and Amanda behind her. Cillian let out a low growl that seemed to rumble along the ground.

Hans tightened his grip on the knife, and Xiomara tensed. A bead of blood dripped down her neck. "Take one step closer, and I'll slit her throat."

Rage pounded through Sofia's veins, blotting out all her fear. "No, you won't. Because another Guardian will be called in her place. Is that really what you want? Another obstacle standing in your way?"

Beside her, she felt Amanda tense. This wasn't part of the plan.

But Sofia didn't care. Hans was a bastard. A coward. And she knew down to her bones that he was bluffing.

And if she could keep him preoccupied while Ruger and Seo-joon got in position, this might go in their favor.

"Are you so sure about that?" Hans hissed, his eyes narrowing. "Are you willing to bet her life on it?"

Sofia's eyes snapped to Xiomara's as if a magnet drew her gaze. The older woman held no fear in her face, her dark eyes pinned to Sofia and widening slightly with emphasis.

Yes, the woman seemed to say. *Bet my life on it.*

Sofia wasn't sure if Xiomara actually knew Hans wouldn't kill her, or if she was angling to be a martyr. Either way, it was all the encouragement Sofia needed.

"You know what I think?" Sofia asked, adopting the casual air that Jayne often used in conversation.

Hans frowned, clearly put off by her tone. He cocked his head, the weapon in his hand lowering just a fraction.

"I think—" Sofia lunged mid-sentence, a trick she'd gotten from an action flick. Bad guys never expected you to attack before finishing your sentence. She crouched low, pressing her fist to the ground as she summoned an Attack spell. The magic rippled in the concrete, sending heat flaring through her knuckles. Behind her, Amanda moved, her hands weaving an intricate spell that she launched toward Hans.

Hans shouted, lifting his blade to Xiomara's throat once more. But Amanda's spell flew toward his face, and he seemed to realize it would strike him whether Xiomara stood in front of him or not. He shoved her away from him just before dropping to the ground to avoid getting hit.

His mistake.

Sofia's Attack spell cracked through the asphalt like roots from a tree, bursting forth and colliding with his jaw.

"Now, Amanda!" Sofia cried, sprinting toward Hans and wrapping him in a headlock, pinning him to the ground with her knee pressed into his spine.

Amanda grabbed Xiomara, who was leaning against the concrete wall. A long gash spread along her neck, oozing blood.

Shit. It seemed Hans had cut her after all. It didn't look fatal, but for a woman her age, it still looked bad.

Amanda's face paled at the sight, but she didn't falter. She pressed her palm to the wall, and a glowing gold circle appeared, spreading wider and wider until a portal formed. On the other side stood Ruger. Amanda gently eased Xiomara forward, and Ruger caught her in his arms.

"The others aren't here," Amanda said in a rushed tone. "Find them."

Ruger nodded once, and Amanda closed the portal.

Unease prickled along Sofia's arms as she realized what Amanda had already noticed. Where were Hans's followers?

This wasn't a trap; it was a distraction to lure Amanda and Sofia. But lure them away from what?

Beneath her, Hans made a pathetic choking nose, but Sofia only tightened her grip around his throat. "Where are your minions, Hans?"

More choking noises. But wait... No, this sound was different.

He was laughing.

Sofia loosened her grip, and he said hoarsely, "You're too late. The city is mine now."

CHAPTER
FORTY-THREE
WE COULD BE HEROES

A s soon as Hans uttered those foreboding words, Cillian
felt the air thrum around him, whipping along his fur
and making his hackles rise.

Something was definitely happening. A wave of dread
washed over him as he glanced around, a low warning growl
rumbling from his throat.

He locked eyes with Sofia. Her face paled, but her voice was
firm and commanding as she said, "Cillian. Griffin."

In a flash, he shifted, his body elongating. Talons formed at
his paws, and giant wings extended from his sides. He threw
back his head and roared as Sofia raced toward him, leaping on
him as if she'd been training all her life to ride a griffin.

Cillian felt her weight atop his back, and it was a
comforting strength. Her magic surrounded him like a veil,
shrouding them both in power and crackling energy.

"You remember where the access point is?" Sofia asked,
leaning close to his ear.

Sure do, Cillian thought to her. *Better buckle up, lass.*

Sofia chuckled, clinging to his fur and mane as he took off to
the sky. The cool clouds of dusk surrounded them, forming a

misty vapor that chilled Cillian's fur and made Sofia shiver. The colorful buildings below them resembled a kaleidoscope of blocky shapes glinting in the fading light of the setting sun.

Even if Cillian hadn't known what direction the access point was, he could see it from here. A shimmering gold energy emanated from a singular spot within the city, the glow intensifying like a beacon. Though Cillian didn't know much about this Guardian stuff, he knew that *wasn't* supposed to happen.

Sofia's grip on him tightened as she noticed it, too. Cillian dived, plunging toward the magic. The wind whipped at his body, and with each flap of his wings, he felt the tension in the air growing.

When he landed, every muscle was tight with a throbbing pain, his body screaming that this was wrong, he was wrong, everything here was wrong. He shook, nausea roiling inside him. A bright light momentarily blinded him, and he realized he'd shifted to his human form, arms trembling as he sank on all fours. A cold sweat broke out on his forehead.

"S-Sofia," he moaned, his teeth chattering.

Her cool fingertips traced along his cheeks and jaw, her blue eyes wide with concern. "I'm here. I know it's painful. But I still need you to do your part. It's not over yet, Cillian. Be strong." She paused. "For me." Her cheeks turned pink as she said it, and Cillian sensed the deeper meaning behind her words.

He'd meant what he said earlier—that he didn't regret parting with Jayne anymore. Because Sofia was so much more than he'd expected. She filled a part of him he hadn't known was empty. A part Jayne hadn't been able to fill—not completely. It was their bond as Master and Rogue—but it was more, too.

Cillian nodded slowly, staggering to his feet, pain rippling along his body in sickening waves. "You can count on me," he said. His voice was strained, but at least it didn't quiver.

Sofia offered a tiny smile, the worry deepening in her eyes.

Cillian bent over and kissed her gently on the cheek. He heard her soft gasp as he withdrew and met her gaze. Shock and uncertainty—and something else; something warm and heady and intoxicating—filled her gaze.

He held her eyes for a moment longer before returning to the problem at hand. "The spell?" he prompted, groaning slightly.

Her cheeks flushed, and she cleared her throat, ducking her head and closing her eyes. A prickle of magic filled the air as she accessed the Torrent, and then her hands glowed green. She stretched forward, and Cillian laced his fingers through hers, his body jolting from the impact of the spell. His blood hummed and sang with energy, his bones rattling as the spell coursed through him. Hot electricity sizzled through his skin and flesh. It made him momentarily forget the pain of being so close to the access point, although this type of pain wasn't exactly pleasant, either.

When the magic completely filled him, Cillian exhaled and tried to relax. But an unfamiliar presence thrummed inside him, like he wore a second skin.

Or a second soul.

He shifted, feeling itchy all over as he adjusted to this strange new feeling.

"Cillian?" Sofia whispered.

"I'm good. Let's craic on, shall we?" He met her gaze. God, those blue eyes were like gemstones gleaming up at him. He couldn't look away. His hand curved against her cheek of its own accord, like he didn't have control over it anymore. His fingers captured a lock of her blonde hair, twisting it around twice before he tucked it behind her ear.

"Be safe," she murmured.

"You too." A knot formed in his throat, but he forced himself to turn away—because if he didn't do it now, then he would never be able to leave her. With a heavy exhale, he strode purposefully down the alley.

He wasn't going far—just around the corner really. But even so, he would be fully separated from Sofia. Unable to help her if she was in peril. It was as good as being thousands of miles away.

Cillian darted past two rows of buildings before circling back and hurrying down the alley they had marked during their plans. Sure enough, there was Seo-joon waiting with the three Guardian children, all of them facing the wall. On the other side of the concrete was the access point.

They would be protecting it from this side.

When they'd canvassed the area before, the alley had appeared completely ordinary; nothing but dirty concrete. But now, the wall glistened with faint gold and green sparkles that Cillian might have missed if he hadn't been looking for it.

No longer held in check by a Guardian, the Torrent's magic was spreading. If it had already bled through the wall, then there was no telling how far it would go before it was stopped.

And on the other side of the wall was Sofia, prepared to face the might of this energy all on her own.

"I've already warded the area," Seo-joon said. "I need to go help Quimby. Are you good?"

Cillian nodded automatically, clapping Seo-joon on the shoulder. "Good luck, mate."

With a grin, Seo-joon ducked around the corner and disappeared down the street.

"Ready, team?" Cillian asked the children, forcing an air of excitement into his voice. As if they were pretending to be superheroes instead of facing mortal peril.

Rebecca met his gaze head-on, no sign of fear in her face. In this moment, she looked like a grown woman, aged with wisdom and hardened by battle.

She looked just like her mother. Different face, but that ferocity was exactly the same. Just as fiery as her red hair.

Cillian smiled at her. The two children behind her—a tall, lanky boy named Trent and a petite brunette named Willow—looked at him with terror in their little faces. They were both smaller and younger than Rebecca, so it was no wonder they were afraid. Cillian crouched on one knee so they were at eye level.

"Listen," he said softly. "I'm here with you. Do I look weak to you?"

All three of them shook their heads.

"I will protect you," Cillian vowed. "We're good at our jobs. You aren't alone. Got it?"

Once more, the children nodded. Trent looked a bit more relaxed, but Willow still looked petrified.

Cillian focused on her and tapped his temple. "It's all in here. Remember?"

Willow swallowed audibly. "Will it hurt?"

To be honest, Cillian didn't know. The spell had never been tested before. He didn't want to lie to her. So instead, he took her tiny hand in his and squeezed it. "If it does hurt, you pinch me as hard as you can so I'll know. Okay?"

"Okay."

Cillian couldn't help feeling nervous. As much as he wanted to appear strong and capable in front of these kids, this was frighteningly new territory for him. He'd heard stories of Adepts accidentally burning up and setting themselves on fire because they dabbled in powerful magic. What if he did the same thing?

The magic coiling in his chest suddenly tightened, cutting off his breath. His throat closed as he choked, desperate for air.

When the magic loosened, he turned to the wall. It was now completely encompassed in a brilliant gold glow.

It was time.

"Rebecca?" Cillian turned to face her. She met his gaze with fierce determination. "You're up first."

Rebecca drew closer and took a deep, shuddering breath, the only sign that she harbored any uncertainty about all this. But her face remained composed, and that fire never left her eyes.

Cillian admired her for it. God, if he had half this girl's bravery, there wouldn't be any problems.

Drawing strength from her—this ten-year-old girl, of all people—Cillian closed his eyes and brought his fingers to her temples. He searched inside himself for that familiar shape—the sphere with the halo and the pattern layered over it—and brought it forward, allowing a few drops of it to trickle into Rebecca's mind.

Rebecca's body jerked, and Cillian tensed, worried he'd given her too much. Then, her breathing slowed, and her frame relaxed slightly. A faint hum whispered in the air, and Cillian recognized it from when he'd accidentally sent her the memory of his first shift. At the time, he hadn't noticed the change in the air, but now that he was focused on it, it buzzed merrily like tiny insects chirping a welcoming song.

A sudden blast of gold power exploded from within Cillian's chest, and he cried out as the magic flowed through him. It felt like a powerful waterfall had torn a hole through his body and was now gushing into Rebecca.

He couldn't turn it off. The force of it was too intense. Too much.

Cillian groaned, hunching over as he tried to stifle the flow of power. *Easy,* he told himself. *Easy now.* He focused on his controlled breathing, his arms straining from the effort. Gradually, a new sensation overcame him, this one cooler and steadier, like a gentle river instead of a chaotic waterfall.

The flow of Guardian magic calmed, tapering off into a thinner and more direct stream of magic. In front of him, Rebecca's body relaxed once more, her muscles no longer straining.

When it was finished and the well of magic had dried up, Cillian released her. She looked at him, and flecks of gold sparkled in her eyes. She raised her hands, and a scorching energy pulsed from her palms as if she held the power of the sun in her fingertips.

It had worked. Rebecca now possessed a fraction of Amanda and Sofia's Guardian magic.

With a relieved exhale, Cillian turned to face Trent and performed the spell again.

FORTY-FOUR

VESTA AND VIVIENNE

Rome

When Jayne and Tristan tumbled through the portal, they weren't alone. Jayne felt it as soon as she landed. There was someone else with them.

In a flash, she was on her feet, facing the intruder, fists raised. She expected it to be Gina or someone else from La Liberté who had hitched a ride through their portal.

But when she saw who it was—a woman with waist-length brown curls and chocolate-brown eyes that were unsettlingly familiar—Jayne froze.

"Vivienne?" Tristan breathed, stepping forward, his face bone-white and full of disbelief.

But Vivienne was staring at Jayne. "You must help." Like Tristan, her voice was lightly accented. And familiar.

This was definitely the screaming woman from Jayne's dream.

"Help with...what?" Jayne asked. "You're here, aren't you? Mission accomplished."

Vivienne looked at her as if she'd sprouted a second head. "No, help Vesta!" She darted forward, and before Jayne realized what she was doing, Vivienne snatched the grimoire in her hands and flipped it open.

"Don't!" Jayne cried, hurrying forward.

But it was too late. A roar filled the shop, and the walls shuddered. But Vivienne held tightly to the book, shooting a pleading look toward Jayne. "Heal her!" she shouted over the roaring. "Please! You're the only one who can."

Jayne's blood ran cold as realization set in. When Medb had ordered her to heal the tortured soul inside the grimoire, she hadn't been referring to Vivienne.

She'd been referring to someone else. Vesta. The Fire Goddess.

Seek the Keeper of Flames, the sibylline texts had told her. *Seek the Goddess.*

"She's dying!" Vivienne screamed. "Do something!"

"I don't know anything about this magic," Jayne protested. In Vivienne's hands, the grimoire started to tremble.

"She is my mentor," Vivienne said. "You have to save her. Without her, I'd be dead right now." Tears pricked her eyes, and her broken, pleading expression told Jayne she was being earnest.

"I believe her," Tristan said, nodding at Jayne. "I know you can do this."

"God help me," Jayne muttered before drawing closer. As soon as she pressed her hands to the grimoire, it went still, though the echo of the screams from within still resonated in the air.

"Heal," Jayne whispered. But as she sent her healing magic, she felt a piece was missing. Like she was missing a limb, or maybe just a finger, something small that could easily be overlooked.

Your magic is not complete, Medb's voice said.

"What the hell does that mean?" Jayne snapped, ignoring the odd looks from Tristan and Vivienne. "I've healed just fine before now."

"But you have never healed a goddess."

"Um, right," Jayne stammered. "This is way above my pay grade."

"It's all right," Vivienne said softly, placing her hand on top of Jayne's. "I will help."

Jayne looked at her doubtfully, but the other woman's eyes were filled with certainty and confidence.

Jayne huffed a breath. "All right. Well, let's heal this goddess-magician-grimoire thingy." She cast a quick glance around their surroundings. "And Tristan, if we die, please make up some story about how we died in an epic battle instead of in this nasty asbestos-filled dump, will you?"

"Not a chance," Tristan said without missing a beat. "If you die, I'm going to say it was in a pizza shop."

Jayne rolled her eyes. "Fine. Not the worst way to go." She closed her eyes and drew her magic forward, focusing on Vivienne's energy in front of her. It smelled vaguely familiar, and Jayne knew that was because she'd sensed it during the Memory spell when they'd interrogated Gina.

God, Vivienne was really here with them. Jayne couldn't believe it.

But she could process that another time. Right now, a goddess was dying inside this grimoire.

"Heal," Jayne said again, and something in her chest jerked forward like she was on a roller coaster. Vivienne's fingers went tense as if she experienced the same sensation. The grimoire quivered under their grasp, and light spilled from its pages, blinding and all-consuming.

A figure formed next to them, shining and glowing like an angel. Except, no wings. Jayne had to admit she was a little disappointed. She'd always wanted to see a real-life angel.

When the light faded, a familiar woman with white hair piled atop her head in a delicate knot stood before them. She looked just like the woman from Jayne's dream. She wore a gold toga and her bronze skin gleamed with power. Her emerald-green eyes fixed on Jayne and then shifted to Vivienne.

"*Ma fille!*" the goddess crooned, rushing forward and crushing Vivienne in a tight embrace. Vivienne returned the hug, clinging tightly as tears streamed down her face.

Jayne only gaped at them. *My daughter.* That was what this goddess—Vesta—had called her. Beside her, Tristan stared with equal bewilderment.

"Does someone want to explain what the hell's going on?" Jayne demanded, placing her hands on her hips.

"One moment," Vesta said, raising a finger. Her voice was heavily accented, but it wasn't French—it was Italian. "Once I restore her power, all will be explained." She pressed a hand to Vivienne's chest, and white light engulfed them both.

Once again, Jayne felt something tug her from the inside, and this time, she couldn't resist its pull. It dragged her forward until she stood right next to the two women. The Torrent's green glow filled her mind, and the white light intensified until it burned against Jayne's eyes.

She'd felt this before. Why did it feel so familiar?

An intense feline smell filled her nose, and then Vivienne no longer stood next to her. Instead, a lioness prowled the length of the room, yawning widely. Jayne felt the pull in her chest intensify, like a rope bound her and Vivienne together.

"Ah, that's much better," came Vivienne's voice in Jayne's ear.

Jayne's mind raced. She could *hear* Vivienne's voice in her ear. Even though she was a lioness. The only other time she'd been able to understand a Rogue like that was...

With Cillian.

Rogue and Master.

Holy *shit*.

"*Putain*," Tristan swore, covering his forehead with his hand. He looked like he was about to faint, his eyes shifting from Jayne to Vivienne and back again.

Reality slammed into Jayne's chest with all the force of a raging bull. She staggered back a step, her head a riot of emotions and thoughts. She turned to Vesta for an explanation, but the goddess was only smirking as if she were enjoying Jayne's reaction.

"I—she—Rogue?" Jayne sputtered.

"Yes," Vesta said, hands clasped in front of her with the air of a queen bestowing a generous blessing on her subjects. "You are her Master. And Vivienne is your Rogue. Your bond is now complete."

FORTY-FIVE

SHOWDOWN

Patagonia

Sofia wasn't entirely surprised to find all of Hans's followers flocked at the entrance to the Torrent access point.

What she wasn't expecting, however, was the Torrent's energy to bleed out, spreading along the street and buildings like a poison. The anti-Guardians were stationed three feet away from the access point, and Sofia knew the wards were keeping them away from it. Their magic had done its job. For now.

So why was the magic so volatile right now? What had the anti-Guardians done if they hadn't even been able to come within three feet of the pocket?

The woman in front, tall and skeletal, turned to leer at Sofia. "You're too late. The deed is done."

"What deed?" Sofia snapped. Perhaps these fools were cocky enough to share their plan. She had to learn as much as she could about this. Even as her thoughts whirled a mile a minute, the gold energy seeped further down the road. It wouldn't take long before it swallowed the entire city.

"We've waited years for this moment," the woman scoffed, her expression smug. "You think we didn't have other ways of infiltrating the access point? Our spells have become more complex and powerful. Nothing can stop us now."

Perhaps this arrogant woman was right. But Sofia had to try. Her Guardian magic had healing properties; she'd learned that from Amanda. And if their plan worked, then the Guardian children would have this same power, too. Together, they could heal the access point.

But first, she had to get rid of these goons in front of her.

Quimby had something sinister in mind with her tech, but Sofia had to get the enemies in position first. She drew closer to them, and they tightened their formation, blocking off the access point.

"Do you really want to fight me?" Sofia challenged, raising one hand and summoning gold light flashing along her fingertips.

The woman in front didn't even blink. "Is that supposed to intimidate us? We've been training with our magic for years. Your puny efforts mean nothing to us. We know you only just discovered your powers."

"Maybe so. But did you know I have a Rogue? And he can shift into any form I will him to."

The woman's eyes flickered with unease. "You're lying. We saw your Rogue, and he's nothing impressive."

"This one has bonded to a Master magician."

The woman scoffed. "Lies. There are no more Masters."

Sofia smiled and leaned closer. "You're wrong. Because you're looking right at one."

The anti-Guardians shifted uncertainly, and the woman's face paled.

Taking advantage of their stunned silence, Sofia struck. She waved her hand, summoning gold sparks to light the air in front of them, then dropped to the ground, sweeping her legs under the woman's to knock her to the ground. When the woman struggled to rise, Sofia struck her in the temple, then the jaw, rendering her unconscious.

The other goons rose to her defense, storming toward Sofia with rage in their eyes. But she was ready for them. Just as she'd practiced in training, she summoned a Shield spell and wove it around herself, creating a protective barrier.

As soon as the anti-Guardians drew nearer, Quimby's attack plan unfolded.

An eerie red mist filled the alley, plunging them into a dense fog. Hans's cronies shouted in alarm as they tried to reach each other to no avail. Music blared through the narrow street, reverberating off the concrete and stinging Sofia's ears. She laughed when she recognized the song: Guns N' Roses's "Welcome to the Jungle." The song grew louder with each beat.

The anti-Guardians were screaming now, trying to drown out the music, but it was incessant. Safe inside her bubble Shield, Sofia could barely stifle her laughter.

Quimby Cain was too much. And Sofia liked her all the more for it.

Electricity crackled in the alley, and Sofia focused all her energy on keeping her Shield spell upright. Green lights danced in the air, and the screams turned into pure terror as Quimby's shockers took them out one at a time. Earlier, Sofia and Amanda had filled Quimby's tiny drones with as much magic as they could, creating small attack pods that could zap a person unconscious with one strike.

And that wasn't all. Quimby had, indeed, been working on a serum to drain an Adept's magic. It wasn't permanent, but it would render their enemies powerless for the time being. This same serum was infused in the attack pods.

Soon, these anti-Guardians wouldn't be able to access their magic at all, even if they *could* wake up from the electric shock.

Genius, really. It was a good thing Quimby was on their side, otherwise she'd be downright terrifying. Hilarious, but terrifying.

When the anti-Guardians' screaming subsided, the red fog dispersed, indicating the all clear from Quimby.

Sofia waved her hands, dismantling the Shield spell, and sent a silent prayer of thanks to her team. With a deep breath, she plunged forward, stepping over the unconscious figures in front of her before she reached the wards protecting the access point. The ground beneath her feet was now a shimmering gold as it continued to spread, and the air felt thinner, as if she couldn't breathe.

Something was definitely wrong. Whatever the anti-Guardians had done must have poisoned the Torrent's magic somehow.

Sofia had to fix it.

"Come on, Cillian," she urged, hoping he'd done his part. "I can't do this next bit without you."

With terror rising in her chest, she pressed her hands against the invisible wards and summoned her Guardian magic. The barrier flared, and heat prickled her palms. Gradually, the wards faded and vanished entirely, allowing Sofia through. Immediately, a blast of heat hit her in the face like she'd stepped into a boiler room. Her face burned and sweat poured down her forehead and neck. She peeled her sweaty hair off her face and drew closer, trying to ignore the stifling heat swelling around her. God, the access point felt like it was on fire.

"How do I heal you?" Sofia whispered. She raised her hands, which still glowed gold, and tried to bring them closer to the warbling wall of energy. But something zapped her skin on contact, repelling her backward. Whatever had poisoned the magic was too intense for Sofia to touch.

Okay, she thought, her head spinning as she contemplated her options. Remembering another spell she'd used earlier, she pressed her fingertips into the hot ground in front of her. Pebbles pricked her skin, but she pressed deeper, trying to infuse her magic into the very earth. She took a shuddering breath and urged her healing magic forward, under the ground and past the wall to reach the access point from underneath. Resistance met her magic, and she strained against it, gritting her teeth.

Come on. She pushed harder, her head throbbing and her skin burning. The magic inched forward, sluggish and hesitant. It felt like wading upstream against a fierce current. Fatigue clung to her bones, draining her. She couldn't keep this up for much longer.

The sudden feeling of a dam being burst swept over her, and her magic flowed freely now. Sofia gasped, inhaling deeply. Whatever had blocked the path was removed, and her healing magic poured into the access point.

She smelled it, then. Sage and moss and something distinctly Cillian. The spell had worked. The children were helping to heal the access point. With a laugh of surprise and relief, Sofia sent more magic through the ground, reveling in the ease with which it flowed. Sweat soaked her shirt, and her back ached from hunching over for so long, but she kept it up. Around her, the air cooled slightly, and the gold threads receded back into the alley.

It was working. They were healing the magic.

"You think you're so clever, don't you?" hissed a voice.

Sofia froze, keeping her hands pressed to the ground. The pocket just needed a little more magic. Slowly, carefully, she turned her head and found the woman, the anti-Guardian she had knocked out. A trickle of blood oozed from her split lip, and she stared daggers at Sofia.

Stay calm, Sofia told herself. *Keep her distracted. The magic has almost run its course.*

"It's not just me," Sofia said calmly. "I have a pretty talented team."

"You have no idea what greater forces are at play here," the woman sneered. "I pity you. One day, you'll wake up and realize you should have listened to us."

Sofia snorted. "Maybe. But for now, I've chosen my side."

"You chose wrong."

The woman lunged, and Sofia stuck out her leg, connecting with the woman's shins. But with Sofia's hands busy, she was at a severe disadvantage. The woman tripped but righted herself, wrapping her hands around Sofia's throat. Sofia gagged, her chest and lungs straining. Her arms itched to rise, to shove the woman off her, but if she did, the spell would be disconnected and the poison would take hold again. She had to keep going, to keep holding on...

Her throat burned, and darkness crept into her vision. With what little strength she had left, she tilted her head back and slammed her forehead against the woman's. It wasn't very forceful, given that Sofia was weak and didn't have much space for a proper headbutt, but it did the job. The woman staggered back, clutching her head in her hands.

Monumentally grateful that Hans hadn't properly trained his followers to fight, Sofia kicked again, her foot landing in the woman's gut.

A sharp silence fell in the alley, and the heat vanished

entirely, leaving a cool breeze in its place. Sofia stilled, her heart racing in alarm and panic. What had happened? What did this mean? The air was so quiet she hadn't realized how loud the humming of the Torrent's magic had been.

The woman moaned in agony, pounding her fists against the ground. And then Sofia realized: the healing spell had worked. The humming in the air hadn't been the Torrent; it had been the poison.

A relieved smile broke across her face. She was so distracted by her success that she didn't see the woman's strike until something heavy and metal connected with Sofia's skull.

Sofia tumbled, her vision darkening, pain splitting through her mercilessly. A dark fog crept over her mind, blurring her thoughts. She just wanted to sleep. To put this pain behind her. Distantly, she heard a woman's voice as footsteps drew nearer.

This anti-Guardian would kill her. But Sofia couldn't move. She tried to rise, but her mind felt disconnected from her body, like she was watching from afar.

"...one less Guardian scum to worry about," the woman was saying, her voice becoming clearer. "Hans will thank me."

Sofia stretched out her arms, struggling to rise as the sensation in her limbs slowly returned. But she was too late. The woman raised the metal bar again, and one more hit could shatter Sofia's skull.

No! Sofia thought.

The woman grunted and then crumpled, her body falling to the ground in a heap. Blood pooled from her forehead. Blinking blearily, Sofia glanced up to find an enraged Amanda wielding a spell along her fingers. A bloody cut ran across her chin, and her shirt was ripped at the collar.

"I'm so sick of these bastards," Amanda growled, extending a hand to help Sofia up. Without thinking, Sofia clutched her in a tight embrace, breathing heavily. She couldn't stop the tears from pouring down her face. God, she'd been so close to dying. And she hadn't been able to do a damn thing to stop it.

"It's all right," Amanda said, awkwardly patting Sofia's shoulder.

"Sorry," Sofia said thickly, withdrawing and wiping her nose. "Just...the emotions catching up with me."

Amanda offered a smile that softened her harsh features significantly. She looked years younger. "Did it work?" She glanced at the glowing access point, which had reduced to a large circle in the wall. Exactly as it was before Hans and his people intervened.

"Yes." Sofia grinned. "It's healed. And Hans?"

Amanda's expression soured. "He had another man lurking nearby. I didn't see him coming. I fought him off, but Hans got away."

Damn. But Sofia shook her head. "Xiomara...?" Fear laced Sofia's chest. If something had happened to the woman...

"She's with Seo-joon. She's alive."

"Thank God." Sofia deflated, all the exhaustion from the fight now settling into her bones. She felt she could sleep for a whole week.

"Let's get you healed and cleaned up," Amanda said, rubbing her shoulder in such a motherly manner that it made Sofia's eyes grow hot once more.

"Cillian... the kids..." Sofia couldn't form a coherent sentence.

"All well and accounted for. We'll be tending to them, ensuring they aren't suffering any lingering effects from the spell. They were amazing."

Sofia nodded. Everyone was safe. The mission was over. She felt so drained that she'd be happy if she went another three years without facing another fight like that.

But, of course, with her line of work, she would never get that lucky.

And, as Sofia thought about it, she realized, surprisingly, that she was just fine with that.

FORTY-SIX

BETRAYED

Exhausted from the ordeal with Hans and the Guardian children, Amanda rubbed her forehead as she returned to the safe house. She was planning on staying at Xiomara's house for a bit longer, to ensure the woman was properly recovered, but she needed to grab a few items first. She had to debrief Joshua and the director, who would not be happy with the damage inflicted from this mission. No doubt he was already in a foul mood because of the incident in Rome.

Amanda was about to insert her key into the turquoise-painted front door when a prickle of energy made her falter. She froze, her magical senses awakening. Frowning, she lifted a hand, and a tiny jolt of electricity rippled along her skin.

Wards. The building was warded. But she hadn't put these up; someone else had.

With a whispered incantation, Amanda waved her hand, bringing the wards down. The air shifted with the change. On the other side of the door, she heard someone speaking. It sounded like Pierce. But his voice kept rising in volume, shouting words Amanda had never heard him speak before.

This sounded nothing like the cheerful, mild-mannered

assistant she was accustomed to.

Amanda reached for the Torrent and grabbed an Extender spell before pressing it against her ears. A thin film coated her eardrums, muffling her surroundings. But when she pressed her ear to the door, she could hear Pierce's voice as if he stood right next to her.

"I'm telling you, there's nothing I can do," Pierce was saying. "It's out of my hands now. The mission is finished." A pause. Then, "I can't do that! I'd be found out immediately. My position here is too precarious, and you know that." More silence. Pierce swore loudly. "You are asking me to risk my life and my livelihood for this. This isn't my fight; it's yours. I have to protect myself." A sharp gasp. "Are you threatening me? You wouldn't have gotten this far without me, I assure you."

Amanda's blood ran cold as the pieces clicked together. It was Pierce. Pierce was the mole inside the TCO. The mole who had been feeding information to their enemies.

And he knew about Rebecca. He knew about the Guardians.

He knew *everything*.

Horrified, Amanda staggered back, her mind whirling as she struggled to formulate a plan. Her mouth was dry, but she knew one thing: she couldn't be caught lurking by the door. She had no idea who else might be inside there or what magical defenses Pierce might have up his sleeve. Someone powerful had set up brand-new wards, and Amanda didn't want to face this on her own.

Footsteps echoed from within the house. Without another thought, Amanda turned and dashed down the street before Pierce found her out. She needed to make sure the children were safe. Then she needed to get back to Langley. She needed to tell the director what she'd learned.

They would trap Pierce together, and the director would see once and for all how vital the TCO was to the CIA.

FORTY-SEVEN

UNWANTED BOND

Rome

"Master and Rogue?" Jayne repeated, dumbfounded. "You must be joking. I don't even know this girl! I should at least buy her a drink first, right?" She gestured wildly to Vivienne, who shifted back into human form with a flash of bright light. Her bewildered expression matched Jayne's.

Vesta, however, looked on with a calm and almost bemused expression. Not for the first time, Jayne got the feeling goddesses enjoyed delivering shocking news. Tristan kept running his hands through his hair, muttering in rapid-fire French.

"The bond between you two is strong," Vesta said. "There is no denying it. You were destined for this, Jayne Thorne. As were you, Vivienne Lowell."

Jayne shook her head, raising her palms. "Look, I didn't sign up for this, okay? The last Rogue I worked with, well, let's just say we mixed business with pleasure and it didn't end well. I'm not messing with that again."

Vivienne wrinkled her nose, looking Jayne over with unveiled disgust.

"Hey." Jayne straightened, offended. "If I swung that way, I'd be a catch. Believe me. Don't look so revolted. You could do a lot worse."

Vivienne sighed, dropping her hands on her thighs. "Can anything be done about this?"

Vesta's smile only grew. "Why would you fight such a powerful bond? You two will do great things together."

"Because I don't know her!" Jayne said.

"Because I don't want this," Vivienne said at the same time.

"See?" Jayne gestured to Vivienne. "The feeling is mutual. We'd like a divorce from this bond, please."

"It doesn't work that way," Vesta said. "You remember what happened when you tried to force a bond that was not there." She leveled a hard look at Vivienne, who ducked her head.

"That wasn't her fault," Tristan said, rising to her defense.

"Tristan, don't." Vivienne lifted a hand. "I might have been young, but I could have refused. I made the decision, just like *Maman* did." She shook her head. "I don't trust her." She narrowed her eyes at Jayne in suspicion. "But I do trust *you*, Vesta." Her expression softened as she looked upon her mentor.

"What happens if we just go our separate ways?" Jayne asked. "I mean, we aren't joined at the hip or anything right?"

"The farther apart you are, the more your bond will call to you," Vesta said. "You can be apart, yes, but the strain on the shared magic will weaken you both the longer you are separated."

So Jayne was now bonded to this complete stranger? So much for her brilliant plan of going off to find her father.

"No," Jayne said, her resolve hardening. "I'm sorry, but I

have an important mission to do, and I can't stand here arguing about dragging around a new friend I'm bonded to for all eternity."

"Ah, yes," Vesta said, her ethereal eyes shifting to Jayne. "Your father, Henry Thorne."

Jayne stilled, her gaze darting to Vivienne and back to Vesta. "What do you know about him?" She didn't know how she felt about Vesta exposing her secrets to a perfect stranger, even if she was Tristan's sister. For God's sake, Tristan's own mother couldn't be trusted, so who knew how many other bad eggs were in the family?

Vesta smiled again, but it was softer this time. "You have healed me, and so, in exchange, I will give you the information you seek. But first, I must warn you." She drew closer, and the warmth of her power emanated from her golden skin. "The creature who roams free is powerful enough to destroy gods and goddesses like myself. It's how I was injured in the first place. Be wary, Jayne Thorne, for you are no match for this creature."

Jayne felt Tristan's eyes on her, and she looked at him in grim realization. "This creature," she said slowly. "Is it a former Master magician?"

Her stomach sank as Vesta nodded. "This Master has lived in the Torrent for a very long time, trapped by my own people many years ago. But it has since been unleashed, and its demonic essence only grows. Now that it is tethered to this world, no one is safe. Not you. Not even me."

A knot of apprehension formed in Jayne's throat. And her own mother was tied to this thing? So not good. "How can I stop it?"

"Only the power of the gods can send it back," Vesta said solemnly.

"Okay...so will you be doing that, or what?"

"I cannot. I am bound to this grimoire and cannot escape yet. Bound by a foul curse."

"Tell me how to break it."

"I cannot. That is part of the curse. You will have to discover how to free all of us. I am not the only one cursed this way. You have done well so far, but there is more for you to learn. Continue seeking the necromantic grimoires." Vesta gestured to the Codex Latinus resting on the floor. "Until you've discovered them all, my kind will never be free. It is up to you, Jayne Thorne."

"Me? Why? I'm not a goddess. I mean, I'm a badass and I'm pretty amazing, but—"

Vesta approached, and Jayne tensed, unsure of how she felt about this goddess standing close enough to kiss her forehead. But instead of kissing her, Vesta pressed her thumb into Jayne's forehead. A searing pain shot through her skull, and Jayne cried out, her skin on fire as Vesta's touch burned right through her flesh.

Just as suddenly, the pain vanished, and Vesta drew back a step with a satisfied nod. "The Fire totem is yours."

Jayne rubbed her forehead. "Another totem? Wow. Um, okay. Thanks? I think." She stared at Vesta. "So now I'm a fire goddess."

"Yes. And I've been waiting a long time for a soul worthy enough to bestow my mark upon."

Jayne's eyes cut to Vivienne, who watched with her arms crossed, her expression unreadable. "And what about your Rogue trainee? Why couldn't you give it to her?"

"That kind of power isn't compatible with my Rogue magic," Vivienne answered for her. Her cutting gaze told Jayne she was still sour about their forced bond.

Well, Jayne was, too.

"With the power of all the totems, you will wield the magic

of the gods," Vesta said. "Retrieve the others, and you can banish the Wraith to his own dimension and spare the world from his destruction. You are the master vessel foretold."

"Um, okay, but there's one problem: Ruth has the Water totem."

"Totems can be removed," Vesta said simply.

Jayne knew this; her mother had tried to tear the Earth totem from her by force. But it hadn't worked. So, how was Jayne supposed to do it? And Ruth could also shift into a hideous demon, which would complicate things just a bit.

God, Vesta sure was asking a lot of her.

"My time is almost at an end," Vesta said, gazing at the Latin Bible with sorrow in her eyes. "I can only be outside of the grimoire for so long. Before I leave, I must tell you the location of your father. He waits for you. He will help you retrieve the remaining totems. He is essential to your quest. You will find his Time Catch near the Jet d'Eau in Geneva, Switzerland."

"The fountain?" Jayne asked. "His Time Catch is in the middle of one of the largest fountains in the world?"

Vesta's form began to flicker. "Be well, Jayne Thorne."

"Wait!" Jayne stepped forward, but Vesta had already vanished. The grimoire glowed, the pages fluttering in an eerie wind before the book went perfectly still.

A stunned silence fell among them. Vesta's lingering presence left the air charged with electricity and energy that prickled along Jayne's skin.

Tristan moved, drawing closer to Vivienne until he clutched her in his arms, his eyes closing in relief. Her arms wrapped around him in turn, her face buried in his shoulder. *"Mon tout petit,"* he murmured, stroking her hair. "I'm so glad you're safe. You don't know what I went through to find you." When he withdrew, he asked, "What happened when you went in there?"

"It was similar to the Domdaniel," Vivienne explained, her eyes shining with unshed tears as she looked up at her brother. "There is another dimension in there, a home where Vesta dwells. That's where I've lived. She's been training me, teaching me how to harness my Rogue magic. I've learned far more than *Maman* ever taught me." Vivienne's gaze darkened slightly before her expression cleared. "Where is she? Did she help you find the grimoire?"

Tristan's face hardened, and he shot a look at Jayne before answering. "No. At least, not willingly."

"Let's just say we're not too fond of your *Maman*," Jayne said with a dark chuckle as she thought of the museum curators bursting into the archives and finding Gina and La Liberté standing there, guilty as hell. Sure, they had magic and could probably get out of the situation easily. But that didn't mean Jayne couldn't get a good laugh out of it.

Vivienne shot her a cold look that said, *This is none of your business,* but Jayne ignored it, inserting herself into the conversation.

"Look, I'm really glad you two are reunited," Jayne said. "But I need to leave. My dad could be in trouble." She turned to Vivienne, at a loss for words. It was clear this girl didn't like her, but what could she do? Assuming Vesta was telling the truth, they were now bonded. Forever.

Perhaps Jayne needed to extend an olive branch.

"You are welcome to come with me," she said softly. "It would be great to get to know you better. Or, if you'd prefer, I can come back and then we can get this whole Rogue-Master thing sorted out. Your choice." She offered a small smile, hoping Vivienne would soften.

Vivienne glanced at Tristan, and Jayne recognized that same impenetrable mask her brother wore so easily. It made her so hard to read. "I'd like to stay here and catch up with my brother," Vivienne said. When she looked back at Jayne, her expression seemed gentler. Much less hostile.

It was a start.

Jayne nodded once. "Okay. Good. Great. I hope you two have a good time. I'll come back to Rome once I've found my father." *Found my father.* God, would she really have Henry Thorne with her when she came back? The idea was so surreal she couldn't wrap her head around it. Suddenly, she was itching to get on a plane right this second and reunite with her dad. It had already been far too long.

Vivienne nodded. *"Bien."*

Jayne smiled again before striding to the door.

"Jayne!"

She turned and found Tristan approaching, running a hand along the back of his neck. Her stomach did an uncomfortable somersault inside her. *Stop that,* Jayne chided herself.

"I just wanted to say...," Tristan began, then stopped, his eyes conflicted. He wouldn't meet her gaze.

"Yes?" Jayne's heart drummed an erratic beat in her chest. She wasn't sure what she wanted him to say. Part of her wanted him to avoid talking about their kiss altogether; the other part wanted him to seize her and make out with her right this second.

Tristan dropped his hand, his eyes locking with hers. Jayne found herself pulled in by his gaze, drawing closer until they stood only a breath apart. *"Merci,"* he said softly.

Oh. She wasn't expecting that.

"For helping me find my sister," Tristan added. "I couldn't have done it without you."

Jayne forced a smile. "Right. Of course. I'm glad she's all right." She turned away again, then stopped. "I guess...I'll be seeing you when I come back? I can't imagine you'll want to leave her side." She tried not to sound too hopeful at the thought of seeing him again.

"You're right." Tristan flashed a grin that made her bones melt. "I'll be here. We will be waiting for you."

"Cool." Jayne strode out the door, not allowing herself to look back at the man who made her feel all sorts of confusing things.

CHAPTER

FORTY-EIGHT

PATERFAMILIAS

Geneva, Switzerland

Two days later, after sending a coded text message to Sofia indicating where she was headed, Jayne stepped off the train and stretched her stiff limbs, inhaling the crisp pine scent mingled with the chill of incoming snow. God, this place would certainly look beautiful encapsulated in white.

Jayne could have summoned a portal using Medb's magic to arrive faster. But she was still drained from healing the Fire Goddess. Not to mention she needed to be cautious; a portal would attract attention, and Henry Thorne had been hiding for years. She didn't want to spook him—or announce his location to their enemies.

So, public transit was the best option. Not that Jayne minded. It gave her plenty of time to read the Song of the Lioness series. Her books had felt abandoned over these past few weeks, and their judgment sank deep into Jayne's bones. She didn't waste a single second making up for lost time, diving into the realm of Tortall and following Alanna's journey to become a knight.

Thankfully, the Jet d'Eau was only a twenty-minute walk from the Gare de Genève. Not only did Jayne secretly want to drink in as much of Geneva as she could—it was her first visit, after all—but she wanted to scent whatever magic might linger in the air. If someone else had gotten to her father first, she would pick up their trail immediately. Tradecraft, as taught by Ruger, was becoming second nature to her.

Her blood thrummed with anticipation, her mind whirling with possibilities. She tried to think through every scenario, not wanting to get her hopes up and come crashing down. It was possible Henry Thorne was already dead—that someone, whether it be Ruth, La Liberté, or another dark baddie, had gotten to him first.

But Jayne had to know one way or another. She was tired of being in the dark. For years, she had believed her parents to be dead. She had wasted time and energy grieving over them when she hadn't even come close to the truth.

It was time for answers. Once and for all.

Jayne wasn't sure if Sofia would get the message in time. For both their protection, they'd kept communication at a bare minimum, leaving Jayne clueless as to her sister's mission or whereabouts. But deep in her chest, an ache had begun to build from the absence of her sister. They had never been apart this long before.

Whether Sofia could join her or not, Jayne felt it was imperative to include her in this. It was their father. Sofia deserved to be a part of it just as much as Jayne did.

Don't worry, sis, Jayne thought with a heavy sigh. *If you can't be here in the flesh, I'll bring him to you. We'll be reunited once more.*

Waves of doubt and unease spread through her. Xiomara's vague warning about Henry being altered didn't tell her much.

Would he be the same as she remembered him? Or had he been twisted into something vile and cruel, like Ruth?

Jayne shook the worries from her mind and focused on the scene around her. She crossed the Pont du Mont-Blanc, a wide bridge with bustling traffic and narrow sidewalks. A breeze whipped at her, and she rubbed her arms to ward off the chill. Across La Rade, she could make out the enormous fountain piercing upward into the sky. The water streamed effortlessly, gushing forth in a beautiful spike of power.

When her eyes first landed on the fountain, a hum of energy tickled her veins, making her blood warm. There was magic here. Powerful magic. Frowning, Jayne glanced around as if she might find an ominous figure in a dark cloak watching her. But of course, there was nothing that obvious.

The power churning in the air cut through the cold, warming Jayne down to her bones. She dropped her arms, suddenly feeling hot and overcrowded, as if the magic had saturated the air and she couldn't breathe properly. She started toward the pier, drawn to the beauty of that power. The Water totem would be of good use here, but for now, she used earth and fire to ground her and warm her from the chilly spray.

When Jayne stepped onto the slick pier, she recognized a familiar blonde figure gazing in wonder at the magnificent water display. Her heart lifted, her insides dancing with excitement as she rushed to Sofia. Her older sister turned just in time to catch her in a tight embrace. Jayne clung to her, relishing that familiar scent of raspberries that she'd missed so much. Sofia wrapped her arms around her, and they held each other for several moments, reconnecting from their time apart.

"You're okay?" Jayne asked when she withdrew, glancing over Sofia's form. She wore a white sweater and a pale blue scarf with matching blue leggings and white ankle boots. She looked like a vision, as usual, whereas Jayne had just thrown on a jean jacket over her black T-shirt along with simple jeans.

Sofia smiled broadly, and Jayne noticed a different air about her. A confidence she hadn't seen before. "I'm great. Xiomara's safe. The team is okay. Everything is fine."

Jayne frowned. "Xiomara's safe? Was she not before?"

Sofia sighed and shook her head. "There's so much to tell. But first, let's track down our father."

Jayne nodded, looping her arm through Sofia's as they walked the pier to the fountain. Jayne cast an Umbrella spell and the water spilled away, keeping their heads dry "So, do you feel it?"

"The magic here?" Sofia asked. "Yeah. It must be the pocket."

"Like what the Guardians protect?"

"Exactly."

"But if there's a Guardian here, where is he?"

"It is—was—Hans Kaufmann. And he no longer serves as a Guardian. Xiomara says Dad came here to protect it somehow, even though he's not bound to this portal but to the one in Patagonia. Apparently, when a portal is in need or under attack, it can be defended by a Guardian who has its best interests at heart."

"Come again?"

"Yeah, it's complicated. Dad has some intense wards in place that even Hans can't get past. Hans has given up on seizing control of this area and is instead moving on to the others. We thwarted him in Patagonia, but it's only a matter of time before he tries again."

Jayne's chest tightened in anxiety at the thought of everything Sofia had endured and learned without her. It felt like they were leading separate lives.

"And you?" Sofia asked. "Are you all right?" Her blue eyes

roved over Jayne with concern and apprehension, and Jayne knew her sister felt the same fears.

"All good. I healed the Fire Goddess and bonded with Tristan's sister, who is a Rogue."

Sofia's head reared back, her expression filling with alarm. "What?"

Jayne laughed. "Like you said, there's lots to tell."

When they stood on the edge of the pier, as close to the Jet d'Eau as they could get without being washed away by the intense stream of water, they paused, gazing at the fountain.

"So, are we supposed to swim?" Sofia asked uncertainly. "I think that would draw too much attention."

"I can cast a Tracking spell, but it might be difficult without something connected to Dad. I barely knew him when he was alive. I mean, when he was *here*."

"Oh! Maybe this will help." Sofia fished in her purse and withdrew a small leather-bound journal.

Jayne gasped and clutched the journal in her hands, nostalgia washing over her. Embossed on the cover were the words *Entreaties and Proverbs*. As she pressed the book to her chest, a tendril of energy spiked through her, making her bones quiver.

Yes, this book possessed magic. And it was all she needed.

Closing her eyes, she reached for the Torrent and found the Tracking spell. Instead of layering it with another, she withdrew it as a simple one-dimensional spell, before pressing it into the journal. The book trembled in her grasp, a current flowing from her to its pages and back again. Electricity danced over her skin like fire.

Some innate instinct told her Sofia needed to be part of this, too. "Your hand," Jayne instructed.

Sofia pressed her hand to the journal, and the energy intensified, buzzing in the air and filling Jayne's soul with light. A beam of gold thread appeared on the ground in front of them, linked to the journal in their hands. Jayne followed it with her eyes, tracking its movement as it weaved along the pier until it disappeared into the depths of the lake.

Sofia and Jayne followed the thread, peering over the edge of the pier and into the water below. Jayne was stripping off her jean jacket before she knew what was happening.

"Jayne," Sofia said in alarm.

"The Time Catch is down there," Jayne said breathlessly, kicking off her sandals. "I'm sure of it. Are you coming or not?"

Sofia glanced over her shoulder, and Jayne cast a Cloaking spell over them. If they were quick, the onlookers would hear a splash and that was it. They'd be none the wiser.

With a groan, Sofia took off her scarf. She pulled a Water-proofing spell around the journal, shoved it back into her purse, which she tucked under her scarf, then kicked off her boots before standing alongside Jayne at the pier's edge.

"You jump, I jump, Jack," Jayne said with a grin.

Hand in hand, they dove over the edge and plunged into the icy depths. The brisk water chilled Jayne to the bone, and she wiggled her arms and legs to warm them up. The gold thread lit their way in the dark waters, and Jayne ensured Sofia was next to her before she dived deeper. From her research, Jayne knew the lake was extremely deep and they wouldn't be able to reach the bottom in one breath. As they followed the thread, her lungs straining, she wondered if, impossibly, the magic expected them to keep going. When she was just about to swim back to the surface for a gulp of air, she found a shimmering gold portal etched into the side of the pier.

Jayne swam through it without a second thought.

A burst of air filled her lungs, and Jayne gasped as she climbed out of the water. Her soaked clothes clung to her, and she shivered, the cool air closing in on her like a tight fist made of ice. A small splash behind her indicated Sofia had followed her in. Jayne did her best to wring out the water from her clothes as she looked around.

They stood in a large laboratory. Shelves and filing cabinets lined the walls, along with tables and several chairs. Stacks of papers, vials, test tubes, and microscopes rested on the tables.

On the opposite wall was a large, transparent film, a rippling stretch of liquid that reminded Jayne so much of the aether in her dream that she had to suppress a shudder. But instead of screaming souls trapped inside, she could just make out a building on the other side. She squinted, trying to discern its distorted features. It was swirled and curvy, like a slab of granite that had been bent into the shape of a wave. After a moment, Jayne was able to place it: the Kryptos sculpture, from the courtyard of CIA headquarters.

But what was it doing here?

Beside her, Sofia inhaled a soft gasp. Jayne followed her gaze. At the table farthest from them, hunched over a notepad and scribbling furiously, stood a man Jayne remembered only from the darkest recesses of her memories. Their father.

At the sound of Sofia's gasp, the man looked up, removing his eyeglasses to squint at them. His hair was still the same dark mass of curls, though much grayer than Jayne remembered. The wrinkles on his face were more pronounced, but there was such wisdom in those brown eyes. She remembered that clearly.

"Dad?" Jayne whispered.

Henry Thorne stood up straighter, his mouth falling open and his eyes widening with shock. In seconds, he'd scooted around the table and hurried over to them, his tall and wiry form knocking against furniture in the process. He scooped them both into side hugs, kissing the tops of their heads and holding them tightly.

"My girls," he murmured, his voice hoarse as if he hadn't

used it in years. "Oh, my darling girls. I knew you would find me."

Tears streamed down Sofia's face, and Jayne felt her own eyes growing hot. But she had far too many questions to focus on the sweet sorrow of this reunion. "Dad," she said again, gently pushing him back to look him over. He looked skinny, like he hadn't been eating properly. And if he was hiding away in this Time Catch performing science experiments for God knows how long, then he probably hadn't. "What are you doing here? What is all this?" She gestured to the lab at large.

Henry cleared his throat, then crossed and uncrossed his arms. After a moment, he said, "I don't know where to begin. I've dreamed of this moment, and now I'm speechless." There was a nervous edge to his voice.

"How about starting with why you're here, in Geneva, instead of Patagonia."

"Oh. Well. It's complicated."

"Right. And the lab?"

"That's less complicated. I'm searching for a new path into the Torrent."

Jayne took a step back. "What? Why?"

"But the access points—" Sofia said, but Henry shook his head.

"The access points aren't enough. They aren't strong enough for what I need."

"And what do you need?" Jayne asked, her heart sinking with dread. She had a bad feeling about what he was about to tell them.

Henry inspected her as if considering whether he should be forthcoming or not. When she fixed her most fearsome scowl on him, he relented.

"The Torrent is a living, breathing entity," he explained, motioning with his hands to illustrate rippling waves. "You know this already, I'm sure. It called to you the first time you accessed it, Jayne. It doesn't call to many. For those of us who aren't careful, we can get sucked inside it."

"Sucked inside?" Sofia repeated, aghast.

But Jayne was thinking of what Vesta had told her: *This Master has lived in the Torrent for a very long time, trapped by my own people many years ago.* Her brain hadn't fully registered it at the time, but Vesta had implied people could *live* inside the Torrent.

Something clicked together in her thoughts as she remembered what Tristan had told her: *All Rudik would tell us was that Thorne is obsessed with locating someone named Alexandra.* "Who is Alexandra? Is she trapped inside the Torrent?" Jayne asked, her voice a hushed whisper.

Henry met her gaze, his eyes soft and full of sorrow. "My mother. Yes. And there are others..." He paused, dropping his gaze before continuing. "Oh, Jayne. How do I tell you this without altering your future? I must, though. I must. Only you can help save them."

"Tell me what? And, *them*? Who else is trapped in the Torrent?"

With a deep sigh, Henry closed his eyes as if in pain. "Your daughter."

A bewildered laugh bubbled up Jayne's throat, and she shot a glance at Sofia, whose forehead was creased with concern. Their dad was clearly unstable. "Dad. I don't have a daughter."

But Henry remained as solemn as ever, that grim look never leaving his eyes.

"But you will."

EPILOGUE

THE PUPPETEER

London

I t had been days since Ruth Thorne could perform even the feeblest of magic. The blow she'd been dealt by her daughter had injured her deeply. She could barely drag herself across the floor of the flat to call for help. And when Lars had appeared, the disdain he'd shown as he dressed her wounds was a warning to her. She'd lost control of her own organization. The Kingdom would never respect her if she couldn't stand up to Jayne and her ridiculous power.

Lars had tended to her for a day and a night, until she could stand without collapsing, then portaled away to rally the troops. He'd shared the news that Hans Kaufman was on the march against the Guardians and went to see what he could do to help.

But at this point, she didn't care about the Guardians or the Kingdom. She was at war with her own being.

Though her body was weak, her mind was clearer than it

had been in days. And she now saw the cage that surrounded her. The cage she had been blind to until now.

The demon had trapped her. He used her as a puppet. She had no more free will. No more power to call her own.

She was enslaved. And there was nothing she could do to alter that fact.

It is all that you deserve, rumbled the voice inside her. *You understood the terms of our bargain. And now, I am calling in my debts.*

Ruth shut her eyes, too grieved to even respond.

You are so weak, the voice went on. *You always were. It is how I conquered you so easily. But our work is not done yet, my dear. We still have a Master to hunt and two totems to retrieve.*

This made Ruth's eyes fly open. Two totems?

Indeed. Because of your incompetence, I've had to spend all my power healing this form. And now we are too late. The Fire Goddess is among us, and we cannot collect her totem. It must be taken by force. But worry not. I have enough power to complete the deed. Step aside, human.

The darkness roiled inside her, and a single tear escaped Ruth's eye as she succumbed to the deadly magic once more.

~

Dearest Reader,

Are you as breathless as I am??? I hope you loved this story, seeing Jayne and Tristan, and Sofia and Cillian, come into their powers together. It's only going to get wilder from here, so buckle up!

Are you ready for more? The next installment, THE PROPHECY OF WIND, awaits!

I am so grateful for your time and support. Thanks for reading, and for being a part of my magical world!

Blessed Be,
Joss

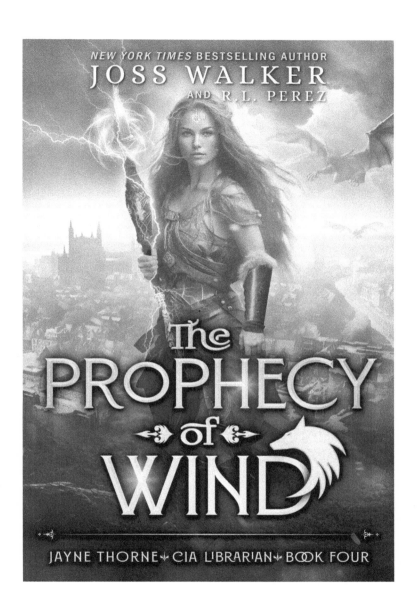

NEW YORK TIMES BESTSELLING AUTHOR

JOSS WALKER
AND R.L. PEREZ

The PROPHECY ⊰ of ⊱ WIND

JAYNE THORNE ⭹ CIA LIBRARIAN ⭹ BOOK FOUR

Acknowledgments

As always, we have many people to thank, folks who've helped us build this world. We are deeply indebted to the following fabulous people for their help bringing this third book in the Jayne series to life:

Laura Blake Peterson; Kim Killion; Phyllis DeBlanche; James T. Farrell; Erin Moon and the whole Tantor Audio team; Salt and Sage Books; Jennifer Jakes; Alisha Klapheke; John McDougal of Murder by the Book; Barbara Peters of Poisoned Pen Bookstore; Jayne Ann Krentz; our Facebook groups—Joss Walker's Readers and Rogues and R.L. Perez's Coven of Readers; our Instagram families; our IRL families: Randy, Jordan, Jameson in kitten heaven, and the parentals; Alex, Colin, Ellie, Isabel, and the whole Perez clan; our favorite librarians, who inspired these tales; and our readers, without whom these stories would not be nearly as fun to write.

Thank you, all, from the bottom of our hearts!

ABOUT JOSS WALKER

Photo credit: KidTee Hello Photography

Joss Walker is the fantasy pen name for *New York Times* bestselling thriller author J.T. Ellison, where she explores her love of the fantasy genre and extraordinary women discovering their power in the world. With Jayne Thorne, CIA Librarian, Joss has created a compelling urban fantasy series perfect for lovers of books, libraries, romance, and of course, magic.

Join Joss Walker's newsletter
https://josswalker.com/subscribe

ABOUT R.L. PEREZ

R.L. Perez is a YA fantasy romance author, perfectionist, anxious Type A worrier, and proud Hufflepuff. She's published three series set in the same world, featuring witches, romance, and time travel. When she's not working on her books, she's either napping, diving into a good book, obsessively watching Netflix, or playing with her two kids. She loves chocolate, loud laughter, and alternative rock music.

Join R.L. Perez's Newsletter
www.rlperez.com/subscribe

ABOUT TWO TALES PRESS

Two Tales Press is an independent publishing house featuring crime fiction, suspense, and fantasy novels, novellas, and anthologies written and edited by *New York Times* bestselling author J.T. Ellison, including the Jayne Thorne, CIA Librarian series under J.T.'s fantasy pen name, Joss Walker.

To view all of our titles, please visit

www.twotalespress.com